The Children in
the Woods

Books by Frederick Busch

FICTION

The Children in the Woods · 1994

Long Way from Home · 1993

Closing Arguments · 1991

Harry and Catherine · 1990

War Babies · 1989

Absent Friends · 1989

Sometimes I Live in the Country · 1986

Too Late American Boyhood Blues · 1984

Invisible Mending · 1984

Take This Man · 1981

Rounds · 1979

Hardwater Country · 1979

The Mutual Friend · 1978

Domestic Particulars · 1976

Manual Labor · 1974

Breathing Trouble · 1973

I Wanted a Year Without Fall · 1971

NONFICTION

When People Publish · 1986

Hawkes · 1973

The Children in the Woods

New and Selected Stories

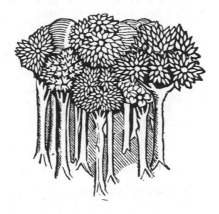

Frederick Busch

Congratulations!
Frederick Busch

TICKNOR & FIELDS

New York

1994

Copyright © 1994 by Frederick Busch

All rights reserved

For information about permission to reproduce selections
from this book, write to Permissions, Ticknor & Fields,
Houghton Mifflin Company, 215 Park Avenue South,
New York, New York 10003.

Library of Congress Cataloging-in-Publication Data

Busch, Frederick, date.
The children in the woods : new and selected
stories / by Frederick Busch.
p.   cm.
ISBN 0-395-64724-x
I. Title.
PS3552.U814C47   1994
813'.54 — dc20   93-5008
CIP

Printed in the United States of America
BP 10 9 8 7 6 5 4 3 2 1

Book design by Anne Chalmers

"Dog Song," "Ralph the Duck" and "One More Wave of Fear" from *Absent Friends* by
Frederick Busch. Copyright © 1986, 1988, 1989 by Frederick Busch. Reprinted by
permission of Alfred A. Knopf, Inc. "A Three-Legged Race," "The Trouble with Being
Food" and "How the Indians Come Home" from *Domestic Particulars* by Frederick Busch.
Copyright © 1976 by Frederick Busch. Reprinted by permission of New Directions
Publishing Corp., to whom the author, for twenty years, has been grateful.

FOR JAMES LAUGHLIN

Note

The previously uncollected stories, sometimes in altered form, appeared in the following publications: "Berceuse" and "The World Began with Charlie Chan," *The Georgia Review;* "Bread," *Gettysburg Review;* "Folk Tales," *Story;* "Dream Abuse," *Michigan Quarterly Review.*

The selected stories first appeared in these collections: "Bring Your Friends to the Zoo" and "Is Anyone Left This Time of Year?" in *Breathing Trouble* (Calder and Boyars, 1973); "A Three-Legged Race," "The Trouble with Being Food" and "How the Indians Come Home" in *Domestic Particulars* (New Directions, 1976); "Widow Water," "The Lesson of the Hôtel Lotti," "My Father, Cont." and "What You Might as Well Call Love" in *Hardwater Country* (Alfred A. Knopf, 1979); "The Settlement of Mars," "Critics" and "Stand, and Be Recognized" in *Too Late American Boyhood Blues* (David R. Godine, 1984); "Ralph the Duck," "Dog Song" and "One More Wave of Fear" in *Absent Friends* (Alfred A. Knopf, 1989).

In addition, "Is Anyone Left This Time of Year?" appeared in *Prize Stories 1974: The O. Henry Awards*, "The Trouble with Being Food" was selected for *The Best American Short Stories 1977*, and "Ralph the Duck" was a selection in *The Best American Short Stories 1989*.

Contents

The Children in
the Woods

Bread

FIRST I WENT from room to chilly room, smoke alarm to smoke alarm. I saw little of the dust-fogged furniture or drapes, or the cobwebs blooming with cluster flies — the slatternly housekeeping for which our mother had been celebrated. Later, we discussed our pride in her carelessness. But this was first. I found the one. It was on the wall, near the molding, above the back-room cellar door. It squeaked like a floorboard, where no one had walked for a week, beneath someone's foot. Every minute or so it squeaked. It was the battery. The battery gives out, and the gizmo makes its little I'm-a-ghostly-footfall cry, and you hunt it down and tear the failing battery away: one ghost less.

It was the next day, in the kitchen, in the chill and in the absence, when I thought, *And not even by terrorists*. I heard my *not even* and I snorted with disgust. I was the man who would complain of his parents' death, of their falling and falling out of the sky, that it was insufficiently political. I snorted again. You make enough such noises, in a house quite suddenly scalloped out by death — by deaths — and the other person with you, in another room, a sister, say, might think she hears her brother weep.

"Chuckie," she called.

"What?"

"Are you okay?"

"Yes."

"Huh?"

❖ 1 ❖

"Yes."

"Yeah," she said. "Okay." Then: "It sounded —"

"I wasn't," I said.

Kendall had decided that the room she couldn't deal with, among the rooms she couldn't deal with, was the kitchen. I'd volunteered. I was the brother. I did that. I had recently enough cleaned out rooms to be used to raking through what mustn't matter anymore — an apartment in Manhattan, four rooms on Riverside Drive, and not a house formerly employed for the storage of four lives and the spirits of six dogs, six or seven cats, the famous rooster flock, some insect-eating plants, and of course, though briefly, the boy whom Kendall so many years ago had smuggled in for the night.

In the city, I'd cleaned up what I finally saw as debris, the still-smoking rubble of a two-year marriage — service booklets on blender and toaster oven, playbills from hundred-dollar theater evenings, a lacy, boy-man's prayer of crimson negligée, the duplicate books, the checks and their sloppy but balanced ledgers: the finally usual. So, though Kendall was close to thirty and I four years younger, I volunteered. I thought of myself as experienced.

Therefore, in the home of my parents who had driven to Syracuse and flown to Toronto and stayed in a hotel on the lake at Harbourfront and had gone to a sort of theatrical evening that involved some visiting English friends, and then had flown from Toronto in a two-engine prop-driven airplane that had come apart over Lake Ontario, I was being experienced. I was fighting the stiff, dark dough I'd taken on the night of our arrival, when I'd offered to do — to do, to *do* — the kitchen, and I was kneading it. Like a semiprofessional mourner, I was conducting myself with dignity and in a manner governed by logic.

"I'm kneading bread," I answered Kendall, who'd been drawn perhaps by my silence into the kitchen she had vowed to avoid.

She sat with staring eyes that jumped from surfaces like hands from hot handles and she lit a cigarette. "You mind?" she asked. She propped her elbows on the narrow wooden table the top of which, once upon a time, my head had been level with. I had swiped hot cookies that my mother had set there to cool.

"No," I said. "I was married to a smoker."

"She never smoked here. Anytime that I saw."

"She sneaked it."

"Did she, you know, sneak around? On you? With guys?"

Kendall's face was a little square, her features slightly gathered at the center of her face. She missed bearing a man's strong face by virtue of the brown-green lightness of her large eyes. They were also our father's eyes. It was nearly his face, though he diminished as she widened her eyes to mock the innocence with which she hadn't asked her question. I turned my back to her and the rest of the kitchen, and I worked at the dough. It didn't yield gladly to my palms as I pushed, then gathered it toward me, gathered, then pushed.

"She did," Kendall concluded.

"That doesn't matter," I said.

"Chuckie, never mind. I shouldn't have, but never mind anyway."

"It doesn't matter anymore. It almost didn't then. Now it doesn't, and everybody moves along."

"That's right," she said. "Listen. How did you learn about kneading bread. Do guys normally *do* that?"

I planted my legs wider and drove hard at the football-sized wad of dough, still cold, unready to be shaped. I picked it up and slammed it onto the breadboard on the long counter. "I watched her," I said.

"A lot? You sat here and just looked at her?"

"No. I don't know. One time, I watched instead of — I don't know. *Not* watching. Isn't that what kids do with their parents? Not watch them a lot?"

I heard her sigh out the smoke. "You're lucky. To remember that."

"*You* remember things, Ken. They're just other things."

I heard her walk to the sink. I looked over my shoulder as she ran water on her cigarette. When she turned, I'd turned back to stare at the dough I leaned on with my palms. I almost didn't hear her say, "But I want to remember everything."

There isn't much of an answer. I nodded over the dough and closed my eyes. I continued to knead. She left the kitchen, swatting my ass, not hard, as she went.

When the flock happened, ours and the nearest other house, a usually vacant rental place in much disrepair, were the only buildings for three or four miles. The rental house burned or was burned. My father had used to snarl about the trash, as he called them, who rented it. They littered the dooryard with green garbage, they used an outhouse, and their goggle-eyed, shabbily dressed, pale-skinned children offended him. One winter, they burned an unsafe woodstove too hot, or lit the house in revenge for an impending eviction over nonpayment of rent. The roar of the fire, the pumper trucks and police cars sliding on the road, the ceaseless dirty gray smoke, scared us all. My father put smoke alarms — expensive in those days, and considered scientific wonders — into every room as soon as they were sold. He forbade us, on the day of the fire, the cigarettes he knew we sneaked. (I stopped, Kendall didn't.) He put a metal emergency ladder into Kendall's room and mine. He made us practice household fire drills. We used to rush about at *Go!*, crawling to doors, crouching from windows, crying out whom we would wake, and with what precautions, and then how we would run for our lives and wait for our parents to find us.

The day after the fire, I returned from — my mother's description — a twelve-year-old's sulk in the woods. I bore a seared, semi-featherless, small-headed, singed-comb little chicken. I brought it home, my parents said, whenever they told the story, to ask if I could give it someplace to die in peace. "He's the only survivor," I was said to have said, referring to the fire in which no one died. I named the chicken Bunny because I'd never been permitted to own the rabbit my mother had promised me as consolation after she'd shattered my sixth year of life by disclosing that the Easter Bunny did not in fact bring jelly beans and marshmallow chicks the color of radioactive rocks.

So we owned a scarred, small-headed chicken whose name was that of some cute, stupid girl with big breasts in some movie about big breasts on a California beach. My father, tall and broad and square-faced, balder than any egg, was business manager and assistant superintendent of the school district on the outermost edge of which we lived. He brought home one night, eight or nine days later, a cardboard box filled with chicks hatched and nourished in the high school biology lab.

The dough was working, now, and I pushed and gathered and then went in search of dish towels to drape on the three balls of dough I would cut from what I'd kneaded and arrange for rising. I was working from a book I had taken from the cookbook shelves. The page was relaxed in the binding, stained and limp. I'd stared at the stains before I'd focused on the words.

So I fed them the feed our father complained the birds ate too much of. Complaining about the cost of lumber, he built and fenced a little hen house, complete with roosting shelf. And Bunny, grown to something like health, with her mean, crazy eyes and the tattered wattle under her remarkably small head, staggered across the yard with her flock to raid the garden, then wheeled with stupid precision to stop occasional cars in our rutted, dusty, unpaved road.

The others didn't lay, though Bunny did. Kendall and I refused to eat her eggs, of course — that would be like eating *people*, Kendall explained for us. All of the birds, though unproductive, were more than willing to crow — on the occasion of a car with a leaky muffler that passed, for house lights spilling yellow down the yard, and for, as my father put it at two or three one morning, "a goddamned harvest *moon*."

Taking advice from his district's high school biology teacher, my father soon enough determined that with the exception of poor, exhausted Bunny, we owned a flock of roosters. "Guys!" Kendall had cried, on hearing the news. As for me, I was busy in school and bored by them all; I remained devoted to the idea of Bunny, but saw as little of her as possible. The rooster flock, and Bunny, soon enough disappeared. Then our parents disappeared. I saw them spilling from the plane. I sent that away. No: he would have reached for her. She would have reached for him. I saw them, then, clutching at each other. I cut the dough into three smaller balls and draped them with the soft, faded dish towels under which they would rise. I left the house by the side door. I could always work in the barn, I thought. I could always be useful in the barn.

He took the roosters and Bunny to a high school janitor who promised, he lied to us, that he would protect them until they died of old age. We knew. He killed them and cooked them and ate them. That was how they disappeared. Bunny au vin. Bunny sautée Basquaise. Bunny, more than likely, fried in lard.

I didn't go to the barn. I crossed the country road, paved now, and too well traveled, they'd complained. SaraJean, who used to be my wife, had liked to laugh when my mother began grousing about cars in the peaceable kingdom. "Where do they find up here to *travel* to?" SaraJean had enjoyed asking. She liked closure. She relished ending conversations, and pushing the button that shut the automatic door on anyone's garage, and terminating laden relationships. Kendall had said that if SaraJean and I had produced children, my wife would have happily inserted them, one at a time, in the trash compactor.

I went up the steep hill across from the house. The pitch was difficult, the snow still thick in wind-driven patches, and elsewhere the thorny stalks and slippery dead leaves and mostly frozen mud made the walking breathless. I aimed myself at an evergreen, fat in a low cluster of sinuous bushes, on the wind-flattened northern slope. In my father's lined denim chore coat, the collar up and a watch cap from the pocket pulled over my ears, I grew sweaty though the wind gusted on my back, and soon I was gasping into all that air. But I pushed hard if awkwardly to get myself up. I was desperate, heaving though I was, to not stop, to get away.

When I was near the tree, I turned to look down along the hill, and then I saw what I'd wanted to: all of it, the white house and garage, the gray wooden tool shed from which the house for Bunny and her flock of roosters protruded, the dead garden, the brown-green dormant lawns that ran to fields that went along the rocky tan hill below the house. It looked, from where I puffed and panted, manageable. It looked as though, if you stared hard and studied the details of cornice and chimney and gutter and sill, you could hold it confidently and summon it as you needed to.

Walking downhill, I had to dig my heels into snow patches and leaf heaps to keep from falling. My knees ached and my shins felt too tight. I walked stiff-legged across the road and around the side to the door. It was when I took off his watch cap and wiped my sweaty face with it that I remembered about his head inside the blue-black wool, his sweat already on the loosened knots of its weave, his fringe of iron hair that I remembered as surprisingly fine, soft to touch, the first time I dared to touch it as a man. I rubbed my head. I felt a way that reminded me of my discomfort on first seeing my father naked. A necessary distance had been shortened. Well, you've got all the distance, now, you'll need: I would have said that to me if I had been someone else.

In the kitchen, I took the towels from the bread and, with a wooden rolling pin that was like a long dowel slightly swollen in the middle, I pressed and rolled until the balls were long, thin ovals. According to the recipe in the cookbook I was to delicately and precisely gather up the edge nearest me and tautly roll. *Delicately* and *precisely* and *tautly*. I rolled up three long loaves and set them on a metal cooking sheet and stuck them in the oven. I'd forgotten to preheat the oven, but the bread would have to overcome the cold just as it would have to overcome its weeks or months in the freezer and my inability to roll it with sufficient delicacy, precision, and tautness. I turned up the heat.

I went upstairs to see if Kendall had made some progress. I, surely, had not. We'd planned to spend a weekend, then had changed our plans, had called in to work to say we'd need more like a week. It looked like a month to me. It looked like lasting into middle age or Social Security.

Kendall was on the floor, near the foot of their bed. Beside her, almost around her, was an explosion of clothing. She looked red-eyed and sore, very pale, maybe ill.

My turn to ask it: "You all right?"

"Where'd you go, Chuck?"

"I walked up over the hill."

"You son of a bitch."

"You would just as soon I hadn't walked up over the hill, I take it."

"I called you and called you."

"I didn't know, of course. Being —"

"Ha ha. Over the hill. Ha ha. Except I was *calling* you."

"I wouldn't have gone, you know. If I thought you needed me here right then."

She slumped, so that she looked as if she were studying their silk and rayon and cotton and wool. Then she nodded.

"You know that," I said.

She nodded again.

I said, "I am going to jump to the conclusion, Ken, that you're not enjoying the sorting out of their bedroom."

"Christ," she said. "You — I don't want to make any snappy re-marks, all right? I feel terrible."

"Sick, you mean, or — you know. About them."

"Them," she said. She gestured at the clothing, then her arm fell on top of it and she went with it, so that she was lying on top of washed-thin half slips and cheap-looking underwear and starchy shirts with cardboard stiffeners and boot socks I knew he'd bought at Agway and slacks she'd ordered from catalogues and shoes that needed to be heeled and cleaned and shined. Kendall said, "I started to take the things out of their drawers and make piles, and I couldn't figure out what I was piling them for. *I'd* never wear her clothes, never mind I couldn't get into a size eight *glove*, much less her dresses. And they're so *cheap*-looking. Ordinary. I thought I learned how to dress from her, and it's all so, I don't know, worn out and faded and not very brilliantly selected. And you hate *his* clothes, don't you? I mean, who wears a suit to work over high-lace insulated *boots*. Let it *be* fucking wintertime: you dress *right*. Right? Or his terrible — they're not terrible. But his ties. That she picked out, with her famous taste.

"So I stopped stacking and I started heaving. It seemed to end up being some kind of revenge thing. So I stopped that, too. I mostly sat here and wailed for you and you couldn't come up and give me a hand, could you? Because you were being Jack and Jill. Whatever you were doing."

The highboy on my father's side of the bed was missing a brass pull on one side of the second drawer down. His bedside table wasn't identical to hers, I noticed for the first time. And they'd never arrested the damp that was ruining the casements of both their windows.

I said, "Whatever I was doing. I'm going to total it up for us, Ken. In about twenty-four hours, we've defrosted a ball of dough and we've made a mound of clothing. I think we're behind our schedule."

"And yet we're both so experienced at this."

"In a manner of speaking," I said.

Kendall propped herself on her elbows and crossed her legs at the ankle. She wore jeans and a cotton sweater, its sleeves pulled up to the elbows, and, despite her pallor and red eyes, she looked young. "Of course," she said, "you're the one used to cleaning up after marriages. I'm the party who slung it all into a duffel bag and two canvas suitcases and moved out in twelve minutes under the standing Olympic record for leaving *any*one. Much less the maniac I *wouldn't* marry."

"No," I said, "I always thought Bobby had a kind of admirable zest. He's the only man I ever knew outside the movies who actually hallucinated at his desk in front of a client."

"The only man," she said, "who ate amphetamines by dropping them into his martini. 'Straight up, babe, no fruits or vegetables in it, and bring me some kind of food with the second drink, all right?' Zest is a fond and stupid word for him. So's admirable."

"From a fond and stupid guy," I admitted.

"You're only stupid, Chuckie."

I sat in the pretty bentwood chair that needed recaning. It leaned as I let my weight down, and I waited for it to collapse, but it held me. I said, hiding behind my closed eyes, "Let's throw it all away."

"Which all?"

"All of it," I said, still hiding. "The clothes, the bedroom slippers, the pajamas — what can we *use*? We don't want to save things — do we? — and put them on like relics. 'Hi, my name's Chuck and I'm wearing a dead man's shirt with sleeves two inches too long. Let's not do that, Ken. Let's toss it out."

"No," she said. Then she said, "All right. Except, we give it to — I don't know. Somebody. People. The Salvation Army."

"No way. They sell it to rag merchants. *They* sell it to clothing makers. *They* get wage slaves in Hong Kong and Costa Rica to use it for new clothes. So you're walking up Park Avenue South, say, and you see one of those overbred undermuscled types with blond eyelashes and about seventeen years of experience at a good college, and they're wearing a casually wrinkled natural fiber outfit, you know, and you stare at it because you see Daddy's *shirt* in there. You say to the androgyne, 'Excuse me, but aren't you wearing my father's shirt?' You don't want that to happen. You don't *want* them wearing Daddy's clothes and Mommy's clothes, Ken. Toss it. Throw it. All of it. If you want me to, I'll start a big son of a bitch fire outside, in the backyard, and we'll burn it."

"Is that called howdah? When the woman throws herself on top of the man who's burning? Or is that what they call burnoose?"

"You're a cultural swinette, Ken. We'll just throw it away."

"All right."

"You mean it?"

"I should have said it first," Kendall said. "It's just that — you know what I have left from when I lived with Bobby? Zip. No souvenirs, nothing. I left everything of mine behind, pictures of him, pictures of you and Mommy and Daddy, everything I brought in with me in the first place. He never called or anything to ask if I wanted anything back. Or if he could have *me* back."

"He's a junkie, Ken."

"He was *my* junkie," she said. And then: "Are you afraid of going through the *real* stuff? Are you scared, too?"

"Their papers? They probably don't have any papers. I mean, insurance things, bank things, that. Sure. But no *papers*. You know, that prove we were adopted, or stolen from kings and dukes or anything. No secret diaries or anything. No."

"So how come you haven't gone through Daddy's upper right-hand drawer?"

I told her, "Good conduct medal. Infantry badges. Two sets of corporal's stripes. Old handkerchiefs."

"You just remember from before."

"From high school," I admitted. "I used to look."

"You're as scared as I am," she said.

I looked at the sloping pile of our parents' clothes. They had nothing to do with how my mother wore my father's flannel shirts on Sunday to cook in, the sleeves rolled and the tails hanging almost to her knees. His flannel shirts looked like anybody's, now, anybody's green tartan from the Army-Navy in New Hartford, anybody's gray and black and yellow and white from the mail-order store.

I said, "I used to look for secret stuff. Dirty things. Pictures or rubbers, I don't know. He didn't have anything. Or he didn't leave it there for me to find. We won't steal their secrets here."

"Where would they hide them?" Kendall asked.

"Why *would* they, Ken?"

"Everyone does," she said. "That's why you're divorced and I live alone, and they went swimming," she said. She plucked at clothing.

I said, "They were together. They stuck together. They died together."

"Maybe they were better at it than we are," Kendall said, "but everybody's a secret from everybody else."

I pulled garbage bags from the box that Kendall had brought up. They were transparent, but they changed the color of the clothes I forced inside them. A watery tone, like what you see on docks or the footing of wooden bridges, went over everything. I felt as though I were drowning their clothes, which looked ugly, distorted, as I crushed them in. And I thought about robbers who pulled nylon stockings over their heads to change their features, which also looked crushed. This, I thought, is what our parents must look like, underwater.

Kendall had stood to take some bags and fill them. I heard us panting, as I had when I'd climbed the hill. This is real work too, I thought. We opened all but one of the drawers she hadn't got to, and we emptied all but one into the bags. My fingers felt sore from pulling at their clothing. I kneeled on each bag to force the air out before fastening it. Under my weight, the bags sighed like people, and the cloth inside went heavier.

When we were done, when we had without relenting thrown away our parents' only surviving skins, and when the room was ranked with sacks, Kendall said, "Look at us. It's like Hansel and Gretel made it back all the way, carrying the witch's whatever —"

"Gold," I said.

"Gold. Gingerbread cake. Whatever."

"You're just *hungry*, Ken."

"And they find out there's nobody home anyway. You know? The parent bastards tricked them *again*, and nobody's *home*."

I said, stupidly, "Ken. They didn't *mean* to."

"Why would I think that?" she said.

We stood there awhile and then, as if we'd made a decision, we left the bags and walked down the hall to the small room over the porch that had been Kendall's before she moved away and they turned it into a guest room.

She went to the closet and opened the door. It was empty, I thought. But Kendall reached in, her eyes still on mine, and her hand emerged to show her trophy: a chain ladder, suitable for escaping from fires or admitting boys on steep, snowy roofs. I apparently made a noise.

Kendall said, "I hate that. You keep doing that. You never used to. Where'd you pick it up?"

"I'm not really aware," I said, "of any unseemly new habits. But thanks."

"Yeah," she said. "You do sound like somebody who's about to hawk one on the floor. You sound like some kid on the street. Is that what New York did for you? Hee-*yach*. Like that. You really didn't know you were doing that?"

"I think I sometimes snort," I said. "Blow air out my nose — not the way Bobby snorted. Just a little sniff, sometimes, maybe."

"New York City on the street, that's your little sniffy snort."

"Tell me something country, Ken. How'd you ever get that kid in here?"

Holding the ladder, Kendall sat down. I think she'd have sat on the floor and hit hard, but there was an old footstool covered with maroon vinyl or leather, and she landed, clanking, on that. It was most of the furniture in the room, aside from the bed and bureau. The room was narrow and decorated with a chocolate brown carpet and off-white walls on which our mother had hung prints they'd brought home from Europe.

Kendall said, "I forgot." She was blushing, and I was glad to see her pallor overwhelmed.

"Poor son of a bitch," I said. "You forget, and the poor son of a bitch probably goes over it, step by step, every other day of his life. How he went up a porch stanchion and along the front porch roof and into Kendall Beaucamp's window. And —" I waited. She volunteered nothing. She shook her head and looked at the chenille comforter, dusty as the curtains, I'd have bet, and the narrow cherry dresser over which a cherry frame, of a slightly different hue, held a mirror in which I watched us stand, sit, remember and try not to. I said, "Ken: did he or did he not get into the sack with you? And what was his name?"

She shook her head. "I can't remember."

"Was he your, you know — was he the first guy you ever —"

"That's plain goddamned prurient, Chuckie, you know that? Yes. We got so turned on by being outlaws in here, we did stuff we didn't know we knew to *do*."

"I remember his name," I said. "Peter."

"No: Preston. Press. Press Leutens."

"The stud."

"He wasn't bad," Kendall said.

"And?"

"This is not the time for telling stories," Kendall said, with no rancor or conviction.

I said, "This is why they *invented* stories."

She said, "Daddy had grounded me for coming home an hour late, after my curfew. We'd been out. Press had the car, his parents' car, and there was some kind of game. Basketball, it was a basketball game, the last league game, we had to win to get into the tournament. So we won. He played a good game, and we didn't get home until late."

"You were the hero's reward?"

"He was *my* reward. I'd had to sit through the game, after all. *And* clap for our cheerleaders. We had more bent, humped, sickly pale, short-legged cheerleaders that year. So we got home late, Daddy all but put me on bread and water, Mommy said those moral things she always said until I said I would leave home unless she and Daddy did first, and that night, the next night, when it happened, I was in my room and Press just showed up."

"At your window."

"At my window."

"Like the movies," I said.

She said, "Exactly like the movies."

"And you let him in with the fire ladder?"

"He didn't really need it. He'd made it up the roof already, most of the way, but I liked the idea of opening my window and unrolling the ladder Daddy used to make me practice unrolling all the time."

"Right," I said. "And?"

"God, Chuck, you're so vulgar."

"I know. Tell me the story."

"Chuck. We acted like we were in Nazi-occupied France and we took our clothes off and went to bed. I was a normal, healthy child and so was he. We'd been warming up in cars and dark corners, and we did what we'd been trained for."

"And I spent my childhood reading dirty books," I complained.

"Not from what I heard."

"Tell me the rest," I said.

Kendall said: "Like the movies. Like the books. Whispering and touching and kissing and talking and screwing, Chuck, until, as a matter of fact, dawn."

"When Bunny crowed."

"Bunny crowed. The cocks all crowed. Press got dressed and went to the window and he was so nervous about making his escape from the Nazis and the Vichy police, he forgot to kiss me goodbye. He went onto the slippery, snow-covered roof, without benefit of the fire ladder, and I was in bed, you know, not *believing* it, and Bunny and that goddamned flock of roosters must have come wheeling into the front yard. Because all of a sudden — one of those icy dawns? when there's nothing to hear except wind? — all of a sudden, every goddamned rooster, *and* Bunny, started in screaming. Like they all were saying *Aww! Aww! Aww!*

"Naturally, Daddy and Mommy woke up. Daddy went to the front door. And naturally he saw dumb-ass Preston Leutens's car, his parents' car, parked square in front of the front walk. He went out to investigate. By then, I was looking out from between these exact same curtains. There's Daddy, he's in his navy blue watch cap and his bathrobe and his chore jacket over it, and the bedroom slippers we just threw the hell away, and he's standing there, looking at the car. And there's Press on the roof above him. Like a statue on the roof, because he's trying not to slide or be seen. And there's the goddamned cock flock, *Aww! Aww!* I betrayed him in my heart, poor Preston."

"Sure you did. You're Kendall Beaucamp. You laughed."

"With Preston's heat still rising from the sheets. I laughed like the witch in *The Wizard of Oz.* I couldn't help it. And Daddy, of course, through the window, in the rooster screams and all that wind, he hears me."

"I was sleeping."

"Of course you were."

"So I missed seeing him kill you and Preston and you're both still dead?"

"Oh, Chuckie. He scrunched up his face until I thought he was going to cry."

"Did he?"

"Mommy claimed he did, later on. He said to Press, 'You get down cautiously. I don't want your parents suing me after I send you to jail.' Then he went inside."

"What'd he *say?*"

"That's between him and me."

"No."

"Goddamned *yes*. That's for him and me."

I had to look someplace else. I looked at what was either a castle in a meadow or something eating the meadow, and then I said, "Weren't you a pistol."

"Wasn't I," she said. "You know what? I just might sit in here awhile. If you don't mind. A little while. All right?"

I didn't know what else to do except lean down and kiss the top of her head, which smelled like a morning's work and herbal shampoo. She bumped her head against my lips, and I went out.

Where I went, of course, was back down the hall and into our parents' room and through the ranked plastic bags to the bureau in the top right drawer of which my father kept the secrets. When I opened it, a sweet, soapy smell came up — the soaps with French names that my mother gave the big, booted school executive for birthdays and Christmases. When they were used up thin, he dried the wafers and broke them into chips and scattered them in his drawers. I thought of the first time I had seen him naked, emerging from the shower, his dimpled flanks and long thighs, the dense hair on his chest and belly, the dangerous mystery of his groin.

What I saw first in the drawer was a small, handled and almost limp, photograph, about four inches tall. It was of a young girl with pretty legs. She wore a dress over a T-shirt, and the dress was hiked up by her straddling of a bicycle. A familar, shy smile composed her face:

you looked from lips to eyes, and you smiled back. It was our mother, aged eight or nine. I had to say "Hello," back through the thirty-six years of their marriage and the long, funny year (as they had often told it) of their courtship — he did the courting, she, as she said, had held her breath and jumped in, trusting (quite incorrectly as it seemed at last) to the probability that everything, after a while, floats to the surface — and back to her childhood in the Korean War, the drills for taking shelter from atomic bomb blasts, and back through World War II, her father in the Pacific, her mother alone with her, chain-smoking Lucky Greens. "Hello," I said, holding the picture he apparently had many times held.

I saw the dark boxes his medals were in, and some wide brown envelopes, an assortment of cuff links and tie clasps presented by us on birthdays, purchased with our mother's money and rarely used. I opened the envelopes, three of them, and found artifacts of children who'd grown older. The envelope on top contained photographs of Kendall in a prom dress, Kendall in her cap and gown at graduation, me in a Cub Scout shirt and jeans, in football uniform, waist-to-heel cast, and my own cap and gown. The envelope in the middle had letters from us: I was ashamed, somehow, of the childish arcs and curves of my hand. And there were pictures of me and SaraJean, or Kendall and Bobby, of New York City and Poughkeepsie, to which Kendall had moved when IBM told her to. I saw that we were happy children. You would call us happy children, if you saw those photographs. And in the envelope on the bottom, there were notes from our mother. I couldn't read them. *Darling*, one of them began, and I folded it shut. There was a drawing signed Kendall in a loopy hand: *My Family*, it said, and there was the vast, big-headed Daddy, with enormous hands and feet and smile, and under him, like shrubs in the shade of a tree, was a labeled *Mommy* with a face-wide smile, and a smaller *Kendall*, her arms spread as if to tell the viewer that here they all were. Under it, folded, was a large Christmas card I had made in elementary school, perhaps in the first or second grade. I could still smell, in the dried smears between the pasted green evergreen shape and the rough construction-paper rectangle, the corrupted vanilla of grade school mucilage. There was more, but I stopped fingering through it. He might have, I thought, hidden cruel, terrible matters deep and far away. But the secrets he had openly kept, in the place a husband and father stores them, where he knows they'll one day be found, had been us.

For punctuation, the smell came up, carried by the draft that went from the kitchen to the stairwell, where it split to go through the dining room and living room toward the back room cellar door, and also to pour upstairs. The odor was dense, and so, then, was the noise. The alarms went off in the kitchen and stairwell, then in the living room — the dining room alarm pitched in late — and I waited for the back room to squeal, then remembered that I'd gutted its alarm.

So much for bread, I thought, running downstairs to a very smoky kitchen. The screaming of the alarms was painful. I turned off the oven, opened the door, and recoiled from the oily black smoke — some of it bread, some the spattered fat our mother wouldn't have cleaned away. I was grinning for her housekeeping, squinting against the smoke, and screaming back at the screaming of the smoke alarms which sounded inside my skull bone like dentist drills.

Kendall, from the doorway, called, "I *told* you that guys don't do bread."

I threw the pan of small black loaves on the floor and retreated to the dining room. She came with me. We stood in the far corner, near a high narrow basket our mother had filled with late autumn grasses, ocher and brown. "It's my mess," I said, "and I will clean it up. It's my fault. I forgot to set the timer. It was cold, you know, frozen, then thawed, then cold, but I knew you didn't do bread *cold*. So I cranked the oven to about 475, and then I forgot."

"You meant well," Kendall said. "I suppose."

I shook my head.

"No," she said, "tell me. You can tell me. I told you."

"You know about yeast," I said.

"In the little envelopes. Mommy always used it."

"They're alive," I said. "Little microscopic plants. Which are alive. Dough rises, the yeast grows. That's what makes the heat. That's why it *needs* heat. So, Mommy freezes the dough. To let the bread rise and bake some other time, she freezes it. So we come here, and it's some other time. So I thawed it. I let it rise. I baked it. Sort of."

Kendall said, "Chuckie."

"That's right. The bread was — well, the yeast in the dough was. You know."

"Alive," Kendall said. "When Mommy was alive."

I nodded.

"Chuckie," she said.

"So of course," I said, "I made sure to take it and kill it, didn't I?"

Kendall was quiet for a long time. I didn't want to look at her, or at the room we'd sat in with company and for Thanksgiving and Christmas dinners. It seemed now such an ordinary room. Like the subsiding smoke as it was drawn through the house to accumulate upstairs and in the back room, then dissipate against the walls and windows there, we were leaving, too.

Kendall, behind me, put her arms around my waist. I felt her along my back. I wanted to turn and pull her in to me, but I didn't. I thought she ought to be as alone with me as she needed to be.

She said, suddenly, with a hoarse, gulping sound, "You know how bad I've been all my life?" She laid her forehead against my back and pushed her head at me as, with her arms, she pulled in.

I said, "I'm going to take you upstairs, Ken. All right? I opened the drawer. I found the secrets. Now I want you to see them, all right?"

I turned, then, and fought her a little until I could take hold of her hand. She stopped resisting, and I led her through the thin current of almost invisible smoke toward the stairs.

"I can't do this," she said. "I don't want to do this."

But I kept pulling her. "Yes," I said. "Really." So we climbed toward their room. In the story, you remember, in the dark forest, when something has inevitably eaten all the crumbs, he leads her home by the hand.

Bring Your Friends
to the Zoo

BECAUSE MANY OF THEM did not know when or how to say no and ate too much and the wrong kind of food — sometimes fatally. They spent the day begging and lost health, too, through lack of exercise. The NO FEEDING RULE has enabled us to establish balanced diets for them, preserve their health and encourage breeding. In one year, while visitors were offering food, the elephants seized no less than fourteen coats, twelve handbags, ten cameras, eight gloves and six return tickets to Leicester, damaging them beyond repair. In the same year one hundred eighty visitors were bitten by other animals — monkeys, parrots, cockatoos and ponies. We want it to be a happy day for you and all the animals.

Present yourself at nine-thirty in the morning as the cashier slides his window up. It is advised that when you ask for two tickets, at eight shillings apiece, you calculate that there are twenty shillings in a pound and you are asking him to change a ten-pound note before he's done any business. Check your fly and clear your throat and look at all the bus stops while he turns his head away and then, because it is an English zoo, offers you apologies, and then commits revenge, smiling: nine pounds four in coin — half-pound pieces, two-shilling pieces, one-shilling pieces, a clanking lump in your sport coat pocket. You should at this point sound like a sack of chains. Watch the bus stops.

Take twenty-four thousand customers on an average summer's day — and one in four brought food for the animals. Six thousand paper bags of food was a *very* large "extra," seven days a week! We want it to be a happy day for you and all the animals. Please Do Not Feed Them, for we want it to be a happy day for you and all the animals. Please.

Then close the guide and say, "Good morning. Hi."

At this time of year she wears a light tan raincoat that is stiff and clean. Her Liberty scarf, a bright blue paisley, shows at the throat. Her hem is too long for fashion and her slender legs are not shown to her best advantage. Her hair blows in the harsh autumn wind that has risen in August, a warning of what the year is to be, but her hair is heavy and it settles about her as the wind wavers, and she still looks composed. She wears her hair simply and does not look stylish; she looks as if she cares to look no other way, and so she carries an air of threat: she is too much her own construction, insufficiently swayed by London modes, or winds of summer, you. Greet her by saying, "Good morning. Hi."

Once through the gate, face right. The Deer House, the Camel House, the Giraffe House, the Cattle and Zebra House and the Antelope House will all be found on your left across the canal and a wild ravine. Water Bus rides on the artificial river start at ten. And for the *little* children there is riding in the Children's Zoo too, on the tiny Shetland Ponies and the diminutive donkeys. As you face your right you see a path before you. Take it. The Cranes and Goose Paddock on your immediate left; you pass, on your right, the Owls' Aviary and the Pheasantry. All of the pheasants have gone away and you can count up fourteen empty cages, waiting. You can listen to the wind across the Reptile House, the Reptiliary, the Gentlemen's Toilets, the Charles Clore Pavilion for Mammals, and Moonlight World. Ahead of you a great fence of wide-mesh wire catches the wind; it is a huge crazy sail that is warped to the ground like a tent and has a door of brushed aluminum. It peaks in twenty places, this mad enclosure, it bulges at its sides; thick steel pipes at strange angles jut like spars and when you walk inside, saying, "You go first. You come first, you always came first for me. You know that," the noise that she makes for you by listening in silence, saying nothing, even when you smirk your sudden words away, is lost. For you are in the Snowdon Aviary, opened in 1965, the first out-of-doors walk-through aviary in the London Zoo, which houses many birds from a variety of natural habitats. The Aviary was designed by Lord Snowdon in association with Mr. Cedric Price and Mr. Frank Newby. A special leaflet about the Aviary is available from the Zoo Shop (price one shilling). Lost, because the wind is constantly a high sighing human voice inside this cage. The ground slopes sharply and the steep bank is cut by a narrow concrete walk. A wide-barred railing keeps you from falling down, as the waterfall goes down, roaring, onto rocks and wet bright vegetation, but you must be cautious at the dangerous rail not to drop like the water down on the rocks and tangled bushes below, very far. There are trees and creepers, everything is twined and seizing and moist and you must take care in the constant wind in which the bellow of her silence is lost.

Shapes and colors move in the transplanted brush, something always is moving off the edge of your vision near a pool or in the shadow of a twisted tree or under something green. Over one hundred forty birds of every color are housed here, and below there are egrets ignoring you, herons and spoonbills, teal and ibises, turacos, kestrel — all were here this morning, will remain tonight, in the breathing wind and faintest rattle, as if chains were shaken, that the fence must always make.

Plans to make the London Zoo the most beautiful and modern zoo in the world have been moving forward. Moving forward, out the final door, leaving you in the Aviary, she will face a wooden wall and large white sign: UNDER REDEVELOPMENT. Beyond and left she should see the West Bridge. Call her and the wind will crush your words. No birds will rise in fright at the sound of your voice. Move along the rail at which you must take care and leave this unique and justly famous structure.

Say to her, waiting at the Regent's Canal before the bridge, "Did you want to leave me there with the other funny birds?"

"No. No. You aren't a funny bird."

"I thought maybe that's why you weren't talking to me."

"I am talking to you."

"Right, yes, you are talking to me. Right. What are you saying?"

"Nothing, I suppose. I don't know. Am I being cruel?"

"What's your best guess?"

"I'm not here to be cruel. I don't want anything bad to happen to you."

"Me neither."

"That's not why I'm here."

"I wonder if I could ask you why you *are*."

"Why I am?"

"Not in general, I mean. We could work out all the metaphysics later, how come you exist, et cetera. I mean why did — no. Dammit. You see? I'm a vicious man. I didn't come here, I didn't ask you to come here, so I could be nasty. Honest."

"No. I know."

"Now *I* don't."

"What?"

"I swear I all of a sudden have no idea why we're doing this. I think I would have stood in front of the gate on Prince Albert Road all day, waiting. I would have called your mother's house, I would have *gone* there and lied my way in. I mean it was crucial, understand? It was essential. Absolutely necessary to see you. Except I don't know why now. Why did you come?"

"Because you cabled me. It was very dramatic. You asked me to."

"But why did you *want* to come?"

"Because you wanted me to. Stupid. Because in America —"

"Please: what happened in America? What did we do? What was it?"

"Oh, that's an easy one. It was a scandal at your university. It was a humiliation to my husband. His students talked about it, your students talked about it. I shouldn't be surprised if you and I didn't manage to talk about it publicly every chance we'd had. Do you remember that oaf of a gibbering something-in-administration of yours, the one with the yellow plastic teeth? 'Ah, the benefits of exchange professorships,' he said. 'Hands and everything else across the waters.' What a pig he was."

"So is that what it was? An embarrassment?"

"You never should whine. I wish you wouldn't."

"But I need to *know* this!"

"You're spoiling your leave what-you-may-call-it."

"Leave of absence. I'm not on leave."

"Why are you in England, then? Your cable said sudden leave or something."

"Guess why I'm here. And I left very suddenly."

"Oh not me. You didn't come all the way over on account of me, that's *hideous!*"

"All right."

"You *didn't.*"

"All right."

"Yes you did."

"I don't want to discuss the mechanics of it."

"But all those miles!"

"Why did *you* fly over all those miles in the first place?"

"But it was end of term. The job was over, we had to come home."

"*He* had to come home."

"This is an ancient conversation."

"And how come you live at your mother's house?"

"Yes. How did you know that?"

"I called your husband on the phone."

"You rang my husband? You made my husband *talk* to you?"

"I'm sorry. You want me to be sorry?"

"I want you to feel like the through-and-through child that you are."

You should not miss the Crane and Goose Paddocks. Cranes fly with outstretched neck and legs trailing behind them. They feed on seeds and small animal life, and nest on the ground.

The London Zoo is now doing its best to correct this lack of breeding by setting up a large colony of chimpanzees at Regent's Park. Here it is hoped to breed enough baby chimps to make it unnecessary to take any further specimens from the wild.

To mention only a few of the fascinating exhibits, there are the stick insects which are masters of protective camouflage. The praying mantis, which preys on other insects, stalking them and finally pouncing upon them with its powerful, sharply spined, grasping forelegs, is a facinating, sinister exhibit. Many of them have been reared in the zoo from eggs sent in masses from warmer lands.

The bactrian camel has two humps. The dromedary has one hump.

While a sparrow has fourteen joints to its neck a giraffe has only seven. Giraffes rarely utter any sound.

Keep to the left on entering the Reptile House; it will help you to make the most of these notes. They store their poison in glands in their head. When they bite. The cobra's hood is produced by the spreading of certain ribs near the neck. Rattlesnakes warn by. Green mamba. Kirtland's tree snake looks like the bark of a tree. Then outside to the Broad Walk, directly ahead. Few people realize there are so many kinds of monkeys and apes. And the Charles Clore Pavilion for Mammals, opened in May of 1967.

Stand facing the door while she looks through its glass at the glass-faced cages where one can ascertain the waking/sleeping rhythms, burrowing habits and jumping capacities of small mammals on display, each in its natural habitat. When she turns from the binturongs and tree kangaroos, by glass twice removed, and the sound of your wordless shout rains onto visitors and the brownish cement of the building, the Otter Pool to your right, the Staff Car Park to your left, the Outer Circle Walk will be at your back. Say, "Why don't you live with your husband now? Why didn't you tell me when you left him? Why don't you let me *love* you?" Noting the stiffness of her stance, the sense she gives, like a smell of imminent flight in wild things, ask her lower, say more secretly, "Why?"

"My husband hates me."

"Did he hit you?"

"*Hate*. Not hit. He doesn't hit."

"Do you hate me?"

"No. I don't know. No."

"I guess I ruined your life."

"Perhaps you did. And if you did you've no need really to be proud. That's simple enough to do. What could be more fragile?"

"Did you love me in America?"

"Please stop asking me questions like that."

"But you don't love me now."

"Now it doesn't matter if I do."

"Oh yes it does."

"I'm sorry. I mean now it makes no difference. No, not that either. I can't really say things cleverly, can I?"

"You can say. You do fine."

"I'm not trying to injure you, you see. I'm trying *not* to injure you. I'm trying — listen to me as if I were a student. A stupid student. A stupid child. Which I am."

"Would you understand what I meant if I started to cry now?"

"Oh, American men don't cry, though, do they? Please?"

"Of course not. You know how I keep forgetting things. Forgive me."

"You me."

"Well, *talk*, talk, tell me. Tell me."

"Have you ever read the personal page of the *Times?* Our *Times*, over here?"

"Sherlock Holmes called that page the agony columns."

"Yes. There's a section headed *In Memoriam*."

"Yes."

"And on the anniversary of someone's death — this always comes directly after *Marriages*, you know."

"Doesn't it."

"On the anniversary of death the family place a message. Usually it's one sentence, headed with the dead person's last name in very dark letters. Sort of '*Smith, W. A. — To the loving memory of William Albert Smith, felled whilst on duty in Bosnia, August 11, 1913, perishing bravely at his Embassy post, ever remembered by all, sacred to the memory of his loving family.*' That sort of thing. I suppose people do read them. I sometimes read them when I've nothing better to do."

"You've recently been having nothing better to do."

"I've spent some time alone."

"I guess you have."

"Most often I feel spooky, sort of, you know, *peeping*. Looking at that sorrow or make-believe sorrow, all of it out on display, like a show or something. Of course it might be real agony, sometimes I think so. And how ghoulish it is of me to finger it and then go away. It's so morbid of me, isn't it? But I do it sometimes."

"And you saw this ad put in by your husband, announcing his death and how he mourned it."

"No."

"I apologize for saying that."

"We both used to say things like that."

"Mostly me, I had less to lose. I used to think like that."

"What I want to tell you is during the time — I mean when my husband threw me out, as soon as we were home, really, and I lived in a room at my mother's. My old room. Lord. Why do you think things always work out like *that?*"

"You can come and live in my room."

"Anyway I read a lot of *In Memoriams.* I suppose I was thinking of writing my own. But do you know, the history of England is there, in those little drizzly horrible squibs of formal language. Things that happened before I was born, or when I was too young to remember. Sacred to the memory of so-and-so, he was shot down thus-and-such, France, 1942. Killed at sea, 1918. On and on. All those people dead, all those people remembering them. And then the little nonhistorical people. Killed in a tragic accident. Felled by a premature stroke. Dead before her tenth year. So *much!* And all those people remembering. Everything is gone, but they keep on remembering. The history is still left. The families are still left. Something is left. Death didn't kill it all, there is such *sadness* left. Like bones in a body when the skin is corrupted and gone all to powders. There *is* something left of what there was and the sad people keep it here."

"I'm trying to marry a widow, you mean?"

"I suppose. I'm so —"

"Well, widows don't mourn at the zoo. They don't stay faithful to some kind of memories — after being *un*faithful — by coming to meet their memories' cuckold that they're supposed to be faithful to after dishonoring what they're honoring *now.*"

"I don't — I'm sorry, really, I really didn't get that. I don't understand what you said. Would you say it again?"

"No. I can't even remember it."

The Pavilion, designed to house the Zoological Society's large collection of small mammals, is a new building with one hundred cages and three outside enclosures, accommodating some two hundred burrowing, jumping, running and climbing animals — marmots, martens, civets, mongooses, lemurs, marmosets, squirrel monkeys, ocelots, wallabies, wombats, porcupines and acouchies. When you follow her inside you can skirt the upper-floor exhibits and walk directly to the stairs that go down. Observe the sign that says DO NOT SPEAK LOUDLY and BEWARE PICKPOCKETS. Put your hand on your wallet, check your fly, walk downstairs with your change adrift in your pocket, rattling.

You will see that this hot wandering chamber is dark, lighted only by tiny red bulbs. A rail divides each crypt of the chamber in half, and each wall is windowed. Several different worlds have been placed side by side, sealed off from one another and discrete, in each glass wall. Follow the wall, keep to the left of the rail. Such creatures as bats, kinkajous, flying squirrels, douroucoulis and bush babies are normally active from dusk to dawn. In this large nocturnal section, known as the Moonlight World, special lighting has been installed, based on a study of these creatures' individual habits. This reverses their days and nights so that they are most active during public visiting hours. When the visitors leave, the lighting gradually increases and the animals fall asleep. They read the *Times* before retiring, and the angwantibos sing at the mouth of the gerbils' burrow as the light bulbs buzz. Visacha. Mouse lemurs. Seldom seen in movement. Seldom seen. For safety a dimly lit green sign on the ceiling warns the visitors to STAND IN PLACE UNTIL YOUR EYES ARE USED TO THE DARK.

Call to her that your eyes are not used to the dark yet.

"Hush, will you? Listen, I have to go now."

She will have moved around several bends of the chamber by now, for her eyes have grown used to the dark. Call to her again. If she silences you, remain silent, for rare Allen's bush babies live here and we want it to be a happy day for you and all the animals.

Still, you should call once more. Note that on the walls around you there are eyes, open eyes, blinking eyes, eyes that flee and return. Note that as you shout, as your feet shuffle, clanking the chains in your pocket, as your hands are held before you while you lurch, always to the left of your rail in the Moonlight World, how you frighten the eyes. They retreat. But they come back. The eyes in silence are the animals awake. When the visitors leave, the lighting gradually increases and the animals fall asleep. This reverses their days and their nights.

Now it is day. This is night to them, they are awake. As long as it is dark they are awake, for their eyes have grown used to the dark. And somewhere in the turnings of the Moonlight World she should say, "We have to go. I have to go."

"I don't want to go unless you come with me."

"No."

"Please."

"No. Hush."

"What about *my* history? Whose memory is that supposed to be sacred to? Who's remembering me? What about me? What good does loving you do *me?*"

But there is so much to see at the London Zoo. Take twenty-four thousand visitors on an average summer's day. As they enter the Moonlight World they obey the sign that tells them to STAND IN PLACE UNTIL YOUR EYES ARE USED TO THE DARK. When you flee them as they enter, you should keep to the left of the rail. The tiny animal eyes are open, of course, as you shuffle, jangling, for the eyes have grown used to the dark. This nighttime is their day. Take twenty-four thousand visitors. Come again and bring your friends to the Zoo. Beware pickpockets. Flee. Climb the stairs slowly and try to find her waiting for you at the top. When the visitors leave it is raw golden daylight. Come up blinking, blind.

Is Anyone Left
This Time of Year?

NOT IN WEXFORD, not in Cork. Not in Limerick, nor Nenagh, Killalo, Tulla, Gort. Nor Galway, under the Spanish arch on slimy cobbles near the bay where gypsy children beg. And not in Oughterard, the clap of crowding Galway gone, the smell of so many hungry breaths. And then there is Clifden. You can drive yourself deeper into the west if you want. You can get yourself nearly into the sea, rip the oil pan out on rocks and scours down to Aughrus More or Kill. But Clifden is far enough, coming in at dusk past the Twelve Bens and the autumn bogs of purple and burnt-brown that go like tide flats away from the cracked road's edge. You keep on driving west at the low red sun and fall into Clifden like a suitcase loaded with stones that falls in the sea.

The Dromaneen is closed. The Ivy Manor is closed. Salt House is closed. Keogh's is closed. The long dark street of Clifden runs to the other long street; they meet at a very sharp angle and point down the hill, over the brick and mortar ruins of the Old Town, over moss-grown steps and broken paving, into the bay. Paper and cans swept from bins by the wind are in the streets, moving. Light from the car shows where on the streets the car, swept in from the east, is moving too. Empty metal kegs of Harp and Guinness crowd the curbings every three doorways and then there is light from the Metropolitan, open, and the light falls onto the street and MAUMEEN'S — HIGH CLASS VICT-UALLER, UNDERTAKER. Closed. The Alcock and Brown is open; this is tinted glass and white stone and Connemara marble labeled

CONNEMARA MARBLE. This is where the red and brown tour buses come, where the lobby is rich with Irish coffee and genuine Irish wool and the booklets on Alcock and Brown, who ended their transatlantic airplane race by landing at Lough Fadda in a bog at an angle of forty-five degrees, sinking.

I land at the Inishturk Hotel, which is always open in the early fall, though most of the tourists are home or at the Alcock and Brown. I come from the dark clenched street past the foyer, where they still have not covered the red and black circuits and switches and fusebox plates that crawl on the high left-hand wall like a network of nerves. And there is the white urn of umbrellas, the bright brass handle on the door to the fireplace room, the Irish china and African hangings and red-flowered wallpaper, hundred-year-old wood of steps and bannister that go up to three floors of rooms. There is the dark carpet that goes past the desk with Peter O'Toole's signature under glass into the empty cavernous unlit lounge — vases and candlestands and feathers on lamp-shades, the wood of dried arrangements, ebony, Waterford crystal, ugly prints in golden frames. The emptiness, silence, absorption of light: what you drive at the sun for, fall to from lichenous mountains, Clifden, *An Clochan*, The Stepping Stones.

If I didn't come at the dusk of a Sunday past silent men who curl forever on donkey chaises, rocked, staring down their cigarettes at the road, and then past only the black road and darkening bogs, I could go down the hill to a ramp where cattle graze above the sea and seem, at a distance and when the sun is bright on the water, to step on the ocean and eat. But at night now I can enter the empty hotel and be noticed in a while and fill in the form and give the registration code and passport number and forwarding address — write *None* — and wait for Sheila to look and smile with her beaked angry nose, eyes with still too much of the dark silver makeup around them, and say, "Oh, *now* so. Of course. You didn't come again yet. We wondered, weeks back. So now you're here. And I've given a single one to you! That's easy to change, this time of year."

And then I must tell her to leave it at a single room.

And she must say, "Oh. A single, then."

And I must say a single, then.

•

She must look away, to Peter O'Toole's modest hand. Then she: "Well, I'll take you up myself, then, if you've no objections. You of all should know how there's nearly no one left this time of year. We do it all ourselves, you'll remember. Mother and me. We shall perish if we don't take care, I suppose. Overwork even in November, to listen to us."

I follow her dark short skirt, bright thighs, up the carpeted stairs to Room Eleven, its dense rich blankets and rug, the squat Victorian bureau, high wardrobe from some other time, the electric fire with ragged cord, the window over the street and the coastal perfume of mildew barely contained, and the usual slatted folding bench on which one lays his suitcase filled with stones.

She says, "We're happy you're back and dinner is always half-seven." I tell her I'm happy I'm back, and dinner at half-seven.

She says, "I remember now all your jokes about my marrying at thirty-three, you know. Well, this year I'm thirty-four." She smiles her angry smile and holds her naked fingers out, like a child in school, for inspection. "Will you tell me *this* is the lucky year?"

Then there is the room and what is in it and the time to wait. Then, still waiting, there is the private bar downstairs, the light-stained wood, bright fabrics, low uncomfortable chairs against the walls, the round china ashtrays and white plastic lightshades and Sheila behind the bar, who draws the Guinness but this time doesn't smile.

Her mother in tinted glasses, who is six feet tall, is smoking short cigarettes on the customers' side of the bar, telling her stories again to the ladies. One, in an open raincoat, leans back low in her straight-back chair and watches her hands on the cocktail table snap a little lighter on and off. Smoke from a frayed butt goes up in a line from her ashtray out of sight. Another lady, in a red plaid tailored suit, sits straight on a high square barstool and stares ahead, out of sight, and nods. The inside of her wrist leans on her collarbone and her fingers hold the cigarette near her lips and she squints inside of its smoke and stares. They have all together done their hair, which is knotted on the nape and parted in the middle, drawn back very tight, very blue.

Sheila's mother puffs and leans against the bar and tells her story of Murray who won a what-you-may-call-it, *letter*, in swimming in the

States. Murray is about to dive from their drifting gondola into the reeking Venetian canal. And she is about to ask the gondolier if he can swim. Then she is going to hold her question, for what if he can't? When she can't either, and at her age and condition of life? And Murray is about to dive and slide, like a pale freckled porpoise, through the stinking waters, then climb back into the boat and shiver and grin. They are about to head back. She is about to learn that the gondolier cannot swim. She will come to say, " 'Our sweet sacred Mother' is what I said, 'And that *still* don't make me your sister, you Roman,' I said," she will say, and they will laugh.

I go out to the dark still lobby and leave them poised — the boy on the hired gunwale, the mother in fear at the Romish canal — and stand in the empty fireplace lounge, with its coal fire silent and reeking; everything metal or wooden is polished, and shapes come back from all around in the coal's low light.

When Sheila comes in, there is only the hiss of coal and the falling of ash through the grate. You of all should know how there's nearly no one left this time of year. Then she puts the half-gone glass of stout on the imitation-ivory-inlaid table near the door and does not look away from what she does and is out of the writhing reflections and the sound of ash gone down. We do it all ourselves, you'll remember. We shall perish if we don't take care.

The small gold cymbal at the stairs' first turning is rung. Twenty-five tables covered with white are in the room, long and oval and sheeted and cold. Five long tables are covered with glassware and silver that crowds to every edge, and there is a bright red paper napkin at each place, and lights above each loaded table, hot on the ceiling, cold and yellow below. One of the tables has napkins and glasses and plates at each place, but silverware at only one, and Sheila sees me to the seat. She says, "I thought it would make for more cheer. We haven't that many people, you know. Two others, only. They're just married. They showed me how Hallowe'en is played in the States. We played Bob o' the Apple and we caught ghosts and lighted a squash. There's only one meal on the menu this time of year, you'll remember. Is that all right with you?"

I tell her only one meal on the menu is all right with me this time of year. The darkened rest of the room is like the hall of a closed museum.

Sheila brings what the meal is and takes the dishes away. I thank her after each course. She looks some other place. She says, "Would you like any more? We have enough for more if you'd like." She pulls at the towel tucked into her apron and her hands caress one another as if there is comfort there.

I tell her no and thank her, and she brings the bitter coffee and then takes the cup away. She brings a cognac and goes away and the newly married Americans come. She has hair the color of the red that is shiny on green pears, and he is bald and tall. His face reacts to everything she does and hers, all earnest frowns, reacts to what he says. They are happy with each other through the cheese and biscuits, and then he orders two sweet cherry liqueurs, and she hesitates and shakes her head. Sheila brings me another cognac, and the husband drinks the liqueur. The wife shakes her head again, and he reaches for her glass. Sheila comes with one more cognac, and the husband finishes her drink and orders one more. His wife says, "No more?" She says to Sheila, "We hardly ever drink."

His face goes red. I watch it change as the burn goes across it. But he shakes his head and finally grins, says, "I didn't really want the first one. It tasted like cherry cough medicine at home. We hardly ever drink."

When they leave, he moves her chair back from the table and helps her away. He leans a shoulder, an arm, toward her as if to shield her from something in ambush. She pulls on his sleeve, and he nods, bending down to her, and straightens and turns to me and nods, says, "Well, good night now." She smiles very widely as if she were trying to say something earnest and useful, something more helpful than only good night.

I say good night.

Sheila comes back when the couple is gone and says, "Could I bring you anything more? Aren't they gentle people? Pardon, of course, but especially for Americans. They have all that love on them like rain on a tree."

I ask her for a cognac and thank her.

She wipes her hands on the towel and says, "You know we have to charge you five-and-three for every glass?"

I thank her for worrying.

"I don't mind worrying, then."

I cough and look at the table and wait.

She says, "Did you enjoy the meal?"

I say that I enjoyed the meal. Then I look at the table and then I ask Sheila if she would like to drink a brandy with me.

She says, "Not until you mean that, thank you just the same, and I haven't driven you to it in desperation. I'm sorry that you've felt so."

Her angry eyes are on my face. I tell her that I'm driven to nothing at all. I tell her not to worry, and I smile. She leaves and returns with the cognac, and I tell her maybe we can have a drink before I leave.

"And leaving already?" she says.

I tell her no. I tell her I don't know. I look at the brandy, which is colored in the dim cold light like the stiffened surface of the dying bogs I came through, burnt-away brown and gold all day underneath no sky. It was the color of ashes in all directions, from the ground straight up, with no cloud and no color and no light reflected — dirty ash gone down on everything, and no sky. Through Maam Cross, Recess, and Ballynahinch, I came under no sky, and at Cashel Hill, among the Bens, the day was punctured by dusk, the sides collapsed, and ashen horizons leaked out, and there was the sun: red and swollen, grazing on the surface of the sea. You drive your car down the final hills and at the sun, to Clifden, where you drink the night's last cognac and see that she has gone — so leave the glass on the table and go to bed.

I go to bed. And later, in the dark, I sit up. I sit in the bay of the window and watch the town and sleep there, falling forward and coming out of sleep with my fingers clawing, my lips wide apart and dry, cracking sounds coming up from my sleep which I don't want to hear. Barefoot and in pajamas, I go downstairs along the carpeting to stand, like a child at night in the big house, before the locked saloon bar door. There are no fires and no lights. The flesh of my feet shines phosphorescent, like fishes belly-up in dark waters. I stand and I look at the door and shrug my shoulders and stand.

Sheila's mother says, "Do you need a drink?"

She wears wide-legged white pajamas under a dark robe and she must have dark slippers on, for she looms above me and all I see to hold her up is an inch of whiteness a little over the floor. Her hair is still up, her brown-tinted glasses still on, a cigarette yet in her hand, its redness moving as she speaks. She says, "Do you need a small something?"

I say I need something.

She says, "I do myself. Almost always now."

Her keys ring as if they are huge, and she opens the door in above the inch of whiteness that moves along the floor. She does not turn the bar lights on, but goes behind the counter — it smells like the closet of a dirty smoker, cigarettes and flesh combined — and she serves me something that I drink. She pours it for herself and then for me, and I wrestle up to a stool while she drinks and pours again.

"Isn't it a pity not to sleep?" she says. "I never knew what peace meant until I lost the power of sleep."

I say it is a great pity not to sleep.

"The rooms you leave at night lose their attraction in the morning somehow," she says. "As if they need your sleep to renew them as well as you yourself needing the sleep, sort of. Do you follow me?"

I say I've noticed it also, rooms eroding.

"Do you pray at night?" she says. "Are you religious?"

I say that I am not religious. I say I don't pray.

"Does that mean you have no hope?" she says. "Would you like another?"

I say I don't mind.

"John Jameson," she says. "Not that Old Paddy — which is genuine Irish, right enough, but it's coarse like most of the genuine Irish. *And* a bad bargain, like the genuine Irish, costing as much as a good whiskey does. Have you tasted the difference?"

I say I've tasted them both and Paddy is coarse. I say I don't mind.

She says, "Do you have feelings over the Belfast problems they're having?"

I say no.

She pours us each another, then says, "Is there anything you'd care to discuss, then?"

I say no.

She says, "Then I'll leave you the bottle, and with our good wishes, and I will be off to my bed if not, Lord willing, my sleep."

I thank her and wish her sleep and she is gone. I leave my drink on the bar and walk around the room. Into my eyes, the pupils large enough by now, and focused, things like chairs and ashtrays come, and then they're out and I've gone around the room again. Soon I stop and finish my drink, leave the glass beside the bottle and go outside, closing the door very gently. On the carpeted steps, a blanket around her head and torso, like a gypsy woman sleeping at someone's door awhile, squats Sheila; her feet are covered, her arms are in the blanket, so only the low brightness of her face shows up — unappeased eyes and angry beak and teeth.

"I see you're having a difficult night," she says. "Who teased me once about long nights."

I say yes.

"I'm sorry," she says. She says, "Couldn't people ever help each other with their lives?"

I tell her I wouldn't know.

"Shouldn't they do what they can?" she says. "Make the try for comfort's sake?"

I tell her no. I go up past her on the steps and from the back and the stairs' first turning she is vanished into her blanket. She is one of the Inishturk's dark fabrics in the slack season, waiting for another year.

I go to bed and fall asleep and my cracked lips wake me up and then I sleep again. Then it is morning and time for breakfast, which the newlyweds don't attend. Sheila has the electric fires on. She brings in coffee and sets it before me in that ballroom of silence. She folds her towel and says to it, "What can I make you for breakfast?"

I ask her how she slept. She nods and I see the sockets of her eyes, silver shadow gone. I tell her some kind of juice and thank her.

She says, "I made my decision last night. Would you like to hear it?"

I say yes.

She says, "I've decided I'm marrying in the time between when we close and when we open in May. It means I'll be a *missus* if you come here again in the fall and notice me about, laughing and all."

I say good, getting married.

"Because it's time now not to live alone. And mothers don't count in such. It's time now not to be living alone anymore at my time and place."

I look at the table, and then I say yes, that's good, marrying.

"Even if I have to find him in a Galway saloon," she says. "Because I *will* find a husband, I decided now."

I fold my red napkin in quarters and nod. I look at the dark brown sugar, tiny useless teaspoons, the stubs of my fingernails folding the fourths into eighths. I nod and keep nodding while she watches me, and I tell her sausages, tomato, scrambled egg.

Then it is the Brandy and Soda Road, with a sky and sun today before lunch at the Inishturk, saxifrage in the heaths showing, cattle and sheep at the stone fences and in the bogs where the Atlantic pushes through the grass in long tidal pools, like the fingers of a lover in a lover's hair. After a while the bright fading grass is level with the narrow road, and the hills have rippled back to where the sea is.

Past a settlement of three square cement houses, one of which has PROVISIONS neatly painted in black on its wall, an unpaved road curves off and goes behind the houses in a wide brown arc. The houses vanish and a hill comes up, high weeds blown by the wind from the sea. The road, grown rockier, heads for the hill and climbs it, toward three shapes outlined on the sky. A small diesel engine covered by tarps is throbbing; it is surrounded by empty jerry cans used for gasoline; wires from the engine run to a high dark van in which no one is sitting, and antennae on the van's roof jump in the steady hard winds. Nearby is a small blue caravan with padlocked door, the sides scratched deep, the windows covered with blinds. The engine pushes electricity out to the van where the radio is, and no one appears. Down the hill and on the other side is a lower hill, and then the Atlantic foaming in at the bleached-bone sand of the small bay. Out on the ocean there are boats that men here call to with their radio, if the men here call, if there are men to call now, warning of winds such as these that now drive the ocean in and rock the trailer and my car and the untended antennae that the throbbing engine feeds.

It is time to go there now, where the ocean never stops banging onto the bone-white beach, the Shore of the Plover, where the sand is made of tiny shells with nothing in them anymore except the wind.

The dirt road goes down to a narrow track with deep furrows, and the car's sides crush against low weeds and high rocks and the track runs off to the right, away from the bay. There are no houses. There is one long hill to the left, low between the ocean and the track, and then the ground on the right rises up to another low hill, and that comes up near the track, while the fields before the car open out and just go on.

The wheel pulls my hands back and forth, and the steel around me makes sounds of things shaking loose. The light brown earth of the track is disappearing as the car falls farther on. A man is very small with no face on the leftward hill as he lifts from the ground and moves a few steps and then returns to where he was before and stoops and lifts. There is nothing on the hill to my right. And far ahead, down the rock field, at the farthest point of my sight, a small white pony is bent to the ground, and a brown pony stands erect. And the car stops, for the track is gone, and there is only rock and some grass. There is track that stops, and a man who endlessly stoops on top of a hill, and two unmoving ponies down the vast stony meadow, and the track ending, a gash or two in the earth and nothing then: the tiny car, the tinier man inside it, the hidden sea, the wind, the immensity coming down.

It is time to turn the car around and follow the track back, pick up the suitcase, and pay them at the Inishturk and leave, to drive up from Clifden back through the Bens and east through Maam Cross and Oughterard, across the Corrib back to see once more if there is some-place, this time in Galway, down in the crowded small streets, where someone is left.

A Three-Legged Race

I HAD SOMETHING TERRIBLE in my eye. It turned red, then the lid lowered until I looked like a pirate. I was sure that's how I looked though I had only heard about pirates, never seen a picture of one. In 1919, Orthodox Jewish girls didn't look at books about pirates. My mother took me to the drugstore. She wore no coat although it was autumn and cold in Manhattan. She made me wear my older sister's handed-down coat. To shame me with her martyrdom? Maybe only because I hated my sister, who made my life terrible. A punishment of warmth.

We couldn't afford to consult the druggist, but we could afford a doctor less. She told me this. So I felt wretched, the cause of more poverty, as we left. Because it was Saturday, all the lights in the apartment were off. The foyer door from our building opened out and wonderful light came in. I was surprised that the street looked so happy. She held my hand, but not with affection. She showed her affection only at night, when she was tired and would have to live until morning with her memories of too little food for us, clothing made of rags, our father's furious noises, all the crying. Then, as we went to bed, she told us stories of Austria and in Yiddish said wisdoms. All she could give. But on the street she held my hand to keep me. As a cat coldly carries its young in its mouth. Efficiency. We didn't talk.

Past the Yiddish theater, the newspaper kiosk, across the trolley tracks we couldn't ride on Saturday, the kosher shops which were closed because on the Sabbath money was not to be touched. Bessermann, a Jew but more a merchant, in his store that smelled of soap and ginger and vanilla, was like a king. Fat-bellied but small in the face, with little eyes and little fingers, a mouth that also smelled of soap, he held my face and turned it, pulled my eyelid up, made me roll my eyeball and weep.

"Tessie," he told my mother, dropping my face from his hand, "you'll leave the eye here overnight, I'll have it ready in maybe two days. Yes?"

I said nothing. I wept harder but I said nothing. Then he folded a shape of blue paper, poured some powder in, told my mother how to use it. She never smiled or spoke, except to tell him that on Monday he'd be paid. He nodded and forgot me. And in the street I howled with horror. My mother took my hand and pulled me home. At night she spoke to me of jokes and teasing. But she left me in her silence during the rest of the long afternoon.

I wonder if I believed him when he said it. I have believed so much. I wonder now, at the middle of the century I started in, whether I was really afraid. How much was I disappointed? That the torture, theft, bereavement, heroism, *magic* didn't take place? Bessermann was only a human male. This is the problem of modern man. My problem too.

Weakness. As when I was working for Liveright, taking dictation, typing, even reading some manscripts. People coming in drunk with cocktails in their hands. The long talks about music and drama. The way they would remember finding Hemingway's stories with their little italicized chapters between a book about African sex and a manuscript on Marxist art criticism. They weren't doing well, then, and I earned very little. But it was the most exciting time of my life. I was alive, in touch with living people and everything important in the world. Sometimes I didn't eat lunch for fear of missing an irreplaceable accidental event.

With this there was Alvin, finishing his residency at St. Vincent's, eating meals in Greenwich Village, where I lived on 11th Street, the most exciting place in the world besides Paris. We would meet sometimes and talk of dreams. He wanted to practice medicine on an island in the Pacific. We wanted everything simple, fundamental. Life could be *touched*, we said. He would heal people and I would write a book about us. We believed that. We believed in Edna St. Vincent Millay, the unbitter parts of her poems. What we wanted, I still believe in that. You could have it now if you wanted to deserve it. Even now.

But his Jew-bitch mother had the soul of an adding machine. I never met her. He never brought me home. She told him that an office with a nurse and a large enough car would cost him $10,000, which he didn't have. Only a girl with money, easily married and jailed at the back of the private house she bought him. Only that. Not me. So Alvin wrote me a letter and explained. I have never accepted explanations since then.

I continued to live on 11th Street, meeting interesting people, seeing plays, refusing to write to my mother. My father by then had left her. A drunken baker addicted to cough syrup. I called myself an orphan. I was dreaming alone. I met Mrs. Miriam and visited often in her wonderful flat on Washington Square. She was elegant. I never thought of her as a mother, of course. I had no mother. But she taught me how to cook, and when I didn't work in the office on Saturdays, she let me sell the jewelry she made in the shop she ran on Grove Street. I loved handling the money, and sometimes, when no customers were there, I rang NO SALE and scooped the dimes and nickels into my hands, let them run like water back down. Her husband was an alcoholic. Weakling. But a very handsome man. He was always asleep when I came. She made him keep out of the way. She introduced me to Eugene O'Neill. Now I talk to janitors and pension clerks. She's old. I don't know where she is. She's ancient. I'm afaid to see her or speak on the phone. There is nothing to say. I wonder how she stays alive. She's alone now. Who isn't?

I married Mac because he was more of a virgin than I was. He was afraid to take me to his mother too. He wouldn't sleep in my apartment until we were married. Then he moved in. I had assumed he would find a larger place for us to live in. But he let me do the finding. Always. The new apartment in Brooklyn. Then the Brooklyn house. He loved me more than I loved him. He joined the Party because I did. Quit when I quit. He followed me everywhere, even in the house. I wasn't surprised. What surprised me was that I needed him. The day after we were married and had finally made love, after a night when he wouldn't let me speak of Alvin anymore, I was standing at the door of the apartment with my coat on. From the day bed he said, "Where are you going?" I told him out for a walk. He said, "What about me?" I told him I'd forgotten. I waited for him to dress.

I had two miscarriages before Harry. They told me I might die if we tried again. Mac said no. But I said yes. We tried again. It almost killed me, but it didn't, and there was my child. There. *Where?*

And when Mac was in the army during the war, Harry had pneumonia. We didn't have the money for sulfa drugs, but I got the money. I always did what I had to. For three nights, I tied myself with Venetian blind cords to the slats of his crib so I would stay awake to take care of him. In the morning Mac's mother would come, with a look on her face as if it was my fault I had to go to work to make the money to keep him alive. Not that she would give me a dime. And at night I would come home and eat standing up beside the crib. And then the ropes, and watching him all night. He lived, and there was my child.

At thirty-two a nearsighted teacher had to join the army. It happened in the movies that way. I'm sure that's where he got the idea. He loved the movies. All that glory and heroism. They always lied, the heroes. They did anything to get in and get shot. Like a man in the movies, he memorized the eye charts, and they took him. So he could leave us behind, I thought. Or wondered. I wondered about that. I had a right to. Where were our dreams of long walks and long talks? Of living an intelligent life of excitement? In the army, being shot. Every day he wrote about how much he missed us. Training in Colorado, then Texas, then going overseas. Telling me, I remember it because it was so stupid and he said it all the time: *I won't get killed. They can't kill me. I'll come home safe.* And I was always surprised, when I wasn't panicked about money or Harry's health, to learn how much I needed Mac to live and return.

So today there's a new disease. Anorexia nervosa. Young girls get it. They starve. They vomit when they eat, even if they're hungry. Once it was polio and pneumonia, now this modern sickness. The girls are the ones who run away from home. Promiscuous, taking drugs. The kind of girl who lived with that killer Manson, the sex maniac. Doing anything with anyone. This is the age of disgust. They look like Auschwitz prisoners toward the end. Living skeletons. And an article in the *Times* blames it on whom? The mother. Of course. I don't remember. Either the mother feeds them too much, says "Eat, eat!" like the Jewish mother everyone makes fun of, our culture's new scapegoat, or she takes her breast away. It threatens them. So how can a mother win, with such "research"? She feeds them or she doesn't, and either way she's a monster. *That's* the disgusting part. Thank God I didn't have a daughter.

I had a son. My mouth used to water when I made him mashed potatoes with milk and butter mixed in. Now he hates mashed potatoes. He had a piano recital in elementary school. I asked him what he wanted me to wear. He told me the plaid dress with the high collar. Made of wool. In June, I wore it. I sweated for an hour to hear him play "I have a little Scottie dog/A little Scottie dog have I." Now he doesn't touch an instrument.

I have studied at Columbia, NYU, Rutgers, and a summer at Harvard, not to mention the A.B. from Hunter, and nothing has prepared me for this. Brooklyn, where we used to live in Flatbush, was green. No cars. Empty lots with trees and bushes in them. The children played in the street and not too many cars came. It was middle class, then upper middle class, then they built the yellow-brick yeshivah on the corner. Then the people across the street, all with red hair and loud voices, the kind who get Jews persecuted, cut their two old maple trees down to build a patio on the front lawn with a high wooden fence for privacy when they gave their parties. Soon the Negroes came, and that was that. Mac got the job at Columbia, we left. I was afraid to stay. Not because of Negroes. Because of *no values*. Nobody respected anything I had learned to respect. Sidewalks, buildings, shrubbery, physical human bodies. Everything was endangered. It was time to go.

Here it isn't much better. People should learn not to dream.

I dieted for months before Mac came home from the service, healed from his wound. I look at pictures of us. I have hundreds and hundreds, maybe a thousand. Pictures. We look ancient. The skirts high, but a childish height. The hair of the women piling over the forehead, or onto the nape, or over the ear. Nothing balanced — *cocky* is the word. No matter how frightened, there was jauntiness in our faces and even our feet. Not like the English. They went crazy when Hitler said he would invade them, and they never recovered. Every morning, ten years later, they tighten their belts in case they're attacked. No. But we were sure. There was Hitler versus us. There was evil, there was good. We were good. We would win. We won, so the A-bomb was good. The Japanese were bad, so the A-bomb killed them and they lost. They were like Negroes to us. Oilier, more elusive. Like Negroes who had forgotten subservience. Pearl Harbor was an early example of Black Power. Only later on we couldn't drop the A-bomb on Harlem in retaliation without killing the landlords and policemen, who then were mostly white.

But we didn't *think* about that. We thought about us versus them and good over bad and we won. In the movies, when I could go, which wasn't too often, I cried. When the uneducated and undereducated wept, so did I. For Myrna Loy and Jean Arthur and Raymond Massey. William Bendix. My God, for William Bendix: the stupid feeling heart of us all. Lloyd Nolan! Because to me in that time of my life, when I might have been half insane, but not knowing it, life unrolled simply before me. No matter how horrible or hard. It nevertheless was clear. It was a road I went down.

So Mac lived through the war. I did. Harry did. I dieted forever and was nearly thin on the day I was to take the BMT to 42nd Street, change for the shuttle, go to Grand Central, and meet his train from the West Coast. I walked to the subway station. On the steel and concrete bridge over the Long Island Rail Road freight line tracks on Avenue H, trees blowing and the sky as blue as a summer snapshot, the tall handsome soldier walked past me. I smiled and so did he. My stomach tightened, I thought of my body as provocative. I thought of *men*. From the other end of the bridge he called me: "Claire! Claire!" Our reunion.

But I recognized him after that. And he knew me. He got his job back at Brooklyn College, though they made him teach freshman composition for years during the slump. I worked at my degree during summers and nights. During the weekdays I worked for Henry Holt. I free-lanced for Harcourt. In Manhattan I was competent. At home in Brooklyn I made meals and interviewed maids. One stole my wallet during the interview. One, a German, Mac felt sorry for her, lived in. Every Friday night I made us go out. To see publishing friends, never his colleagues. I never met his colleagues except by accident. We came home early one night to see her drunk with two men. Two clients. With Harry sitting on the hall steps, listening. So I have been a kind of madam too. I studied and I went to school. I taught part-time at night on an assistantship. I nearly went crazy. I won my Ph.D. But no one hired Jewish ladies in English departments. I edited books for men who were editors.

Mac in his bed dreamed of death. He rolled, he bit his lip, he cried and whimpered. I woke him when the nightmares came and asked him to tell me what it was. He said, "The war." For years he told me nothing. It was his. I had my bed and my own nightmares. We met in the morning. Two pieces of toast with peanut butter and marmalade. Two cups of coffee. Every morning he ate that meal and on the way to school, he never told me where, had another cup of coffee. He read Freud for help in analyzing his dreams, and they stopped. For him it was always that simple. My dreams went on in the daytime.

He was promoted, and I was given raises, though never better jobs. I stopped applying to teaching posts and taught myself Russian. Everyone said the Russians would conquer the world. Maybe they would let me teach. Then postcards came from my mother. She lived on the Lower East Side, still. "Dear daughter" they began. In the middle they always said, "I know you will try to send what you can." At the end, "I hope Mac and the children are well." I never told her Harry was all that we had. Mac sent her money at the end of every month. And then my father sued us, all the children, for support. We sent nothing. Mac went to court. I couldn't. I couldn't. We didn't hear from him again until my youngest sister wrote me that he died in a county hospital. I didn't tell Mac for a month.

Mac's parents lived with his sister, Ida. She and Dick drove them back to New York from Monticello where they were sick. His mother hated me, always. She blamed me when he went to the war. She blamed me whenever Harry was sick. When Mac was in the hospital for his back, she told me I didn't take care of him. They didn't know how sick she was. She died in horrible pain and I hated them — his sister and his brother and him. Letting her die. Alone. Yes, in a room where her daughter lived. Yes, visited by her children. Yes, attended by the weak old man, her husband, who in Russia was an anarchist, quailing now and flimsy and full of fear. But alone.

I made the arrangements for the wake. He was strong for his brother and sister, and he held his father as if his father were his child. Then he wept and coughed when we were alone in the house. He let me hold him in our living room and on the stairs. When we pulled Harry's covers up on his shoulders. In our bedroom beside my bed. Then he told me his heart was pounding. He shook and sweated, felt his own pulse. He told me that his chest hurt. He couldn't breathe. He lay in his bed and I watched him till he slept. We never went to bed together again.

We went to the nineteen-fifties. Arguments about Eisenhower. Mac thought he looked like Ike and voted for him, though his colleagues all voted for Stevenson. I didn't vote. Everyone we'd seen in leftist theater in the thirties was turning everyone else in to congressional committees. We got Harry a TV set, and the programs were about Communists trying to subvert the American way. The TV went in the semi-finished basement near the furnace. I let Harry watch an hour a day during the week, an hour and a half on Saturday, two hours on Sunday. Mac watched the "Colgate Comedy Hour" with Harry and howled at Jerry Lewis until the tears ran on his face. I read upstairs. I liked Mister Peepers: he reminded me of me. Mac said there was no resemblance. And at Brooklyn College, the left-wing teachers were purged. Mac kept his mouth shut and survived.

We had pretty much stopped going to parties by then. We sometimes went to museums or on a Sunday field trip, but Harry hated that and I hated his sulking. We stayed home. They did. I went to the city by myself as often as I could. I wanted to go on field trips with the Brooklyn Bird Club by myself. But Mac insisted on coming. He never initiated. He always went along. Which meant Harry had to come, because who can you trust with a pre-adolescent all day long? They were hateful days, and I was happy to come home so they would watch their Sunday television.

When I complained that Mac never took me to lunch near the

campus, or had his colleagues over, he planned a party. All I had to do was complain. Then he'd act. He invited six army buddies and their wives or girlfriends for a Friday night. I came home from work in the early afternoon and cooked. A *crème caramel*, hot beef hors d'oeuvres in cream, veal birds stuffed with ham, fresh broccoli, bottles of liquor and soda, freshly ironed tablecloths and napkins. Harry wore a sport coat we had bought because Mac said a boy of eleven should own a sport coat. He whined when I made him put it on, but then he got excited. He got ready to be cute and winning for the guests, I could see that.

They came in their business suits and party dresses. They had never met me. Mac had never brought us together after the war. We sat in a ring in the living room and I made each one a highball, measuring the ounce and a half of liquor in a silver cup, two ice cubes per drink so we wouldn't run out of ice. Mac wasn't home by six, and then he wasn't home by seven. At nine they were itchy with embarrassment for me. Harry chattered and amused them. Then he bored them. We ate. I made more drinks for them. I wouldn't drink anything. I pressed my hands in my lap and waited. At ten-fifteen the phone rang and they watched me answer it in the hall. It was Mac, so drunk he hardly could talk. He said, "Claire? Claire? I'm at a corner. Can you see me? What's the corner called, Claire? I don't know where I am. Do *you* know where I am?" I made him describe the street and I told him to stay there. Then I called the police and asked them to find him.

So I met Mac's friends. They met Harry. They all disapproved of me, and we didn't invite them again. When we had people over, they were my friends. Mac would sit at the table, listening to us but not really listening. He was always by himself.

Harry turned twelve. He was fat and pimply, oversexed, full of worries that girls didn't like him. He couldn't dance, so I tried to teach him the box step. He wouldn't learn. He didn't like dancing with his mother, he said. He always was unhappy, very fresh to us, stayed by himself. On Fridays after school, he either played stickball in the street with his friends — all in dungarees, high greasy pompadours, swaggers, Eisenhower jackets, and turtlenecks — or he did what he really preferred. Went to the library, came home with a pile of science fiction books, drank some milk and ate some cookies, went upstairs to lock himself in his room with the toy pistols he still kept. Reading fantasy trash in his room by himself.

For his twelfth birthday I planned a surprise party. Carefully learned his friends' last names so I could telephone them. Even the girls he liked. Made my plans with Mac. He said it would be nice. Nice. Because frankfurters made me sick, I wouldn't trust them. I shaped hamburger meat at night into long tubes. Mac brought home charcoal for the grill. On a Saturday in July I sent Harry on a complicated series of errands to Avenue J which would keep him away for an hour or more. He grumbled, of course. He was always grumbling, half in tears, fearful, mad. While he was gone, as arranged, his friends came. Three boys who looked like bums. And one was the son of a high school principal! And four girls, all looking the same. Fluffy hair, sleeveless flaring dresses that swished. One of them had breasts as large as mine. Mac played his avuncular personality like a matinee part. Laughing with them, getting them to help him make the fire, setting out paper plates and plastic forks on the backyard table.

It was a bright hot day; the trellises which screened us from the neighbors were green and shining. Those wonderful high ancient trees rolled in the wind. The children had stacked their presents for Harry and were talking awkwardly among themselves. Mac pruned hedges and dug up weeds. He loved to do that. Sit on the soil in his army coveralls and push his fingers into the dirt. I had the cake in the icebox and was starting to cook. The beef smell and charcoal were mixed with the slow fire Mac had started in a garbage pail for weeds and old leaves. It got hotter and everything smoldered. The air in the back-yard shimmered. I was happy, and happier when Harry drove home on his bike, carrying a high bag of groceries in one hand, braking and putting his foot down in imitation of motorcyclists he'd doubtless seen on TV.

His friends waved to him without speaking. Then one of the girls went up to him and kissed him on the cheek. They shouted Happy Birthday. They all shrieked laughter. I thought that he would weep. But Mac came up and broke the uneasiness, hugged Harry's shoulders, made one of his little unfelt speeches and then a joke. They laughed more easily, came to the table to watch him open his gifts. He followed very slowly. The girl who had kissed him was holding hands with one of the thugs. He rubbed her buttocks when they thought I wasn't looking. Then: aftershave lotion for my boy! A necktie thin as a string. A paperback book by Isaac Asimov from the girl who had kissed him. How could she know him so well and let a hoodlum rub her body like that? A child. Or a wise child. She made me angry and sad.

They ate in silence, the moment of emotion over — or the imitation they had resolved to create. It was over. Even during the cutting of the cake. They had sung "Happy Birthday" in cracked soft voices. Then they ate as if their embarrassment choked them. Harry looked at his book on the table. His face looked panicky. Mac was throwing weeds on his fire. I acted fast.

I went into the house for the ropes and showed them to the children. All cut into the right lengths. I told them some games would be fun. The boys smirked and raised their eyebrows. Pushing pimples up. The girls smiled at each other when they thought I wasn't looking. Harry sat at the table, red as if with sunburn. Finally he said, "Ma. *Ma.*"

But I knew what to do. I called two of the boys to the far end of the garden while Harry shook his head and hung it. Mac stayed to watch, then went into the house. While I positioned the boys side by side and tied their adjacent legs together, Mac came back out and went to his fire. Then we were ready for the three-legged race. I called, "Ready, get set, go!" and they hobbled through the garden to the birthday table and back toward Mac and me. One pulled the other forward, one dragged the other back. They didn't work together well, as if they pulled another body between them. They made rude comments and sweated, tripped. I said, "Make the ropes *help* you. Some tough guys. You act like you're in a chain gang!" I untied them. Because I knew what preadolescents were like, fifty percent sex maniacs, I made up two teams, a boy and a girl on each team. Better to let them feel each other's legs in your own backyard than at some party with stolen liquor.

I tied Harry's leg to the leg of the girl who had kissed him and given the science fiction book. For fun, I set them opposite the tallest boy whom I tied to the littlest girl. Mac went into the house and came back out. Harry was still bright red. The girl smiled a tolerant smile. She acted as if Harry were her brother. He didn't protest anymore, and I thought to myself that the party would end up successful even if I had to run in a three-legged race myself. I said cheerfully, "All right. Now you've got the idea. Let's see which is the best team!" I love parties, and I hadn't minded the hours and money spent to make this one work. *I* would make it work.

Mac went back into the house and returned as I started them off. Harry and his partner tripped right away and lay in the dirt as the other couple hopped and dragged each other from the fire to the birthday table and back. They won. And Harry lay with tears in his eyes. I could see them. The girl whispered to him and then sat up to untie them from each other. Mac went into the house and came out with Harry's basketball. He threw it over and said he thought they ought to walk over to Wingate Field and have a coed game. Two of the girls said ritual thanks as they left. The boys waved. Harry, red and moist-eyed, called, "Thanks for the surprise birthday, Mom. Thanks, Dad." He said it as his back was turning, so the words went with him. They were gone.

Mac went into the house and returned to his fire. I looked at a piece of frankfurter-shaped hamburger meat which I'd left on the grill. It was charred black, it looked like a tiny piece of wood, smoking. The gifts were on the table, and dirty paper dishes, smeared plastic forks and spoons. Most of the fruit punch I'd made them was gone. I felt sick.

Mac came over from the fire and sat on the bench of the table. He said, "I thought it was a pleasant party."

"Harry hated it," I said.

"No." He said it the way a father comforts a child.

"Stop it, Mac. It was a flop. That's that."

"Claire? Don't be so upset. He's growing up. It's awkward. That's all."

"That's all. That's all. I tried so *hard*. I *love* to make parties for him. I wanted this to be so *happy*."

He said, "Well." Well.

I saw the afternoon again and hated it. All I felt was humiliation. All he'd wanted was to get away. I saw everything again. Then again. I turned my head. Mac always looked at me a certain way when I turned my head a certain way. We were doing that. Then I walked over to his fire in the garbage pail, which had more smoke than before. He called, "Claire?"

I pulled one of the books from the fire. It was only a little blackened, only the fringes of some pages were burned. *Johnny Got His Gun* by Dalton Trumbo. I pulled another out and beat the embers from it: *Heroes I Have Known* by Max Eastman. More, then. Engels on the Manchester working class. *Progress and Poverty.* A study of Beatrice Webb. Some of the pamphlets I used to push under doors in the thirties on my way to work. The books of all that dreaming. All those years in the Village. High hopes and big talk and the sureness we were right.

I walked to the hedges and looked into them. All I saw were insects and droppings and leaves. The books made my hands hot. Mac said, "It's the only way to be safe."

"So now we're safe."

"They're firing people who even went to meetings and never *joined*. We were *in* the Party, we were in the Nature Friends, we were in Youth Against Fascism. They're fronts, Claire. People are making lists. Would you like me to get fired?"

"*Fronts.* You sound like a German. Like a senator. Fronts. I never asked for a front. I *wanted* to be a Communist."

"But now you don't."

"Now things are different."

"Tell *them*, Claire."

"All right."

He sat and looked at me. I waited for him to argue, but he almost never argued. It reminded me of my father if he shouted. He knew that. We wouldn't fight. I stood at the hedges and looked at him and he sat at the birthday table and looked down the garden toward me. He held his hands out at his sides, like an old Jewish man in the neighborhood I'd lived in as a child. He smiled.

I said, "All right." I went over and put the books back into the fire and then walked toward him and past him and up the steps to the dark kitchen. He came in with a tray of paper plates and cups, the leftover food, even the short lengths of rope. He always was meticulous. He was old. He put the ropes into the drawer where he kept his hammer and nails and pliers. Everything was taken care of now. Our family was safe.

The Trouble with Being Food

I WAS A VERY FAT BOY and always had to tolerate mezzanines in clothing stores called Big Guys and Muscle Builders, and in smaller shops in our neighborhood I would suffer comments from little men and women, spoken at my parents from between my legs, such as "He needs a lot of room in the seat, huh?" Then in college I grew thin without trying, and loved it, and wore as little as I could to show as much of my smallness as was possible. When I left school I ballooned again, and as I've wandered I've swelled. But Katherine, whom I travel to in Montpelier, Vermont, where she lives with her kids, from Cicero, New York, where I live with myself and the usual upstate ad agency — no talent in the shop, and little income — says she loves my stomach, which stays round when I lie down. She holds it sometimes between her hands. I try to cram it all inside her cold palms. I'm not in good health. I try not to pant on the pillow after love.

On the pillow after love at night in Vermont I hear my heart knock, and it wakens me. Katherine snores. It's the same wet growl as my father's, which I heard twenty years ago or more, in our house at night. It's the same dream: the long thin lighthouse with its corrugated metal steps, and up the steps and around and up, *rumpty-dump* and *rumpty-dump*, here comes Casper the Friendly Ghost, footless but marching, *rumpty-dump*, and I waken to hear my father snore. I didn't know for twenty years that my pillow is a drum, I hear my heart. It haunts me out of sleep.

Katherine stops snoring and says, "What is it?"

I say, "Me."

She says, "Oh." Then: "I thought it was one of the kids." Then: "Or Marlon Brando." Then she snores.

I say it to myself: Tomorrow morning I'm going on a diet. I'm losing seventy-five pounds. I'll become superb. Because when I have the heart attack I don't want my nurses making jokes about me.

I fold the pillow so it hurts the back of my neck, and I lie against my rock, a holy man, impressed that I'm not afraid, but earnest about staying up all night so as not to hear my heart do what it does in the darkness: surge to the base of my throat and rap like fists, race my pulse up, cover my forehead and neck with sweat. I am no longer impressed, and I *am* afraid, and I wonder if Katherine will waken to find my body in bed in her home, but no one home in the skin.

This is not a fertile pursuit. I consider her sons — slender like her, like their long-gone crazy father whom we often discuss, calmly and matter-of-factly, because Katherine and I are adults and this is her history: what can we do but discuss? (We can burn his clothing, cauterize her cervix of his trace, defile his name in the children's ears, and hire assassins to hunt him into terror and slow death.) But we discuss, it's what she needs. And in her old farmhouse surrounded by potato fields, wind with the smell of snow lying up against our breathing, I lie against Katherine, blink against sleep and the dreams of my fat body, consider her sons.

The question is whether Sears and Roebuck will question my lie that Randy and Bob are my sons too. They're listed on the application I returned, which came to tell her about life insurance for less than seven cents a day, which everyone needs because in America there's death by accident every five minutes. It said, "Think what a check for $100,000 can mean to your loved ones at such a time." All right: a fertile pursuit.

What I'm waiting for, of course, is the burst of pain up my neck, the tingling fingers. What I'm waiting for is a way to fall beneath a truck before that happens: accidental death, and an end, by the way, to nighttime snacks and the sneaking of seventh helpings — the ultimate diet. As Randy said, "Hey Harry? I think Santa Claus is fatter'n you, isn't he?" Not by much, kid. And when I show up in your fireplace you'll see who knows about ashes.

So here I am now, insured but still breathing, though not awfully well, at Katherine's living room window. The coffee is made, the house is in its early Saturday morning ease. Upstairs Bob rolls against the bars of his crib and they rattle, but everyone sleeps. The light swings through the town. It squeaks over fog frozen onto cornstalks that flap, and over the telephone wires fencing in the leafless trees on either side of the road. Everything had just been blue, and then it was ashen with cold sun on houses and fields. And now it's morning, the truck is idling at the trees beside Purdy's Bridge while its cherry picker hoists a man on its platform to prune the branches which in winter might fall under snow loads and snap the cable into silence.

While one man from the telephone company uses his chain saw and hooks, another in an orange safety vest gathers fallen branches and throws them into the back of the truck. Then he waits for the hoist to come down, then gets inside and drives to the next stand of trees, gets out and places the yellow sign in its metal frame on the road in front of the truck. It says MEN WORKING IN TREES and he gathers more gray wood as the saw tears. I think of men in the crotches of all the trees on the town's main street, repairing shoes, restringing guitars, mitering wood, filing down ignition points. All of them are loved by fine women, everyone is smiling, and chamber music makes the shape of a room above the road and fills it. Yellow light from the top of the cab, in its squeaky swinging bubble, jumps through the town. And here comes Katherine, softly through the cold morning in her wooden house while children breathe upstairs and flatter us with their serenity. By keeping silent we pretend to give them cause for calm sleep: that lie of family love.

Think what a check for $100,000 can mean to your etc.

Heart disease makes you look *in*. So as Katherine walks across her living room — tall in a fleecy blue bathrobe that ties beneath the breasts and makes her look pregnant, big of foot in slippers of fleece that make her slide: long-faced, shining, glad — I hear my heart rock wetly in my chest. The pulse feels fast, I want to clock it, but I smile. She watches my eyes, she feels me sliding in and hooks me out as the light of the truck creaks by: "Good morning, good morning. Are you leaving us for good?"

I shake my head and smile. Good child.

She says, "Are you leaving us for a quickie back home?"

Shake.

"Are you tired of older women? Am I scary-looking in the morning?"

Shake again. Reach for her furry front and pet it.

"So why are you sneaking around the house? You make coffee at dawn like a husband. Pad-pad-pad in your bare feet. Clank the pot like a cymbalist."

"That's me. Your community orchestra. Music to get laid by."

She pushes into my palm, says "Shut up," and we hug in until our crotches dock through cloth. We spill coffee, chunk the mugs onto the white-painted windowsill, back off and circle around the sofa which is at right angles to the window: she goes her way around, and I go mine, and we meet at adjacent cushions. When I sit, my stomach presses up inside my body and squeezes my lungs. It feels like that. I pant, looking at the framed prints, the brown pots, cherry wood and clear-grained maple, cloth that wants to be touched. The hope, I guess, is that she'll look where I do, instead of at me. Or do I want her to watch me, and say *What's wrong?* so I can be brave, and start a fight in defense of not complaining — and thus complain while chalking credits up for courage, strength, great pain?

She looks at the walls and I grunt up onto my feet — a lesser stegosaurus in glasses and corduroy pants — and then I walk around, breathing. I bring our coffee from the windowsill and hand a cup over her shoulder. When she bends to drink, I bow to graze on her long neck. She puts her cup on the mahogany table, but I can't reach there and, bending as I am to chew, I still can't set the cup on the floor. So I hang as if fastened by my teeth at great height. She feels this, then she feels the coffee droplets, then she turns — her face knocks my glasses from one ear — and when she sees my athlete's smile of teeth and flare of nose, she laughs so loud she wakes the children up.

Think what a check for etc. can mean.

So we go upstairs and get hugged by sleepy kids. Randy is talking already: he wonders if we can find an Indian long house or at least a war canoe buried in the backyard field which goes to the looping river.

Bobby's trying to climb from his crib. Washcloths, turtleneck jerseys, miniature dungarees, small shoes, and all the time — "No, honey, put his hand through *here*" — as I help to dress someone else's children in a house he signed a mortgage for, there is a two-room apartment in Cicero, New York, where I am not listening to good opera on a bad record player while starting my survey of the week's new *TV Guide* to see what films I'll watch at 9 and then 11:30, 1:15.

Downstairs, Bobby watches Katherine fill a bowl with cereal and milk. He drops his spoon on the floor, smiles a sly one at me, bends to his bowl, saying "More?" Randy drinks orange juice and says, "Mommy, I have dripping sinuses, I can't eat. Okay?"

Katherine says, "No."

I say, "Perhaps this isn't wise —"

Katherine, looking at my face, says, "No to you too."

"I would like to marry this."

Randy says, "I'll *up*chuck if I eat."

Katherine says, "You better not, boy."

"Which one, Kath?"

"Both of you."

Which leads us to stacking the dishes, brushing our teeth — Bob chews a small brush ropy with ancient Crest — and the zipping of quilted jackets. Then, Katherine towing Bob in a wagon with wooden sides, we walk down the road toward the postal substation, Randy speculating on what happened to the Indians: "Then after the settlers shot their buffaloes, they got extinct. Like dinosaurs. They went into the ground."

"No," I tell him, "there are lots of Indians left."

"Uh-uh."

"Yeah, Randy. A lot of them live near Syracuse. A lot live everywhere."

"Then where's their spears and bow-and-arrows?"

"They're like us now, hon. They wear the same kind of clothes and work in offices —"

"Do you have any in your office, Harry?"

"Oh sure. Chiefs, too. Chiefs all over the place."

"Do they got any knives?"

"*Knives?* Listen —"

Katherine says, "Let's be quiet for a while, Randy, okay? Let's listen to the morning for a while." Bob in his wagon is a motor, pukketing to the motion of his ride. Randy and I keep still. We hear woodpeckers and the snarl of jays, local dogs, cars on distant roads that are aimed for the Saturday errands I crave: the lumber yard drive, the haul to the local dump, the station wagon mission with kids in the back and no hurry, and then home to soup and soda and the wind blowing back from the river to gather about the house.

At the post office, which is someone's garage, Katherine and Randy go in for the mail while I stand with my legs apart and, holding Bob's wrists, swing him below me and back and forth. He shouts and laughs his wicked laugh, he's a lump of heavy cloth and knitted cap and scarf, his breath is small white smoke puffs. Then I put him back in the wagon — "More?" he says, holding his hands up, "more?" — and I listen to the knock in my chest, the brain pan's steam-whistle noises. I work at my breathing. I have eaten no breakfast and promise to starve all day. I breathe.

Randy stoops at the post office door and plays with a cat. The cat doesn't want to play, but Randy nails it down with his hand, crushing the soft neck to the ground, cooing "Ah, ba-by." Katherine comes out with some magazines and an opened letter. Her eyes are like the eyes in a drawing: almost like life, but too flat. She sends Randy ahead with the wagon, weaving in the road toward home, Bob an impossible engine.

"Dell's coming," she says. She shakes the letter out; it crackles and refolds. "He'll be here tonight or tomorrow. He wants to see the kids. Sure he does." We walk back between the two rows of houses on the town's main street, which is a road that runs in the country between larger towns. We say nothing, and her face is nearly not familiar, like the palm of someone else's hand.

Which leads us to the long lunchtime — I eat three sandwiches — and then we carry the boys upstairs for early naps. Bob's resigned, Randy is angry and wants to dig up Indians. The sky is smoky with early snow, and through Randy's window I see the black field hands nod their heads and tighten up. The farmer comes from his truck and lays a row of brown burlap bags beside a quarter-mile furrow which the tractor has made. They come from Burlington to work for thirty-five cents a bag. Now the snow comes down, a fine fast grainy fall, and Katherine and I lie down on her very historical double bed and listen to her children bounce around as the tractor changes gears and returns from the river over the field toward the road, pulling earth and potatoes up.

We're dressed. She's under the quilt, waiting. I say, "Kath? You think I ought to go home?"

She doesn't answer.

I'm still breathing heavily from climbing the stairs, and I know she's listening to that too. I fight the lungs, the heart in its damp wrappings. "Listen," I tell her, "you should decide about this. It'd be easier, wouldn't it?"

She says, "Easier for Randy and Bob, I guess. Less embarrassing for me. Weaker."

"No. What weak? It's your *life*."

"By now I should be able to deal with him. And you're a fact now, Harry. I don't have to get married for you to be a fact."

"But you *could*."

"I don't want to be married anymore, kid. Shut up."

"Katherine: *I* want to be married anymore." She doesn't answer, the tractor roars, a field hand's voice comes up. When I look over, her eyes are closed. I think of her driving me to the bus stop, and then the ride to Burlington with travelers and their old suitcases, shopping bags, cigars, then the wait in the gray terminal, the longer ride to Albany, then Syracuse, in darkness, and the half-lighted Greyhound station, all the people there not knowing me or that I've left a New England farmhouse and a family and people grunting over food dug up from cold soil. I tell her, "I don't want to go back."

"What?"

"Go back. Leave."

After a while she moves on the bed, says, "Then that's the decision."

"What's *yours*, Katherine?"

"I don't want to make love."

This requires a delicate pause, partly for the sake of dignity, and also because the idea now utterly seems to call for the act. I say, "Well, I don't recall inviting you, ma'am. Thanks anyway."

"Don't be lousy."

"Don't be private."

"No?"

Fat but not stupid, I say, "It *is* a fairly private problem."

"That's right."

"*Fairly* private."

"Harry, would you believe it, I know what you mean?"

"I know you do. I'm sorry."

"This is dumb, Harry."

"Come on, Katherine, I'm apologizing. For thinking you don't know what's going on. And for your having to live through a weekend like this. For trying to get you to say it."

"You're always trying to get me to say it."

"Sometimes you do."

"Porky Pig, I always do. Kind of."

"Kind of."

"How's your chest?"

"Beautiful. Bigger than yours."

"It's pretty nice."

She turns over and with one hand unbuttons my shirt, puts her icy hand inside, draws her knees up and becomes a small girl falling into sleep. We lie like that, and I reach to the bedside table for something to read — an old *Newsweek* with a puzzled article on heroes of the Green Berets recently dead in South Vietnam. Think what a check for $100,000 can mean to your loved ones at such a time.

And then four o'clock in the far western corner of the field, the burlap sacks in their rows, the tractor cutting the porridge of snow — it still falls lightly — and the hands in their thin jackets or only shirts, pulling up potatoes with the curved-metal long-handled forks, making deep noises, talking sometimes. We are near the river; its rich cold smell comes through the dense little forest on its bank, and Randy with a shovel impossibly long for him is digging with total seriousness through snow and hard ground to find an Indian long house or a fallen warrior's skull. Bob is on my back in a nylon and aluminum baby carrier, solid and happy and still, swathed in woolen cap and long scarf. I pant as I move with him, he listens to my rhythms and pants to my time: he says it.

A short coal-gleamy field worker in an aqua-colored windbreaker stands, stretches his back, blows on his hands. He calls over, "You got yourself a burden, now."

I nod, smile. I have what I want for a minute, and he knows that. I say, "Not as bad as yours."

He shakes his head. He calls, "You want some of these for the missus?"

"Do I look like I need potatoes?"

He laughs and shakes his head. Bob laughs too. Randy comes over with a small lump of limestone. "Harry, is this from the bones of someone?"

I say, "Probably. But put your *mittens* on, will you? Aren't you cold?"

His lecturing face comes on as he ignores mere weather to say, "See this mark over here? This is where the bullet from the settler's gun went in. Isn't it, Harry? Here. You hold this while I go back to find the bullet. It probably fell out when his brains got rotten."

The field worker drinks from a pint of something dark. The cracks on his hard hands are white. Wind comes across the river to blow him into motion again. The tractor rips slowly past and Bob says, "Choo!"

Then the man who harvests potatoes nearby says, "This is a bad-ass day for living. You give me some other day for that."

Down the row a heavier man who is drunken — he slips whenever he moves from his knees — says, "Pick the day with care, son. They coming bad more often. I noticed that."

The short one says, "Your cold black ass told you that, isn't that right."

The drunker one says, "My cold black *life*, son."

The snow is thicker — Bob says "Rice!" — and Katherine's house moves farther away, diminishes. Randy pokes with the tall shovel. An old green truck with snow chains in the southeast corner, near the road, is loaded with filled brown sacks. Bob says "Rice!" and then pants to my rhythms. The tractor starts toward us.

Then far away, at the distant house, a small car is in the drive, a man beside it. I see Katherine on the back porch. The man comes up the steps, stands below her, and they talk. She points toward us in the field. The tractor comes closer, Bob in the backpack stirs to watch. The man raises his hand, drops it, walks past the swing set in the backyard, then past the swings which the wind has set drifting on their chains, then over the chewed land in a fog of blown snow toward Randy and Bob and me. Arms across her chest, Katherine watches.

I look at the field hands and their long lives and think of *TV Guide*, of Katherine at my skin. Randy digs for dead Indians, Bob sucks for air because I do, the tractor comes closer, its steel fork tears up food and huge stones and think what a check for $100,000 can mean.

But the people in the story include that baby tied to the fat man's back. Everyone stands still, including Dell at the edge of his former freehold. Then Randy drags his shovel toward the man who waits, not looking anyplace but down, and I lug Bob back too, walking in the path the shovel makes. The tractor is past, there has been no accident. And Katherine watches us all come home.

Now there are the usual backstage noises: clatter of stainless steel and crockery, the battle of the kids being fed, the utter politeness of conversation among adults who cannot imagine how to survive the hours flat ahead of them — stony field they have to somehow work. When the children offer a chance, they drop all over them like sudden snow. There is the sound of corks being pulled and the tops of beer cans exploding. Now: here are the grownups at the kitchen table (it's a litter of chicken death and vessels), and here are the sounds of Bob in his crib too early to sleep, and Randy upstairs playing Odetta's song about it's good to be home.

There is one partly nibbled drumstick on my brown pottery plate, and the wreckage of some servings of salad. My wineglass is scalloped from recent pourings. Dell, who has removed his sport coat and tie and rolled up his sleeves, drinks ale from a can — he's stowed a case in the refrigerator. His ironed-in shirt creases are still firm, and in his oxford cloth he looks like Katherine's date, warming up for the evening's abandon. I feel as if I look like me: an ocean of rumples. Katherine drinks more wine. Some of it has run onto her thick tan sweater, and her hair is up, and I consider how important it is that I lick the wine from her front.

Lean pale Dell, with his left eye bloodshot, his large hand wrinkling empty Red Cap cans, his legs jiggling up and down, a smile on his long face — I sneak my looks at him. He says, "Harry, you didn't eat much." The host.

"Well."

"I *know* you tend to put away more than that."

"Well, I've got big bones."

Katherine, now my mother or my aunt, says, "He ate a lot of salad. Didn't you, Harry?"

"Yes, ma'am. A good deal of salad."

Two wall lamps light the big room and Dell inspects the shadows. He says, "You forget how intimate the kitchen looks."

"*You* forget," Katherine says.

Odetta celebrates the freedom of the eagle.

Katherine says, "I didn't mean to be rotten," and pours more wine for her and me. My stomach cheers for political triumph, since Dell is excluded by his ale. But he pours water from his goblet into mine and holds the glass out for Katherine to fill, and she does. She looks at my plate. I slump in the chair and stretch my legs for better breathing; it doesn't work, and I sit up straight.

"So I'm a success," Dell says. "I'm a dean of students. What do you think of that? I'm into administration and right guidance." He drinks ale. "I will deftly guide them through the thickets of life."

"And along the abyss, don't forget," I say.

"Absolutely. Abyss, and crumbling ledge. *And* gorse and hawthorne and virulent ivies. Never ignore the virulent ivies. You get really fucked over if you fail to keep the virulent ivies in mind. I've always found that to be true, haven't you, Harry?"

"It's a safe rule to live by, Dell."

Katherine pours us more wine, and Dell holds his goblet up for more too, though he hasn't drunk any. She says, "So here we are. The extended family." This is consummately humorous, and we all laugh.

Odetta discusses peace in the morning sunrise.

She puts her glass down and pushes at the stem with one finger, which suggests that she's about to suggest something. She says, "I wonder why you came here, Dell."

I say, "I think I'll take a walk. I'm taking a walk."

As I get my coat from the wall hook, not looking at Katherine, Dell stands up and takes his long black tweed dean's overcoat down. Katherine says, "No."

Dell says, "But it's your answer — that's why I came. I wanted to address the gentleman currently in your life."

"And see the children, of course," she says.

He says, "Of course."

She says, "Let's all stay inside."

But he is pushing my arm at the door and we go, not drunk enough yet, but going, and then already down the back steps and into the snow in our street shoes which fill with slush, walking past the swings and onto the field. There's a shape out there I wonder about, and a bright white moon, strong wind.

"Dell, don't you think someone should keep Katherine company?"

He strolls a little ahead of me, says, "Why, someone always does, you see."

Now even though he's a dean, he's a dangerous man. He has beaten Katherine with his hands and once with a rolled-up newspaper they were using to train a Dalmatian which was killed by an electrician's truck. Of course, she's beaten him too — he's a dean. But Dell is drunk in a gaseous loose-jointed way that thin men have which frightens me. And he hates the history of their house. And he has to hate me too — unless he thrives by dining on pain which his liver, by habit, can turn into strength. He grips the cloth of my sleeve as we walk toward the river and — the moon turns it on like a lamp now — the stubby chipped station wagon snuggled into hard mud.

Dell says, "I don't think my wife hates me anymore, do you?"

"Me? No. No, I don't think so, Dell."

"Did you ever get divorced, Harry?"

"No, I never got married, actually."

"So you couldn't of gotten divorced, then."

"Right."

"Yeah. You're pretty young, still. So you don't know what me and Katherine are talking about."

"Well —"

"Unless you think fucking and playing house's the same thing as what Katherine and me're talking about."

"Look, Dell. This is very embarrassing."

"It *is?* Oh, I'm sorry there, Harry. It was not my intention to drive all the way here at risk to life and limb just to throw shadows on your soul."

"Dell, you want us to go back inside and have some more to drink, maybe? I don't know what to *say* to you. Maybe if we all got very drunk I would find it easier."

"Actually, old Harry, I am fairly well drunk at the present moment. And I don't honestly give two pounds of llama shit what makes anything in the whole world easier on you, kid." He lets my sleeve loose so he can indicate the whole world. "You got shadows on your soul because I'm a long-term cuckold on account of you. You put the shadows on your own soul, Harry."

By now I have stopped, and he stops too, near the light-colored station wagon. Around us the wide white field spins out, and the furrowed potatoes, the unfilled bags, curved forks. I decide not to discuss the logistics and amenities of divorce, or the question of when precisely a man is allowed to need the presence of someone without being digested by the major figures of her history. I do consider the gleaming points of potato forks, and Dell's deep craze, and how much a check for $100,000 can mean at a time like this. Does homicide count as an accident if you really don't want to die? My chest is shaking at my clothes; breathing is serious business again.

Dell walks closer; he stands before me, takes my glasses off and puts them in his back pocket. "Being in the academic trade," he says, "I appreciate what these could mean to you." His breath is camphor and old cheese.

I have watched too many TV shows about the immorality of unpremeditated violence to be unwary. I am on my wet cold toes, moving backward, squinting at her blurry husband. And when he moves in again I scream a judo karate jiujitsu noise to paralyze his reflexes, I spin on my left foot and kick backward with my right for the nerve complex just below his sternum. I strike nothing, something collapses in my ankle, I go down. He cries, "You terrific bag of weakness, you don't snort the scraps off my plate!" And his knees or elbows land on my chest, my face is opening up beneath his hands. I push up, strike up, swinging wide loose powdery punches, get lucky, and something slicker than mucus streaks on my hand. He shouts — no words — and I stick up fingers as if I were a maddened typist. He screams, and then his breath is in close, his teeth on my cheekbone, he bites down and though I roll and kick and punch on his skull he bites in harder. I scream in his ear; I want to tear it with my teeth but can't.

He's off. His spit and our blood run along my cheek. I'm helped to my feet by people I can't see. I stand on one leg and hold to someone's hard shoulder. There's a smell of deep cold and blended whiskey, sweat. Dell sits before me on the field, a blurred face. I see the tail gate of the station wagon open — courtesy light, I remind myself. There are brown unfocused faces in the light, and much commentary.

Dell says, "Like it's an academic situation, brother, dig? Much as I appreciate your interest, I don't think you see the subtleties here."

A deep voice near him says, "I don't believe we your brother, *man*."

The potato picker I hold to says, "You own one chewed face, you know that, mister? I don't wonder if you got yourself some rabies."

The one with the deep voice far away says, "Yeah, well that's the trouble with being food, son."

I listen to my body breathe and I whisper, "Are my glasses broken?"

"If not, they the only things that's whole now. So come on to your home."

We slide and lurch to the house I can't see, me thanking and he saying never-you-mind, and both of us laughing once and then, by the time we reach the drifting swings, gasping in the cold air, silent. In the window above the back porch, there's a dim brown light. I say, "Who is that? Upstairs?"

"A small kind of Indian. Red and yellow feathers. Watching you drag home."

"I wish he wasn't."

"Yeah."

"Hey — thank you."

"Uh-huh."

"*Really.*"

"Yeah, all right."

The clicking of the storm door, and Katherine's face — fury? fear? no: pain — and alcohol on the eaten face, an elastic bandage on the ankle, Randy's wagging headdress, the hobble upstairs, the weight of blankets. Katherine's insistence on silence, sleep, the sound of Dell's car starting down the drive: they wash into morning, the gray and golden early light in her still house, the curl of her body on the bed. Rather than consider, I twist down.

Rather than consider that an accident — by civil law, papal bull, Torah, or the New York Builders' Code — is what you don't make plans for. Rather than consider that the final sentence of the Sears and Roebuck contract no doubt says, *In the event that the Insured is counting on this Policy for a measure of design in his little story, the Contract is nullified — it becomes just one more Cold-Assed Petition to end whatever pickle, puzzle, plot or unofficial war Insured can't deal with.* Rather than consider, truly, whether I heard Dell whine away. Rather than consider that I first heard Dell and Katherine yowl and sigh, make a long silence, and maybe leathery love, before he rode for home with part of my face in his war bag. Rather than consider shadows on my soul, or the thickets and abysses and the crumbling ledge.

My cheek feels hard and swollen, the ankle complains, but I twist down, slowly diving, and nose beneath the covers for her flesh. I push at the nightgown, kiss her cool thigh and crotch then stomach as she stirs. I come up onto her chest and suck a smooth nipple, turn at it.

She slams me, under the covers, and I sit up, the quilt like a shawl all over me. "Goddammit! Will you stop biting me?"

I wait, and my insides surge. Because here it comes.

She pushes her nightgown partly down, but not enough to pretend that we aren't naked, haven't been. And then she covers her eyes with her hand, whispers, "I don't want to live with anyone, Harry. Not even weekends for a while. All right? I think just alone right now. All right?"

Her bare thighs and pubic hair and stomach sadden me, like spurious jukebox mourning songs. I cover her with the blanket and put a pillow over my lap and belly-mound, I hold it with a hugging arm, she squeezes her eyes with her fingers, we wait. Bob bangs his crib slats to start the day.

It will not be a fertile pursuit. It will finish with a near-sighted ride to Syracuse, the bullet-whipped fragment of a Mohican's skull another truth and trophy wrapped in my clothes. I will finish with an elevated leg, some great living stack of sausages and eggs and chocolate milk, and lean men easily breathing on the TV screen who smile. I'll use the extra glasses, an old prescription, nearly strong enough, which I've kept in a drawer with my socks for emergencies.

Katherine says, "All right?'

Sure.

How the Indians
Come Home

PICTURES FROM THE FORTIES make him sad about his parents: those baggy wrinkled unsynthetic fabrics, the graininess of the photographs, the hair pushed away from the faces — everything is frail, too much exposed, vanishing. He told me that on his eighteenth birthday his mother left a package at his breakfast place for him to find in the morning. It was a shirt box containing some pictures of him and his parents after his father came home from the war. And there was a long bright patterned apron string; pinned to it was a note: *Now you're not tied to this.* Doubtless, he felt free.

Before I divorced him (and almost didn't), we lived in our early days in a one-room apartment on Morton Street in the Village. He sat there once from six at night until the next morning, not speaking. We had just been married and both of us were scared. I kept thinking about the woman with two kids, he'd had a long affair with her — as if he were just divorced, and I had arrived in time to be his therapy, diversion. I stopped believing that, it wasn't true, but *then*, with no money, and no plans, and just us and the little room, I thought of some earth-mother witch in New England, all breasts and belly, eating on his mind. It wasn't true. He told me later that he'd sat all afternoon and night not speaking because he didn't know what to say about being married. And because he was thinking about his parents — how he'd never know them now.

That wasn't our honeymoon. We didn't have money for a honeymoon. We went uptown and saw a Jack Lemmon movie, then had an ice-cream soda at a nearby Schrafft's. He was pale and funny in his sport coat (it was too small, he was getting good and fat), and his collar was too tight. He leaned over to me and said, "I don't think I'll ever be free. It's my mother. I don't think —"

"You mean you love her funny?" I rehearsed everything I'd read about Oedipus in one psychology course at the New School and ended up saying it again: "You love her, in a kind of funny way?"

He laughed and held my hand. His hand was sweaty. He said, "Freudyanna. I want to *mar*ry you. I want *you*. But I keep feeling like I deserted her. Both of them. I feel bad."

I told him something useless (I could have said the identical words about the death of a beloved dog, or the loss of a favorite scarf), and we continued — from jobs to other jobs, from the Village apartment to another one, from one hospital to another, from wound to wound, from childlessness to child to child. We tried.

We found out that we were in the West at the same time, as tiny kids. My father was in San Diego at a naval base. He wrote home that he was "traveling well," which got through the censor to tell us that soon he'd be shipped out with the division he was working for. My mother took everyone's gas coupons and drove in a 1937 Dodge, nonstop, through smelly motor courts and snowstorms and communities quarantined with flu scares, missing the cable which told her not to come, that he was being sent out immediately. The newspapers tried to warn her, the state police tried to stop her, but she went. And he wasn't shipped out, and we lived in San Diego and ate oranges together for months. I don't remember it — except a blizzard somewhere, when the car wouldn't go, and my mother sat at the wheel, crying. His mother took him on a train out West to see his father in training camp, and as soon as they arrived, Harry got sick. She had to take him home. He remembers ruining his parents' reunion. Why?

He remembers himself in a little khaki uniform worn under a bathrobe, walking through the aisle of a troop train in little slippers, talking to soldiers. Or he remembers his mother telling him about himself. He doesn't know which. Because he told me once that all he could remember from the war is himself and his mother and another woman, crouching in an elevator during an air raid, being scared. But America wasn't bombed. He really doesn't know how much of his past he's been in.

He remembers lying on a canvas cot in their dining room in Brooklyn, the walls full of bookshelves, light shining on the cherry table, but the room very dark. He remembers eating giant pills which tasted horrible, and his mother watching him whenever he wakened. She told him she was going to make him a surprise out of folded newspaper — an army field cap, a paper boat, a crown: he can't remember which. He says — he said this in Schrafft's, I didn't know then if we'd last for a week — the doorbell rang and his mother, who had sat beside him, her hair piled on the back of her neck, folding, cutting, went to see who it was. He can't remember the emotion, but he does remember the speed and sureness of it, tearing at the cap or boat or crown, rending it, undoing it, wadding it to trash. He remembers that when she returned, she wept. He remembers that in the dark room, between their table and their books, she said, "Oh, I'm sorry. I'm sorry." In Schrafft's, the night of the day we were married, he said, "I shouldn't have done that. I wonder why I did that."

He remembers the dream he had when he was very small. It was after his father came home from the service, and their house was filled with dreams. He would see, in his sleep, the flesh-colored blanket folded at the foot of his father's bed. It was almost flat and smooth, but there was one wrinkle in it. He would see the wrinkle and be sickened with terror. He would see the wrinkle and whimper to himself in catastrophe. Then he'd get up and walk very quickly across the hall to his parents' room, stand at the head of his father's bed — never, he remembers, looking at the blanket there — and touch his father's forehead, saying, "Daddy, Daddy, I had a nightmare." His father would waken in fear; he remembers that whenever he was suddenly wakened his eyes looked frightened. Then he'd hold his arms up and pull him into bed and hold him for a minute. Then, holding his father's hand, he'd be led down the hall to the bathroom where they both would stand and urinate, then spit afterward into the toilet. This, his father explained, would make the dream go away. Then he'd be led to his own bedroom and would fall asleep, at peace. He remembers not wondering if his father went to sleep again.

After the separation and divorce he came in very frequently, sometimes every week, to see the boys and sit with me in our old apartment
(I shifted the furniture so he wouldn't feel too sentimental), and talk
about what we all "needed": money for clothes for the boys, a vacation
trip, new drapes, whatever he could provide, so long as he received no
benefits. The idea was for all of us to conspire that he hadn't ruined
our lives. And he hadn't, we had all worked together on that, and the
boys were surviving (I think they were relieved), so we had a couple of
our pleasantest months since the early days. As he relaxed, he came in
less frequently, and after a while we lived on a schedule instead of by
our needs. Or the schedule *was* our need. It was something of a relief
to finally be a typical couple, divorced.

This Tuesday he called, that Thursday the boys called him, on
Saturday we met if he was in town, twice a month he made sure to get
in from upstate, and once a month he took the boys for a long weekend,
picking them up in his car and driving to places I hadn't heard about,
where they stayed up late and ate motel food and were happy together.

It was going all right. Ian often wet his bed, but he did it less and
less, and I refused to believe that Harry and I had all that much to do
with it. So few fifty-year-olds wet the bed, Harry always said, when
we discussed it on the phone, and we agreed that he would grow away
from it when he was older. Stuart had no problems. He ate incessantly,
beat on his older brother when he felt like it, and asked for his Daddy
when he woke. I hated that, and I hated his confusion, and my days
always started wrong because of it. But you can't have what you want,
and sometimes you live with wrong mornings. Ian cried at school
sometimes. All right, you sometimes cry at school. I wondered when
Harry cried. And I knew when I did.

One night, when we were married and not asking questions out
loud, I patted Harry on the shoulder in bed and said, "It's all right, it's
all right, sweetheart." He'd been whimpering like a baby, the saddest
long moans.

In the darkness he said, "Thank God. Thank you, I couldn't
have —" and he rolled over onto his side, then onto his back, said,
"Thank God you did that. Thank you." I rubbed his head, which was
wet with sweat, and he started to fall asleep again. Then, suddenly, he

said, "We were in a hotel room, it was all white. You were dressed up, very elegant. You were dressed up for other people. Not me. And you kept walking around this bright room. You looked so *tall*. You kept saying you were leaving me. That it didn't make any difference — you really didn't care, Anna. You were completely independent."

"I'm not leaving you, Harry. It's all right. I'm staying right here."

"I felt abandoned. Totally abandoned. I mean, it was *grief*. I didn't know what I would ever do. Then you noticed — you pointed it out to me, like you were *appalled* — you told me I was urinating in the bed. I saw the top sheet going all dark. But I was so relieved. I felt so much easier. Then you woke me up." I stopped rubbing his head and lay back. "Oh, Jesus," he said. "Jesus, I was like a *baby!*"

"And I was like your mother? Abandoning you?"

"Jesus," he said. Then: "No. It was *you*."

"Yes, but it still could be —"

"No, Anna! You didn't *feel* like my mother. You felt like you."

"That's who I am," I said brilliantly.

And after a while he said, "That's scary, if it wasn't about you and me. I mean, it's scary *enough* if it was you and me. Horrible enough. But if —"

"No. Never mind. You shouldn't do that with dreams. Just have them and get them over with and forget them."

"You don't think it was anything else?"

"No."

"Really?"

"I'm staying right here. I'm here." And soon he rolled over and reached across my shoulder into my nightgown, seizing, squeezing, holding on, and we made love.

Harry remembers, and I do too, the night, before we had Stuart, when Ian stood in the doorway of the kitchen, his pajamas too short, his feet so long and bony, face too white. He kept rubbing the corner of his mouth, his lips were so delicate and swollen then, his fingers so long, the nails all bitten away. He was holding the imitation army rifle made of metal and hardwood that Harry had bought him for Christmas. He held it by the barrel and stood like a sentry at the edge of the kitchen — *our* sentry, almost guarding us from us: because for a minute we stopped. Harry was in his plaid wool bathrobe, I remember, and I was wearing blue tights and a dark blue woolen shirt, half open, the buttons torn because he'd been tearing at me. A family portrait. I turned away so Ian wouldn't see my eyes: "Hey, Ian, you're up so *late*."

Ian said, "I heard noises." I guess he was looking at Harry, or me, I didn't watch. He said, "Did you hear a shouty kind of noise?" After a second he said, "I thought I heard kind of shouts."

I was washing my eyes with cold water. I remembered when Ian was supposed to be napping and Harry and I sneaked into the bathroom. I had his pants open, and my dungarees were down, when Ian pushed the door in and it caught on Harry's foot. He knocked and said, "Hey, what are you guys *doing?*"

By the time Harry let him in, he was squatting on the floor, like an Indian, and nearly zipped. I was sitting in the tub, the water was running, I was splashing it into my blouse as it rose above my half-closed jeans. Harry said, "I'm watching Mommy take a bath. What're *you* doing?"

Ian said, "Watching you watch, Daddy." And then, knowing something — his eyes got that sly look — but knowing nothing, he said, "Aw, you guys are silly," and went to bed.

So, anyway, I washed my face that time in the kitchen and moved as fast as I could so he'd see as little as possible. I tucked him in and kissed him and told him something about a little argument, but don't worry, and then went back. While that was happening, Harry was standing in the kitchen and looking at the brown bean pots and white pottery vases and dark blue bowls. The copperware hanging on the brick above the stove caught a lot of light, and the beauty of the apartment, its investment, made him bow his head down. When I came in he was saying, "The usual self-pity. And it's right on time."

I said, "What": a dull heavy stroke . . . the weariness I really felt, and then the weariness I wore for effect, to show how much he'd exhausted me, and also to show how little his statements could mean.

He answered with the same weighted voice, because by then we were puppets on the fingers of our arguments. We were left with nothing to say. The arguments were having *us*. We must have looked like kids at the end of a street fight, panting and drooling, surrounded by cold-eyed watchers: us. He said, "I was feeling sorry for myself. And hoping you'd hear me. So you'd feel sorry for me."

"That's fair."

"It wasn't supposed to be fair."

"No," I said, "I mean it *was* fair. That you told me. I have to have a cup of tea, my stomach hurts. Do you want some?"

So we sat in our little dining alcove, drinking sweet tea and not fighting. We were exhilarated by loss and fatigue and we were talking very quickly about the people next door, making jokes about the neighbors calling the police. Then we grew silent, shook our heads, rubbed at ourselves. Then we just sat. The sounds of sirens from the street came in, and the horns of fire trucks, the humming of the elevators going past our floor. I felt process going on, and us being sheltered away from it. It all felt very easy. We drank our sweet tea, got drowsy, were still.

I remember noticing myself, but not thinking anything. I stood up, and he got frightened. I took the tea mugs away to the kitchen. He said, "I thought maybe we'd talk?"

I felt such confidence, it was like punching him: "Oh, we talked."

"No, I mean together. Come on — you know: not fighting."

I said, "Well, we *don't* not fight, friend. Do we?"

Harry said, "We've been doing a lot of it. We've been doing it. But I keep thinking" — he closed his eyes and laid his fists on the table — "it's so *temporary*. Really. You know? We get past this time, we work on it, we get back into the *marriage*. That's what we have to do, Anna."

"Long distance."

"What?"

"From away from each other. If we think, we can think in different rooms. Different cities, probably. I don't know. But different. Away."

"You're pulling that on me again?"

"I'm not pulling anything again."

"Oh no. Just the old Now I'm leaving, so you shape up — that's all."

"Harry, I'm not pulling."

"That's blackmail, Anna."

"No. It's moving out of the apartment."

"With Ian, of course."

"With Ian."

"And that's kidnapping. He's my boy too."

"Listen, Harry, you can call it murder if you want to, but in the morning Ian and I are taking a trip."

"You'd threaten me with this."

"No, I'm doing it. If you think it's threatening, maybe you should think about what makes me do it."

"God, Anna. Look: first of all, I don't want you to go. Second of all, if you're so dumb and you have to go because you want to *hurt* me. Uh, third, you can't take Ian."

"Second, third, eleventh, a million, who *cares?* You're such a big-mouth, Harry, you know that? Kidnapping, murder, blackmail — you make that little boy cry in his bed —"

"Don't you use that on me. You were there too, remember? You were there. Don't you tell me I made him cry."

"You did."

"You made him cry *too*. Don't *tell* me that."

"Don't you believe it, friend — that you can cry your way out of it this time. This time you pay. So you can cry *blood* if you want to and I don't care. Because you terrified that baby."

"We can't do this, Anna."

"Done. Consider it done."

"You're crying too."

"So *what?* Somebody's always crying here. So what? See, the idea is *not* to cry. The father makes the wife and child *not* cry. The wife makes the husband not cry. It's called being happy. We don't *do* that anymore. So you and your words and your crying — oh, do break it, Harry. Break it. You can throw everything in the apartment at me and smash it and break it and everything and I *still* —"

I saw Ian's rifle come around the corner of the doorway as I held my hands in front of me and Harry crushed the round brown pot against the sink. I made a noise as if he'd kicked me. So he kicked me in the leg. I kicked him back. He hit me where the jaw goes into the neck. I swung back with both hands moving, and he caught my wrists and held them in the air. I screamed, I bit my lip, I cried and kicked at him. He dodged my feet and bent my arms back. I heard it over the noise: *Shh.*

Ian was in the doorway, making his playtime rifle sounds, holding his gun awkwardly because we didn't let him watch war movies yet. Elbows pointed out, and long feet, the white tight face with its giant eyes, his mouth rubbed red, pointing his rifle and shooting: *Shh. Shh. Shh.* We heard him.

We also heard Harry that night, later, when he decided to exhibit all of the characteristics for which I did not marry him, or love him, or find him more than tolerable. He pouted, always where I could see him (in an apartment, not difficult), and he looked like a sullen ape; instead of peering through banana trees, he sulked over sofa and chairs, from around the refrigerator door. He sighed very loudly and talked to himself, but always less than audibly, trying to tempt me to ask him "What?" and open the conversation again. I put Ian back to bed and calmed him down. He was eager to sleep and make his escape. I took a shower and stayed in the bathroom a long time. Then I went to bed and had stopped shaking enough to read our old magazines, one after the other, while Harry sat in the dark living room, going past the bedroom corridor from time to time for more ice. He was widening the purview of his exhibition to include the Drunken Husband in Grief. I read the old *Times* magazine supplements; struggling Africa and threatened Kurds fell through my head like garbage down the dumbwaiter.

I don't know what he drank, but he must have drunk a lot of it, and I must have fallen asleep. His voice from the bathroom, echoing, woke me up. I heard the water splash in the tub as if an elephant were taking a foot bath, great slopping wallops. Then it dripped on the tile floor, very loudly, and then he stood in the corridor, fully dressed and soaking wet and in his shirt and pants and shoes. He came in and turned the bedroom lights on, whistling, and I just watched. He tore his shirt buttons off, pried off his shoes without unlacing them, dropped his trousers onto the mound of wet clothes. When he was naked he said, "That's a comfort," sighed very loudly, and lay on the bedroom rug.

I was thinking about rape, and making love, and how cold he must be — his big nipples on his hairy fat breasts had shrunk and tightened — when Ian walked slowly into the room, pale and blinking, his pajama bottoms in his hands. A smear of moisture ran halfway up his tops, which he still wore.

He said, "Did you wet yourself, Daddy?"

Harry said, "Oh, hon —"

"Did you wet yourself too? I did." He wept, and his noise was uncontrolled, as if his body still were asleep. "I did too."

Harry, still naked, with a very frightened face, moved before I did, picked him up, carried him through the hallway to his room. I followed, listening to "I got you" and "I'm taking care of you, love" and "Don't worry, it's just an accident" and "Here I am, I'm here." He was tender and very worried, clumsy, not so awfully drunk-sounding then. I loved them both. And I didn't know how to tell them apart. I stood in the doorway as Harry crooned to him, taking off the pajama tops, folding him in a curve on the bed, rubbing his flanks, talking. He opened drawer after drawer in the half-darkness until he found underwear and fought him into the shorts and shirt. He tore the wet bottom sheet from the bed and nearly knocked Ian to the floor. Ian began to cry again. Everything fell out of Harry's hands, he had to do everything twice.

I whispered, "Let me help."

He said, "Stay there. Anna! I'm here! I'm *here!*"

He pushed the door shut and I leaned my shoulder against it to listen as he slammed the drawers of the blanket chest, saying, "Okay, Ian, I'm taking care of you. Daddy's here, love, you're fine, you're fine." And Ian, mostly asleep, still cried.

After a while it was silent on the other side. Then Harry said, "Hey, Ian."

"What, Daddy. What?"

"Remember that time you went for a walk with me in Prospect Park and I told you about —"

"Go way, Daddy. Go way."

He said, "Ian?"

"What! Go *way!*"

I went into the living room and cried. There were bottle and glass, moisture rings on the coffee table, the feeling that something sordid had happened on the cushions and carpet. He would follow me here, puzzled, not very drunk now, without an idea of what to do. He would follow me anyplace else. He would follow me into the living room and then I'd take him to bed. In the morning I wouldn't leave. I cried harder. And then he came in, still naked, tousled, bewildered, sorrowful with guilt for all the moments of the evening — mine, and Ian's, and his own. I looked at him and rubbed my face and said, "Very nice."

He smiled his kid's grin and said, "I haven't a thing to wear."

It was after Schrafft's, and during his first month at work, when he told me why his mother, whom he never saw, might be troubled. I hadn't asked. I was sitting on the bed, being exhausted (we had no couch) and he was doing the dishes in our only room. I said, "Maybe you haven't done anything wrong."

"No, I probably have," he said.

"Maybe you *didn't* do anything wrong."

"Maybe." He stood with his hands in the water, amputated by the suds, and he sighed, his shoulders slumped; he shook his head. When I remember this he looks so young to me, much younger than a man in his thirties, inexperienced. He said, "It's scary. It's like I'm always looking down two tunnels at once, two tubes. One has what *we* feel, how pissed off we get by all that — *that*. And down the other there's all this information, I don't mean that. Excuses. Or, I don't know — *possibilities*. You know: she doesn't feel well? Her kid's grown up and away? Her life isn't too fine for her anymore? She's in trouble? Lonely? You know what I mean. I was standing here, looking down the tubes. I sort of moved my head to the left, I always see ours on the left. The one on the right is hers, right? It went dark. But that's not it. I *made* it go dark. I knew I was doing it. Just now. I just stopped looking there. I don't want to *know* that side anymore. It's either us or them, so it's us. Finished."

"Harry, I never heard of anything like that. I don't believe it."

"No? *I* believe it. I said to myself, Hey Harry, that's too easy. You just don't want to work at seeing both sides. You know what I answered myself, just now?"

"How could I know anything like that?"

"I told myself, Okay. Call it easy. Be *bad* from now on. But all you see is *your* side, yours and Anna's. Otherwise you're dead. So now I'm not dead. But maybe they are. Maybe she is."

· "I don't understand."

"No? Well, why should you? Why should you? That's what happened, though."

"Does it make you feel bad?"

"I don't know. Really, I don't know. It makes me feel *good*. But
maybe bad also. I don't know."

We're civilized, we see each other a lot now (or we're *un*civilized and
see each other a lot, I don't know). He misses the boys, and me, and I
miss him and hate that he's so sorry. And he's admitted to me that as
tough as it is for him to be away from his sons, it's tougher to be with
them now, though he's doing a pretty good job of being with and being
without. We remember each other, and treat each other well. We're
both still confused. In some ways he always was a child about sex —
our first two years together were difficult for him, for me. He grew up,
though, and I did too, and that part was all right. But I know that he
remembers it, still is sad and ashamed for what we were in the beginning. And I'm certain that he wonders now about the men I know, and
how I know them. We only discuss the past.

He remembers so many books, he always remembered them: *The
Book of Fascinating Facts*, Red Randall on chipped yellow pages fighting
the Japanese, Gregor Felsen's *Navy Diver*, with sheath knives cutting
air lines for the sake of democratic life. He read them after the war, of
course, when he lived in his imagination in his room. He memorized a
book called *America's Fighting Planes*, which had full-page pictures of
the B-24 Liberator dropping bright red bombs on German cities, and
the Grumman F4F Wildcat pumping tracers through the canopy of a
Japanese Zero and into its thrashing pilot's back. In the fifties he
wanted to join the Civil Air Patrol as a ground spotter to help intercept
a Communist sneak attack; he was disappointed for weeks when they
told him he was too young. He remembers Zane Grey and Edgar Rice
Burroughs in old torn editions he brought home from his Boy Scout
library. He knows the plots and names of so many of them, and he
hardly remembers his life.

When I think of what he's told me it's like watching an inferior print
of a very old film — jumps, splices, long illogical gaps. He remembers,
and yet he's mostly forgotten. A lot of him is lost. I asked him when

his grandmother died and he didn't remember. I asked why she died and he didn't know. He does recall that he dressed for school on the day of her burial, and came downstairs and ate his breakfast and went to the door, while his father watched him and his mother watched them both. He didn't know about funerals, or doesn't remember knowing; or, if he did understand, he didn't realize that he was going to school on the wrong day. His father silently looked while he stood at the door. His mother said, "Aren't you coming to Grandma's funeral?"

He doesn't remember speaking, but he knows he went to school. Twelve years later his mother told him he answered, "What'd she ever do for me?"

I told him he'd never have said it. I said she shouldn't have told him, even if he had. I told him plenty more about her, and he said his recollections probably didn't do justice to his parents, he simply couldn't remember enough.

I said, "Harry, what do you feel *good* about?"

He smiled a helpless little boy's smile and said, "Just you."

I have never been so frightened since then — not even during my operation when they cut me apart, and not during the divorce when something similar happened. Not even now, when I sit on our furniture at night and think I could marry him again if I got crazy enough. Who's sane?

He remembers so much and so little. Well, I remember too: the Christmas when Ian was so sick and we gave him phenobarbitol and penicillin and he always slept. We put him on the living room sofa and took turns watching him. He cried sometimes when he woke, and once he said, "I have to make a teepee!"

Harry said, "Bathroom, honey? You have to go to the bathroom?"

Ian pointed his finger down at the blue and white blanket: "The Indians don't have any place to *live!*"

So I fed him cream soda and Harry took the elevator down and went to gather twigs on the city streets. When he came back, Ian was sleeping, he looked flat beneath the covers, his white face on the white pillow was completely still. Harry sat on the rug and tied three wet crooked sticks together with twine, then looped the twine around the sticks at the base so the teepee would stand. Then he very carefully cut out shapes from the Sunday *Times* and taped them on as walls: Richard Nixon and Archbishop Makarios for the Indians to go through to get home.

Ian woke up crying. Harry rubbed at him, he kept pushing the hair away from Ian's forehead as if he wanted to see him better. Ian turned his face away from the hand and kept crying. Harry said, "Look, baby. Hey: here's a house for the Indians to live in. Pretty good, huh?"

Ian looked at the little wood-and-paper tent and his face twisted in, his lips looked redder. He cried and shook his head; he said, "It isn't good enough, Daddy."

Harry didn't know what to say. I don't know what he remembered, but he had counted on his medicine working and he'd failed; I thought that he'd cry too. He said, "Ian, hey — tell me what's wrong and I'll fix it."

Ian said, "You didn't make a *door*, Daddy. Why did you do it like that?" He tore at the teepee and the newspapers fell from the frame of twigs and twine.

Widow Water

WHAT TO KNOW about pain is how little we do to deserve it, how
simple it is to give, how hard to lose. I'm a plumber. I dig for what's
wrong. I should know. And what I think of now as I remember pain is
the fat young man and his child, their staggering house, the basement
filled with death and dark water, the small perfect boy on the stone
cellar steps who wept, the widow's coffee gone cold.

They called on Friday to complain that the pump in their basement
wouldn't work. Theirs is shallow-well country, a couple of miles from
the college, a place near the fast wide river that once ran the mill that
all the houses of the town depended on. The railroad came, the town
grew, the large white clapboard houses spread. By the time their
seedlings were in the middle growth, the mill had failed, the houses
had run to blisters of rotted wood on the siding and to gaps in the black
and green roofs. The old ones were nearly all dead and the railroad
came twice a day, from Utica to Binghamton, to Utica from Binghamton, carrying sometimes some freight, sometimes a car of men who
maintained the nearly useless track. And the new people came, took
their children for walks on the river to the stone foundations of the
mill. They looked at the water and went home. People now don't know
the water as they should. I'm a plumber, I should know.

I told him I couldn't come on a Friday afternoon in April, when the
rains were opening seams and seals and cellars all through the county.
Bella was making coffee for us while I took the call, and I snapped my
fingers for her to turn around. She did, all broad — not fat, though —

and full of colors — red in her face, yellow in her hair going gray, the gold in her tooth, her eyes blue as pottery — and I pointed at the phone. She mouthed a mimic "Today, today, today," and I nodded, and she nodded back and poured the almost boiling water out into the instant coffee, which dissolved.

He said, "So you see, sir, we can use your help."

I said, "Yessir, sounds like a problem."

"No water, and we've got a boy who isn't toilet-trained. It gets kind of messy."

"I imagine."

"So do you think you could . . ."

"Yessir?"

"Come kind of soon?"

"Oh, I'll come kind of soon. It just won't be today."

"You're sure you couldn't . . ."

"Yessir?"

"Come today?"

"Yessir."

"Yes sir, what?"

"Yessir, I'm sure I can't come."

Bella rapped on the table with her big knuckles to tell me to come and sit. I nodded, pointed at the telephone, waited for him to try once more. He was from the college — he would try once more.

He said, "But no water — for how long? The weekend? All week?"

I heard a woman whisper in the background with the harshness of a wife making peace, and then he said, "Uh — I mean, do you know when you can come?"

I said, "When're you up?"

"Excuse me?"

"When do you wake up?"

"We'll be up. Just tell me when."

I said, "I'll be there tomorrow morning, early, if that's all right."

"I mean, how early?"

"You get up, Mr. Samuels, and you have yourself a comfortable breakfast, and I'll be there for a cup of your coffee."

He hung on the line, waiting for more. I gave him nothing more, and he said, "Thanks. I mean, we'll see you tomorrow, then. Thank you."

"Thank *you* for calling, Mr. Samuels, and I'll see you soon."

He said, "Not soon enough," and chuckled and didn't mean the laugh.

I chuckled back and meant it, because coffee was waiting, and Bella, and a quiet hour before I went back out to clear a lonely lady's pipe in a fifty-foot well. I said, "Goodbye, Mr. Samuels."

He said, "Yes," which meant he was listening to his whispering wife, not me, and then he said, "Yes, goodbye, thank you very much, see you soon."

I blew on my coffee and Bella turned the radio off — she'd been listening to it low to hear if she'd won the fur coat someone in Oneida was giving away — and we sat and ate bran muffins with her blueberry jam and talked about nothing much; we said most of it by sitting and eating too much together after so many years of coffee and preserves.

After a while she said, "A professor with a problem."

"His pump won't turn off. Somebody sold him a good big Gould brand-new when he moved in last summer, and now it won't turn off and he's mad as hell."

"Well, I can understand that. They hear that motor banging away and think it's going to explode and burn their house down. They're city people, I suppose."

"Aren't they ever. I know the house. McGregory's old place near the Keeper farm. It needs work."

"Which they wouldn't know how to do."

"Or be able to afford," I said. "He's a young one and a new professor. He wouldn't earn much more than the boys on Buildings and Grounds. I'll bill him — he won't have the money in the house or at the bank, probably — and we'll wait a couple of months."

Bella said, "We can wait."

"We will."

"What did you tell him to do?"

"I told him to unplug the pump."

"He wasn't satisfied."

"I guess I wouldn't be."

"Abe," she said, "what's it like to be young as that?"

I said, "Unhappy."

She said, "But happy, too."

"A little of that."

She bent her gray and gold head over the brown mug of dark brown coffee and picked at the richness of a moist muffin. She said, still looking down, "It's hard."

I said, "It gets easier."

She looked up and nodded, grinned her golden tooth at me, said, "Doesn't it?"

Then I spent the afternoon driving to New Hartford to the ice-cream plant for twenty-five pounds of sliced dry ice. I had them cut the ice into ten-inch-long slivers about three-quarters of an inch around, wrapped the ice in heavy brown paper, and drove it back to Brookfield and the widow's jammed drill point. It's all hard-water country here, and the crimped-pipe points they drive down for wells get sealed with calcium scales if you wait enough years, and the pressure falls, the people call, they worry about having to drill new wells and how much it will cost and when they can flush the toilets again. They worry how long they'll have to wait.

I went in the cellar door without telling her I was there, disconnected the elbow joint, went back out for the ice, and when I had carried the second bundle in, she was standing by her silent well in the damp of her basement, surrounded by furniture draped in plastic sheets, fire-wood stacked, cardboard boxes of web-crusted Mason jars, the growing heaps of whatever in her life she couldn't use.

She was small and white and dressed in sweaters and a thin green housecoat. She said, "Whatever do you mean to do?" Her hands were folded across her little chest, and she rubbed her gnarled throat. "Is my well dead?"

"No, ma'am. I'd like you to go upstairs while I do my small miracle here. Because I'd like you not to worry. Won't you go upstairs?"

She said, "I live alone —"

I said, "You don't have to worry."

"I don't know what to do about — this kind of thing. It gets more and more of a problem — this — all this." She waved her hand at what she lived in and then hung her hands at her sides.

I said, "You go on up and watch the television. I'm going to fix it up. I'll do a little fixing here and come back tonight and hook her up again, and you be ready to make me my after-dinner coffee when I come back. You'll have water enough to do it with."

"Just go back upstairs?" she said.

"You go on up while I make it good. And I don't want you worrying."

"All right, then," she said, "I'll go back up. I get awfully upset now. When these — things. These — I don't know what to do anymore." She looked at me like something that was new. Then she said, "I knew your father, I think. Was he big like you?"

"You know it," I said. "Bigger. Didn't he court you one time?"

"I think everybody must have courted me one time."

"You were frisky," I said.

"Not like now," she said. Her lips were white on her white face, the flesh looked like flower petals. Pinch them and they crumble, wet dust.

"Don't you feel good now?"

"I mean kids now."

"Oh?"

"They have a different notion of frisky now."

"Yes they do," I said. "I guess they do."

"But I don't feel so good," she said. "This. Things like this. I wish they wouldn't happen. Now. I'm very old."

I said, "It keeps on coming, doesn't it?"

"I can hear it come. When the well stopped, I thought it was a sign. When you get like me, you can hear it come."

I said, "Now listen: You go up. You wrap a blanket around you and talk on the telephone or watch the TV. Because I guarantee. You knew my father. You knew my father's word. Take mine. I guarantee."

"Well, if you're guaranteeing."

I said, "That's my girl." She was past politeness so she didn't smile or come back out of herself to say goodbye. She walked to the stairs and when she started to shuffle and haul the long way up, I turned away to the well pipe, calling, "You make sure and have my coffee ready tonight. You wait and make my after-dinner coffee, hear? There'll be water for it." I waited until she went up, and it was something of a wait. She was too tired for stairs. I thought to tell Bella that it looked like the widow hadn't long.

But when she was gone, I worked. I put my ear to the pipe and heard the sounds of hollowness, the emptiness under the earth that's not quite silence — like the whisper you hear in the long-distance wires of the telephone before the relays connect. Then I opened the brown paper packages and started forcing the lengths of dry ice down into the pipe. I carried and shoved, drove the ice first with my fingers and then with a piece of copper tube, and I filled the well pipe until nothing more would go. My fingers were red, and the smoke from dry ice misted up until I stood in an underground fog. When nothing more would fit, I capped the pipe, kicked the rest of the ice down into the sump — it steamed as if she lived above a fire, as if always her house were smoldering — and I went out, drove home.

I went by the hill roads, and near Excell's farm I turned the motor off, drifted down the dirt road in neutral, watching. The deer had come down from the high hills and they were moving carefully through the fields of last year's corn stumps, grazing like cattle at dusk, too many to count. When the truck stopped I heard the rustle as they pulled the tough silk. Then I started the motor — they jumped, stiffened, watched me for a while, went back to eating: a man could come and kill them, they had so little fear — and I drove home to Bella and a tight house, long dinner, silence for most of the meal, then talk about the children while I washed the dishes and she put them away.

And then I drove back to the house that was dark except for one lighted window. The light was yellow and not strong. I turned the engine off and coasted in. I went downstairs on the tips of my toes because, I told myself, there was a sense of silence there, and I hoped she was having some rest. I uncapped the well pipe and gases blew back, a stink of the deepest cold, and then there was a sound of climbing, of filling up, and water banged to her house again. I put the funnel and hose on the mouth of the pipe and filled my jeep can, then capped the check valve, closed the pipe that delivered the water upstairs, poured water from the jeep can through the funnel to prime the pump, switched it on, watched the pressure needle climb to thirty-eight pounds, opened the faucet to the upstairs pipes, and heard it gush.

I hurried to get the jeep can and hose and funnel and tools to the truck, and I had closed the cellar door and driven off before she made the porch to call me. I wanted to get back to Bella and tell her what a man she was married to — who could know so well the truths of ice and make a dead well live.

Saturday morning the pickup trucks were going to the dump, and the men would leave off trash and hard fill, stand at tailgates, spitting, talking, complaining, shooting at rats or nothing, firing off, picking for scrap, and I drove to see the professor and his catastrophe.

His house was tilted. It needed jacks. The asbestos siding was probably all that kept the snow out. His drainpipes were broken, and I could see the damp spots where water wasn't carried off but spilled to the roof of his small porch to eat its way in and gradually soften the house for bad winter leaks. The lawn at the side of his drive was rutted and soft, needed gravel. The barn he used for garage would have to be coated with creosote or it would rot and fall. A child's bright toys lay in his yard like litter. The cornfield behind his house went off to soft meadow and low hills, and everything was clean and growing behind where they lived; for the view they had, they might as well have owned the countryside. What they didn't own was their house.

He met me at the back steps, all puffy and breasted in his T-shirt, face in the midst of a curly black beard, dirty glasses over his eyes like a mask. He shook my hand as if I were his surgeon. He asked me to have coffee, and I told him I wouldn't now. A little boy came out, and he was beautiful: blond hair and sweetly shaped head, bright brown eyes, as red from weather as his father was pale, a sturdy body with a rounded stomach you would want to cup your hand on as if it were a breast, and teeth as white as bone. He stood behind his father and circled an arm around his father's heavy thigh, put his forehead in his father's buttocks, and then peeped out at me. He said, "Is this the fixing man? Will he fix our pump?"

Samuels put his hand behind him and squeezed the boy's head. He said, "This is the plumber, Mac." He raised his eyebrows at me and smiled, and I liked the way he loved the boy and knew how the boy embarrassed him too.

I kneeled down and said, "Hey, Mac."

The boy hid his face in his father's behind.

I said, "Mac, do you play in that sandbox over there?"

His face came out and he said, very politely, "Would you like to play with me?"

I said, "I have to look at your pump, Mac."

He nodded. He was serious now. He said, "Daddy broke it last night, and we can't fix it again."

I carried my tool pack to the cellar door — the galvanized sheeting on top of it was coming loose, several nails had gone, the weather was getting behind it and would eat the wood away — and I opened it up and started down the stone steps to the inside cellar door. They came behind me, then Samuels went ahead of me, turning on lights, scuffing through the mud and puddles on his concrete floor. The pump was on the wall to the left as I came in. The converted coal furnace in front of me leaked oil where the oilfeed came in. Stone foundation cracking that was two hundred years old, vent windows shut when they should have been opened to stop the dry rot, beams with the adze scars in them powdering almost as we watched: that was his cellar — and packing cartons and scraps of wood, broken chairs, a table with no legs. There was a stink of something very bad.

I looked at the pump, breathed out, then I looked at Mac. He breathed out too. He sounded like me. I grinned at him and he grinned back.

"We're the workers," he said. "Okay? You and me will be the workers. But Daddy can't fix anymore. Mommy said so."

Samuels said, "We'll leave him alone now, Mac."

I said, "How old is he?"

Mac said, "Six years old."

Samuels said, "Three. Almost three and a half."

"And lots of boy," I said.

Mac said, "I'm a worker."

Samuels said, "All right, Mac."

Mac said, "Can't stay here? Daddy? I'm a *worker*."

Samuels said, "Would we be in the way? I'd like to learn a little about the thing if I can."

Mac shook his head and smiled at me. He said, "What are we going to do with our Daddy?"

Samuels said, "Okay, buddy."

Mac raised his brows and shrugged his little arms.

Samuels said, "Out, Mac. Into the yard. Play in the sandbox for a while." He said, "Okay? I'll call you when we need some help."

"Sure!" Mac said.

He walked up the steps, arms slanted out to balance himself, little thighs pushing up on the steps. From outside, where we couldn't see him anymore, the boy called, "Bye and I love you," and ran away.

Samuels held his arms folded across his chest, covering his fleshy breasts. He uncrossed his arms to push his glasses up on his face when they slipped from the bridge of his flat nose. He said, "The water here — I tried to use the instruction book last night, after I talked to you. I guess I shouldn't have done that, huh?"

"Depends on what you did, Mr. Samuels." I unrolled the tool pack, got ready to work.

"I figured it wouldn't turn off on account of an air block in the pipes. The instructions mentioned that."

"Oh."

"So I unplugged the pump as you told me to, and then I drained all the water out — that's how the floor got so wet. Then it all ran into that hole over there."

"The sump."

"Oh, *that's* what a sump is. Then that motor like an outboard engine with the pipe —"

"The sump pump. The water collects in the hole and pushes the float up and the motor cuts in and pumps the water out the side of the house — over there, behind your hot-water heater."

"Oh."

"Except your sump pump isn't plugged in."

"Oh. I wondered. And I was fooling with the motor and this black ball fell off into the water."

"The float. So it wouldn't turn itself *off* if you did keep it plugged in. Don't you worry, Mr. Samuels, we'll pump her out later. Did you do anything else to the well pump?"

He pushed his glasses up and recrossed his arms. "I didn't know what else to do. I couldn't make it start again. We didn't have any water all night. There wasn't any pressure on the gauge."

"No. You have to prime it."

"Prime it?"

"I'll show you, Mr. Samuels. First, you better let me look. Right?"

"Sorry. Sorry. Do you mind if I stay here, though?" He smiled. He blushed under his whiskers. "I really have to learn something about how — this whole thing." He waved his arms around him and then covered up.

I said, "You can stay, sure. Stay."

I started to work a wrench on the heavy casing bolts, and when I'd got the motor apart from the casing, water began to run to the floor from the discharge pipe over the galvanized tank.

He said, "Should I . . ."

"Excuse me?"

"There's water coming down. Should I do anything about it?"

I said, "No, thank you. No. You just watch, thank you."

After a while the trickle slowed, and I pulled the halves apart. I took the rubber diaphragm off, put the flashlight on the motor, poked with a screwdriver, found nothing. I expected nothing. It had to be in the jet. I put the light on that and looked in and saw it, nodded, waited for him to ask.

He said, "You found it?"

"Yessir. The jet's blocked. That's what it sounded like when you called. Wouldn't let the pressure build up, so the gauge wouldn't know when to stop. It's set at forty pounds, and the block wouldn't let it up past — oh, twenty-eight or thirty, I'd say. Am I right?"

"Uh, I don't know. I don't now *anything* about these things."

I said, "When this needle hits forty, it's what you should be getting. Forty pounds of pressure per square inch. If you'd read the gauge you'd have seen it to be about thirty, I calculate. That would've told you the whole thing."

"I thought the gauge was broken."

"They generally don't break. Generally, these things work. Usually it's something simpler than machines when you can't get water up."

He pushed his glasses and covered up, said, "God, what I don't know."

I said, "It's hard to live in a house, isn't it? But you'll learn."

"Jesus, I hope so. I don't know. I hope so. We never lived in a house before."

"What'd you live in? Apartment houses?"

"Yeah — where you call the janitor downstairs and he comes up while you're at work and you never see him. Like magic. It's just all better by the time you get home."

"Well, we'll get this better for you."

He frowned and nodded very seriously. "I'll bet you will," he said. It was a gift he gave me, a bribe.

I said, "So why don't you go on up and ask the missus for about three inches of aluminum foil. Would you do that? And a coat hanger, if you don't mind."

"Coat hanger?"

"Yessir. If you don't mind."

He walked across the floor to the wooden steps that went upstairs above the furnace; he tried to hide the sway and bounce of his body in the way that he walked, the boy coming down the outside concrete steps as the father went up the inside ones. "Do you need any help?" the boy said.

I said, "Mac, you old helper. Hello."

"Do you need any help?"

"I had a boy like you."

"A little bit big, like me?"

"Little bit big. Except now he's almost a daddy too."

He said, "Is he *your* daddy now?"

I said, "Not yet."

"Not yet?"

"Not for a while."

"Oh. Well, then what happened to him?"

"He just got big. He grew up."

"Does he go to the college?"

"He's bigger than that, even."

Mac smiled and showed his hand, fingers held together. "*That* big? *So* big?"

"Bigger," I said.

Mac said, "That's a big boy you have."

Samuels handed me the foil and coat hanger. I rolled the foil around a cigar until it was a cylinder, and I stuck it in the well side of the nozzle. I opened the hanger and straightened her out.

Mac said, "What's he doing, Daddy?"

Samuels said, "I don't know. I don't know, Mac. Why don't you go outside? I don't know."

I said, "Mr. Samuels, I wonder if you would hold that foil firmly in there and cup your hand under it while I give her a shove."

He held. Mac watched him. I pushed at the other side of the jet, felt it, pushed again, and it rolled down the aluminum foil to his palm: a flat wet pebble half the size of the nail on his little finger. He said, "That's it? That's all it is? This is what ruined my life for two days?"

I said, "That's all it ever takes, Mr. Samuels. It came up with the water — you have to have gravel where there's water — and it lodged in the jet, kept the pressure from building up. If it happens again, I'll put a screen in at the check valve. May never happen again. If it does, we'll know what to do, won't we?"

Samuels said, "I wonder when I'll ever know what to do around here."

I said, "You'll learn."

I fastened the halves of the pump together, then went out for my jeep can, still half full from the widow's house. I came back in and unscrewed the pipe plug at the top of the pump and poured the water in, put the plug back on, connected the pump to the switch.

Mac jumped, then stood still, holding to his father's leg.

The pump chirred, caught on the water from the widow's well, drew, and we all watched the pressure climb to forty, heard the motor cut out, heard the water climb in the copper pipes to the rest of the house as I opened the valve.

I was putting away tools when I heard Samuels say, "Now keep away from there!" I heard the *whack* of his hand on Mac's flesh, and heard the weeping start, in the back of the boy's throat, and then the wail. Samuels said, "That's *filthy* in there — Christ knows what you've dragged up. And I *told* you not to mess with things you don't know anything about. Dammit!"

Mac wailed louder. I watched his face clench and grow red, ugly. He put his left sleeve in his mouth and chewed on it, backed away to the stone steps, fumbled with his feet and stepped backward up one step. "But *Dad*-dy," he said. "But *Dad*-dy." Then he stood on the steps and chewed his sleeve and cried.

Samuels said, "God, look at that."

I said, "There's that smell you've been smelling, Mr. Samuels. Mouse. He must've fallen into the sump and starved to death and rotted there. That's what you've been smelling."

"God. Mac — go up and wash your hands. Mac! Go upstairs and wash your hands. I mean *now!*"

The small brown lump of paws and tail and teeth, its stomach swollen, the rest looking almost dissolved, lay in its puddle on the floor beside the sump. The stink of its death was everywhere. The pump cut in and built the pressure up again. Mac stood on the cellar steps and cried. His father pushed his glasses up and looked at the corpse of the rotted mouse and hugged his arms around himself and looked at his son. I walked past Samuels, turned away from the weeping boy, and pushed up at the lever that the float, if he had left it there, would have released on the sump pump. Nothing happened, and I stayed where I was, waiting, until I remembered to plug the sump pump in. I pushed the lever again, its motor started, the filthy reeking water dropped, the wide black rubber pipe it passed through on the ceiling swung like something alive as all that dying passed along it and out.

I picked the mouse up by its tail after the pump had stopped and Samuels, waiting for my approval, watching my face, had pulled out the plug. I carried my tools under my arm and the jeep can in my hand. I nodded to Samuels and he was going to speak, then didn't, just nodded back. I walked past Mac on the steps, not crying anymore, but wet-faced and stunned. I bent down as I passed him. I whispered, "What shall we do with your Daddy?" and went on, not smiling.

I walked to the truck in their unkempt drive that went to the barn that would fall. I carried the corpse. I thought to get home to Bella and say how sorry I was for the sorrow I'd made and couldn't take back. I spun the dripping mouse by its tail and flung it beyond the barn into Keeper's field of corn stumps. It rose and sank from the air and was gone. I had primed the earth. It didn't need the prime.

The Lesson of the
Hôtel Lotti

MY MOTHER'S LOVER was always exhausted, and yet he generated for me, and I think for her too, a sense of the most inexhaustible gentleness, and the strong calm I grew up thinking a prerequisite for love. He was a lawyer with offices at the foot of Manhattan, a neighborhood he knew intimately and talked about compellingly. The son of Austrian immigrants, a Jew, he lectured gently on Trinity Church and practiced maritime law, a field not famous for its renunciations of the more vulgar bigotries. He was the same age as my mother, fifty-five, when they started practicing deceptions and certainly cruelties upon his wife. And when my mother died at sixty-two, a couple of years after he did, she had suffered the most dreadful solitude, for he was necessary.

I was unplanned, unexpected, and apparently less than desirable. Born when my mother was thirty-nine, I was doubtless part of what happened not long thereafter. My father, who owned yards — a pleasure-craft boat yard, two lumberyards, and part of an undistinguished California vineyard — left my mother, and me, for a woman with inherited land in a suburb of London called Edgware. I have been there, for reasons I don't need to make clear; it looks like Flatbush Avenue in Brooklyn, though less permanent — every other house seems to be in a state of rebuilding or repair — and I never will need to go back. I grew up as much my mother's younger sister as her child. And the older I became, the more accomplished I was said to be, so my mother grew more fatigued by the world, more easily dismayed.

I have composed some recollections, for the sake of sentiment — I don't want to lose *anything* now — and so I think that I recall him standing silently at the door of our apartment on East 50th Street, late one night, as they returned from the theater. He seemed reluctant to walk farther in. I think I remember his smile: lips tightly closed (he had bad teeth), the long frown-lines from the nose to the corners of his mouth (they later became the boundaries of jowls), the pale blue eyes content but ready not to be. I think I can call him ironic, in the sense that he inspired, and dealt with, several emotions at once; he never surrendered to sarcasm. He looks larger in this possible early recollection than he was but, then, I feel smaller, when I remember him, than I am. He was nearly six feet tall, but because of his short legs he looked less large when I knew him well. His head was bald, the fringe gone chestnut and white. His face was square, his neck solid but not thick. His nose was wide without being bulbous. He was a slender man with a broad chest and strong shoulders, and he dressed in dark expensive suits. His voice was deep; it could snap and yap and snarl, or it could rumble soothingly as he spoke of what he loved, and nearly always when he talked to me it was with a graveled gentleness I have heard no other man use.

For years, my mother spoke of "my attorney," or "my legal adviser," or, as I grew older, "our lawyer." Then it became "Leonard Marcus says" and then "Leonard." He came to my graduation from the Brearley School, and I introduced him as "my Uncle Leonard," although my mother had never called him that. The night of my graduation, the three of us had dinner at the Russian Tea Room and went to a revival of *Our American Friend*. I thereafter left for a party with classmates, and when I came home early because I had decided to age quickly by finding myself bored with my intimate companions of four years, I found my mother waiting in the living room for a talk.

For a talk: a separate category in our lives, signaled by a silver drinks tray on the coffee table, a round stone ashtray, and a packet of Player's cigarettes, which my mother had come more and more to smoke too many of — perhaps to remind her, in distress, of the England my father had fled to. The sailor on the packet had blue eyes, and on his hatband was the word HERO.

She wore a long challis housecoat and no slippers, and sat in a corner of the sofa with a plaid blanket held across her lap; I had bought the blanket for her in England during my pointless pilgrimage there the summer before. We greeted each other matter-of-factly, per our tacit agreement not to become hysterical until it was clearly a necessity, and for a few minutes we discussed how remarkably mature I had become, in contrast to my friends, in the course of a single evening. She made herself a drink — Calvados and soda with ice — and I made my own sophisticated bourbon and ginger ale. She lit a Player's Navy Cut, hissed smoke out at me, and then caught her breath as I took a package of Kools from my bag and lit up too.

"Well, well," she said.

I shrugged.

"About Leonard," she said.

"Where is he?"

"Leonard's at home with his wife."

I puffed as if the cigarette were a pipe. My face beat hot, and I'm sure I felt the same sense of landslide felt by children who in their teens are asked, "Did you ever think you might be adopted, darling?" But I managed to say, as if it weren't the second commencement of the day, "Gee, I didn't know he was married, Anya."

"Leonard is a married man," my mother said, nodding, and with a note of pride in her voice — a sound I would hear again when I came home from Vassar to discuss with her my first and unspectacular coupling, with a boy from Union College.

"Has he been married — uh — all the time?"

My mother nodded and drank some brandy, said across the rim of her glass, "We have always been having an *affaire*." Her French was manifest and overaccented; she was an educated woman, and never untheatrical. "He is not your uncle, darling."

"Well, that's all right, Anya."

"Susu," she said.

"Anya, would you mind very much calling me Suzanne?" I said.

So I was Suzanne, and he was not Uncle Leonard, nor simply our attorney, Leonard Marcus. And shortly, we were a domestic routine. Once the declaration had been made, it wasn't mentioned again — by me, because I was in awe of an *affaire* conducted by a woman with varicose veins who was my humdrum, pretty, and flustered mother; by her, because I tried very hard that summer to rarely be home.

I worked at the neighborhood Gristede's during the day, and at night I kept moving — the evening jazz concerts at the Museum of Modern Art, or Shakespeare in the Park, or films at the Thalia, or shopping for frights on Eighth Street in the Village, or posed and dramaturgical dates ending with kisses on the Staten Island ferry slip and several near-misses — and near-disasters — in the cars and homes of boys who belonged to poetry clubs at Lafayette or to rugby clubs at Yale.

I felt, in part, like an elder sister, or a mother even, who was giving Anya as much privacy as possible with her beau. And then, in late August, when I was beginning to shop for school and to face the fact that going to Poughkeepsie frightened me, I returned to the apartment on a Saturday afternoon after swimming at Rye with friends — I had, by then, forgiven them their youth — to find Leonard on the sofa in the living room, and Anya in a true state of fear.

His head was what I saw first, propped on a crocheted pillow that leaned against the arm rest. It was white, and I saw blue veins near the surface of the skin, and beads of perspiration that looked like oil; they didn't run or drip. He wore his polished black wingtips, and it was their position that frightened me. They didn't touch, nor did they lie as if he sprawled at rest; they were apart because his legs were slightly apart, the dark blue poplin suit soaked onto them by sweat, to show how thin his thighs and calves were. There was a terrible weakness in his posture, a sense of the exhaustion of resources. His hands lay on his stomach, barely, as if he hadn't strength enough to lift his arms. His breathing was shallow — I looked to be certain that he breathed. He opened his eyes, and their blueness made his pallor seem worse. He smiled and then his lips made the shape one makes to whistle. He was showing me that he knew how he looked, and that he felt as ill as he appeared, and that he, and disability, and us together — me poised over and before him in uselessness and perplexity — were something of a joke we each understood. But no noise came from his lips. I touched my own lips with my index finger, as if hushing him, as if dispelling the confession he would make, and I turned away quickly to find Anya in the bedroom, where I knew she would be, smoking Player's and crossing her legs.

I sat on the bed beside her. But she sat up taut, so I moved away. "It's the heat," she said.

"It looks like more than the heat, Anya."

"It's the heat *because* it's more than the heat. He has a bad heart. He's been seeing doctors."

"What are they planning to do?"

"Nothing. Medication. They say he's too old for the kind of surgery he needs."

And that, as much as Leonard's condition, was what made her start to weep. I think she had been waiting in that darkened bedroom filled with cigarette smoke and the hum of air conditioning for someone to whom she could state that cruelty: that she, a slender woman in shorts and a halter, a woman with a young throat atop a body that was no disgrace despite the varicose veins, a woman who for years had conducted in perfect French an *affaire* with a man of gentle elegance — she, such a woman, now faced the continuation of a lesson she had received when my father left us years before. The lesson was about things running down — respect and trust and strength, and finally time.

I said, "Anya, can I ask you something?"

She sniffed and wiped her face with the back of a pale beautiful wrist. "When you ask if you can ask, Susu — Suzanne — it means you know you shouldn't ask it. Do you really need to?"

I said, "Do you and Leonard make love?"

She exploded into tears then, perhaps because her answer — not the impertinence or heartlessness of the question — was another segment of the lesson she must learn. "We used to," she said, as she tried to catch her breath.

"He can't anymore?"

"Suzanne!"

And her genuine dignity, a surprising muscularity of tone, her wonderful slight carriage, the beauty of her hair and neck, and certainly the specter of Poughkeepsie and my sense of the blackness beyond what I managed to know — all brought me into her arms, leaning over her, smelling her hair, wishing that I wept only for her.

Her letters to school described his frailty and determination. My visits home confirmed them. They were together a great deal, and Leonard came to 50th Street with gifts — a book, a pen from Mark Cross, a scarf purchased at Liberty on one of his transatlantic trips. I grew accustomed, over that first year of school and then the others, to his slower walk, a loss of tension in his bearing, his need to pause and catch his breath, the permanent pallor of his face, his need for naps. His illness aged my mother, and I accepted that as well: I felt ten years older than I was, and it seemed appropriate to me that my mother should not look young. Leonard worked harder than before, and Anya tried to convince him to retire.

I was studying in my room at home one weekend, with the door ajar, when I heard her ask him, again, to slow his pace. He snapped at her, "I have to provide for a *wife* — remember? She's getting on, like us."

That was in my sophomore or junior year, and on the New York Central to Poughkeepsie that Sunday evening I stared out the window at the Hudson, which in the last sunlight looked like ice although it was nearly May, and I thought as hard as I could about Leonard's wife. I knew that he had been married to her for some thirty years. I knew that their child was grown and away. I knew that they maintained a home in Westchester County but that Leonard, complaining of fatigue, had furnished an apartment in the East Forties where he stayed during the week. I knew that he often found a reason for staying in the city over weekends as well — that is, he found an alibi to broadcast in Westchester; I knew the reason. I wondered how much his wife knew, and I fell asleep refusing to believe that she didn't know it all.

I spent a week preparing for final exams, and made use of one of Leonard's lectures. This one had been on the Dead Sea scrolls. He had lent me three books and had told me what he knew. As I studied, I heard the low sweet voice, smelled the breath of decay, saw the round-shouldered posture he more and more assumed, and the sad ironic smile — a kind of shyness, I concluded — on the handsome white face. And I studied history, and Platonic posturings — " 'But, sirs, it may be that the difficulty is not to flee from death, but from guilt. Guilt is swifter than death' " — and thought, again, that Dryden really needn't have bothered. I was studying Leonard Marcus, my mother's lover, and wondering why he, who had in spirit left his wife, was of a different category of being from my father, who had left his wife in fact. It pleases me to remember that, although I couldn't answer the question, I knew that Leonard Marcus *was* different. And thinking of my small rattled mother, or of Leonard's low devoted tones caressing the history of the Jefferson administration, say, or of the angry assertion of his wife's need for money in old age, I am now — callow an impulse as it is — proud.

Leonard was not allowed to drink, and I had sworn myself to ignore his married life. We renounced those imperatives together in New York after he had returned from a business trip to Paris, and after I had begun my first semester at Columbia Law. Leonard called me at John Jay Hall and asked me to meet him at the Top of the Tower. I dressed nervously and too stylishly, and was quiet as we rode the elevator to the top of the Beekman Arms. We sat at a little table on the terrace and looked over the stone balustrade at the river, which, from that enormous distance, looked clean. The entire city looked clean and manageable, and knowing that it was an illusion helped me swear to myself that for this shrinking man who always, now, was out of breath, I would sustain whatever illusions he required of me. The winds up there were strong, despite the heat of late September, and I thought Leonard shivered. But when I suggested that we move indoors, he smiled that shy smile, shrugged his shoulders, and ordered drinks. He bought me a brandy Alexander, as if I were half child and we were combining the magic of a milkshake and the necessity that a dignified law student enjoy strong drink.

I felt like someone's daughter.

Leonard held my hand, then put it down as you would place Baccarat on a marble table — with deference to its quality, with care because it was fragile. And he began — precisely as if he were telling me of the rebel zealot Jesus, or of the building of Washington, or of the regulations governing off-shore fishing in Europe — to deliver another lecture. But this one was about his life.

"My wife is named Belle. Did you know that? She's a very tall woman, nearly as tall as you are. But she has bad feet, something to do with the instep, it's terribly painful, and she tends to shuffle. For some reason, that makes her look shorter. When I tell you this, you should try to see her as someone who is short. She has friends on Long Island, younger than she — younger than I — who are very much involved in the restoration of Colonial furniture. Do you care about Colonial furniture?" He actually paused, waited to know, and I am quite certain that he did wonder, even at the moment, about my interests. I shook my head and lit another Kool — he had to cup his hands around mine to shelter the flame from the wind — and then Leonard continued.

"This happened last week, before I went to Paris. Did you know I'd been there? I'll have to tell you about it. A ship seems to have disappeared, although the client insists it was sold to the Egyptians, under Panamanian registry, for purposes involving proscribed shipments to Northern Ireland. Our adversaries insist that the bill of lading was received and entered at Marseilles. The original owners are Americans — it's out of Eric Ambler, did you ever read him?" He laughed and threw his hands up, shook his head. "It's nonsense, and they're all crooks. But I want you to know about last week, before my trip. Belle was supposed to spend the weekend with her friends, and they asked if I could drive out with them. It was time to say yes, and I did, and we met at their apartment, at University Place, to go together to their house on the Island. You know how I've been — sometimes my energy is pretty poor." This time he didn't smile.

"Without going into details, let me say that I was pretty punk about it. Just as we were about to leave, I told Belle that I was too tired for the drive and that I'd go back to my apartment. She was furious, but she wasn't surprised." He looked at me so intensely that I looked away. "I want you to understand some of the complexities of our assumptions, Belle's and mine. At any rate, I did go back, and they went on to Long Island.

"My understanding is that Belle became worried about me" — he signaled for more drinks, brandy Alexander for me, white wine for him — "and woke up the poor host and made him drive her all the way back to New York at two in the morning, in a nasty rain. She has a key, of course, and let herself into my apartment."

"You weren't there," I said.

"No."

"Because you moved in with Anya after I went uptown to Columbia."

"That's not inaccurate."

"You keep the other place —"

"As a cover. In an Eric Ambler novel, it would be called that, yes." Leonard tried to smile, sipped his wine, frowned at it.

"And you sort of live part-time with Anya?"

He shrugged, raised his eyebrows, said, "It's a simple clarity for a complex situation — but, yes. Yes."

"Can I be your law clerk, Leonard?"

He grinned, with all his teeth this time, saying, "You mean you're my student? You flatter me that much?"

"Meaning I admire you very much."

He said, "You'll be *Law Review* and start someplace so prestigious —"

"Can I? Can I ask you again at the end of the year?"

He blushed, like a young man having drinks with a girl at one of the city's romantic saloons, and he said, "Yes. Please."

"Thank you, Leonard."

"But listen," he said. "She came into an empty apartment and looked around — it's tiny, a sofa bed, a kitchenette, a bathroom and closet. But she looked. And not only wasn't I there, there were barely signs that I'd *been* there. I don't know precisely what she began to know, but she began to know it. It was four in the morning by then. She sat there, by herself, not reading, not looking at television. She simply sat. Probably in the dark. And then, around six, she called the police and asked what to do. They told her she could file a missing persons report. What would that achieve? she asked. Nothing, they told her, except list me as missing and cause my name to be checked in emergency rooms and at the medical examiner's office. She thought there was no point in that, she said. She said she knew that if I were sick or dead she'd find out fairly soon. Then she went down to Grand Central and rode home. She reached me at the office later that morning. I assured her that I had been all right. I told her not to worry herself."

"And she accepted that?"

"She said she supposed foreign clients had arrived on a late plane and that I had to meet them."

"You let her believe that?"

"I didn't really answer. I told her I'd be home that weekend and told her to take care of herself, and we hung up."

"Leonard, she believed you?"

"We believe what we need to, I suppose."

"Is that true?"

He clasped his hands before him, in the air. The tips of his fingers were white and substanceless beneath the skin; they held the imprint of whatever they pressed upon. Shrugging his shoulders, he said, "It *sounds* true."

Leonard, everything sounds true if you say it right."

"Dealing with other people's truth *can* be a self-indulgent process," he said. And then, as if to assure me that his remark was not meant merely to discipline me, he added, "We have been self-indulgent, I suppose, in a sense. Though we've been waiting for this. We're waiting now." And I didn't know which *we* — my mother and he, or someone else's mother and he — he meant.

I finished my drink, and he ordered another round, and then he finished his. We sat in silence through the arrival of the drinks, and through our consumption of them, and through the waiter's arrival with more. I smoked a lot and tried to think hard. Leonard waited patiently for me to have a reaction, or to discern what it was. I lit another cigarette — he cupped his hands for me again — and I blew smoke out, feeling that my tongue was raw, my throat sore, my head filled with childish exclamations and masterful formulations and the tune of a Robert Hall radio jingle. It was dark over the river now, but bright on the terrace, and ships were glimmering like fish as their superstructures caught the light the river absorbed. I said, "Life is confusing, Leonard," and he was decent enough to try to keep his lips from curving. But he couldn't, and then I couldn't, and we laughed — whooped, really — until he walked around to my chair, leaned from behind to kiss my cheek, and then gripped my arm to help me up and get me to a cab.

A year after his death — he died in his sleep, and in Westchester —

I was spending the weekend helping my mother clean and cook for a party she'd decided it was necessary to give. As I vacuumed and put things away, grinding my teeth because I should have been uptown at my desk, I looked, thinking of my books, at the bedside bookcase. I saw *Judgment on Deltchev* by Eric Ambler. I thought of the Beekman Tower and Leonard's lesson; I had been trying to understand it since he'd offered it to me, and particularly since his death — since the funeral we felt we couldn't attend. I think our absence would have provoked his hesitant smile, but also grave pity for Anya and, I think, actual understanding of her relief at not having to watch him buried. Anya learned of his death when she read it in the *Times*.

With the vacuum cleaner bellowing, I opened the book, saw Balkan names and descriptions of fear and subterfuge, and then a shade of baby blue — a piece of notepaper. I laughed, because only in stories and in the most arcane probate cases will a letter from the dead fall from among the pages of a book. But I was sure that I had found such a letter, and I did not laugh anymore. In the roar of Anya's Electrolux, air pouring from an unstoppered vent, the old motor getting louder as it got hotter, I sat on my mother's bed and opened the folded single sheet. It was six-by-nine — perhaps half an inch longer each way — and where it had been folded, yellow-brown had supplanted the blue. A lion was engraved in the upper left-hand corner, and in the right it said *Hôtel Lotti, 7 et 9, Rue de Castiglione, Paris*. And below, nothing. No message I could read, no reminder, no clue. It was simply a bookmark, a convenience — it had nothing to say.

I smelled the motor grinding and meat cooking in the kitchen and the harsh intimate scent of Anya's Russia Leather. I was made physically sick by the blankness of the paper, its near precise folds in which the brown discolorations pooled. I folded it and put it back in the book, and I thought of Leonard in a hotel room that smelled of paint. He lay on the long wide wooden bed in the Hôtel Lotti. Over a chair hung his trousers, wrinkled from the airplane, and on the bathroom doorknob hung his jacket, heavy with passport case and pens. He was in under-shorts and undershirt, and his long black hose were held to his thin white calves by garters, black and tight. His feet nearly touched, and one arm lay on his chest while the other held *Judgment on Deltchev*. He was reading of failures and fealties, the corruptions of the sub-rosa world, and Anya was on 50th Street, and I was studying torts, and the man who had fathered me was living in Edgware, and I knew who my father was. I heard the shallow breathing and saw his thin white skull on the wide pillow, the dwindling body enclosed by the patterned wallpaper of the Hôtel Lotti.

I was holding the paperback book when Anya came in to find me sitting on her bed. The noise of the vacuum cleaner broke around me like beach thunder. Her throat was slack now, and the flesh of her upper arms soft. In her black dressing gown she seemed pretentious and pathetic, too made up, as if she had costumed herself for solitude and, at the same time, me.

She turned her head to the side as she looked at me; it was a dog's motion of puzzlement, a gesture new for her, another sign of age in us both. She asked me, I think, what the matter was. But her voice did not carry through the sound of the machine.

That was when I whispered, into all that mechanical rage, to all her worn-out loneliness, that I'd been studying too hard and needed to rest. I thought of Leonard Marcus's wife and tried to picture her as short.

That was when Anya mimed across the machine to me the question I read on her lips.

She said: What? What?

My Father, Cont.

IF ANYTHING WAS GROWING just because it was March, it was growing under cover like the rest of us. Snow still rode the eaves and trembled in the skies, the banks of black-grained ice stood three feet tall at the sides of the roads and over all the lawns. But the calendar said spring, and the local newspapers said spring, and even the TV shows from New York, piped into Syracuse and Utica, then out among the small winding roads and old hills to the brand-new pastel trailers and the old gray clapboard farmhouses — the farmers lived in the trailers; the city people, in heralded perpetual retreat, lived in the farmers' abandoned homes — said spring. What made it worse was that when all the official organs of the world's conspiracy for early spring made their announcements, the Solsville Cooperative Nursery School Book Sale made theirs. When that happened, I kept my mouth shut tight. I had read my "Hansel and Gretel," and I knew what parents did with kids when there wasn't enough — and never mind *what* — to go around.

My father was a doctor and an ex-convict. That's how he used to describe himself to people he had just met and had drunk a couple of George Dickel sour mash whiskeys with: "I'm a doctor of children and an outcast of the people. I sat out the war because I didn't believe in killing, and sometimes the care these troglodytes up here give their children is enough to drive me past Korea and my conscientious objection and into the pits of pure murder."

He had been divorced, and I had a couple of older half sisters someplace in the Middle West. He had married a pretty young woman who wrote a children's book when she was twenty and who never wrote a word again unless it was on a sign announcing a nursery school book sale or a rummage to benefit the local members of the Future Farmers of America. I was their issue, and I knew what was coming since it was calendar spring but actual winter, and my mother had just told him he should go upstairs to his study, an extra bedroom really, and take down his old paperback duplicate books and this year give in, for God's sake, and donate them to the Solsville Nursery School Book Sale and be charitable for once.

"Listen, Edna," my father's voice said. It hummed on the floorboards upstairs in my room and poured up through the old-fashioned heating vents. It was Sunday and I was waiting for the Celtics' game and looking at the horrible illustrations in "Hansel and Gretel." It's the story about the family with too little to eat. They kept taking the kids into the forest and leaving them there because there wasn't enough to go around. It's the saddest story about families. It's the one that says hunger comes first. "Listen, Edna," my father said, "I don't mind taking their calls at six in the morning, and I don't mind chugging out at midnight to an obscenely underequipped rural emergency ward. I'll treat their kids and wait three years for them to pay their bills. All right —"

"Hold it, Hank," my mother said. She was closer to my age than his, I always thought, and smaller, like me, and nearly as smart as he was, which I wasn't. She had also said, one night, when I could hear them, that if it wasn't for me, she'd be long gone from his bucolic infantilism. I didn't look it up because I didn't want to know. But I wasn't pleased with how things were going for us. My mother said, "You won't be giving your precious thirty-five-cent paperbacks that are fifteen, twenty years old to the same pasty-faced potato-fat kickers you cure, Dr. Schweitzer. They don't read, remember? You're giving books that will be sold by the nursery school so it can keep the profits and stay open another few months and take care of the children of some faculty members at a small and undistinguished state college who nevertheless are the only friends you've *got*. Remember?"

He didn't whine but he seemed to, nearly, when he said, "Honey, it doesn't *feel* right to give my books away like that."

There was a little silence, and then she said, very low, "They're my books too, aren't they?"

And then another little silence, and then he said, "I'll do it. Do that again, and I'll do it."

And then another little silence and a long silence.

I went back to "Hansel and Gretel" — the part where the father gives in and says, "Ah, but I shall regret the poor children."

Later on, my father thumped up and down the creaky wooden stairs of the old farmhouse — between the phone calls he always got on Sundays from patients who should have seen him on Friday or waited till Monday — and he carried some cartons of books out to the station wagon. I heard the doors slam as he loaded the old paperbacks into the car. I was watching a basketball game on TV because I had finished my schoolwork and needed something full of team spirit — Bob Cousy being given the ball because he was lighter than air and he glowed in the dark and he *deserved* the love he was getting. I didn't want to think anymore because I didn't understand what I was thinking. I didn't want to read any more about those kids in the forest because I did understand what I was reading. And that's why my heart was poisoned like a witch's pancakes when my father said over drinks in the living room — I could hear him breaking their long silence, which was hard on all three of us — "Let's go up into the hills, in near Brookfield, and see if the deer are coming down yet."

I hoped that when my mother answered, "It's too early," my father would drop the idea. She pushed him: "It's too early for the deer to come down, Hank. What they want is corn stubble, and the fields are still covered with snow. And they sure don't want more snow. They can get plenty of that up where they are."

As soon as he started to answer, I could tell from the swollen sound of his voice that she had made a big mistake.

Cousy glided in from fifteen feet out, it felt like, for a slow-motion shot that made me hold my ears and shake my head. The Celtics surrounded him and they all slapped each other's buttocks and nodded and walked around with each other. I thought, *Ah, but I shall regret the poor children.*

My father said, "Well, Our Lady of the Charitable Mysteries and Reliquary Book Sale, if it's too early for deer, then it's too early for books, on account of both depend on spring, which has to do with the pagan notion of the earth reborn, and the Christian's juvenility about his Lord. If the deer won't come down, being a medieval symbol, then the Christ is not arisen. And if *He* won't be bothered, then I surely don't have to commemorate a spring which hasn't come by carrying my private property down to Solsville to watch them give it away."

My mother said, "You never should have stayed away from the war. You were meant for it."

I turned Cousy off and went for my coat and boots. When they called me, I was ready. They were surprised.

It was getting colder, and the air smelled wet, like snow coming. My father drove slowly and sighed, as if he were relaxing. The back seat of the wagon was down, and I sat with my back against their seat, my legs on the floorboards pointing out the back window, my elbows propped on cartons of books. I listened to my parents breathe and thought about the father saying, *We are going into the forest to hew wood, and in the evening, when we are ready, we will come and fetch you.* Of course I was intelligent and enlightened and, according to my mother and father, I lived in a climate of reinforcement, so all I had to do was lean back in the darkness of the car and the darkness of the ending day and watch as we crossed Route 12 and drove up the rutted icy roads, past gray houses with dull yellow lights in the windows, past mobile homes with eighty-foot antennas, to see how too smoothly we slipped into the woods.

In the summer there, you'd mostly see the maples and ash and beech, what elms were left, and the evergreens filled the spaces between. But in the early autumn, as the leaves fell, there was a kind of dance. First the trees weren't bare, because they bloomed bird's nests, vacant and ragged. Then the wind took some of the nests, or you stopped noticing them, and there was a lot of emptiness around. Then it was winter, and the evergreens seemed to step forward, the annual bearers seemed to recede, and then what you saw was snow, the hard brown roads, the evergreens covered in white, and the scraggly wisps of deciduous trees waiting for spring so they could step back into full sight. It was a slow exciting dance, and I miss it, but I won't go back to watch.

My father smoked his pipe, the car filled with smoke, my mother

sneezed, and he drove up steep roads, past all houses now, into darkness, the lights still off. The car shivered and slid on its heavy snow
tires, but he pushed it up. My mother said, "I think we should go back,
Hank. It's early for deer, it really is. We always do this. We always
come looking too early."

The tires whined, but he kept the car moving. I drew my knees up
on the floorboards beside me and leaned over the seat, looking forward
now, sniffing in the pipe smoke, letting an elbow touch each parent's
shoulder in the fragrance and darkness of our ride. I saw the branching-
off of our snowy road; in the darkness, the snow seemed to glow with a
light from underneath it, and then the secret light went out as my
father turned the car lights on, and we were coasting downhill slightly,
but pretty fast, at a fork.

I would have stopped. My mother said it very clearly, that she
thought we ought to. He let the car slide left, and we went downhill
farther, maybe fifty or sixty yards. The car slid hard, then stopped —
as if cement had just that moment turned from fresh to ten years old
around the wheels.

"Okay," my mother said, "we're stuck."

"No," my father said. He floored it in forward gear, then shifted to
reverse, floored it again, then shifted forward, then into reverse, and
the wheels whined, the motor roared, a cloud of snow and exhaust
blew up behind us, and the car stayed where it was. "Maybe not," he
said.

The heater was on full, and it was getting sweaty in there, and the
smoke from his pipe seemed suddenly a little sweet. I thought of
sweets, of poisoned pancakes, and I said, "Hey, Dad, are we really
trapped here? Can we get home?"

My mother said, "Shh," but it was too late.

My father, who was tall and heavy, and whose hair was an unkind
color, like a metal you might find in a factory or a hospital but never
around the house, shouted, "Well, of *course* we're going to get home!
For Christ's sake. Do I really have to answer that kind of question now?
Of *course*, dammit. And we'll get home in the goddamned *car* is how
we'll do it."

I didn't answer, and he said, "Right?"

"What, Daddy?"

"I said *right?*"

"About what, Daddy?"

"*Jesus!*" he said. He slammed the door closed when he got out, and he walked through snow that looked sometimes to be up to his calves and sometimes his knees as he went to open the tailgate, pull out the folding army-surplus shovel, and bend behind the steady red shine of our taillights to stop and push, rise and heave — I can see that now, at any time, in a crowd or in my sleep, that steady red-tinted rise and fall of my father in the forest, hewing. My mother held to the forearm of my heavy jacket. But I moved away. I watched.

The shovel flashed red as it crossed in front of the light, and so did his hands, and so did his face as it dipped to rise. He was chopping us out, and once he looked in, panting, blowing, the sweat on his face a bloody wash in the taillights' falsifying glow — he would have loved to see himself like that, and perhaps he was looking at his reflection in the glass — and he smiled at me and asked forgiveness with his grin, as he usually did. But then he got angry again, frustrated, and his head bobbed up and down again, his face was hidden, as he dug at all the snow in the Brookfield forest.

After a while my mother said, "I hope he doesn't have a heart attack."

I said, "Can I dig? Can I take a turn? That'll keep him from having a heart attack."

My mother said, "He is so determined to have a heart attack, neither one of us can do a thing to keep him from having his way. Your father's a baby."

I said — and I don't know why; it was no wisdom, it was only *talk*, and yet maybe it was my memory of the woodcutter's wife — I said, "Should you be saying things like that about your husband?"

My mother squealed. Her head retreated, like a turtle's. She opened her mouth wide, and I saw her tongue quivering. The door boomed and my father hurled himself in behind the wheel, panting, heaving against his clothes. My mother closed her mouth.

I said, "Don't have a heart attack, Daddy."

"Absolutely not," he said. He rocked the car forward, then from forward to reverse, reverse to forward. But we didn't move. The metal of the motor screamed, and he stopped. He said, "One more shot at it." I thought of the family who didn't have enough to go around. I thought of wandering among the thick, self-reliant trunks of trees which went so far up I couldn't see their tops. Making no progress. Wandering in terror. Gagged by my own tongue. My mouth freezing open, yes, the tongue iced to the roof of the icy mouth. I thought of the snow turning black, the tree trunks white, my body going from white to black. My black tongue frozen in my mouth, my black teeth biting at nothing. Black wind pouring in and out. Everything black down past my tonsils to my teeth and stomach and my bowels. Then I saw my eyes, and they were black marbles. I thought of people knowing that I was there forever and not mourning — but regretting it.

My father, leaning over the seat, interrupted me by saying, "Give me the books."

"What?"

"The goddamned *books*, goddammit!"

My mother said, "Don't take it out on him, he's frightened enough."

"I'm not frightened," I said.

"I'm not taking it out," my father said. He stopped moving, then started again, this time talking in a higher voice. I guess he thought what was higher was lighter as well. He reached in past my arms and legs and hauled things into the glow of the glove compartment light: "A soupçon of Thomas Hardy, I think. Ah, just right: *Jude the Obscure*, famous family man. Never did get his degree, as I recall. Yes. And some *Dickens!* Come on, Chuck, let's have the old *Bleak House* there and — oh, my land, how generous, he's giving us *Tale of Two Cities* too. Now that's what I call *giving* — somebody needs books, you give *books*. Am I right? And Miss Brontë, I believe? So kind of you to hurl yourself into the effort." He chuckled like what a mad scientist is supposed to sound like, and I guess that was meant to reassure us. I passed a few more over to him, and he took them and went around to kneel behind the rear wheels. We heard him grunting even though the motor still chugged in a ragged neutral.

Without asking permission, I got out. I took the flashlight with me, but I kept it off. I stood with the whole world behind me, and maybe because the road sloped, it felt as if everything could tip upon us, pour down onto us, and sweep us farther along. The snow was glowing again since he'd turned the car lights out, the all-but-darkness of the forest seemed to make the snow burn brighter from within. My mother looked through her window at me. She smiled a kind of smile, and I did it back.

My father had finished wedging the paperbacks beneath the tires — his last hope for traction — and then he got in to put the car in gear and floor it. I stayed where I was, my hands cupped over my ears so that I wouldn't hear the engine scream this time. Jude and his babies and Ellen and Sydney Carton and Catherine Earnshaw and Heathcliff flew from beneath our wheels, were torn by the deep treads into tiny fragments and blown behind us and up into the air. They sailed there, half in darkness, then down into the brightness of the glowing snow, and then they were carried by the wind and were ridden away. They were gone by the time my mother and father, ponderous in their snow gear, came out. Bulky as they were, they were as prone to flight and disappearance as the tiny papers and their black invisible words.

A couple of chunks of the stronger covers lay in odd designs behind the wheels. I was looking at what was left, and thinking of the family where hunger was foremost, and where there simply wasn't enough to go around. My father, I saw at last, was looking at me. He was grinning.

He said, "Ain't I something?"

"We go looking for deer," my mother said, "delicate gentle little hungry deer, and look what we end up with. A dead car and" — pointing at my father, at the woods — "this."

I said, "You really messed up, Daddy. You got us lost in the woods and everything." He shrugged, then turned to shut off the motor, lock the car up. I watched him as he walked around the car, being certain. I said, "I guess we didn't get *that* messed up."

He came back and stood before me. He said, "You think I screwed things up for you?"

I was shivering by then. I turned the flashlight on and pointed it at his face. There was no body and there were no woods. There was my father's face, and the darkness.

He looked into me the way some people peer into rooms. He saw what I was seeing. Looking away from me, and down at his vanished body, then into me again, he said, "Do I look like a ghost to you? Are you really good and scared?"

I started to cry. I let go of all of it and cried very hard.

"I'll get you home, love," he whispered down onto the top of my head as he hugged me. "I'll get you out of the woods and I'll get you into your house and before you know it, you'll be laughing. I can do that for you, love."

I felt my mother move in to hug us. She pulled at the flashlight and I let it go. I kept my eyes closed and felt the dark woods tilt upon us.

My father — who was not a woodcutter, and for whom the hungers did not consistently come first — said, "It's all right. I'm not a ghost. There aren't any ghosts."

And for some good time he was right.

What You Might as Well Call Love

JUST LIKE A CURSE, rain fell for two weeks, hissing on shingles and in nearly naked trees, and the river, dammed by brush and rotted elms, began to rise. Sun sometimes shone, and sometimes the rain held off an hour, but the ground was always spongy, and mud was on everything. The river wound around the hamlet, in some places close to backyards, in others separated from yards by hillocks and cabbage fields. It was a dark autumn, and always cold; the cabbage stank in the early mornings and late at night. And the water table rose in response to the rain and pushed through deep foundation stones and up through cracked cement cellar floors, pooled around furnaces and freezers and water heaters, triggered sump pumps which gargled out the water which ran back into the ground and reappeared inside, rising slowly, in the darkness of the cellars looking black.

On the second day of flooding, Ethan came home from school with the mimeo'd message about the outbreak of head lice in the elementary grades. Marge had come up from sweeping pooled water in the cellar and her black boots glistened as she read the notice and cross-examined Ethan about school, while, forcing his head down, she raked through the fine brown hair, seeking nits.

"What's a nit?" Ethan said.

"You're clean," she said. "A nit is the egg of a louse."

"Louse?"

"A louse is one lice. Lice are a lot of louses."

"What's a *person* who's a louse, then?"

"A nitwit. Please go up and change your clothes."

"Can I look at the flood?"

"There *isn't* any flood. There's water in the cellar and go upstairs and change your clothes. Please. Everything's fine."

"How come you were down there, then, Mom?"

"I was sweeping water into the sump. It collects some places, and doesn't go into the sump. If that happens, it doesn't get pumped out. See? Please go up?"

"But doesn't it come back *in?*"

Marge sat on the floor and took one boot off. "That is not a nine-year-old question," she said. "Up."

Ethan said, "It's a nitwit question." He gave her his grown-up smile, irony and all, ruffled her thick light hair, and went up. Marge took off her other boot and leaned against the wall, stretching out her legs, to wait for Ben to come home.

He came in a red-and-black woolen shirt that was darkening with rainwater, and wire-rimmed glases that were sheeted over, and thirty feet of black plastic pipe taped in a big crooked circle. As Marge held the door, Ben backed and sidled and swore — "Sell. We sell, and we move someplace where we can live on top of a hill and *nothing* runs in" — and then he was inside their small kitchen, talking in a low rant and forcing the pipe around the table to the cellar door.

Marge said, "According to Ethan, who is correct, the water is welling *up*."

"What?"

"That water's coming *up* from the ground."

"You noticed that too, huh?" Ben was down on the cellar steps now, pulling the pipe after him and grunting.

In a far, partly lighted corner, water ran in black smears down the wall stones and onto the cement floor. In the center of the floor, a hole three feet deep, about eighteen inches in diameter, received the runoff from the walls and floor. Tied to various beam jacks and ancient wooden posts, some with bark still on them, held in a web of white sash cord, was the sump pump with its copper float. When water in the sump reached a certain level, the float came up and the pump started.

Water ran from it through black plastic pipe such as Ben wrestled with, and up through a broken storm window above their heads, and out onto the ground beside the house. The motor went on and off twice as they watched, and Ben cleared his throat and sniffed as if the need for pumping, the sound of the little motor, the invasion of water, were making his sinuses pour.

He lugged the pipe around the furnace to the other side of the cellar. There water pooled deeper than anywhere else, in a declivity that didn't permit it to run to the sump. They looked at it, and as Ben began to swear Marge went upstairs and put her boots on.

Ben stood above the center of the pool which shimmered, bubbled slightly, in the light of a bulb on the ceiling. In the pool was a silted corroding pipe. He leaned the circle of black plastic pipe against the furnace, squatted in the water, almost sitting in it, and jammed a plastic joint into the pipe in the floor. "It fits!" he called. "I guessed, and I was right, and it *fits!* I'm telling you, Marge, I'm going to pipe the goddamn water right the hell out of this old well or whatever the hell it is, *directly* into the faithful sump and its obedient pump, and we are *home!* There will be *no* pooling of water in my house without written permission. The furnace will continue to roar, *all* the necessary machines will function, including us, and the home fires will burn."

Marge stood a few feet away from him, and when he noticed her he smiled, and then they both were silent as he pushed the elbow joint deeper into the rusted socket. There was the sound of dripping, and of the pump cutting on and off, and then the louder yammer of the water pump forcing water upstairs from their well because the pressure to the faucets was low, and then, at the same time, the whir of the furnace fan. Then the machines completed their cycles and stopped, and there was only the sound of their breathing, of trickles and drips.

Ben cut the tape from the black plastic pipe and Marge took one end to stretch it away from him. She wove it among lolly columns and beam supports to where it would empty into the sump. "Mere victory," Ben said. "Nothing great. Maybe a small cathedral's worth of vision and ability and strength. Thank you."

Marge, looking at the open end of the pipe, which still was dry, which carried nothing from the rusted drain into the sump, said, "It does flow up."

"Water doesn't flow up."

"It *wells* up. It seeps. It's like a spring, Ben, when the water table's high. It comes up around the pipe you put there. It just comes up."

"Jesus, Marge."

She walked back to where he stood at the elbow joint and, stooping, pointed. In the silt around the pipe into which he had shoved the white plastic joint, water was bubbling up, stirring mossy brown sediment. The pool of dark water widened. Ben took the big janitor's broom that leaned against the furnace and he began to sweep, long hard angry strokes, so that the pool ran over the lip of its margins and flowed along the inclines of the cellar, into the sump. He said, breathing hard, "It doesn't work."

"Nice try, though."

"I really thought it would work. I thought seventeen dollars' worth."

"It was a good idea," Marge said.

"I should have listened."

"Ethan figured it out."

"Yeah? He's nine and I'm thirty-five."

"He has the advantage of years," she said.

He threw the broom into the pool, which was widening again, and said, "I don't really think it'll get into the furnace."

"No," she said, "it probably won't."

"We'll check on it."

They were walking up the narrow steps.

"There's an epidemic of head lice in school," Marge said.

"Ethan's okay?"

"So far. But it's really contagious."

"Son of a bitch!" Ben said.

Marge said, "I'd rather have locusts than lice."

"You're right," Ben said at the top of the stairs. "There's a better tone to locusts than lice."

"And it seems more suitable to floods, anyway," Marge said.

Ethan was waiting in the kitchen. "I thought you said there wasn't any flood, Mom."

She sat on the floor, thin, with long arms, looking like a child as she took her black boots off. She said, "There isn't."

"Didn't you and Dad just talk about one?"

"It's a flood for grown-ups," Ben said. "It isn't a flood for kids."

"Nitwit," Ethan said.

And Ben roared, *"What?"*

Marge said, "It's a joke, Ben. It's a joke Ethan and I were having. Ethan, why don't you go upstairs and change your clothes?"

"I just did. Remember?"

"Why don't you go upstairs and read *John Sevier, Pioneer Boy?*"

"I finished it last night. Mom, would you and Dad like some privacy? I can go upstairs and work on my carrier."

Marge told Ben, "It's an atomic supercarrier which is capable of holding a hundred and ten assorted fighters and long-range patrol planes, plus surface-to-air missiles. One inch to forty feet. Goodbye, Ethan. I love you."

They were sitting in the kitchen with whiskey and ice, and Ben said, "Substitute teaching may just be the worst work in the world, and *I* wouldn't do it. I don't blame you for hating it. I'm saying, for *me*, right now, even though I did worse work in New York, my job is ugly, boring, stupid, and horrible. I mean, I think I'm running out of sick leave from calling in with phony flus every other day."

"And you don't get paid enough," she said.

"Nope."

"And neither do I, when I do get work."

"Nope."

"And we're out seventeen bucks for plastic pipe."

Ben said, "Do I need another drink or do you?"

"Why don't we both do that, and skip the fight we don't even feel like having, and discuss what to have for dinner."

"Let's go out for pizza," Ben said.

"It'll cost more money."

"Which we haven't got."

"Almost. We almost haven't got it, you're right."

Wind threw rainwater, as if it were solid, at the back-door window, and Ben said, "Fucking rain."

Marge stood, poured more whiskey over fresh ice for them, pulled at the hem of her sweater, and remained standing as she said, "I would like us to consider having another child."

Ben said nothing, drank a large swallow, stared at her. He offered a smile, the sort you use in case a bearer of bad news might be joking, then he withdrew it. The pump went on and off, then on again, then off. "It always sounds like it's grinding something," Ben said.

Marge said, "I realize this isn't the best time to broach the subject. But it's not a complete surprise."

"No."

"The rain keeps making me think about babies. It's the *threat*. Do you know what I mean? What if something, I keep thinking, what if something happens."

"You mean to Ethan?"

Marge's eyes filled and instantly were red at the rims. She nodded.

"We won't *let* anything happen to him," Ben said, as if he were accused of neglect.

"We can't stop the lice," she said. "We can't stop the rain."

"We're *old*, Marge. Aren't we pretty old to be having kids?"

"We're poor, and it's a nuisance, taking care of a baby again. But a thirty-five-year-old woman can deliver a child safely, a normal child, without risking her health."

"Not without risk."

"Without risking that *much*."

"Is that true?"

She drank some whiskey. She said, "I can find out."

In a khaki slicker and rubber boots, wearing a tweed hat, Ben walked the river. Behind him, the cabbage fields went slightly up-hill and then descended to their yard and the backyards of seven other small box-shaped hundred-and-fifty-year-old farmhouses that had rank-smelling cellars and sodden lintels and rotting beams. In the late summer, when the cabbages were young and small, aquamarine, not stinking, thousands of small white cabbage butterflies hovered in the field, invisible until one of them caught the sun and then drew attention to the others, and what had seemed to be hundreds of rows of blue-green vegetables set into rock-studded light brown soil suddenly would seem an ocean of little butterflies that surged around the houses and their small yards. Now the cabbages were bulbous and dark, part of the muddy field that, despite its slope, could not keep the water table from rising through stone toward a furnace's fuel jet.

Ben broke through a natural fence of brush, some red poisonous berries still glistening but most fruit gone, and the vegetation a tangle of blackthorn and exploded milkweed and powdering log, pulped fungus. He sank in down to his calves and had to work himself loose. His boots freed with slow-motion sucking sounds, and there was a released smell of gases from the rotted roots and weed. He went downhill the last few yards, a steep muddy incline leading to the river's edge — higher than it ever had been — where sinuous dying elms stood on both sides of the river, which roared like machines. Debris floated past, chunks of log, plastic milk bottles, a bran-colored kitten, turning. The surface was like a skin, for although it sped, there was an undercurrent, other water, deeper, moving more quickly. The surface was Prussian blue and silver, bright, dangerous-looking, like a reptile's skin. The water below was muddy and poisoned by cesspools rising with the flood.

It was deeper than ever, and faster, high enough to cover a tall man, swift enough to drown him as it had the kitten. Ben threw a heavy rounded chalky rock into the water. It made no ripple or splash, but disappeared. Slowly, as if he balanced at a great height, Ben walked along the river toward the red iron bridge at the south end of town. He passed behind the homes of two widows, and the only man he knew who was always glad — Henry Quail, seventy, fat, smelling of chewing tobacco and sweat and Irish whiskey. Because of his cleft palate, Henry was hard to understand, and few people asked him to speak. Henry patrolled the roads in his long green pickup truck, answered fire alarms in his red reflecting vest and yellow hardhat, helped repair tractors, collected his Social Security, made large and undeclared sums for cutting the horns off cattle, and was always bright-faced drunk.

In the large backyard of the second widow, water had collected six inches deep at least. A pyramid of logs, waiting to be split — probably by Henry Quail — had fallen, and some of the logs were submerged in the pool. Then the field between the river and the hamlet climbed again, steeply, and there was no cabbage; at first there were rows of corn stubble which, as the snows melted, the deer might come to crop at dusk, and then there was only tangled brush and high weed as the land rose to close Ben in at the river's turning.

The elms were bare above him, close together, soon to die and fall. Some willow flourished there, the empty branches hanging like awful hair, suddenly shuddering as the wind picked up. The temperature was dropping as darkness fell, and a mist hung above the water, higher than a man could reach, thick and smelling of cabbage and silt and old plants. The fog looked yellow in the dusk light. The roar of the river grew as Ben went on and arrived at the dam.

At first it looked as if the silver-blue skin of the water had grown tumorous. Then he saw, just under the surface, tangled trees, woven vines, and bushes locked into one another, small logs and larger ones, pieces of siding, detergent boxes, green garbage, bones. All were holding the river high, though a million gallons flowed past him as Ben watched. He closed his eyes and opened them, lost the peculiar focus he'd found, and saw simply a silvery blue skin that writhed.

He went on to the bridge, from which children in summer fished and where Ben had stood to watch Ethan and some friends wade on the sun-heated slippery rocks. Now, as soon as a foot went into the water, they would be seized and beaten, pulled away, spinning, to surface half a mile downstream, under the railroad trestle, features erased by rocks and trees, bloody tubes of meat digested and released.

Ben reached toward a stump and knocked on it three times. He said, "Please."

They ate dinner in the living room, in front of the Franklin stove. The third time Ethan smacked his lips while chewing hamburger Stroganoff, Marge made good on her threat and marched Ethan into the kitchen, where he sat in the yellow light of one lamp and finished his meal alone. Ben and Marge, in the living room, said nothing; they ate and looked at the bright flare of fire visible where the stove doors met. Ethan's chair scraped, something creaked, and then there was a silence.

"Where's he going?" Ben whispered.

"Maybe his room."

"I didn't hear him on the steps."

"Well, there's noplace else to go. He has to go past us to get to the TV —"

"Yeah," Ben said, standing, "but he doesn't have to go past us to go *out.*"

"Ethan takes care," Marge said. "He wouldn't want to get soaked — oh, come *on*, Ben, he is *not* going to the river."

Ben said, "If the sump pump starts in now, to punctuate all this dread and criminality, I'll disconnect it." The sump pump started in, they heard it grinding downstairs. Ben said, "I can't disconnect it or the cellar will flood and the furnace'll go out."

"What dread?" Marge said. "What criminality?"

"No, it's just, with the river rising, with the goddamn *cellar* rising, I don't like it that we aren't together. Happy."

"Ben," she said, "do you know how unhappy he would be if there weren't consequences? Discipline? Rules he has to follow?"

"Yeah, but he can't follow them."

"He will. It's called learning."

Ben put another log into the stove and sat down again, then stood up. The sump pump was on. "But what if he does go to the river?"

"He won't. Go look for him if you're worried. It isn't such a big house. You know, go look."

Ben sipped coffee and rubbed the back of his neck. "Do you understand that when you talk to me like that, when you patronize me, even if it's *Ethan*, I can't go do what I think is right?"

"You asked me and I told you."

"Bitch," Ben said. He put his coffee on the table in front of the sofa and went around it, clumsily and blushing. He leaned over, one knee on the cushion, to kiss her on the cheek chastely. "I forgive you your transgressions," he said.

Marge said, "Asshole." She held his head and stuck her tongue out slowly, and slowly licked his lips from side to side. Ben sat down beside her, moved in closer, and kissed her mouth.

"That's right," he said when they'd stopped.

"That's right," she said.

As if to hold her trophy up, while Ben breathed deeply on the sofa beside her, Marge called, "Ethan!"

When there was no answer, Ben shook his head. She called again.
Ben shouted, as if in rage, "*Ethan!*"

The high small voice came back from far away: "Yes?"

"Where is he?" Ben said.

"Yes?"

Ben said, "Is that from outside? He *is* outside."

But Marge was already up, walking toward the kitchen and the cellar
door, and she was on the steps before Ben had stood to follow her.
Downstairs, in the light of the one bulb at the far end of the cellar, in
the grinding chatter of the pump, Ethan swept water from the drain
that Ben had uselessly capped. The water rolled with a loud hush
across the gray floor and spilled over into the sump and was pumped
out to seep back in again. There was a new smell downstairs, among
the smells of wet wood and soaked stone and hot motor — the sharp
tang of mildew. Ethan, in Marge's high black boots, continued to
sweep. Marge in her fur-lined slippers, Ben in his still soaked boots,
both with wet feet, stood watching him — the long pale intelligent
face, the slender arms and legs, big hands. In Marge's boots, in the
weak cellar light, in the pool of black water, Ethan looked small.

"Hi," he said. Then he smiled, and his ill-brushed teeth shone beige.

Ben said, "We thought you went out, honey."

Marge reached back to slap Ben's buttocks, to warn him into silence.
"How's it going?" she said.

Ethan said, "I don't think I'm making any progress. But you guys
were so upset about the water, I thought maybe I could, you know, do
something."

"No," Ben said, "you're doing fine."

"Really fine," Marge said.

Ben rubbed the back of his neck and stepped away so that Marge
couldn't reach him. "Ethan," he said, "you know where babies come
from?"

Ethan said, "Mom told me. You could check with her if you want
to."

The boy swept more water into the sump, and the pump went on
again.

"Okay," Ben said, "I will."

Marge turned and walked to the foot of the steps. Ben stood, watching Ethan sweep. Then he turned too and followed his wife. When Marge was in the kitchen, and Ben was halfway there, Ethan called, "Hey, Dad? Dad?"

"Yes, sir."

"Tell me what she says, okay?"

That night the skies shook and darkness was total: no moon, no stars, no road lights visible from the bedroom window, the bedroom itself extinguished, and their eyes squeezed shut. They did not touch; when they rolled on the mattress or tugged at blankets or pushed a pillow flat, they grunted as if hurt. They slept finally, then awakened to hear field mice running in the eaves and between the walls at the head of the bed. It was the dry scraping sound of panic. It rhymed with the grinding chirr of the pump in the lath and beams and floorboard between them and the flooded cellar. Marge turned her bedside lamp on, and the walls jumped in toward them. Ben whispered, "Don't read. Just lie there. If you say you're awake, you won't be able to sleep at all."

Wearing Ben's undershirt and squinting from the blackened eyes of an exhausted athlete, Marge reached up to turn off the light.

"You look nice," he whispered.

"You always like me to wear your clothes."

"So I can own you."

"So you can *protect* me."

"Probably that too."

Marge said, "If the mice desert it, and come in here, does that mean the world is sinking?"

Ben said into his pillow, "The world will be fine."

After a minute, after another minute, with the darkness humid around them and expanding into the darkness of the flooded world outside, Marge said, "Can you promise me that? Can you *promise*?"

"I promise," Ben said.

"You better mean that."

"I do. But no babies. No more babies."

She said, "Then you better mean it, Ben."

He lay still and saw the yellow school bus, Ethan on board, rolling off the rain-slicked road. Ben opened his eyes so as not to see the children bouncing in the bus, pips in a fat collapsing gourd. He saw the darkness. He closed his eyes and against his will he looked closer, supplying details. He saw the battered heads of bleeding children, and black hair, yellow hair, brown hair, hair cut short and hair tied in thin bright ribbon, all of it pasty with blood and teeming with lice, the lice jumping in blood and tracking it tinily on the wrinkled brown lunch bags that lay on cracked seats and in muddy aisles. He heard Ethan cry, not in the house with them now, but in his dream, in the future, in the world that possessed more of him than Ben thought it right to have to yield, and he pushed himself from the pillow. He almost said *I do*. But he turned — Marge said, "Ben?" — and in the darkness, with the pump going on and off, with mice hurtling furiously between the walls, he wrestled her, tore at the shared shirt, buried his mouth in her neck and labored with his lips and teeth, dropping upon her with no question and no answer, hearing nothing for the first time that night, making what you might as well call love.

The Settlement
of Mars

IT BEGAN FOR ME in a woman's bed, and my father was there though she wasn't. I was nine years old, and starting to age. "Separate vacations," then, meant only adventure to me. My bespectacled mother would travel west to attend a conference about birds; she would stare through heavy binoculars at what was distant and nameable. My father and I would drive through Massachusetts and New Hampshire into Maine, where he and Bill Brown, a friend from the army, would climb Mount Katahdin and I would stay behind at the Brown family's farm.

And it was adventure — in the days away from New York, and in the drive alone with my father in the light green '49 Chevrolet, and in my mother's absence. For she seemed to be usually angry at someone, and my father struck me as usually pleased with the world, and surely with me. And though I knew enough to understand that his life was something of a secret he didn't tell me, I also knew enough at nine to accept his silence as a gift: peace, which my mother withheld by offering the truth, in codes I couldn't crack, of her discontent.

I remember the dreamy, slow progress of the car on heat-shimmered highways, and my elbow — this never was permitted when we all drove together on Long Island — permanently stuck from the high window. We slept one night in a motel that smelled like iodine, we ate lobster rolls and hot dogs, I discussed the probable settlement of Mars, and my father nodded gravely toward my knowledge of the future.

He gave me close escapes — the long gray Hudson which almost hit us, because my father looked only ahead when he drove, never to the side or rear, as we pulled out of a service station; the time we had a flat and the jack collapsed twice, the car crashing onto the wheel hub, my father swearing — "God*damn* it!" — for the first time in my hearing; and the time he let the car drift into a ditch at the side of the road, pitching us nose-down, rear left-side wheel in the air, shaken and stranded until a farmer on a high tractor towed us out and sent us smiling together on our way. My father bared his teeth to say, "It's a lucky thing Mother isn't here," while I regretted the decorum I had learned from him — I was not to speak without respect of the woman with binoculars who had journeyed from us.

I thought of those binoculars as we approached the vague shapes of weathered gray buildings, wished that I could stare ahead through them and see what my life, for the next little while, might offer. But the black Zeiss 12 x 50s were thousands of miles from us, and really further than that: they were in my memory of silent bruised field trips, when my father's interest would be in covering ground, and my mother's would be expressed in the spraddle-legged stiffness with which she stared at birds up a slope I knew my father wanted to be climbing.

Bill Brown was short and mild in silver-rimmed glasses. He wore a striped engineer's cap with a long bill, and he smiled at everything my father said. Molly Brown was taller than Bill, and was enormously fat, with wobbling arm flesh and shaking jowls and perpetual streaked flushes on her soft round cheeks. Their daughter, Paula, was fourteen and tall and lean and beautiful. She had breasts. Sweat, such an intimate fact to me, stained the underarms of her sleeveless shirt. She wore dungarees that clung to her buttocks. She rolled the cuffs to just below her knees, and I saw the dusk sun light up golden hairs on her shins. She had been assigned to babysit me for the visit. I could not imagine being babysat by so much of everything I had heard rumored, and was beginning to notice in playgrounds, secrets of the other world.

We ate mashed potatoes and a roast that seemed to heat the kitchen, which, like the other rooms in the house, smelled of unwashed bodies and damp earth. I slept that first night on a cot in Paula's room, and I was too tired even to be embarrassed, much less thrilled, by the proximity; I slept in purest fatigue, as if I had journeyed on foot for weeks to another country, in which the air was thin. Next day, we walked the Browns' land — I could not take my eyes from Paula's spiny back and strong thighs as we climbed fences, as she helped me, her child-assignment, up and over and down — and we ate too much hot food, and drank Kool-Aid (forbidden, because too sugary, at home), and we sat around a lot. I rejoiced in such purposelessness, and I suspected that my father enjoyed it too, for our weekend days at home were slanted toward mission; starting each Saturday morning, we tumbled down the long tilted surfaces of the day into weeding and pruning and sweeping and traveling in the silent car to far-off fields to see if something my mother knew to be special was fluttering over marshes in New Jersey or forests in upstate New York.

My father, who made radio advertisements, spoke a little about his work, and Bill Brown said in his pleased soft voice that he had heard my father's ads. But when Bill said, "Where do you get those crazy ideas, Frank?" my father turned the conversation to potato farming, and the moth collection which Bill and Molly kept together, and the maintenance of trucks. I knew that my father understood nothing about engines. He was being generous again, and he was hiding again while someone else talked of nothing that mattered to the private man who had taught me how to throw a baseball, and how to pack a knapsack, and how — I know this now — to shelter inside other people's words. And there was Paula, too, smoking cigarettes without reprimand, swinging beside me on the high-backed wooden bench that was fastened by chains to the ceiling of their porch. I breathed her smoke as now I'd breathe in perfume on smooth, heated skin.

In reply to a question, my father said, "Angie's in Colorado."

"All the way out there," Molly said.

Bill said, "Well."

"Yes, she had a fine opportunity," my father said. "They gave her a scholarship to this conference about bird migration, I guess it is, and she just couldn't say no."

"I'd like to go there sometime," Paula said, sighing smoke out.

"Wouldn't you, though?" Molly growled in her rich voice. "Meet some Colorado guys and such, I suspect?"

"Give them a chance to meet a State of Maine *girl*, don't forget," Paula said. "Uncle Frank, didn't you want to go to Colorado?"

My father's deep voice rumbled softly. "Not when I can meet a State of Maine girl right here, hon. And don't forget, your father and I already spent some time in Colorado."

"Amen that it's over," Bill said.

"I saw your father learn his manners from a mule out there, didn't I, Bill?"

"Son of a bitch stepped so hard on my foot, he broke every damned bone inside it. Just squatted there, Frank, you remember? Son of a bitch didn't have the sense to get off once he'd crushed it. It took Frank jumping up and down and kicking him just to make him wake and look down and notice he already done his worst and he could move along. Leisurely, as I remember. He must of been thinking or something. I *still* get the bowlegged limps in wet weather. I wouldn't cook a mule and eat one if I was starved to death."

"Well, didn't she —" Paula said.

"Angie," I said. I felt my father look at me across the dark porch.

"Didn't Angie want to come up here and meet us?" Paula asked.

Molly said, "Couldn't you think of any personal questions you would like for Frank to answer for you?"

"Well, I guess I'm *sorry*, then."

"That's right," Molly said.

"It was one hell of a basic training," Bill said. He said it in a rush. "They had us with this new mountain division they were starting up. Taught us every goddamned thing you could want to know about carrying howitzers up onto mountains by muleback. How to get killed while skiing. All of it. Then, they take about three hundred of us or so and send us by boat over to some hot jungle. Ship all our gear with us too, of course. So we land there in the Philippine Islands with snow-shoes, skis, camouflage parkas, light machine guns in white canvas *covers*, for gosh sakes, and they ask us if we'd win the war for them."

"It took us a while," my father said.

"Didn't it now?"

Bill went inside and returned with a bottle and glasses. He sat down next to my father, and I heard the gurgle, then a smacking of lips and, from my father, a low groan of pleasure, of uncontrol, which I hadn't heard before. New information was promised by that sound, and I folded my arms across my chest for warmth and settled in to learn, from the invisibility darkness offered, and from the rhythm of the rattle of bottle and glass.

I was jealous that Paula wanted boys in Colorado when I was there, and I was resigned — it was like fighting gravity, I knew — to not bulking sizably enough. Their voices seemed to sink into the cold black air and the smell of Paula's cigarettes, and I heard few whole words — nothing, surely, about my vanished mother, or about my father and me — and what I knew next was the stubbly friction of my father's cheek as he kissed me goodbye and whispered that he'd see me soon. I thought that we were home and that he was putting me to bed. Then, when I heard the coarse noise of Bill's truck, I opened my eyes and saw that I was on the canvas cot in Paula's room in a bright morning in Maine. I was certain that he was leaving me there to grow up as a farmer, and I almost said aloud the first words that occurred to me: "What about school? Do I go to school *here?*" School meant breakfast, meant wearing clothes taken from the oak highboy in the room in Stony Brook, Long Island, meant coming downstairs to see my father making coffee while my mother rattled at the *Times.* The enormity of such stranding drove me in several directions as I came from the cot, "What about school?" still held, like scalding soup, behind my teeth and on my wounded tongue.

Paula, at the doorway, shaking a blouse down over her brassiere — I could not move my eyes from the awful power of her underwear — called through the cloth, "Don't you be frightened. You fell asleep and you slept deep. Frank and Daddy're climbing, is all. Remember?" Though the cotton finally fell to hide her chest and stomach, I stared there, at strong hidden matters. We ate eggs fried in butter on a wood-fired stove while Molly drank coffee and talked about a dull moth which lived on Katahdin and which Bill might bring home. I stared at Paula's lips as they closed around corners of toast and yellow runny yolks.

We shoveled manure into the wheelbarrow Paula let me push, and we fed their dozen cows. One of them she'd named Bobo, and I held straw to Bobo's wet mouth and pretended to enjoy how her nose dripped. I listened to the running-water noises of their stomachs, and I looked at the long stringy muscles in Paula's tanned bare arms. Her face, long like her mother's, but with high cheekbones and wide light eyes, was always in repose, as if she dreamed as she worked while naming for me the nature of her chores and the functions of equipment. I watched the sweat that glistened under her arms and on her broad forehead, and she sounded then like my father, when he took me to his office on a school holiday: I was told about the surfaces of everything I saw, but not of his relation to them, and therefore their relation to me. In Jefferson, Maine, as on East 52nd Street in Manhattan, as in Stony Brook, New York, the world was puzzling and seductive, and I couldn't put my hands on it, and hold.

We went across a blurred meadow that vibrated with black flies and tiny white butterflies that rose and fell like tides. On the crest of a little hill, under gray trees with wide branches and no leaves or fruit, Paula lay flat, groaning as if she were old, and stared up through bug-clouds and barren limbs and harsh sun. "Here," she said, patting the sparse fine grass beside her. "Look."

I lay down next to her as tentatively as I might lie now beside a woman whom I'd know I finally couldn't hold. Her arm was almost touching mine, and I thought I could feel its heat. Then the arm rose to point, and I smelled her sweat. "Look," she said again. "He looks like he's resting awhile, but he's hanging onto the air. That's work. He's drifting for food. He'll see a mole from there and strike it too."

Squint as hard as I might, there was nothing for me but bright spots the sun made inside my eyes. I tried to change the focus, as if I looked through my mother's binoculars, but I saw only a branch above us, and it was blurry too. I blinked again; nothing looked right.

"I guess I saw enough birds in my life," I told her.

"That's right, isn't it? Your mother's a bird-watcher. In Colorado, too. I guess there's trouble *there.*"

"They're taking separate vacations this year."

"They sure are. That's what I mean about trouble. Man and wife *live* together. That's why they get married. They watch birds together, if that's what they do, and they climb up mountains together, and they sleep together in the same bed. Do Frank and Angie sleep in the same bed?"

I was rigid lest our arms touch, and the question made me stiffer. "I don't see *your* mother climbing any mountains," I said.

"Well, she's too fat, honey. Otherwise she would. And if this wasn't a trip for your father and mine to take alone, a kind of special treat for them, you can bet me and Momma would be there, living out of a little canvas tent and cooking for when Daddy came back down, bug-bit and chewed up by rocks. And you won't find but one bed for the two of them. I still hear them sometimes at night. You know. Do you?"

"Oh, sure. I hear my mom and dad too." That was true: I heard them talking in the living room, or washing dishes after a party, or playing music on the Victrola. "Sure," I said, suspecting that I was soon to learn things terrible and delicious, and worried not only because I was ashamed of what I didn't hear, but because, if I *did* hear them, I wouldn't know what they meant. The tree limb was blurred, still, and I moved to rub my eyes.

Then that girl of smells — her cigarette smoke lay over the odor of the arm she'd raised — and of fleshy swellings and mysterious belly and the awesome mechanics of brassieres, the girl who knew about me and my frights, about my parents and their now-profound deficiencies, said gently, "Come on back to my room. I'll show you something."

When she stood, she took my hand; hers was rough and dry and strong. She pulled me back over field and fences, and I thrilled to the feel of flesh as much as I hated the maternity with which she towed me. But I thought, too, that something alarming was about to be disclosed. I couldn't wait to be told, though I was scared.

Molly was putting clothes through a mangle near the rain barrel, and she waved as we passed. We went through cool shadows into the room Paula had decorated with Dick Powell's picture, and Gable's, and on the far wall a blurred someone with a mustache wore tights and feathered hat and held a sword.

"My library," she said, opening the closet. "Here." And on shelves, stacked, and in shaggy feathering heaps on the closet floor, were little yellowing books and bright comics and magazines that told the truth about the life of Claudette Colbert and Cary Grant. I doubt that she knew what I needed, for she was mostly a teenage kid on a little farm in Maine. She wasn't magical, except to me in her skin, although she was smarter than I about the life I nearly knew I led. But something made her take me from the swarm of sun and insects, the high-hanging invisible bird of prey — that place where, she possibly knew, I sensed how much of my life was a secret to me — and she installed me on the dirty floor of a dirty house, in deepening afternoon, half inside a closet where, squinting, I fell away from the world and into pictures, words.

I read small glossy-jacketed books, little type on crumbling wartime paper, with some line drawings, about Flash Gordon and Ming the Merciless and the plight of the always-kidnapped Dale. I read about death rays and rockets that went to Mars from Venus as quickly as they had to for the sake of mild creatures with six arms who were victimized by Ming's high greed. Dale and the other women had very pointed breasts and often said, "Oh, Flash, do you really think so?"

And there was Captain Marvel, whose curling forelock was so much like Superman's, but whom I preferred because I thought we looked alike and because he never had to bother to change his clothes to get mighty: he said *Shazam!* and a lightning bolt made him muscular and capable of rescuing women with long legs. I read of Superboy, whose folks in Smallville were so proud of him. Littler worlds, manageable by me, and on my behalf by people who could change, whether in phone booths or storerooms or explosions of light, into what they needed to be: Aqua-Man, Spider Man, the Green Lantern, wide-nostriled Wonder Woman in her glass airplane, and always Flash and Dale, "Oh, Flash, do you really think so?"

For a while, Paula sat behind me, cross-legged on her bed, reading fan magazines and murmuring of Gary Cooper's wardrobe and the number of people Victor Mature could lift into the air. When she went out, she spoke and I answered, but I don't remember what we said. I leaned forward in the darkness, squinting and forgetting to worry that I had to screw my face around my eyes in order to see, and I stayed where I was, which was away.

They had a radio, and we listened to it for a while after dinner, and then Molly showed me, in a room off the kitchen, board after board on which dead moths were stiffly pegged. I squinted at them and said "Wow," and while Paula and Molly sat in sweaters on the porch and talked, I squatted in the closet's mouth, under weak yellow light, and started Edgar Rice Burroughs's *The Chessmen of Mars*. When Paula entered to change into nightclothes, I was lured from the cruel pursuit of Dejah Thoris by Gahan of Gathol, for the whisper of cloth over skin was a new music. But I went back with relief to "The dazzling sunlight of Barsoom clothed Manator in an aureole of splendor as the girl and her captors rode into the city through the Gate of Enemies."

When Paula warned me that the lights were going off, I stumbled toward my cot, and when they were out I undressed and went to sleep, telling myself stories. And next day, after breakfast and a halfhearted attempt to follow her through chores, I walked over the blurred field to the rank shade of Paula's room, and I sat in the closet doorway, reading of Martian prisons, and heroes who hacked and slew, unaware that I had neither sniffed nor stared at her, and worried only that I might not finish the book and start another before my father and Bill returned. They didn't, and we ate roast beef hash and pulpy carrots, and Molly worked in the shed on the motor of their kitchen blender while Paula listened to "Henry Aldrich" and I attended to rescues performed by the Warlord of Mars.

It was the next afternoon when my father and Bill returned in the truck. They were dirty and tired and beaming, and they smelled like woodsmoke. My father hugged me and kissed me so hard that he hurt me with his unshaved cheeks. He swatted my bottom and rubbed my shoulders with his big hands. Bill presented Molly with a dirty little moth and she clapped her hands and trilled. Paula smoked cigarettes and sat on the porch between Bill and my father, listening, as if she actually cared, to Bill's description of how well my father had done to follow him up Abel's Slide, where the chunks of stone were like steps too high to walk, too short and smooth to climb, and up which you had to spring. My father broke in to say, "Like a goat in a competition. I thought my stomach would burst, following this — this *kid*. That's you, Bill, part mountain goat and part boy. I don't know how you stayed young for so long. You were the oldest man in the outfit, and what you did was you stayed where you were and I got ancient."

"Nah. Frank, you're in pretty good shape. For someone who makes his living by sitting on his backside. I'll tell you that. You did swell."

"Well, you did better. How's that?'

Bill swallowed beer and nodded. "I'd say that's right."

And they both laughed hard, in a way the rest of us could only smile at and watch.

"Damn," my father said, smiling so wide. *"Damn!"*

My head felt hot and the skin of my face was too tight for whatever beat beneath it. They were shimmering shapes in the afternoon light, and I rubbed my eyes to make them work in some other way. But what I saw was as through a membrane. Perhaps it was Paula's cool hand on my face that did it, and the surge of smells, the distant mystery of her older skin and knowledge which I suddenly remembered to be mastered by. Perhaps it was the distance my father had traveled over and from which, as I learned from the privacies of his laughter, he still had not returned. Perhaps it was Molly, sitting on the porch steps next to Bill, her hand on his thigh. Or perhaps it was the bird I couldn't see which hung over Jefferson, Maine, drifting to dive. I pushed my face against Paula's hard hand and I rubbed at my eyes and I started to weep long coughing noises which frightened me as much as they must have startled the others.

My father's hobbed climbing boots banged on the porch as he hurried to hold me, but I didn't see him because I knew that if I opened my eyes I would know how far the blindness had progressed. I didn't want to know anything more. He carried me inside while I wailed like a hysterical child — which is what I was, and what I'm sure I felt relieved to be. I listened to their voices when they'd stilled my weeping and asked me questions about pain. I swallowed aspirin with Kool-Aid and heard my father discover the comics and the books I'd read while on my separate vacation. And the relief in his voice, and the smile I heard riding on his breath, served to clench my jaw and lock my hands above my eyes. Because he knew, and they knew, and I still didn't, though I now suspected, because I always trusted him, that I wouldn't die and probably wouldn't go blind.

"Just think of your mother's glasses, love," he whispered while the others walked from the room. He sat on the bed and stroked my face around my fists, which still stayed on my eyes. "Mother has weak eyes, and these things can be passed along — the kids can get them from their parents."

"You mean I caught it from her?"

The bed I was in, Paula's bed — I smelled her on the pillow and the sheets — shook as he nodded and continued to stroke my face. "*Like* that. Just about, yes. I bet when we go home, and we go to the eye doctor, he'll put a chart up for you to read. Did you have these tests in school? He'll ask you to read the letters, and he'll say you didn't see them too clearly, and he'll tell us to get you some glasses. And that's *all.* I promise. It isn't meningitis, it isn't polio —"

"Polio?" I said. "*Polio?*"

"No," he said. "No. No, it isn't a *sickness.* I'm sorry I said that. I was worried for a minute, but now I'm not, I promise. You hear? I'm promising you. Your eyes are weak. Your head'll feel better from the aspirin — it's just eyestrain, love. It's nothing more."

"Yeah," I said. "Some dumb vacation. I should have gone with Mommy."

I lay in a woman's bed, and in the warmth of her secrets, and in the rich smell of what was coming to me. And my father sat there as his large hands gentled my face. His hands never left me. I dropped my fists, though I kept my eyes closed tight. I felt his strong fingers, roughened by rocks, as they ran along my eyebrows, touched my cheeks, my hairline, my forehead, then eyebrows again, over and over, until, with great gentleness, they dropped upon the locked lids, and he said, "No, no, this is where you should be." So I hid beneath my father's hands, and I rested awhile.

Critics

I USED TO SAY to my father, "Are you famous?"

And he used to smile his slow almost-frown — I understand now that he enjoyed the question, admired his own struggle for proportion — and he would answer, "Maybe a little. But not with the critics." Then he would finish with what I learned early and by heart: "And just about everybody's a critic, pal."

When I was ten, we rented a house on the coast of Maine, as far northeast as you could drive without entering Canada. It was a cottage, really, small and dark and cold, but a picture window in my parents' bedroom opened on the Atlantic, which, in fog or bright sun, made my father stretch and wriggle with delight. He was a sedentary man, wiry and pale, with bright red hair that looks to me now, in the colored photographs I don't often examine, like a cheap synthetic wig. He made little motions, that summer in Maine, which were new to me — in the openness with which he flopped shirtless on rocks near the water; in the smallness he suggested by bowing his head to stare at kelp on the tide; in the happiness with which he heard my mother sigh at the sight of diving cormorants; in his willingness to do no work, to only read green-spined Penguin thrillers and scribble postcards and broil fresh fish over driftwood fires on the beach.

My mother seemed taller than he, though I think they were both the same size, average height. She was beautiful and blond and angry. She was married to a writer of nearly successful novels; she herself wrote essays for the glossy magazines and she practiced patience with his moods — the dreaming energy he drifted upon when he was working, the anxious chatter of his fright when he couldn't produce — and surely she loved him as I did, though neither of us found it easy to do when he snarled and yapped between the end of one book and the start of another. When they were published, and he moaned over Kirkus Reports, crowed for *Book World,* stammered with rage at his publisher's refusal to pay for ads, she listened without answering; there was nothing safe to say. And it was her silences that provoked his anger, the *disloyalty,* he called it, of her failure to respond. Then they would fight. It once went so far as her packing bags for herself and me and demanding that he drive us to the airport. And then he would sulk, and then repent, and then apologize, and then we all would wait for the next time.

The summer in Maine was paid for with my mother's check from *The Atlantic* for a two-part article on a family of migrant grape-pickers as they traveled from California to New York State. It was my father's idea, though — to go to someplace new, where he would give us vacancy: no expression at all of the usual needs. When he thought I wasn't listening, he said to her, "This is for you." Gesturing at the ocean, the black and purple rocks, high tamarack: "This is for you."

Naturally, I was bored. There was the rowboat in the tide pools, the fishing from high rocks, the building of forts on the beach, the riding up and down our country road on my bike, occasional trips to a sand beach, the rainy afternoons — soaked dog fur reminds me of their smell — spent mooching up and down the aisle of small-town pharmacies and hardware stores. But there was, I complained one rainy late afternoon after a day of sitting around while rain hung over us in a cold suspended mist, nothing to do.

"Nothing to do," my mother said. She was reading a magazine in the small living room, her feet tucked up on the sofa. My father was playing with his fire in the Franklin stove. "Nothing to do?"

I was biting my nails again, which was a pleasure I had pretty well learned to renounce except when my parents fought, and when we traveled. On his knees, face red from blowing at the dying coals of driftwood I had hauled from the beach, my father said, "Terry, this is the last stronghold of pirates and smugglers, and you're telling me you're bored here?"

He was skilled at that — dropping in a little detail I could *almost* count on his having made up, luring me from the privacy of a mood and into his constructions. I dutifully said, "Pirates?"

"Well, smugglers, anyway. You know Dennis's Point?"

"No. And there aren't any smugglers anymore, Dad."

"No? Look: Dennis's Point — well, you can't see it in this weather. It's the spit of land you can just make out across the bay, when the sun shines. It's almost in Canada. But it isn't." He was in an Indian squat, and he was in control. "That's the point, it's kind of a border. Well, if you get your heroin and cocaine — drugs."

"I know about drugs."

"Oh, yeah?"

"They're bad for you. You go crazy and you die."

"Exactly. Well, there are these ships, they come from France and Singapore, places like that, druggy places. And somebody on one of those boats has a deal with somebody who lives in a house that *looks* deserted, but isn't, over on Dennis's Point. Well, the sailor on the big ship drops this waterproof bag filled with drugs over into the ocean, close to the Point. It floats, see. And then the guys from the hideout across the bay take off in a very powerful boat, probably forty feet at least, probably run by a couple of big Ford engines, and they pick up the bag. They pull it in, go back to the hideout, and then some family-looking people, you know, a father and a mother and a kid, say, a boy — they just steam up to the house like a bunch of tourists on vacation, and they put the bag inside, oh, maybe a dark blue sleeping bag" — like the one I slept in upstairs — "and then they go home with a million other tourists. Nobody looks in the back of their station wagon" — like the dark blue wagon we'd driven to Maine — "and *boom*: all the drug addicts in the city of New York are crazy and joyful again, and very very sick, because the Jones Man came."

My mother, listening along with me, and doubtless in spite of her wish to read every page of *Family Circle*, said, "Jones?"

My father smiled the silly grin and said, "Cop-talk for junk. Addicts' talk. Drugs. I think, specifically, heroin."

"Well researched," my mother said.

"Thank you, Caroline."

"You're telling me there are crooks doing that out *here*, Dad?"

"Ask Mom. There was a big article in the Eastport papers. The FBI arrested half a dozen of them."

"Right over there?"

"Ask Mom."

I looked at her, but she was reading the magazine again. "I think he made it up," she said.

I looked at my father, who was staring at her. So I tried. I said, "Everybody's a critic."

My mother put the magazine down a little harder than I'd have wanted her to, but before she could speak, the door thumped, as if someone had struck it with the side of a fist and not knuckles.

"It's the landlord," my New York mother said.

"It might be the cops," my father hissed. "Terry, get rid of the Jones!"

"Terry," my mother said, "please answer the door very politely."

Standing in the mist, with weak sun behind him, the man at the door had a kind of rainbow shine on his shoulders. His wire-rimmed glasses were wet, and his hair was slick on his head. He wore a navy-blue T-shirt soaked black, and jeans over heavy boots, and the tight straps of his knapsack made the muscles of his shoulders and upper arms look very large. He peered past me to say, "Mister Philip Maslow? Is he staying here?"

My mother said, "Phil." I said, "Yes." My father said, "Coming. Coming."

"Mister *Maslow*," the man said, pushing his arm past me to shake my father's hand. My father stood behind me, moving his free hand through my hair. "Mister Maslow, I heard you were here this summer. I'm Philip Hansen. We have the same first name."

"Hey," I said.

"Mister Maslow, I read your novel."

"Oh, great — which one?" I heard my mother blow her breath out in an ugly noise.

"I only know the one, sir. *Morning Glory*. I think it's a wonderful book. I'm a real fan of yours. So when I heard you were renting here, I walked out from town to say hello. You've written more books, then?"

Without turning, I knew that my father smiled the way he did when I asked him about fame. "I've written a number of novels," he said.

"Well, gee," Hansen said. "It's a standout pleasure to meet you. *Morning Glory*'s one of my favorite books. I'll have to read the others."

"You walked a long way," my father said.

"Oh, no problem. I do a lot of walking. I collect mineral specimens, and I help take the census on the osprey. I walk down here a great deal."

"Well, I'd sure hate to turn you out in the rain," my father said. "Especially after a walk like that —"

"We're in the middle of *dinner*," my mother called from the living room.

"No problem," Hansen said. "I'll get down here again sometime. I do a great deal of walking."

My mother had come to stand behind us. I felt my father shift as she arrived. "He'll probably be writing," she said very loudly.

"I wouldn't want to disturb you," Hansen said.

My mother said, "But it's nice of you to call."

My father said, "Well, hey — thanks a lot, eh?"

"No problem," Hansen said, looking through his spotted glasses as I looked through the little shimmer of red around his head and knapsack straps. "Just wanted to express my admiration."

"Really nice of you," my father said.

"Sorry about the dinner and all," my mother said.

"No problem," Hansen told them both.

And then we were in the living room, where I looked out the window to see Philip Hansen walking. When I looked in, and saw mother fall back to the sofa, and my father crouch at his fire and ferociously blow, and when I saw their faces, I started on my fingernails again.

My father said, "You know how many times anyone ever walked someplace in the rain to talk to me about something I wrote?"

"Very flattering," my mother said. "But he was weird. Did you see his eyes? He's weird, Phil, and I don't want him around here, at the end of a dirt road in the middle of noplace — you know what happens out here?"

"No," he snapped. "Do you?"

"I know what *could* happen out here. But I don't think Terry has to worry about it, do you?"

"His eyes, huh? That was what made you chase him? Those baleful glittering eyes you could see through my back from the living room sofa that made you tell him a little story about dinnertime?"

"Everybody tells stories," she said. "I thought telling stories was an aceptable practice around here. I seem to recall a perfectly *fraught* little tale about Oriental smugglers and the dreaded Jones Man."

"That happens to be *true*, Caroline. And that wasn't the same as what you did, and I think maybe my motives for telling it were slightly different from yours. You think so? You think that's a possibility?"

"We're out here to *not* worry about what some people write and what other people think about it. I mean, that's the story you told me during three days of hot driving. That's what I remember. Maybe I didn't understand that one?"

"Maybe I *do* understand it. Isn't it the one about making sure I don't engulf you and the other victims with my omnivorous needs?"

She hiccupped a small laugh. "We're talking about the same story, all right."

"Yeah, well, what if he came out to see *you?*"

"Philip: I don't need him to."

"And I do?"

That was when I went to the hook near the door for my yellow slicker, and I called out, "Going down to the beach. I'll see if there's any dry driftwood left. No more fighting, okay?" I got out before I could be cautioned to mind my business, or manners, or to be careful of the nameless dangers they thought resided only outside.

The path to the beach was slippery, and the low-hanging spruce branches dripped. I stopped to watch the moisture run down the trunk and needles of the trees as I had seen water run off buildings in New York. Then I moved on to the beach, which was all dark stones, some of them enormous; and in the center there was a great green-gray mass of some different kind of stone that was an island I often stood upon as the tide came in. I went past shattered pieces of telephone pole and rough timber, thrown up, my father said, by winter storms. I climbed down along the boulders, then up the green-gray rock, and I stood there, frowning in imitation of my father, looking into mist and the fog that had begun.

The tide was out, so there wasn't much sea-sound, and I could hear the evergreens dripping. The fog poured swiftly, and I grew frightened; I always did. The fog sealed me up, it hid me, from home. But I stayed where I was, nibbling at my fingers. "Hello," someone said, and I knew that it was Philip Hansen.

He was down on one knee just a few feet behind me, looking at the knapsack mouth in which his hand moved. I wondered whether he could carry drugs from Dennis's Point in the knapsack, and whether he might try to convince me to sneak them back to New York in our station wagon, wrapped in my dark blue sleeping bag.

"Finish your dinner already?"

Another story, I remember saying to myself. "Oh, sure. We eat really fast. We're — fast eaters," I said.

"Want to see something — what was it — Terry? You want to see something I found?"

"I don't know. What?"

He came closer, and I backed toward the edge of the green-gray rock. Then he extended his hand and opened it, showing me a small and many-faceted purple shining stone, a crystal of some sort. "I dug it out of the rocks up there, where the beach bends." He smiled so simply, though with invisible eyes, as if he wanted only that I smile in return. I tried. But I was also trying to remember whether they made drugs out of any varieties of stone.

"It's pretty," I said. "I have to go back for dinner. I think my Mom's making dinner now."

"I thought you folks already bolted that," he said.

"What? Oh: *dessert*. I mean. We always take a walk before dessert. My Dad likes us to do that because of blood pressure and everything. Mom and Dad are walking back now and I have to catch up with them, okay? We're ready for dessert now."

He was closer to me, and his wet glasses tilted down as his fingers opened and closed on the stone. "Well, fine," he said. "No problem. I wish you'd tell your father how much I enjoyed meeting him."

"Oh, I will. Sure will. Thanks for letting me see your rock."

"No problem. Don't get lost in the fog."

"No, sir," I said.

"You can really get fog around the Point."

"Yes, sir," I said. I slipped on the rock as I started to run, but I kept running, over the pebbles and larger stones, up the slithery trail, under fingery branches and along the meadow floating in mist. I slammed the front door, locked it behind me, dropped my slicker on the floor, and went into the living room to find them sipping wine and looking at the fire.

"All clear," my mother said.

I sat, panting, and they waited for me to speak. But there was nothing to tell them that was true except my strange and nameless feelings, and I suspected — now I'm guessing — that they were as much of a story as anything else had been, that long day of vacation. The silence went on, and then my father said — I know it now as an offering to her — "He was some weird guy, that whatshisname, Hansen."

I gave my father one of his smiles back and reached for something to say. "He's probably the Jones Man, Daddy."

"Nah," he said. "That was just a story, pal."

And the way he took it back — desertion of me, gift to my mother, one more tale chipped out and extended and then withdrawn — sent my fingers to my mouth, then me from my chair, toward the stairs.

"Terry," my mother called.

"What's wrong?" my father asked.

She called again, but I was in my room and closing the door. I looked out my window toward the beach. I wanted to see Philip Hansen. I wanted no one who loved me to call again from the rented sofa or walk up the stairs to say a single word.

Stand, and
Be Recognized

❖

I DELIVERED LENNY just as I delivered a hundred or more pieces of mail during the war. And I sent the letter that brought him into mourning and risk. I wrote it care of the school in Rome, saying that when our Opel hit the doe, the deer stood still and the car ricocheted off the road, then across it, and up an incline of shale. We rolled back, I told him, and then we stopped, and I was certain that before I fainted I saw the bone of Ariana's forearm slide through her flannel sleeve.

Lenny Levine, in 1971, was teaching American servicemen's children abroad because his country had tried to draft him twice, before he took up teaching and was therefore classified Essential to the National Effort. I knew that if he came home he would invite conscription. But I sent the letter, and five weeks later he flew from Rome to Boston, rode the bus to Montpelier, Vermont, saw me in the Trailways waiting room and butted me in the chest. Weeping, he said, "I'm here. I'm here."

He wept again as I drove us in my Volkswagen bus, and he sniffled at the end of the drive, outside Irasville, at the house that Ariana had bought for us after her mother drowned off Providence, drunk on white Burgundy and widowhood. I fried old ham and poured neat whiskey for us in the damp kitchen. Lenny was letting his whiskers grow again; his pale face was framed as if in a locket by the sparse red hair and beard. In his greasy suede sport coat, he slouched in a chair and studied the room, and I knew he was thinking that if the light were brighter, he would see the old canisters Ariana had bought, and the William Morris wallpaper, the stripped chairs she'd refinished. Lenny wore the dimness of the room like a quilt, he pulled it upon himself as he leaned one shoulder at the wall and huddled, peered.

And then as I served us he chattered — because, I guessed, he was frightened of what he had done, of how much safety he'd renounced, of what emotions I'd require. He talked about Italian girlfriends and war-loving officers and nuclear artillery shells and his trip to Venice. "There was this boatload of German tourists on Murano," he told me. "They all marched into one of the *fornaci*, one of the factories where they blow the glass? I'm standing there with them, we're all lined up on a kind of bleacher, three tiers of steps, and this sweaty little guy opens one of the ovens — I didn't *know* they were Germans, did I say that? So he opens the furnace door and all this heat comes out. There are these middled-aged people around me in very good lightweight tweeds, and when the oven door opens up, they sigh. They *love* it! And I'm standing with them, and they're moaning. German tourists always moan when they appreciate something. And all of a sudden I think, wait a minute, hold it: all these people are swooning for an oven. They have to be Germans. And they had to be there when it happened. They damned well probably were *there*. Now, I know they weren't about to pick me up and put me in the oven —"

" 'Alice in Wonderland,' " I said.

"What?"

"No, I meant — which one is that? 'Hansel and Gretel,' I guess. Is that what I meant?"

"What you meant was I'm telling you a lot of stories because I'm afraid you're about to tell me something about Ariana."

"More ham?"

"No, no more. More whiskey."

"I don't think so," I said. "Not for me. I want to drive tomorrow. Are you coming with me?"

"Sure. Yes. That's why I'm here."

I was cleaning my nails with a paring knife. I looked past Lenny, along the wall at which he leaned. Lenny turned to look there, but he could see just a pair of muddy black boots, a long propped shotgun, a corner. "You're here because of Ariana," I said.

"Where are we driving?"

"I've been doing mail runs," I told him. "I go up to Montreal, sometimes other places. I did Toronto once. I take letters from people in the States. I deliver them to people who didn't want to get drafted. And then I take mail back. I take it into Vermont, New York, sometimes New York City. Sometimes I drive to Boston. Tomorrow I'm going to Utica, some towns near there. Would you like to come?"

"That's why I'm back, Bill."

"No it isn't, dammit. Now, I want you to tell me the *truth*."

"But why?"

"Why?" My anger made me feel that if I took a breath and bellowed, I would say something pivotal and salient. But I had so little to say. And this was my friend, I told myself. This was my friend; I wanted to tell him I remembered that. And I wanted to hit him, then. I stood, and I was much bigger than he whether I stood or sat. I decided to at least tower. And finally I poured more whiskey for him and said, "Find a bed, Lenny. I'll wake us up."

"I thought maybe we'd talk a little," he said.

I shook my head. "We did."

So he gave up, finished his whiskey and asked, "Any room's okay?"

That was a question I'd been waiting for. I took considerable pleasure in saying, "Ariana was sleeping upstairs in the little room, the second door on the right. You're welcome to it."

I enjoyed his silence, and then his little syllable: "Bill?"

"Lenny, good night."

But he persevered, and he fooled me. "It was something I used to teach to the seniors. Chekhov said, if there's a shotgun at the beginning of a story, you should make sure it gets fired by the end. You remember that?"

"You duck out of the army, and all those cannons, Lenny, and you end up teaching children about shooting off shotguns?"

He looked so dirty in that suede coat, so sparsely haired, so like a gosling, so lonely in a kitchen he had known at other, brighter times, that I wanted suddenly to talk about college and the years afterward in

New York, and our long silly drunken conversations, our truer sober ones. But instead I moved toward the kitchen door and put my hands above its frame, leaning in at him, but staying away. I said, "You do keep on not telling me what you're telling me."

Lenny closed his eyes as if he were a stutterer who had to measure out sound. "Don't do anything rash," he said.

That was Lenny: words, little wisdoms, the fearing for the worst. I heard myself say with great calm, "I had a concussion. I wasn't conscious. I couldn't tell them. She was out too. Nobody knew. The bone tore through the skin. They were afraid of infection. They gave her a lot of penicillin. She's allergic to it. I could have told them. They didn't wake me up to ask. She's allergic to penicillin and she had a reaction. So she died. Her throat closed. Everything closed. Now: you think, is this it? You think I'm going to take a breech-blocked shotgun that's fifty years old and put it in my mouth and try blowing my brains out on account of a woman's secret allergy?"

Lenny was panting as if he had run up the stairs. "I'd consider it," he said.

"Maybe that's why we're here. Because I know that you would," I lied. "Would you go to bed now, please? And stop telling me Russian stories and German stories and Italian stories and fairytales and lies?"

It was supposed to be my time of grieving, just slightly his, and we were supposed to understand that and not talk about what we understood, so he rose and walked to me and squeezed my arm, and I squeezed his, and then he went up. I knew what he would do — turn on the lamp in the room she'd been using, and see the mattress on the floor, its sheets and blankets mounded, and see no clothes in the closet, and see no pictures on the walls, and no sign of Ariana or anyone else. He would stand in the room that was abandoned and he would fear to lie on the mattress. I went upstairs and got into the bed we'd moved from New York in a rented truck, years before. I heard him walk softly downstairs to sleep on the living room sofa. I knew he'd pause, on his way, and stare in the darkened kitchen at the shotgun I would never use. And that was Lenny: he was the man who indicted me — the man whose indictment I nearly wanted to share — for having no desire to load a gun and suck on the muzzle and make my story neat.

The weather was good for driving — a low, overcast sky with little glare on the Albany Northway and New York 20 — and the driving was simple and fast. In a New York town called Schuylerville, we delivered a letter addressed in a hand so looped and dark with effort, we both expected hysterics from the addressee, Mrs. Adolph Yoder. But she smiled and shook her head, as if her hiding-out son were a naughty fourth-grader, and before she read the letter, she served us iced Kool-Aid. "Isn't this war *confusing?*" she crooned. At a house on a hill outside Cooperstown, we slid a letter underneath a door. Circling back to Route 20, near an abandoned gas station, at what used to be a diner, we presented to a very old unshaven man who chewed tobacco and didn't speak, three envelopes, numbered in sequence and held together with a hinge of masking tape.

We drove as far south as Norwich on Routes 12B and 12, stopping at Deansboro and Madison, where a short woman in a trailer park turned her back and told us to leave the letter in the mailbox outside her mobile home. She said, looking away, "You'd think grown men would have a regular job."

Between deliveries, we stopped at bars, eating kielbasa and pickled eggs and drinking beer, filling ourselves each time as if we hadn't stopped before, as if we had performed hard labor and were emptied. We were driving north again when it was well past dark, and Lenny had told his stories about Salerno and Lake Como and Rome, and I had told a number of stories about how Ariana had paid for the house and we had lived there, as he knew, on her mother's money, one year raising two pigs and killing them, thereafter planting a garden each year but keeping no stock.

On Route 20, outside Madison, I turned into 12B, and Lenny said, "That leaves the big envelope for Clinton."

I said, "That's the last one. But first we pause for replenishment."

"We just did that, Bill."

"I want us to wait awhile for the Clinton delivery. The woman we're delivering to doesn't always get home until later on."

"That's custom-tailored service."

"Service is service," I said.

So we stopped in a town that was a large crossroads lined with

shabby small houses that were close together, many for sale. A long
high factory sat on a river that ran through the town, and its open
windows let out light and the surf-sound of machines. The street-
lamps, instead of shining the blue-green radiance of highway lamps,
cast a hard brown-yellow glare, and the town was an old tinted photograph at night. Men on the street wore white undershirts and stared.
The women we saw looked older than the men, but not as old as their
children.

At the clapboard Antique Mirror Bar, the only functioning part of a
closed hotel, we parked the van and walked on stiff legs. Inside, we
drank beer in a booth across the large room from an ordinary bar
counter backed by the customary mirrors. We looked away from one
another at the wallside booths: we commented on the size of the
glowing jukebox, the silence of the bartender and his only other patron,
a small man in a yellow slicker who drank something green at the bar.

"I'd like to commend us," Lenny said. He left the booth and returned with two double shots of whiskey.

I took one and said, "That sounds like the beginning of a comment."

"No, it's the beginning of a commendation. Which is different."

"Not with you, it's not. Let me instead remind you of the night you
became impotent in Hanover, New Hampshire."

"I was never impotent in Hanover, New Hampshire. I was impotent
at a small hotel on Torcello not too long ago, and I was less than
efficient about a year ago in the Vaucluse. But never in Hanover."

I signaled to the bartender, raised the shotglasses, and he reluctantly
brought more drinks. "Yes," I said, enjoying myself. "Hanover, New
Hampshire. You were upstairs with a nurse, the one who had beautiful
brown hair. I was downstairs, I don't even know whose house it was.
We were supposed to spend the night studying for something. A
classics course we were flunking, I think. So, you were up there, and
all of a sudden I heard you singing your sad little song — 'I can't *do* it!'
Right? Remember? And the nurse you were with, she had amazing
brown hair, I remember, she screams back, 'Honey, you sure can't.' "

Lenny didn't laugh. He nodded, smiled, stopped smiling, and said,
"I would like to commend us."

"I'm not going to be able to stop you, am I?"

"I'd like — no, you can't. I flew about ninety-seven thousand miles to say this. I'd like to say, we are the only two men I know who can do this."

I looked at the room.

"And without talking about her," Lenny said.

He lifted his glass; I held mine on the table. The door opened out and the women arrived, entering single file and in silence. They wore red shiny warm-up jackets trimmed in white cloth. On the back of each jacket, in small and unevenly applied white letters, was KADETTES. Their slacks were tight on their calves, and they wore ballet flats or sneakers. The one who carried the largest bowling-ball case, made of bright red plastic, wore curlers in her hair beneath a pink translucent scarf. It was she who went to the jukebox at once and put the money in.

Lenny said, "What year is this?"

"This is where I want to go when I die," I said.

The women stood at the bar and drank beer. They smoked a lot, quickly dipping toward their cigarettes to sip the smoke. And songs I hadn't heard for years came out of the wide high jukebox, and everyone listened to Jerry Lee Lewis and Paul Anka, to cha-chas and mambos and mostly to songs that required the twist and the lindy, or the Jersey bounce.

And then, while the leader towed a taller, thinner woman by her red satin sleeve, another member of the team put more money in the Disney-glow jukebox. The women stood at the end of the table and smiled at Lenny and me with shy but certain expressions — *Only Dance* — and each held out a hand. Without speaking, we moved to the center of the room, bobbed our heads at one another until we agreed to the beat, and then began.

We thumped on the soft boards of the Antique Mirror Bar with our knees cocked, our elbows locked, eyes avoiding our partner's. We turned, stamping, gripping moist hands, then releasing, then gripping again, pulling hard, each trusting the other to support the bent weight hanging as we spun, shoulders banging down as heels did, to signal or celebrate the rhythm, or the act of dancing, or the speechlessness in which we agreed to move.

There was no arrangement for the tenure of each dance. Women in red satin jackets walked up as they wished, tapped a teammate on the shoulder, moved, head nodding, into the music and then the dance, and then danced with Lenny or me. The music was constant, and each member of the team danced with one of us several times. Lenny and I huffed and blew, but the women, though sweaty, only smiled or frowned with effort; the women made no sound. So there was the music of the lindy-hop, the squeak and shuffle of shoes, and the panting of men.

The little person at the bar in his yellow slicker turned, twice, to look over his shoulder at us, then went back to his drink. The bartender watched a small soundless television set at the corner of his counter, set in among beef jerky and potato-chip packets. Chuck Berry roared.

Then the music stopped. Lenny said "Thank you" to everyone. No one replied. The women reassembled at the bar, a couple of them nodding to Lenny and me, one offering a small wave at shoulder height. They worked at their hair and lips, pulled the hems of their red satin jackets, the cuffs of their sleeves, and then, each retrieving a bowling-ball case from the floor among bar stools, they left.

"The guys are coming home from the four-to-twelve shift," I guessed. "They'll make dinner for them now."

"I believe it," Lenny said. "I believe anything."

From outside the partly open door, a woman called, "You're welcome, boys," and the team giggled as the door closed.

Lenny said, "I believe it."

I brought drinks from the bar, and we sat in the booth, sweating, drinking warm whiskey, and chasing it with cold beer. "There are nights like this, anything like this," I said, "and some fishing, and sometimes I go out with a gun that isn't breech-blocked and I shoot something, and sometimes I see a couple of movies in a row."

"And then go home and watch another movie on TV until you fall asleep?"

"Unless it's a sad one. I turn them off."

"Right," Lenny said, "or an offensively happy one. Right? For me, anyway. If Gene Kelly starts in kissing her, and she smiles with tears in her eyes, then I fall apart."

I put my hand on Lenny's wrist, squeezed it, released it, wiped my mouth, and said, "That's all I'm telling you, Lenny. Fill in the rest. You know me well enough, all right? That's all of the details for now."

"We can do that," Lenny said. "You and I are the only guys I know — you know that wasn't true about Hanover, I don't remember that at all. But the time I was talking about on Torcello did happen. After I got your letter, about the crash."

"That did it to you? Are you surprised I'm not surprised?"

His pale face reddened, and I thought he might cry once more. But he said, "I wonder if this wouldn't be a good time to deliver the last letter."

"Oh, fine. Fine. You don't care about sleeping in the van, do you?" I was almost sorry, then, for having written to him. But there was, as he had pointed out, the last delivery.

"One more drink and I can sleep on the roof," he said.

"You probably won't have to."

We stood in the Antique Mirror Bar and waved at the bartender, who didn't wave back. "Nobody answers you in this part of the country," Lenny said. "Have you noticed that? They do not perform the little motions of grace to strangers around here."

The little man in the slicker, drinking his green fluids, called, "You be careful, boys."

I said, "You too."

"Oh, hell," the little man said, "I always am. You don't see *me* churning around with no half a dozen girls in pajama tops."

So at half past midnight, pitching up hill roads in a northeast backwater, Lenny calling out names on rural mailboxes, as if I didn't know where to go, we came to the small farmhouse on the broad plain that sat above the valley we'd driven through. Route 12B below gleamed gray in hard moonlight and looked like a nail that lay on a board. Up there, the land was silage crop, golden even at night with the coming-on of autumn, blown by steady winds. The house was at a crossroads, in a square of shaved lawn, flanked by balding maples. The leaves rattled, insects called through the slamming of our car doors, and it wasn't long — we hadn't yet rapped at the metal knocker — before an upstairs light went on, and then a parlor light, and then the light above the door.

She said, "I guess I got more mail."

I said, "My friend's delivering with me."

She wore a bathrobe meant for a man, and her feet were bare. Her hair looked shiny and tight, and it held to the curve of her head the way her large toes gripped at the floor. Her nose was narrow, nearly beaked, and she looked like someone — she always did — fresh from inconsequential angers. "Hello, friend," she said.

I said to Lenny, "This is Miss Waldren."

"You can call me Loretta, friend," she told Lenny. "The man who writes to me is not my husband. We never made agreements, really." She looked at the mailing envelope I held out. "I don't think I want that."

"The guy who sent it thought you would," Lenny said.

"Do you think he's a victim of something?" she asked him.

Lenny said, "I don't much care what he is. I hope he doesn't die of something in Asia sometime. He's in the dead letter department already."

"Well, that tone of talk doesn't make much sense," she said. "And nobody's dead, for heaven's sakes." Then she looked at me and raised her eyebrows at her own mistake and shook her head.

Lenny said, "How about this — we came about a hundred and fifty miles the long way around to give you that?"

She said, "All right. Then I'll take it from you." She was looking at me. I wasn't able to turn to look at Lenny and dare him to say something more.

I stood in front of her, waiting, and then Lenny went back to the van. I watched him lean against the door. She raised her eyebrows, this time for fun, and she went inside.

Lenny called, "You bastard. You son of a bitch. How am I supposed to handle this?"

I turned around and folded my arms. It was all I could do.

Lenny said, "Sure." He climbed into the van. I went inside the house.

Next morning, I woke him very early, bringing a thermos and a brown bag filled with cinnamon toast. I threw the envelope from Canada into the back of the van and, as we ate and drank, I drove. We listened to the radio, we watched the traffic form, we didn't speak.

Turning onto the Northway, I looked at him. Lenny said, "Get much?" and I sprayed a mouthful of coffee onto the instrument panel. But he didn't laugh. So I said, "I'm sorry, Lenny."

"You're so sorry, you're taking that poor bastard's letters back to him, right? All the way back to Montreal? Do you think he'll find that form of penance touching?"

"She doesn't love him," I said.

We listened to a Phil Ochs song and looked at the cars. And in a little while, I said, "You know, you realize this: I'm not the one around here doing penance."

"Leaving me the penitent?"

"Lenny, you're the guy who came over an ocean for her. You're the one who rode the bus. You're the one who couldn't get it up, and you are the one who is stuck so deep into grieving, you have to hang on to Ariana's husband who she probably would have ditched. Might have. I don't know. But I'm right about this. You loved her for so long."

Lenny looked out the window.

I put my hand around the back of his neck and I squeezed. He bent forward. "I like it that you loved her," I said. "It's fine."

"Do you love Miss Waldren?"

"We're friends. We get along. You don't understand it all, about me and Ariana. It's confusing."

"You brought me over, didn't you, just so I could see her? I believe that's called confession, in certain churches. Except I'm not —"

"No! You keep on having what you had for her. I'm driving you to a bus station, Lenny. I'm taking the goddamned envelope north, and that's my problem, and forget it. But you get onto a bus and go someplace for a while. We're friends."

"Who?"

"I'm talking about you and me."

"Okay."

"And we'll connect in a while."

"You are not about to shoot yourself, that's pretty apparent."

"And it isn't the reason you came here."

"Part of it."

"All right. Part of it. But you know why you really came here."

"Because you wanted me to," Lenny said. And a few minutes later, he sighed and said, "Listen, why don't you save me the carfare and get me over the border into Canada? You can drop me off up there. Because I'm sure to get drafted if they catch me in the States. I'm not Essential now. Get me over, and I can stay up there for a while."

"You wanted to come home, Lenny."

"Fine."

"Lenny, you *did*."

"You can carry my mail back and forth."

"I didn't force you home, Lenny."

He said, "That feels better, doesn't it?"

I'm here. I left Canada because I was tired of people who said *oat* instead of *owt*, and because I didn't like ice hockey, or any place named Mastigouche, and because too many people complained to me about acid rain that came from the States, as if I didn't get rained on too. I didn't eat dog food in Canada: I worked, and made good wages. I wrote some pretty bad stuff for the kiddy shows on television — they took my sour prose as wry charm — but I worked, and I drank fresh milk and ate marbled meat. But what I *felt*, at night, on some of those nearly-in-Europe Montreal streets, was the misfortune of those old people who eat dog food because they're so poor.

As a matter of fact, I never saw anyone eat dog food. But I did hear a lot about people who did. It seemed to be America's fault in general, and mine in particular, that they had to, no matter what country they lived in. It was like the story I heard from a terrifically handsome woman named Rosa. She told me that her way of working against the Vietnam War was to walk these kids, draft dodgers, over the bridge at Niagara Falls from New York State into Canada. The customs officers weren't apt to stop newlyweds, at least that's what the antiwar workers thought, and they often were right. Rosa never got caught. And she used to walk these trembling, green-faced little American boys over the bridge, and then she'd wave and deposit them there; they'd seem like a married couple with one of them looking for a bathroom. And he'd be gone, and she'd walk back after a while. She'd have a drink first, if she could, she told me. She came to Montreal to look one of them up once, and we met, and she told me this. We got friendly. She never found the guy, and then the war ended and we were all a good deal older. That's the story she told, and I guess if that's true, and I don't see why it shouldn't be, if something like the *war* was true, then I believe it, and I believe about the folks eating Alpo out of cans.

It doesn't smell that bad, when you first open the can. I was on my way out of Canada, traveling down on 133, aiming for 89. I wanted to find out if I was part of the president's amnesty. No one had told me, and I didn't know who to ask anymore. And if you asked the wrong person, and you weren't pardoned, you might find out in federal jail — that's where the counterfeiters beat on the draft dodgers because of their pride in our flag.

I was hitching in, because hitching was a habit, and so was saving money up, and this man in a very sedate Ford Galaxie 500 of some age who picked me up had a little white dog in the back. When we stopped at the Vermont state line, and I was sweating out the border patrol-man's eyes he fed his dog, and I smelled the stuff. It made me think of stories about old folks eating dog food, and it made me think of Rosa and how she remembered things. And it made me — all that remembering, regretting as I sometimes did that the body kept the brain alive at its pleasure and the brain had no independence — it made me think of Bill Gruen, who used to be my friend. This was particularly true when his wife, Ariana, was alive, since I loved her dearly. I mean: I was in love with his wife.

And while I was sitting next to the decent, fat, dog-bound and sentimental salesman of cigars who was driving me in a long Ford toward any place south of Canada, I realized that I had no one to come sidling silently home to. I realized how much I regretted that I had outlasted my family — except my sister, who wished not to speak to me again, and whose husband agreed. There weren't friends, no one I'd want to sit next to, describing exile in Canada. *About* my time there, I had no solid feelings yet — except that I was homesick, and uncertain of what distance I could make toward home, if I could name it and then get there. So I thought of Bill Gruen. I might have hated him. And, surely, he felt some kind of strong and possibly dark emotions toward me. But we *knew* one another. And I had a great need, then, to be known. I got out of the Ford near Swanton, Vermont, and I stomped around in my worn-down boots, dragging my old duffel bag behind me like a kid who'd been thrown out of camp. I found a bus station, and I sat around and drank coffee until it was light enough to see the cars, and be seen, and then I thumbed and walked and thumbed and walked, from Swanton to St. Albans, St. Albans to Georgia Plains, and then all the way through Winooski and Burlington to Montpelier, where I could look for locals going west on the small roads toward Irasville, and the only person in America I could think of to visit.

I had hitchhiked half asleep, then had slept for real in a stranger's car. He delivered herbicide for Agway, and he didn't care, he said, what it killed or polluted, as long as his wife and his chickens were all right. I saw this short, round, freckle-faced man who had remarkably long arms, my Agway driver, waking up in an old four-poster bed, his chunky wife alongside him, and the two of them under a living blanket of Leghorns and Rhode Island Reds. I laughed, and then he woke me, or I'd been awake and then he spoke, but, anyway, I had made it into the gut of northern Vermont, which in summer looked green and frisky. It had always seemed on the verge of dying out, like a giant creature that had eaten its food supply and that waited in hunger for the vegetable world to decide on its fate. Grass was always sparse there, it had seemed to me when I was living in Canada, writing for kids about Uncle Nelvin who talked too much and fell down a lot. I thought of the grass in Vermont as thin, like the wisps on a balding person's scalp. And yet here was the lush dark green I associated with France or the flat fields in the south of England. Instead of meadows where rocks were the crop, I saw rye and corn fields, and a lot of growth I couldn't name, and from a distance it all looked healthy and thick. The road to Bill Gruen's house was still a stony track, and dust kicked up almost before my boots thumped on the surface. There were midges to swat, and a red sun to signal high heat, and a massing, around the sun, of thick clouds.

I had forgotten how, as you came closer to his house, the brush grew denser and rose higher around the road. It felt as though the air supply lessened in that dark and green and brambled channel that approached the house. I had forgotten how, beyond the long and narrowing road that rose with the land, there were foothills crouching, so that air had a hard time moving out when a high-pressure front oppressed this part of Vermont, as it surely was doing right now. I nearly couldn't look forward, but I could look up, as if I walked in a trench, and there was the sun, rising to catch up with me, and as red as infection. The clouds closing in around it looked purple and matted, transparent but growing thick very quickly. I was sweating, and I was nervous because of the time that had passed without our speaking. Five years before, I had come back to the States from Italy, where I'd skipped the draft by teaching — Essential Service, they called it — the kids of military people stationed near Rome. I had come back because I thought Bill needed me after Ariana died in a manner too ridiculous to think about. But I do not think about her dying. I don't think about that. My return had meant the end of my deferment, and a sure trip to Southeast Asia. I returned to comfort Bill. That's what I told him. That's what I pretended to believe. We both knew that I'd come because Ariana was who I loved — a reason for going away to Europe, and a reason for returning to mourn. And Bill, on one of his runs through northeastern country to deliver mail from draft evaders in Canada to their parents and girlfriends and wives, had stopped off to screw someone, a fine enough woman I'm sure, and I had withdrawn my trust. Like a prig at a bawdy party, like a miser at a shaky bank, I'd taken away the deposits of friendship made over years and years, and I'd stuck in Canada while Bill went back to the States. And here I was. Without a right to be where I was, and without too much of a reason I could state without shame. I was here to be recognized. *Halt! Who goes there?* Me. Me. *Stand, and be recognized.* Me.

Then the high hot bushes ended, the path spilled out into a low hilly lawn before the small wood-frame farmhouse that was backed by a meadow and then the hills that held the house in something like a palm. Even the hills were knotted like knuckles, and even the lawn before me was like the thick ridge of muscle at the base of a person's hand. I stood, therefore, at the edge of the wrist and I stared up the narrow path, worn only by feet and not tools, that went to the house; it was like one of those lines you're supposed to read so you know the future, but I didn't know whether the pebbly path was called Career, or Life, or Love, or Hope, or just something to do with breakfast. I was hungry, hollow with trepidation, and waiting for someone in America to look me over and say that of *course* that's who I was: the famous and oft-remembered me.

What I saw was a belly I thought I recognized. It was in front of the house, and part of a body so still and slender and dark that in heat waves, and next to the doorway's vertical lines, it had seemed to be a piece of the picture I saw, and not a living thing, that belly's body. I looked again, and I saw, below a stomach that ever so slightly protruded, a small red rag of cloth. I saw very long thighs, knobbed knees, though not unsightly ones, and slender calves. I saw the rag again, the belly again, lean stomach and rib cage and small breasts in matching red rag, and then a set of braids, and dark hair tight on the scalp. The face, at that distance, looked like a child's, perhaps a teenager's or that of an older adolescent. The nose looked bobbed, which for a nose in my generation is not an unusual state: it was something of a national hobby in the late fifties and early sixties, cutting down the beaks of upper-middle-class girls. It was a ghost. It was Ariana.

I thought that if I went closer — or, probably, just closed my eyes and focused within the little stereopticon of my madness — I would see, it was returning now, that the suit was made of terrycloth. Ariana had sewed that suit, I remembered. So, naturally, her ghost would be wearing it. In that regard, this was a practical delusion, I thought, since clothing could be recycled and natural resources saved. *Who goes there?*

"Bill?" the ghost called in a high, nasal voice. The voice tried to emulate softness and calm, but it sounded worried. I wondered if a man who thought he saw a ghost could make it think that it was frightened. It moved, and for an instant it was gone in the lines of the cracked gray door and its unpainted sills, the sun-scarred creosoted cedar shingles of the house, the densities of heat that rose in the air around the dooryard. Then it was back, and calling for Bill again. It

seemed to be looking directly at me, and it did seem, really —
really? — to be scared.

I thought I was going to fall over. I was standing in the dreadful
downward push, like that of a hard hand, that the heat and mugginess
exerted. I held the duffel bag on my shoulder, still, and my lightweight
jacket was knotted around my waist. Inside my boots, my feet felt
ankle-deep in water. I wanted to tear my clothes away, but instead I sat
down, on top of the bag, and unbuttoned my shirt to nearly the waist.
It looked at me steadily, the ghost, and its legs didn't move. I studied
its nose and its stomach. It called again for Bill.

The door opened out and he came. It was Bill, tall, though shorter
than I'd remembered him, yet big enough to tower over most men,
which was something he liked to do in markets and bars. He was burly
as ever, covered with graying blond hair and whiskers, wearing only
shorts and sandals, so that the hair all over his body glowed with sweat
in the sun. He looked annoyed. That was something of a permanent
expression, I remembered, because he was nearsighted but refused to
wear glasses. He swiped at midges as if they were persecuting him. He
saw her. He saw me. He looked. His tensed shoulders and big arms
relaxed, then slumped, and he smiled, the wonderful smile that made
people less frightened — me included — in his vast and often grouchy
presence. He smiled and held his arms out as if we would hug like
fellow bears, which we often had done, drunk and sober, in trouble
and out, over many years. Then his arms went to his waist, and he said
something — my name, I thought — out of the corner of his mouth.
The ghost nodded — the woman, someone like Ariana, I thought, as I
walked toward them, someone very like Ariana but not resembling her
nearly enough to be her twin, just a woman who was long and slender
and whose belly was doppelganger to hers: belly-ghost, I thought,
laughing a belly-laugh. Which was when Bill did walk over to me and
seize my shoulders and hug me, as if he'd decided that, no matter what
I wanted, I would be embraced. *Stand, and be recognized*, I thought, as
he squeezed me against his smelly wet chest. Well, I was.

"Lenny Levine!" he called to her, as if confirming what he'd earlier
whispered. "Lenny Levine!"

I stepped back, wrinkling my nose and wiping sweat off my lips. He nodded, as if to confirm that as usual he wouldn't bathe until forced to by the niceties of a trip to town, or by local pressure.

The ghost — well, she wasn't one, was she? The woman looked at a distance like Bill Gruen's long-dead wife: that was all. The woman came closer, after squatting awkwardly for a shirt that lay on the lawn. As she walked, she buttoned it over her and rolled up the sleeves. It was a huge shirt, Bill's, of course, and she looked more interesting in it than diminished by it. It was a bobbed nose, a nose job, we'd called it at home when we were high-school kids, and it was a lived-in face. Bill was older than I was, and she was closer to his age than mine. She was very pretty. In spite of the heat, however, her face was frozen: she smiled, but not above the nose; she talked, but not with flexible lips; she asked me questions and heard what I said, but her forehead and eyebrows never moved to signal that she cared. I envied her such coolness in that temperature and humidity.

Her name was Kelly. I hated her name. Everyone was being named Kelly and Erin and Shaun, spelled Shawn, and they wrote me letters care of the program, asking idiot questions about whether Captain Goldfish was as much of a Pike-er as I'd said. They signed their letters Kelly, and I knew they would have to grow up into airline hostesses or footsore hookers in Saskatchewan. Her name was Kelly, all right, and she wasn't glad to be interrupted in her working vacation with Bill. She took photos for a living. Well, she took photos, and for a living she taught students at the University of Vermont how to take photos for course credits. She was an artist, Bill made clear. I was to see her portfolio later. Neither she nor I had spasms at the prospect.

The house was almost cool because of its screened windows and because of the mountain ash that served as shade trees. What moving air there was came in the shaded rear windows and blew across to the front. But the sun was still a hot red circle and I sat and sweated, dripping, yawning with fatigue and apprehension. They pointed me toward the bathroom, though I quickly remembered where it was, and I took a cool shower, enjoying the smell of a household's soap and drains and hair and old shampoo that clung to the shower tiles. Someone lived here, even if one of them was wrong. And it was a house. I wanted one. I had enough money for a down payment on one, and it was there, in the small cramped bathroom that Ariana had used and that someone named Kelly, enamored of strawberry gels, had usurped, that I decided on my course of action. I would stay awhile with them, until I felt American again, or accustomed to being in the States, and then I would leave them to one another and go someplace cooler, maybe Maine, or someplace near the White Mountains in New Hampshire, and I would buy myself a small house and a lot of land, and I would live there until someone came who loved me, and we would sleep in a four-poster bed under chickens, and I would never have to think about television, or children named Kelly, or people going *oat*, and I would write a book about being an expatriate so close to home. When the money ran out, I would write radio ads, or travel folders, or even teach a language course — Italian for beginners, say, at a Berlitz franchise in Peterborough, New Hampshire. *Ecco i miei bagagli. Ci sono solo effetti personali.* I stood under the showerhead as, with closed eyes, I saw one of my students presenting his luggage at the border for inspection — just personal effects, he'd say, with my handmade accent. I did have a future, a plan. *Viaggio solo.* But what the hell. Here I was. *In camera mia non ci sono asciugamani!* I stuck my head out and shouted for towels, please, and Kelly came, her smile a piece of ice, *ghiaccio*, on her lips. I had a plan, though. I was going to be alive in America, and alive in a house with one hell of a bathroom, and one day teach Italian and make love under chickens to someone terrific in a red bikini.

And be a jerk. By the time I was dressed in khakis, and loafers without socks, and a cotton T-shirt that said RCMP BALLBOY — our station had played the Mounties to raise money for a children's hospital — I was depressed again. I put my sweaty clothes back in the duffel and shut my jacket and toilet kit inside of it too. I was ready to move if I had to.

Kelly had dressed in baggy shorts and had tied Bill's shirt high up on her stomach, so that we were treated to her youthfully middle-aged muscles a-ripple. Bill had washed his face in the sink, I thought, because water still dripped from his beard, and there was soap in his ear. He was carving with a Pukko folding knife at pencils, probably just because he needed to do something with his huge, beat-up hands. He was a man who had to work away at the world, and with dangerous tools. If he wasn't breaking something because it needed removal, or building something only marginally necessary, or shooting something down, or digging something out, he became nervous. He had to feel useful. He was one of his implements, and he needed to feel that he was utilizing himself in such a manner as to earn her praise. But I was thinking of Ariana, for whom he used to show off, and whose love he had felt it was required he must daily earn. Now he was with Kelly. And here she was. She was scooping frozen lemonade from a large, long can.

"Lenny, will you have lemonade?" she called from the old trough sink.

"Thank you," I said. "Yes, I will. Thank you."

"I'll put two spoonfuls in, then," she said. "I won't have any." And that's what she did. In a small stoneware pitcher she dropped two tablespoonsful of frozen lemonade concentrate. She put the tin back in the freezer of the old Kenmore refrigerator, and then she stirred the concentrate in the pitcher.

"Very economical," I said.

That made her smile. She had beautiful teeth and a wide mouth, and when she meant her smile it was lovely to see. I understood how attractive she must be for Bill. Of course, there was also the fact that, given the right atmospheric conditions, she could pass for the ghost of his beautiful wife. How proud she seemed about saving money, too: that might be a source of her beauty, not a defrosting of reserve. Time was money, after all, in America. Next, I thought, I'd be telling them of the threat to Canadian forests posed by pollutants that American industry released into the jetstream. *Who goes there, dummy? Stand.*

I stood. I sipped at the artificial citrus taste — she'd put no ice cubes in the pitcher; I had seen, when she opened the freezer, that there were two trays of ice, so she was saving them — and I walked from the kitchen past the hall and toward the foot of the old, narrow stairs. Up there was a room in which I had wanted to sleep after Ariana's death. I wondered if Kelly kept away. It seemed to me that she could make good use, economical use, of Bill's need to earn his salvation in the daily world. Salvation through sex after performing useful acts, it might be called. Sex withheld, it might be called, until the acts were performed.

He had followed me. He stood in the doorway and put his hands on the molding at the top of the frame. "Whaddya think," he said, his Scandinavian eyebrows, all woolly and peaked, jumping on his face like wings. "I mean Kelly. What's your verdict?"

"Beautiful," I said.

"For a lady in her advanced condition of age — you know she's almost as old as I am? Who's better looking than her?" His tongue rolled in his mouth as if he were going to butter her up and pop her in. "She's got to be the best damned looking woman in the whole Northeast."

"Are you guys married?"

He shook his head. "She can't get a divorce. Her ex-husband, he's still her husband, but I can assure you he's ex. He won't give her a divorce. He calls her up and whines when he gets broke. Doesn't matter. Good stuff's good stuff, married or not. Her father was head of the glass museum, you know. Did I tell you? He's still about as important in glass as Ansel Adams is in photography." He whispered: "And what a piece she is."

I remembered, then, that he had used to talk of Ariana in the same way, and with the same phrases. She, then, at the start and even past the middle, had been good stuff. She, then, had been a tempest in bed. The things she knew, the things she *did*, he would sing. And she too had been one of the five — he'd never named the other four — most beautiful woman in all of the American Northeast. Well, Kelly was Number One now, Kelly the gorgeous, with her fake nose and her ghostly stomach and her two scoops of concentrate, and save the ice for later, and I would have to stop. I would have to: I hadn't been invited, and I'd felt a need to intrude, and he had been my friend.

I think that I might have wanted to make some somber announcement about the confirmed death of a friendship after long illness, had Kelly not come in behind Bill with a fine smile on a face that was red with pleasure. There was a sincerity in her eyes that made me think I was a liar and fool. She stood on her toes and he stooped, and she whispered in his ear. She was flushed, as if she'd been baking. Bill said, "It's naptime, isn't it?" He stretched and yawned. I remembered the terminology. In their good days, Bill and Ariana had taken frequent "naps" — which meant that strangers and friends had to move a discreet distance away as they went upstairs to make love. It had been important to them, the announcement, and I used to wonder if they had much sex when no one was about to know.

I said, "I'll take a walk down to the river, the little stream in the meadow. I'm not sleepy right now. I think I'll drop my feet in there and cool off and make some plans."

He smiled at me, and there was just the glimmer of a much older man, who would dodder after lean flanks and nose jobs until he was dead. I closed my eyes because I knew that I'd mourn him if he were dead, just as I mourned, while he stood before me, radiant with health, ready to rut on the floor of his farmhouse, so much that had to do with his being alive. They started up the stairs, and I went out to the hot buggy meadow.

It was rumpled land, I saw, as I walked it again. Although it lay in flatland surrounded by hills that blocked it from good breezes and, in winter, collected snow, the land itself was corrugated into millions of one- and two- and three-inch hills and their valleys, and I tripped as I walked through high grass and the clouds of gnats and other little bugs that flew up like living dust at each step. Where the garden had been, where Ariana had worked in a passion for rows of order in her life, and rows of babies in her fallowness, I'd always thought, nothing grew. The fence was there, chicken wire on old pine sticks, so Bill had made at least the empty outline of it whole again, and maybe in her memory. There was no produce. There were stones and dry clods and blown pollen that didn't take, some weeds with tightly furled brown pods, and some black long leaves where something had flowered some years past her dying and that now lay like flags along the sad surface that she'd dug at so hard. *Il giardino*, I would tell my students, moving my lips like a drunk old husband in a bad Italian movie: *jardee-noh*.

In the meadow, a hundred yards or so from the little hill and garden behind the house, the stream ran in oxbow shapes beneath its shallow bank. I didn't dangle my legs, but I did lie on my back under the sun, surrounded by the wideness of the unused fields, as ripe for crops as the garden was blasted and black, and I pulled my shirt up to my neck to catch the sun on my fish's belly, and I closed my eyes. I would leave tomorrow and spend some money on clothes and maybe one of those swanky small bags that travelers carry, and something light to wear on my feet, and I would go to Logan Airport in Boston, and get myself fetched overseas. Either Venice airport, and then the *vaporetto* to my favorite place, Torcello, where in the church on that island the Christ is a pagan's drama of dying gods, all rolled eyeballs and thick blood — or the Santa Maria del Fiore in Florence, where there is a Last Judgment worthy of the notion of *last*. Yes, a pair of white running shoes, maybe, that I would wear on the plane and while I walked around, before I settled into — wait a minute, I told all the little chirring, chugging, peeping, whistling insect engines that were loud around me: Wait. I'm talking about going all the way back, back overseas. What about Peterborough, New Hampshire, and the Berlitz franchise for nervous tourists? That's it, dear: he says *Passaporto, prego,* and you smile and hand it over, and then you say *Viaggio solo* to tell him you're traveling alone.

There seemed to be a difference of opinion among the staff in Expatriate Command.

It was the lemonade, I realized, that had me as wild as anything — everything? — else. It was the cheapness of two scoops of frozen lemonade concentrate instead of, say, a whole pitcher of lemonade with ice cubes and fresh-baked cookies and a kiss on the cheek and a roll in the hay, and maybe she *was* Ariana's ghost. Because even though I hated her, and resented her intrusion, and despised Bill's unfaithfulness to the dead, I was as convetous of Kelly as I'd been of Ariana. Could all this mean that the common denominator between these women was their husband and boyfriend? Was I queer for Bill? I thought not. On the other hand, I'd never thought I'd live that long in Canada, either, and anyone who could live in that enormous small town of a nation that long, talking *aboat* American imperialism, could just as well be lusting after men when he never thought he would. All right, I told myself, sighing up into the sun, put the sexuality issue on hold, but don't ignore it. At your age, and at your station of life — which is to say: being too old, with too little achieved, and with too few prospects — you mustn't ignore any clues. All right. But meanwhile, and of course keeping this famous open mind, consider that you've come a long distance over a good many years, to see someone who knows you. You know him. You knew him. Be patient. Find out.

Where's the bathroom? The question was asked by Ariana, who was wearing one of those crinoline-lined wide skirts of the fifties. It was gunmetal gray, with a pink felt poodle on it. The blouse was a matching pink, with piping on the collar that matched the body of the skirt. She wore long black ballet slippers, and in her ponytail were pink ribbons. Her fingers were bleeding. Her eyes were bloody holes with little glass beads in them, and they looked like the Christ in the medieval cathedral on Torcello. *Where's the bathroom?* she asked, and from her angry tone I realized that we were having a disagreement. I tried to tell her where it was, but she didn't understand my Italian. I tried English, but all I could say were the embarrassed laugh-noises that no one really makes, but that are represented in *Archie and Veronica* comics by bubbles emanating from teenage mouths with *Heh heh* inside them. *Heh heh*, I told her. In the dream, I knew as I spoke that it was necessary to cry to her something more important. I couldn't and, anyway, her eyes were so bloody, her fingers were dripping, and she was angry at me.

I woke with sun in my eyes and I closed them and fell asleep again, to the sound of my voice: "She isn't angry. You're having a nightmare. Anyway, she's dead. Go back to sleep." When you live alone, you're the only one who can wake you from hard dreams and send you back to sleep again without them, and that's what I did. I wasn't deep in sleep. I was riding sleep's surface and remembering, as I lay along it, how once, wonderfully, Ariana and I, in the Gruens' apartment in New Haven, with sun rolling in from the fire escape, had sat together while Bill went out to buy something for dinner. We were on a little sofa that we'd pushed up close to the window so that we could put our feet up on the window's low ledge and still see pedestrians across the street. The neighborhood was filled with students and poor people, so the radios throbbed like drums in the early evening as we sat, our shoulders touching, and each at once, I think, grew aware that they touched. I moved away and looked at her. She was smoking cigarettes and looking at the street. I moved back, and she must have felt my shoulder lie along hers again, but she made no sign. I stayed that way, seeing nothing of what she saw outside, and breathing shallowly so that my body wouldn't jump and make her understand that we — no other description will do — were intimate.

I felt her: tough muscle that moved easily under the skin. I smelled

her: harsh cheap bath soap, the Balmain perfume her mother brought
her from Paris, the scent of her shampoo, which was something used
on infants' hair and which had the delicate fragrance I associated with
the innocence in little bodies. When she spoke, I smelled her mouth:
cigarettes, the spiciness of coffee we'd been drinking, and her body
itself. Her body smelled like cooking herbs I've held on a hot bright
street in Provence.

Then she moved, she tilted her head back, breathed out smoke and
rocked in place beside me in the big room that overlooked an ordinary
street. She said, in her low voice, "Were you glad when Bill left?"

I stood, as if I'd done something daring and offensive and must
move. I watched her. I was certain that my face was bright. Hers
wasn't; she was calm, and she was clearly enjoying herself. I was
certain I looked young to her. I said, "You mean was I happy to be
alone with you? Why are you asking?"

"You're right," she said.

"No, no, *I* don't mind. I didn't mean I minded. Yes. You know that.
Don't you?"

"You're right," she said. But she was smiling such an innocent smile.
I seemed to give her such pleasure that she smiled broadly enough to
make my chest squeeze. That was it. My entire body winced. "You're
right."

"I'm — always glad to be with you. This isn't what I mean."

She was wearing a shirt she'd made from some very coarse home-
spun-looking tan cloth, and her jeans were faded almost powder blue;
they made her thighs look softer than her torso, and I wanted to put
my hand on her leg, just to touch her, to see whether her legs were as
tender as they seemed. "I know it isn't," she said. She smiled, and the
sun and her clean hair, the hazy filigree of her drifting cigarette smoke,
everything made her words feel warm as I heard them. "I know it
isn't." She beamed, as if with pleasure. "I wonder," she said.

That was it. We spoke on other topics, not hastily, but carefully, and
in a manner that was considerate to everyone, but especially to me. She
did, always, try to take good care of me. But I waited on the precipice
of her statement. I carried her smile, and her hair, and her exhaled
smoke, the stiffness of her shirt, the softness of her jeans, the glow of

her language and its promise unfilfilled: I bore them all with me to
Rome, and I bore them back when Ariana died; they went, as surely as
my GI duffel bag, from the States up to Canada and now down to
Vermont, and they were with me in the field that she had owned, they
were over me as surely as the sun and heavy air and little flies.

I heard jays and crows fly up and make their protests, so I knew that
someone was coming. I heard Bill grunt as he walked past me on the
corrugated field to plunk something heavy in the stream. It would be
beer. Bill conducted business in a context of alcohol. I looked at
Ariana's smile and I knew what I could easily have known at other
times, but had decided not to. No: I hadn't told myself that I could
know. But now I did, and I knew it for absolute truth as I lay in the
field, and I know it now, as I say this to myself again. While I had
always carried with me the possibility, the outside chance that we, had
we tried, might have loved, Ariana hadn't wanted me to think that way
at all. She had seen me as wounded and youthful and sweet. She had
enjoyed my deference, my supplication, and my quiet love — it had
been flattery, it had been whatever she needed. She hadn't, however,
needed Lenny Levine. And I had carried with me from place to place
and time to time what was finally nothing more than a wish.

Bill came up and he nudged me from my almost-dream, which had
turned into more of an almost-waking, by prodding me with his foot.
He pushed me with his toes and I opened my eyes.

When I moved my mouth to tell him, again, that I was going away,
and as I tilted up to prop myself on an elbow, my skin felt taut and
stretched and mildly burned. The sun was balanced on the top of the
hill. The air was starting to swirl and make the meadow a little cooler.
From the stream, Bill pulled up a couple of cans of beer, which he
opened for us. He sat beside me, on his haunches, and he smiled.

The beer was cold and it tasted good. I was glad to take some
pleasure in it. "Where did you say you were going?" Bill asked.

I shrugged, sat, pulled my shirt down over the sunburn and bug
bites, then shrugged again. "It isn't clear yet," I said. "You know, you
sometimes feel like you should really be getting on your way, but you
don't have any plans? I think either New Hampshire or Venice."

He laughed and laughed, as if I'd made a good joke. Maybe I had.

"But there's someplace else," I said. "It was the wind picking up that made me think about it. I went there when I was teaching in Rome. I took a train down there, and then there was a bus that went to a market town in the south of France, Salon de Provence. A pretty place. They have a fountain inside of a huge bushy tree in the market square, and I used to sit there and drink pastis until I admitted that I wasn't Hemingway and anise gave me the runs. But you could get a bus out of there that went to a place called Les Baux. It was once like a country up there, with most of Provence right under it. A giant castle, walls all the hell over the place. Some king named Philip, I think, had it leveled, just to make sure everyone knew he was the only king they had — he was the Lyndon Johnson of France. Well, the chapel's still there. It's built right into the rock of the mountain. They have shops and even art galleries there now. When I went, it was like a carnival, and kids were running around, and tourists, and all that pretty Provençal cloth — didn't I send some to Ariana from there? A scarf or something? There were some doorways left, you know: arches going into rooms, just doorways and some stones. And the chapel. It was so dark and low. And off to one side, they'd left it the way it must have been when knights with big noses went in there to really believe in God and be scared. Cold, and dampness, and darkness, a low ceiling. There was a little stone cross, and that was it. It was the second-best church I ever was in. It made me cry. Good churches make me cry," I said, starting to sniff and get teary, "so I got the hell out and drank white wine and looked down on everything from way up. That place and Torcello. Don't I seem to be going on about churches today? Well, in my sleep, anyway. Never mind."

I drank more beer. He sat, then, and stretched out his legs, which were in brown duckcloth carpenter's pants, all loops and toggles and pockets and flaps, and held together with big rivets. He said, softly, "What was Canada like?"

"Oh," I said, "it was okay, if you like nothing-special. It's a nothing-special place and everyone there is determined to do something about that. You're okay there if you aren't black or Pakistani or something, and if you can piss and moan about America — American TV, American books, American industry, American foreign policy. They spend so much time, in Montreal, anyway, trying to be either France or not-America, they don't know *who* in hell they are. It was like living in a doctor's waiting room. It wasn't bad. It was long."

"So how come you stayed there? I mean, besides the draft? The war."

"That's a lot to say besides about. But I didn't know where to go, was one thing. I didn't know what they'd done about my passport. And then it was expired. And I had to learn how to save money. Which I did. I'm loaded. I've got traveler's checks all over my person and inside my shaving tackle and everyplace. I can go where I want to, for a while. Anyway: there wasn't that much going on out here that I missed. I guess."

Bill said, "And you were pissed at me because I wasn't faithful to the memory of Ariana Gruen."

"Come on, Bill. I mean, she was dead. I'm sorry. But she is. Right? And you can fuck whoever you want."

"We were in trouble before she died. You know that. It didn't make it easier when she died. It was tough on me. You know about this thing, guilt?"

"My people brought the industry to America, remember? Anyway, that's why I came in from Europe."

"Nah," he said. He walked to the stream and brought two more beers back. "You came on account of her. It was on account of her."

I drank my beer because he was probably right and because there wasn't much to say.

Bill said, "I might marry her some time."

"Kelly?"

He nodded.

I said, "Great."

"She's a little shy," he said.

"I'd have thought she was a little resentful."

"Nah," he said. "She loves you. No, it's when someone from before her time comes up here, she feels like she's competing with Ariana."

"And she is."

"I guess that can't be helped," he said.

"She looks like her. A little like her, anyway."

"Really? I'd never have thought so."

"Well, something like her."

"Two legs and a crotch," he said.

"And Ariana's bathing suit," I guessed.

Bill looked down at his beer. Then he looked up and smiled all his teeth and his big wet lips. He waggled his eyebrows and blinked his small bright eyes. "I never said I wasn't careful with a dime," he said.

"Very practical," I said. "What the hell, why not? Why not? Why *not?*"

He raised his can of beer and toasted me. I raised mine and toasted him back. Our beer cans clanked, and we drank. It was what we had done, years before, over and again. For we had achieved much of our friendship in the rituals of bars and activities connected with the consumption of alcohol. We hadn't talked much, after the first year or two of knowing one another. It had been a long and easy silent friendship, and the assumption always had been that we'd progressed past language. As we toasted and drank, I understood that we had evaded language, out of embarrassment and probably emptiness. We had danced a dance of friendship, and the music had been habit, and — just as now, I realized — we had spent a lot of our time in not discussing what was difficult and maybe therefore important in the lives of adults. I was moved when I understood how easily the silent companionship that men grow up in search of, that they admire in films and books, can turn into the silent politeness of strangers who sit at the same long bar and drink.

We went back, and Kelly was out on the lawn, this time in crisp chino trousers and a soft halter top at which her nipples prodded. I watched her nipples for a while, and then I got tired of the stimulation. So I cut back on my focus, and I watched her and Bill set deck chairs up on the lawn near a folding table. On the table went a bottle of inexpensive gin and a small bottle of domestic vermouth, and half a bowl of ice cubes — Kelly would be saving the rest, I thought, for something important.

Bill made a fire at the brick fireplace near the end of the house, feeding it hardwood that popped and cracked, and, as he let the coals accumulate, we made martinis and ate synthetically flavored onion-

and-sour-cream potato chips, diving right into getting drunk enough to act at ease with one another. Kelly, with all the graciousness you could ask of someone set to entertaining an uninvited and relatively undesirable guest, passed the package of artificial chips toward me once or twice, and she even made my first drink. She gave me one ice cube, but didn't protest when I took a second without asking permission. The fire hissed and exploded, and dusk settled over the bowl of hills, and then the meadows, and then the lawn; the insects changed pitch, or maybe different ones began to sound, and it nearly was night. The vermouth was oily, the gin was sour and strong, and, if I used my imagination, the little ice available to us did reduce the temperature of our martinis.

Bill was telling me, soon, what a simply brilliant photographer Kelly was, and how at faculty meetings her colleagues were often heard to praise her at the level of extended song. The bugs at night were worse than the ones that had bitten me in daylight. I remembered where Ariana had kept bug spray and, without asking permission, I went to the door, reached around to the low shelf just inside the kitchen, and found an old orange can. I brought it back to the table, sprayed my arms and neck and face, spat out the residue that had leaked onto my tongue, put the can beside its cousins, the flavored chips, and made myself another drink. I smelled like a drugstore, or a gas station. I held my breath while I drank. Bill checked the fire, then decided to delay cooking by piling lots more wood on. He'd have to wait for more coals he could heap up, which meant another couple of drinks. Kelly was trying to channel the conversation back to her teaching and her photography, and Bill was eager to cooperate — his little eyes swiveled and danced as he watched us, hoping for the best, no doubt expecting only the worst, and drinking and talking, and working, in general, quite hard.

I was asking about his car, an old International Harvester, that guzzled gas. He was telling me about a winch on the front. We were going on about body rust when Kelly stood and stretched. I had hitherto seen such moves in films, but never on a live person before me. Having composed a face that generated concern about the starving children of the Indian subcontinent, or perhaps certain lost canvases of

Winslow Homer, she continued to stretch, so that she gave each breast its turn and each nipple its due; then she gave notice of her flanks and her loins, and then she sighed — all those hungry kids! I stopped talking and I watched her and, as she sat, I said, "Yes?"

"I didn't say anything," she said, smiling.

"I thought you did." And she had. For Bill had shut up as she'd begun to move, and he now dutifully concentrated on the topic she had raised. And now that she was sitting again, now that his leash had been tugged, he didn't know what to say. So he added more gin to his glass and he drank it.

Kelly smiled at me, all fang. I showed her a tooth or two in return. We talked about the presidential election, and I expressed my regret that Richard Nixon wouldn't be available for service to his nation once again. "I miss him," I said. "He's been in my life or on the fringes of it as long as I can remember. It's like not having Satan anymore. How am I supposed to remember who God is if I don't have the Devil for comparison-shopping?"

Kelly said, "My father feels the same way, about the first part of what you said. He misses Nixon too. Except, he thinks he was railroaded out of office."

Bill said, "He tried to kill Lenny by drafting him, he *did* notch up a couple of hundred thousand bodies to his credit. Anyway, you don't believe that, Kel."

Kelly said, "I'm talking about my father, strange one. Lenny, my mother's in the DAR, you understand? That's her chief attraction for my father. He thinks it was the blacks and the Jews who railroaded Nixon out. My father has a lot of trouble with Jews," she said, staring at me and not blinking.

I sprayed bug stuff up into the air, as if there were an all-out attack of giant flies. Bill panted loudly, like a large dog, reminding us that anti-Semites were a joke, and here we all were friends.

I said, "Yeah, I know a lot of people who've got trouble with Jews. They're called bigots. Or assholes, maybe. In Europe they call them either the village mayor, or Sir, or fascists, depending on who does the calling. They've got them in Germany and Italy and France and Rumania, where they do a first-rate job of hating, I can tell you, and let us not forget the oft-victimized but always stalwart Poles, who could do you a valve job, lube and change the oil on a Jew before you can say DAR."

Bill panted, poured more gin, and escaped to check on the fire. He was too responsible to us, though, to stay away, and as Kelly was describing for me this document her father owned several copies of, and as I was howling like a second large dog, but with a certain cheerfulness, I have to admit, Bill returned and sat down on his beach chair to pour more gin, then fled for the kitchen, saying "Ice."

By the time he lurched back with an ice-cube tray, the final one, by my count, I was explaining things to Kelly. *"The Protocols of the Elders of Zion* was imported by Henry Ford. He did business with Czarist Russia to buy thousands of copies because he was so impressed. He didn't understand the book was a fake. He didn't want it to be. But it wasn't, it *isn't*, an actual account of these vicious old rabbis sitting around and cackling into their beards and drinking the blood of small Christian children as they plan to control the currencies of the world. It is possible that many distinguished people have believed this, including your father, maybe, and several selected members of the general staff, and conceivably Richard Nixon. But it isn't true. George Wallace knows it isn't true. The American Nazi party knows it isn't true. The KKK thinks it might be true. And your father knows it *is* true, is that right? Are you kidding me?"

Bill dropped ice into our glasses and Kelly said, "Save some, sweetie."

I said, "Hitler did believe it, of course. Fine, that was his job. He was supposed to behave like Hitler. Okay. But how can your father — how, after they killed all the goddamned Jews in Europe, nearly, can your father *talk* like that?"

Kelly was blithe. I have to give it to her: she was the blithest. She said, "Daddy's hard to convince. It takes a lot to change his mind. You have to understand: he hardly ever met a Jew until he went to college, let alone a good Jew."

"A good Jew?"

Bill said, "I'm gonna smear a lot of mustard on some very thick chuck steaks and broil them over the fire and we are gonna have a *feast*."

"Kelly," I said, "a *good* Jew?"

She turned toward me. She smiled with all of her mouth. She nodded her head. " 'Scuse me," she said, still smiling, "while I go in and make us a green salad to go with the steaks."

"A good Jew," I said to Bill.

He said, "Look. It's how she was brought up. She didn't *decide* to think that way."

"You don't think that way."

"You should know better than to talk about that to me, Lenny."

"Yeah, but you're living with this woman, Bill, and she has some kind of dividing line in her life. Good Jews, bad Jews. Doubtless we have good blacks and bad blacks, good spics and bad spics, bad Indians and dead ones, semi-tolerable Greek Orthodox — Bill: what've you got in your *life* now?"

"I love her, that's all. So forget it. All right? Some people have bad breath and other people keep living with them. Kelly was brought up by dumb people, that's it. She's working it out. This'll help her. Lenny: she did a whole photographic essay on people in New York, she must have half a dozen Hassidim in there, these old Jews with braids."

"I think Goebbels had a Jewish wife, Bill. Braids and all, little leather party dresses, wooden shoes. He still liked the smell of Jew-smoke."

Bill was too gentle to hit me in the face or body. He flailed with his paw at the tumbler I was holding. He pressed his lips together and his eyes narrowed and he batted at me with his arm straight out, his torso unmoving. He wasn't malicious. He was trapped, he was desperate, and he had no more words. I went to my knees, and I was hurt. The glass had apparently shattered when he struck it, and the shards were in my fingers. I was on both knees, then, seeing bright lights go on and off as Kelly called, "Wow!" Bill went down onto his knees too, snuffling, holding my sliced hand as he picked the glass out as well as he could while we both panted and trembled. "Oh, Jesus," he said. "Don't bleed to death, all right? Don't die." He stood and raised me and herded me into the house. Kelly was at the door, and she looked pretty because there was that pink flush under her slow-baked front-lawn tan. Her nostrils were wide with excitement, her eyes were immense, I thought she was going to swallow the night. I thought I was going to faint, and I made the announcement. Bill shoved me onto a chair and then pushed my head down between my legs with such strength I thought one of my vertebrae threatened to pop. I leaned all the way forward to save my spine, and I went off the chair, face-first onto the floor. I lay there and tasted blood in my mouth from a slice of the lip I'd apparently bitten when I threw myself down.

Bill laughed, a forced and purposeful "Hoo" like the sound a man in the spin of good times might make. But there was nothing funny, only Lenny Levine being ridiculous, and I didn't join in, and he stopped. I became aware of odors — cheap, store-bought dressing for the salad, and the damp rancidness of the unswept wooden floor, and the sweat that came off Bill's big body, and the sweat that came off my own. They sat me up where I was and leaned me back against the chair. I let my head rest on the seat while Bill held my hand still and Kelly, with tweezers and then hot needle, took splinters of glass from my palm and my fingers.

"Leave my thumb," I remember gasping. "Take the others off if you have to *ow!* but leave the thumb."

"So you can hitch," Bill said grimly.

"You guys are crazy," Kelly said. I wanted to take my bloody palm and smear it on her face. I smiled, though, and nodded.

"That's what always got us through, Kel," he said.

"But then we got old. We grew up. Remember?" I said. "Bill? You remember what Ariana told us? You remember that? In New Haven? You went out and you came back — *ow! ow!* — with Chinese food? I think you were in the place on Chapel Street. You sat down across from me and you took out these about fifty eggrolls and a quart of cream soda, and Ariana made herself a cheese omelet and told us we'd be okay acting like that as long as we didn't get older. *Dammit*, Kelly! I'm sorry. *Woof!* Thanks for trying to be gentle. Are you trying?"

"No," Bill said.

"What, hon?" Kelly said, and she knew what he would tell us.

"I don't remember, that's all."

"Well," I said, "what the hell. What's eggrolls."

"I'm sorry I swung like that," Bill said. "I panicked."

I said, "Me too."

Kelly said, "Ariana was probably right."

"I don't remember that," Bill said. He let my hand go and he helped me up by my arm. Kelly was pouring merthiolate on the palm and daubing it on the fingers. Her hands were shaking more than mine, and I think it was excitement. I think that she was galvanized by the picture she must have retained: her big Bill, her own, swinging his massive arm in a wide, powerful arc to swat the buzzing Jew-boy and smite him where he'd lighted. Bill was shaking too, I could see him vibrate — even his knees were going. He couldn't breathe right, and he was pale. I knew how much he regretted hitting me, though the blow was also a gift to Kelly, and he'd treat it as such to woo her, and he'd take her praise with thanks. That was Bill. That was how he achieved the affections of women. American men were famous for doing that, I had been told by Europeans, and Bill was all of an American man. I wondered, of course, if I purchased my loves by getting hurt.

He hugged me. We used to be conspicuous in that regard. People in bars would sneer when we got joyous and squeezed one another's shoulders. We did do that, and he did it now. We went outside, my thanks to Kelly and her response colliding in the air between our turned backs. We sat at the table again, and he spilled gin as he poured it into the yellowish vermouth, trying to make a proper martini and start our evening off all over again on a ceremonial note. I couldn't look at him, even when he shakily left the table and went into the house, then returned with gauze bandage and adhesive tape. He wrapped my hand, patted my cheek and then my shoulder, and he raised his glass to signal our toast.

My hand was throbbing, and the gin wouldn't help. My head was starting to throb in rhythm with my hand. I raised the glass and then put it down. I said, "I'm sorry. I didn't mean to come here and criticize your — I was going to say wife. But you know what I mean. I hope it really works out terrifically for you. I do."

He sat at the folding table on his lawn and watched me walk inside. He probably thought I was going to drop my wriggling benediction onto Kelly too. But I hadn't gone in search of her. I went in — the flashing lights I'd seen were still behind my eyes, and I'd finally decoded them — to find her camera. It was one of those large 35mm professional instruments, sleek and black and, in the right circumstances, as menacing as a gun.

"Hi!" she said brightly, showing the most affection she'd displayed to me — I was her subject, now, not just an intruder.

I picked up the camera, which was near some cellophane-wrapped lettuce on the counter next to the sink, and I fumbled at it.

"What are you doing, Lenny?"

"I'm trying to open your camera, Kelly, and get the film."

"No, don't do that."

"You're right," I said. I put the camera on the softwood floor and stepped on it as hard as I could. Kelly wailed. I jumped on the camera, and something popped open while a lot of delicate glass and machinery crunched under my feet like bugs. I saw a piece of film and pulled at it, and the spool unwound into a twisted mess that was torn up the middle by something projecting from the shattered box. I held it up and said, "I bet you got good shots, Kelly. But of course you had a good Jew to work with."

I went into the hallway and found my bag, tied my jacket around my waist, and walked past Bill, who sat at the table and didn't act surprised. I went along his lawn, and down his road, and through the clouds of midges that seemed to never cease their swarming onto anything that moved. My eyes grew accustomed to the dark, my hand hurt worse, my feet chafed because I wasn't wearing socks, and I was alone at home in America, well met by the only person alive with whom I had much history, and greeted by the ghost of what I'd sought.

It remains for me once more to say the obvious. I'm an American in Europe, residing on the cheap above a trattoria run by Spaniards in Venice, close to the Rialto Bridge. I earn a living as a teacher of English to the children of wealthy Venetian restaurateurs, summertime guide for British tour groups, and occasional travel writer — "Northern Italy Without Pasta!" — for American food magazines. I get by. Sometimes I take a few hours and sit with a bitter coffee at the Locanda Cipriani on the Island of Torcello, as now, and I watch the gasoline shimmer on top of the canal.

I walked away from Bill Gruen's house in Vermont and, by the time I'd stopped hyperventilating, I counted myself lucky that he hadn't come after me to batter me for insults to Kelly and her equipment — or, worse, to ask me to stay. I didn't expect to catch a ride, but I did. An old guy in a new pickup stopped for me and made courteous conversation before I left him at Montpelier. He had a son, he said, who worked at IBM in New York.

I went there too, though not to work for anyone. I made Manhattan a full day later, and I checked myself into the Waldorf-Astoria because that was the fanciest hotel I could think of when I caught the cab at the Port Authority bus terminal. I felt that I owed myself some luxury, and I graciously accepted the gift. I stayed there in a cool peach marble room for a week, enjoying the air conditioning and good showers, room service, and even the barber, who washed my hair and shaved me as gently as you'd like to be stroked by a stranger. I bought a first-rate pair of running shoes and some lightweight trousers and shirts, and even a suit that Brooks Brothers fitted for me with a minimum of fuss. Then I moved over to the West Side, after soliciting the advice of a cab driver, and I checked into a very dusty, very shabby, but un-verminous hotel, where they did scrub down the bathrooms and change the sheets, and where the bill was low. I went to a joint on West 45th and had my picture taken. I applied by mail for a passport, knowing that if it took a long time, then I would not have been pardoned, and had better make my way up north, and at least into Montreal, if not all the way to the Gulf of St. Lawrence. I went to a lot of films and I saw a revival, in Greenwich Village, of a Harold Pinter play that made my jaws ache just under the ears, as if I'd been sucking on lemons. A week went by, and there was no passport in the mail for me. I bought myself a paperback copy of Hugh Honour's Venice book because I thought that I might hack a living as a guide of some sort, and Honour knew everything I'd have to say about the pictures in Venice. It was well into the third week, when I was truly considering fright and flight, that my passport came.

At Macy's I bought myself a canvas suitcase. I picked up some toilet supplies and more shirts, a seersucker sport coat and summerweight dark slacks, and then I was off for the Pan Am office, where I booked my plane. I left, two days later, for the place where ghosts are said to be more at home; even the buildings in Europe are constructed as if to house them. Though certainly I knew as I went what I'd learned on coming home — that you cannot be haunted by the ghosts of your choosing. You take what you get. It's up to them.

I shuffled from the departure lounge at Kennedy Airport to display my passport and tickets at the Pan Am gate. Ariana seemed more mine than she'd been. But she was air, she was argument, and there was no consolation in possessing her with words. The young Pan American Airlines clerk, skin the color of saddle leather, eyes very dark and very intelligent and consummately bored, sat sweating in his dark blue uniform in the wet heat that crushed New York. He looked at my tickets. The music of a long-defunct Broadway show was playing from the speakers in the ceiling as he looked at the passport, but not at me, and then nodded to no one in particular, returned the little book, and motioned listlessly that I could pass. *Eccomi qui.* I'm here.

Ralph the Duck

I WOKE UP at 5:25 because the dog was vomiting. I carried seventy-five pounds of heaving golden retriever to the door and poured him onto the silver, moonlit snow. "Good boy," I said because he'd done his only trick. Outside he retched, and I went back up, passing the sofa on which Fanny lay. I tiptoed with enough weight on my toes to let her know how considerate I was while she was deserting me. She blinked her eyes. I swear I heard her blink her eyes. Whenever I tell her that I hear her blink her eyes, she tells me I'm lying; but I can hear the damp slap of lash after I have made her weep.

In bed and warm again, noting the red digital numbers (5:29) and certain that I wouldn't sleep, I didn't. I read a book about men who kill each other for pay or for their honor. I forget which, and so did they. It was 5:45, the alarm would buzz at 6:00, and I would make a pot of coffee and start the wood stove; I would call Fanny and pour her coffee into her mug; I would apologize because I always did, and then she would forgive me if I hadn't been too awful — I didn't think I'd been that bad — and we would stagger through the day, exhausted but pretty sure we were all right, and we'd sleep that night, probably after sex, and then we'd waken in the same bed to the alarm at 6:00, or the dog, if he'd returned to the frozen deer carcass he'd been eating in the forest on our land. He loved what made him sick. The alarm went off, I got into jeans and woolen socks and a sweatshirt, and I went downstairs to let the dog in. He'd be hungry, of course.

.   .   .

I was the oldest college student in America, I thought. But of course I wasn't. There were always ancient women with parchment for skin who graduated at seventy-nine from places like Barnard and the University of Alabama. I was only forty-two, and I hardly qualified as a student. I patrolled the college at night in a Bronco with a leaky exhaust system, and I went from room to room in the classroom building, kicking out students who were studying or humping in chairs — they'd do it *anywhere* — and answering emergency calls with my little blue light winking on top of the truck. I didn't carry a gun or a billy, but I had a flashlight that took six batteries and I'd used it twice on some of my overprivileged northeastern-playboy part-time classmates. On Tuesdays and Thursdays I would waken at 6:00 with my wife, and I'd do my homework, and work around the house, and go to school at 11:30 to sit there for an hour and a half while thirty-five stomachs growled with hunger and boredom, and this guy gave instruction about books. Because I was on the staff, the college let me take a course for nothing every term. I was getting educated, in a kind of slow-motion way — it would have taken me something like fifteen or sixteen years to graduate, and I would no doubt get an F in gym and have to repeat — and there were times when I respected myself for it. Fanny often did, and that was fair incentive.

I am not unintelligent. *You are not an unintelligent writer*, my professor wrote on my paper about Nathaniel Hawthorne. We had to read short stories, I and the other students, and then we had to write little essays about them. I told how I saw Kafka and Hawthorne in a similar light, and I was not unintelligent, he said. He ran into me at dusk one time, when I answered a call about a dead battery and found out it was him. I jumped his Buick from the Bronco's battery, and he was looking me over, I could tell, while I clamped onto the terminals and cranked it up. He was a tall, handsome guy who never wore a suit. He wore khakis and sweaters, loafers or sneaks, and he was always talking to the female students with the brightest hair and best builds. But he couldn't get a Buick going on an ice-cold night, and he didn't know enough to look for cells going bad. I told him he was going to need a new battery and he looked me over the way men sometimes do with other men who fix their cars for them.

"Vietnam?"

I said, "Too old."

"Not at the beginning. Not if you were an adviser. So-called. Or one of the Phoenix Project fellas?"

I was wearing a watch cap made of navy wool and an old Marine fatigue jacket. Slick characters like my professor like it if you're a killer or at least a onetime middleweight fighter. I smiled like I knew something. "Take it easy," I said, and I went back to the truck to swing around the cemetery at the top of the campus. They'd been known to screw in down-filled sleeping bags on horizontal stones up there, and the dean of students didn't want anybody dying of frostbite while joined at the hip to a matriculating fellow resident of our northeastern camp for the overindulged.

He blinked his high beams at me as I went. "You are not an unintelligent driver," I said.

Fanny had left me a bowl of something made with sausages and sauerkraut and potatoes, and the dog hadn't eaten too much more than his fair share. He watched me eat his leftovers and then make myself a king-size drink composed of sourmash whiskey and ice. In our back room, which is on the northern end of the house, and cold for sitting in that close to dawn, I sat and watched the texture of the sky change. It was going to snow, and I wanted to see the storm come up the valley. I woke up that way, sitting in the rocker with its loose right arm, holding a watery drink, and thinking right away of the girl I'd convinced to go back inside. She'd been standing outside her dormitory, looking up at a window that was dark in the midst of all those lighted panes — they never turned a light off, and often let the faucets run half the night — crying onto her bathrobe. She was barefoot in shoe-pacs, the brown ones so many of them wore unlaced, and for all I know she was naked under the robe. She was beautiful, I thought, and she was somebody's red-headed daughter, standing in a quadrangle how many miles from home and weeping.

"He doesn't love anyone," the kid told me. "He doesn't love his wife — I mean his ex-wife. And he doesn't love the ex-wife before that, or the one before that. And you know what? He doesn't love me. I don't know anyone who *does*!"

"It isn't your fault if he isn't smart enough to love you," I said, steering her toward the truck.

She stopped. She turned. "You know him?"

I couldn't help it. I hugged her hard, and she let me, and then she stepped back, and of course I let her go. "Don't you *touch* me! Is this sexual harassment? Do you know the rules? Isn't this sexual harassment?"

"I'm sorry," I said at the door to the truck. "But I think I have to be able to give you a grade before it counts as harassment."

She got in. I told her we were driving to the dean of students' house. She smelled like marijuana and something very sweet, maybe one of those coffee-with-cream liqueurs you don't buy unless you hate to drink.

As the heat of the truck struck her, she started going kind of clay-gray-green, and I reached across her to open the window.

"You touched my breast!" she said.

"It's the smallest one I've touched all night, I'm afraid."

She leaned out the window and gave her rendition of my dog.

But in my rocker, waking up, at whatever time in the morning in my silent house, I thought of her as someone's child. Which made me think of ours, of course. I went for more ice, and I started on a wet breakfast. At the door of the dean of students' house, she'd turned her chalky face to me and asked, "What grade would you give me, then?"

It was a week composed of two teachers locked out of their offices late at night, a Toyota with a flat and no spare, an attempted rape on a senior girl walking home from the library, a major fight outside a fraternity house (broken wrist and significant concussion), and variations on breaking-and-entering. I was scolded by the director of non-academic services for embracing a student who was drunk; I told him to keep his job, but he called me back because I was right to hug her, he said, and also wrong, but what the hell, and he'd promised to admonish me, and now he had, and would I please stay. I thought of the fringe benefits — graduation in only sixteen years — so I went back to work.

My professor assigned a story called "A Rose for Emily," and I wrote him a paper about the mechanics of corpse fucking, and how, since she clearly couldn't screw her dead boyfriend, she was keeping his rotten body in bed because she truly loved him. I called the paper "True Love." He gave me a B and wrote *See me, pls.* In his office after class, his feet up on his desk, he trimmed a cigar with a giant folding knife he kept in his drawer.

"You got to clean the hole out," he said, "or they don't draw."

"I don't smoke," I said.

"Bad habit. Real *habit*, though. I started smoking 'em in Georgia, in the service. My C.O. smoked 'em. We collaborated on a brothel inspection one time, and we ended up smoking these with a couple of women —" He waggled his eyebrows at me, now that his malehood was established.

"Were the women smoking them too?"

He snorted laughter through his nose while the greasy smoke came curling off his thin, dry lips. "They were pretty smoky, I'll tell ya!" Then he propped his feet — he was wearing cowboy boots that day — and he sat forward. "It's a little hard to explain. But — hell. You just don't say *fuck* when you write an essay for a college prof. Okay?" Like a scoutmaster with a kid he'd caught in the outhouse jerking off: "All right? You don't wanna do that."

"Did it shock you?"

"Fuck, no, it didn't shock me. I just told you. It violates certain proprieties."

"But if I'm writing it to you, like a letter —"

"You're writing it for posterity. For some mythical reader someplace, not just me. You're making a *statement*."

"Right. My statement said how hard it must be for a woman to fuck with a corpse."

"And a point worth making. I said so. Here."

"But you said I shouldn't say it."

"No. Listen. Just because you're talking about fucking, you don't have to say *fuck*. Does that make it any clearer?"

"No."

"I wish you'd lied to me just now," he said.

I nodded. I did too.

"Where'd you do your service?" he asked.

"Baltimore. Baltimore, Maryland."

"What's in Baltimore?"

"Railroads. I liaised on freight runs of army matériel. I killed a couple of bums on the rod with my bare hands, though."

He snorted again, but I could see how disappointed he was. He'd been banking on my having been a murderer. Interesting guy in one of my classes, he must have told some terrific woman at an overpriced meal: I just *know* the guy was a rubout specialist in the Nam, he had to have said. I figured I should come to work wearing my fatigue jacket and a red bandanna tied around my head. Say "Man" to him a couple of times, hang a fist in the air for grief and solidarity, and look terribly worn, exhausted by experiences he was fairly certain that he envied me. His dungarees were ironed, I noticed.

On Saturday we went back to the campus because Fanny wanted to see a movie called *The Seven Samurai*. I fell asleep, and I'm afraid I snored. She let me sleep until the auditorium was almost empty. Then she kissed me awake. "Who was screaming in my dream?" I asked her.

"Kurosawa," she said.

"Who?"

"Ask your professor friend."

I looked around, but he wasn't there. "Not an un-weird man," I said.

We went home and cleaned up after the dog and put him out. We drank a little Spanish brandy and went upstairs and made love. I was fairly premature, you might say, but one way and another by the time we fell asleep we were glad to be there with each other, and glad that it was Sunday coming up the valley toward us, and nobody with it. The dog was howling at another dog someplace, or at the moon, or maybe just his moon-thrown shadow on the snow. I did not strangle him when I opened the back door and he limped happily past me and stumbled up the stairs. I followed him into our bedroom and groaned for just being satisfied as I got into bed. You'll notice I didn't say fuck.

He stopped me in the hall after class on a Thursday, and asked me How's it goin, just one of the kickers drinking sour beer and eating pickled eggs and watching the tube in a country bar. How's it goin. I nodded. I wanted a grade from the man, and I did want to learn about expressing myself. I nodded and made what I thought was a smile. He'd let his mustache grow out and his hair grow longer. He was starting to wear dark shirts with lighter ties. I thought he looked like someone in *The Godfather*. He still wore those light little loafers or his high-heeled cowboy boots. His corduroy pants looked baggy. I guess he wanted them to look that way. He motioned me to the wall of the hallway, and he looked up and said, "How about the Baltimore stuff?"

I said, "Yeah?"

"Was that really true?" He was almost blinking, he wanted so much for me to be a damaged Vietnam vet just looking for a bell tower to climb into and start firing from. The college didn't have a bell tower you could get up into, though I'd once spent an ugly hour chasing a drunken ATO down from the roof of the observatory. "You were just clocking through boxcars in Baltimore?"

I said, "Nah."

"I thought so!" He gave a kind of sigh.

"I killed people," I said.

"You know, I could have sworn you did," he said.

I nodded, and he nodded back. I'd made him so happy.

The assignment was to write something to influence somebody. He called it Rhetoric and Persuasion. We read an essay by George Orwell and "A Modest Proposal" by Jonathan Swift. I liked the Orwell better, but I wasn't comfortable with it. He talked about "niggers," and I felt him saying it two ways.

I wrote "Ralph the Duck."

Once upon a time, there was a duck named Ralph who didn't have any feathers on either wing. So when the cold wind blew, Ralph said, Brr, and shivered and shook.

What's the matter? Ralph's mommy asked.

I'm *cold*, Ralph said.

Oh, the mommy said. Here. I'll keep you warm.

So she spread her big, feathery wings, and hugged Ralph tight, and when the cold wind blew, Ralph was warm and snuggly, and fell fast asleep.

The next Thursday, he was wearing canvas pants and hiking boots. He mentioned kind of casually to some of the girls in the class how whenever there was a storm he wore his Lake District walking outfit. He had a big, hairy sweater on. I kept waiting for him to make a noise like a mountain goat. But the girls seemed to like it. His boots made a creaky squeak on the linoleum of the hall when he caught up with me after class.

"As I told you," he said, "it isn't unappealing. It's just — not a college theme."

"Right," I said. "Okay. You want me to do it over?"

"No," he said. "Not at all. The D will remain your grade. But I'll read something else if you want to write it."

"This'll be fine," I said.

"Did you understand the assignment?"

"Write something to influence someone — Rhetoric and Persuasion."

We were at his office door and the redheaded kid who had gotten sick in my truck was waiting for him. She looked at me like one of us was in the wrong place, which struck me as accurate enough. He was interested in getting into his office with the redhead, but he remembered to turn around and flash me a grin he seemed to think he was known for.

Instead of going on shift a few hours after class, the way I'm supposed to, I told my supervisor I was sick, and I went home. Fanny was frightened when I came in, because I don't get sick and I don't miss work. She looked at my face and she grew sad. I kissed her hello and went upstairs to change. I always used to change my clothes when I was a kid, as soon as I came home from school. I put on jeans and a flannel shirt and thick wool socks, and I made myself a dark drink of sourmash. Fanny poured herself some wine and came into the cold northern room a few minutes later. I was sitting in the rocker, looking over the valley. The wind was lining up a lot of rows of cloud so that the sky looked like a baked trout when you lift the skin off. "It'll snow," I said to her.

She sat on the old sofa and waited. After a while, she said, "I wonder why they always call it a mackerel sky?"

"Good eating, mackerel," I said.

Fanny said, "Shit! You're never that laconic unless you feel crazy. What's wrong? Who'd you punch out at the playground?"

"We had to write a composition," I said.

"Did he like it?"

"He gave me a D."

"Well, you're familiar enough with D's. I never saw you get this low over a grade."

"I wrote about Ralph the Duck."

She said, "You did?" She said, "Honey." She came over and stood beside the rocker and leaned into me and hugged my head and neck. "Honey," she said. "Honey."

It was the worst of the winter's storms, and one of the worst in years. That afternoon they closed the college, which they almost never do. But the roads were jammed with snow over ice, and now it was freezing rain on top of that, and the only people working at the school that night were the operator who took emergency calls and me. Everyone else had gone home except the students, and most of them were inside. The ones who weren't were drunk, and I kept on sending them in and telling them to act like grown-ups. A number of them said they were, and I really couldn't argue. I had the bright beams on, the defroster set high, the little blue light winking, and a thermos of sourmash and hot coffee that I sipped from every time I had to get out of the truck or every time I realized how cold all that wetness was out there.

About eight o'clock, as the rain was turning back to snow and the cold was worse, the roads impossible, just as I was done helping a county sander on the edge of the campus pull a panel truck out of a snowbank, I got the emergency call from the college operator. We had a student missing. The roommates thought the kid was headed for the quarry. This meant I had to get the Bronco up on a narrow road above the campus, above the old cemetery, into all kinds of woods and rough track that I figured would be choked with ice and snow. Any kid up there would really have to want to be there, and I couldn't go in on foot, because you'd only want to be there on account of drugs, booze, or craziness, and either way I'd be needing blankets and heat, and then a fast ride down to the hospital in town. So I dropped into four-wheel drive to get me up the hill above the campus, bucking snow and sliding on ice, putting all the heater's warmth up onto the windshield because I couldn't see much more than swarming snow. My feet were still cold from the tow job, and it didn't seem to matter that I had on heavy socks and insulated boots I'd coated with waterproofing. I shivered, and I thought of Ralph the Duck.

I had to grind the rest of the way, from the cemetery, in four-wheel low, and in spite of the cold I was smoking my gearbox by the time I was close enough to the quarry — they really did take a lot of the rocks for the campus buildings from there — to see I'd have to make my way on foot to where she was. It was a kind of hollowed-out shape, maybe four or five stories high, where she stood — well, wobbled is more like it. She was as chalky as she'd been the last time, and her red hair didn't catch the light anymore. It just lay on her like something that had died on top of her head. She was in a white nightgown that was plastered to her body. She had her arms crossed as if she wanted to be warm. She swayed, kind of, in front of the big, dark, scooped-out rock face, where the trees and brush had been cleared for trucks and earthmovers. She looked tiny against all the darkness. From where I stood, I could see the snow driving down in front of the lights I'd left on, but I couldn't see it near her. All it looked like around her was dark. She was shaking with the cold, and she was crying.

I had a blanket with me, and I shoved it down the front of my coat to keep it dry for her, and because I was so cold. I waved. I stood in the lights and I waved. I don't know what she saw — a big shadow, maybe. I surely didn't reassure her, because when she saw me she backed up, until she was near the face of the quarry. She couldn't go any farther.

I called, "Hello! I brought a blanket. Are you cold? I thought you might want a blanket."

Her roommates had told the operator about pills, so I didn't bring her the coffee laced with mash. I figured I didn't have all that much time, anyway, to get her down and pumped out. The booze with whatever pills she'd taken would make her die that much faster.

I hated that word. Die. It made me furious with her. I heard myself seething when I breathed. I pulled my scarf and collar up above my mouth. I didn't want her to see how close I might come to wanting to kill her because she wanted to die.

I called, "Remember me?"

I was closer now. I could see the purple mottling of her skin. I didn't know if it was cold or dying. It probably didn't matter much to distinguish between them right now, I thought. That made me smile. I felt the smile, and I pulled the scarf down so she could look at it. She didn't seem awfully reassured.

"You're the sexual harassment guy," she said. She said it very slowly. Her lips were clumsy. It was like looking at a ventriloquist's dummy.

"I gave you an A," I said.

"When?"

"It's a joke," I said. "You don't want me making jokes. You want me to give you a nice warm blanket, though. And then you want me to take you home."

She leaned against the rock face when I approached. I pulled the blanket out, then zipped my jacket back up. The snow had stopped, I realized, and that wasn't really a very good sign. It felt like an arctic cold descending in its place. I held the blanket out to her, but she only looked at it.

"You'll just have to turn me in," I said. "I'm gonna hug you again."

She screamed, "No more! I don't want any more hugs!"

But she kept her arms on her chest, and I wrapped the blanket around her and stuffed a piece into each of her tight, small fists. I didn't know what to do for her feet. Finally, I got down on my haunches in front of her. She crouched down too, protecting herself.

"No," I said. "No. You're fine."

I took off the woolen mittens I'd been wearing. Mittens keep you warmer than gloves because they trap your hand's heat around the fingers and palms at once. Fanny had knitted them for me. I put a mitten as far onto each of her feet as I could. She let me. She was going to collapse, I thought.

"Now, let's go home," I said. "Let's get you better."

With her funny, stiff lips, she said, "I've been very self-indulgent and weird and I'm sorry. But I'd really like to die." She sounded so reasonable that I found myself nodding in agreement as she spoke.

"You can't just die," I said.

"Aren't I dying already? I took all of them, and then" — she giggled like a child, which of course is what she was — "I borrowed different ones from other people's rooms. See, this isn't some teenage cry for like *help*. Understand? I'm seriously interested in death and I have to stay out here a little longer and fall asleep. All right?"

"You can't do that," I said. "You ever hear of Vietnam?"

"I saw that movie," she said. "With the opera in it? *Apocalypse*? Whatever."

"I was there!" I said. "I killed people! I helped to kill them! And when they die, you see their bones later on. You dream about their bones and blood on the ends of the splintered ones, and this kind of mucous stuff coming out of their eyes. You probably heard of guys having dreams like that, didn't you? Whacked-out Vietnam vets? That's me, see? So I'm telling you, I know about dead people and their eyeballs and everything falling out. And people keep dreaming about the dead people they knew, see? You can't make people dream about you that like that! It isn't fair!"

"You dream about me?" She was ready to go. She was ready to fall down, and I was going to lift her up and get her to the truck.

"I will," I said. "If you die."

"I want you to," she said. Her lips were hardly moving now. Her eyes were closed. "I want you all to."

I dropped my shoulder and put it into her waist and picked her up and carried her down to the Bronco. She was talking, but not a lot, and her voice leaked down my back. I jammed her into the truck and wrapped the blanket around her better and then put another one down around her feet. I strapped her in with the seat belt. She was shaking, and her eyes were closed and her mouth open. She was breathing. I checked that twice, once when I strapped her in, and then again when I strapped myself in and backed up hard into a sapling and took it down. I got us into first gear, held the clutch in, leaned over to listen for breathing, heard it — shallow panting, like a kid asleep on your lap for a nap — and then I put the gear in and howled down the hillside on what I thought might be the road.

We passed the cemetery. I told her that was a good sign. She didn't respond. I found myself panting too, as if we were breathing for each other. It made me dizzy, but I couldn't stop. We passed the highest dorm, and I dropped the truck into four-wheel high. The cab smelled like burnt oil and hot metal. We were past the chapel now, and the observatory, the president's house, then the bookstore. I had the blue light winking and the V-6 roaring, and I drove on the edge of out-of-control, sensing the skids just before I slid into them, and getting back out of them as I needed to. I took a little fender off once, and a bit of the corner of a classroom building, but I worked us back on course, and all I needed to do now was negotiate the sharp left turn around the Administration Building past the library, then floor it for the straight run to the town's main street and then the hospital.

I was panting into the mike, and the operator kept saying, "Say again?"

I made myself slow down some, and I said we'd need stomach pumping, and to get the names of the pills from her friends in the dorm, and I'd be there in less than five or we were crumpled up someplace and dead.

"Roger," the radio said. "Roger all that." My throat tightened and tears came into my eyes. They were helping us, they'd told me: Roger.

I said to the girl, whose head was slumped and whose face looked too blue all through its whiteness, "You know, I had a girl once. My wife, Fanny. She and I had a small girl one time."

I reached over and touched her cheek. It was cold. The truck swerved, and I got my hands on the wheel. I'd made the turn past the Ad Building using just my left. "I can do it in the dark," I sang to no tune I'd ever learned. "I can do it with one hand." I said to her, "We had a girl child, very small. Now, I do *not* want you dying."

I came to the campus gates doing fifty on the ice and snow, smoking the engine, grinding the clutch, and I bounced off a wrought iron fence to give me the curve going left that I needed. On a pool table, it would have been a bank shot worth applause. The town cop picked me up and got out ahead of me. He used his growler and siren and horn alternately, and I leaned on the horn. We banged up to the emergency room entrance and I was out and at the other door before the cop on duty, Elmo St. John, could loosen his seat belt. I loosened hers, and I carried her into the lobby of the ER. They had a gurney, and doctors, and they took her away from me. I tried to talk to them, but they made me sit down and do my shaking on a dirty sofa decorated with drawings of little spinning wheels. Somebody brought me hot coffee, I think it was Elmo, but I couldn't hold it.

"They won't," he kept saying to me. "They won't."

"What?"

"You just been sitting there for a minute and a half like St. Vitus dancing, telling me, 'Don't let her die. Don't let her die.' "

"Oh."

"You all *right*?"

"How about the kid?"

"They'll tell us soon."

"She better be all right."

"That's right."

"She — somebody's gonna have to tell me plenty if she isn't."

"That's right."

"She better not die this time," I guess I said.

Fanny came downstairs to look for me. I was at the northern windows, looking through the mullions down the valley to the faint red line along the mounds and little peaks of the ridge beyond the valley. The sun was going to come up, and I was looking for it.

Fanny stood behind me. I could hear her. I could smell her hair and the sleep on her. The crimson line widened, and I squinted at it. I heard the dog limp in behind her, catching up. He panted and I knew why his panting sounded familiar. She put her hands on my shoulders and arms. I made muscles to impress her with, and then I let them go, and let my head drop down until my chin was on my chest.

"I didn't think you'd be able to sleep after that," Fanny said.

"I brought enough adrenaline home to run a football team."

"But you hate being a hero, huh? You're hiding in here because somebody's going to call, or come over, and want to talk to you — her parents for shooting sure, sooner or later. Or is that supposed to be part of the service up at the playground? Saving their suicidal daughters. Almost dying to find them in the woods and driving too fast for *any* weather, much less what we had last night. Getting their babies home. The bastards." She was crying. I knew she would be, sooner or later. I could hear the soft sound of her lashes. She sniffed and I could feel her arm move as she felt for the tissues on the coffee table.

"I have them over here," I said. "On the windowsill."

"Yes." She blew her nose, and the dog thumped his tail. He seemed to think it one of Fanny's finer tricks, and he had wagged for her for thirteen years whenever she'd done it. "Well, you're going to have to talk to them."

"I will," I said. "I will." The sun was in our sky now, climbing. We had built the room so we could watch it climb. "I think that jackass with the smile, my prof? She showed up a lot at his office, the last few weeks. He called her 'my advisee,' you know? The way those guys sound about what they're achieving by getting up and shaving and going to work and saying the same thing every day? Every year? Well, she was his advisee, I bet. He was shoving home the old advice."

"She'll be okay," Fanny said. "Her parents will take her home and love her up and get her some help." She began to cry again, then she stopped. She blew her nose, and the dog's tail thumped. She kept a hand between my shoulder and my neck. "So tell me what you'll tell a waiting world. How'd you talk her out?"

"Well, I didn't, really. I got up close and picked her up and carried her is all."

"You didn't say *anything*?"

"Sure I did. Kid's standing in the snow outside of a lot of pills, you're gonna say something."

"So what'd you *say*?"

"I told her stories," I said. "I did Rhetoric and Persuasion."

Fanny said, "Then you go in early on Thursday, you go in half an hour early, and you get that guy to jack up your grade."

Dog Song

I

HE ALWAYS THOUGHT of the dogs as the worst. The vet's belly
heaved above his jeans, and he cursed in words of one syllable every
time a deputy tugged a dog to the hypodermic, or trotted to keep up as
a different one strained on its chain for its fate, or when a dog stopped
moving and went stiff, splayed, and then became a loose furry bag with
bones inside. The deputies and the vet and the judge, who also did his
part — he watched without moving — did it twenty-six times, in the
yard behind the sheriff's offices. The air stank of dirty fur and feces as
though they were all locked in. The yelping and whining went on.
When they were through, one deputy was weeping, and the vet's red
flannel shirt was wet with sweat from his breastbone to his belt. The
deputies threw the dogs into the back of a van.

They might be dangerous, Snuyder had decided. They might have
been somehow perverted, trained to break some basic rules of how to
live with men. So they had died. And Snuyder, doing his part, had
watched them until the last lean mutt, shivering and funny-eyed, was
dead. He thought, when he thought of the dogs, that their lips and tails
and even their postures had signaled their devotion to the vet or to one
of the deputies; they'd been waiting for a chance to give their love. And
as the deputies flung them, the dogs' tongues protruded and sometimes
flopped. When their bodies flew, they looked ardent.

The dogs in the yellow trailer had drawn the attention of the people in the white trailer across the unpaved rural road: their howling, their yapping, the whining that sometimes went on and on and on. Lloyd and Pris, the man and wife in the trailer with the dogs, came and went at curious hours, and that too attracted the attention of the neighbors, who had their own problems, but somehow found time — being good country Christians, they *made* time — to study the erratic behavior and possible social pathology of the couple in the bright yellow trailer edged in white, propped on cinder blocks, bolstered against upstate winters by haybales pushed between the plastic floor and the icy mud. The neighbors, one working as a janitress, the other as a part-time van driver for the county's geriatric ferrying service, finally called the sheriff when there was a February thaw, and the mud all of a sudden looked awfully like manure, and an odor came up from the yellow trailer that, according to the janitress (a woman named Ivy), was too much like things long dead to be ignored by a citizen of conscience.

But only one of the dogs was dead, and it died after the deputies had kicked the door in, and after it had attacked and had been shot. It died defending a mobile home that was alive with excrement and garbage. Turds lay on the beds and on the higher surfaces, counter and sink. Madness crawled the walls. Lloyd, the husband, had written with dung his imprecations of a county and state and nation that established laws involving human intercourse with beasts. Twenty-six dogs were impounded, and the couple was heavily fined by the judge.

The awful part, of course, had been the dogs' dull eyes and duller coats, their stink, their eagerness to please, and then their fear, and then the way they had died. Later he decided that the nurse with her hair that was thinning and her arms puffed out around the short tight sleeves of her hissing uniform was the worst part so far. The first sight Richard Snuyder had seen, when he fell awake like a baby rolling from its crib, had been a man on crutches at his door, peering. The man had sucked on an unlit filter cigarette, adjusted his armpits on the crutches, and said, "I heard you did one *jam*-jar of a job. Just thought I'd say so. I was raised to express my appreciation of the passing joys."

Snuyder, hours later, had thought that the man on crutches, apparently a connoisseur of catastrophe, was the worst. He wasn't. The worst became the orderly who brought in a plate of mashed potatoes and open hot roast-beef sandwich in glutinous gravy, who was chased by the nurse who brought the doctor, whose odor of dark, aged sweat and stale clothing did little to dispel that of the roast beef, which lingered in the room as if the pale orderly had hurled it on the walls to punish Snuyder for being on a liquid diet.

The doctor, who had mumbled and left, Snuyder thought for a while, was really the worst part of it: his dandruff, his caustic smell, his dirty knuckles that gave the lie to the large scraped moons of fingernail above the tortured cuticles. This is the worst, Snuyder had thought, though not for long.

Because then the candy striper with her twitchy walk and bored pout had stood at his door, a clipboard in her hand and an idle finger at her ear, though carefully never in it, and had looked at him as though he weren't open-eyed, blinking, panting with pain, clearly stunned and afraid and as lost while being still as dogs are that stand at the side of the road, about to be killed because they don't know what else they should do.

After the candy striper had left, the balding nurse with great arms, and no need for such forms of address as language spoken or mimed, came in to adjust something at his head and something at his leg. His neck didn't roll, so he couldn't follow her movement except with his eyes, which began to ache and then stream. Looking at his legs, she wiped his eyes and took the tissue away. He was about to ask her questions but couldn't think of anything that didn't embarrassingly begin with *Where* or *How*.

He tried to move his legs. That was next, as soon as the nurse left. He worked at wiggling his toes and each foot and each leg. They moved, though they were restrained by something, and he called aloud — it was a relief, during the cry, to hear his own voice and to know that he knew it — because the right leg was pure pain, undifferentiated, and the left, though more flexible, hurt only a little less. His legs, and the stiffness at the neck, his aching eyes and head, a burning on the skin of his face, the waking to no memory of how he had come there, or why, or when, or in what state: *he* was the worst so far. He suspected that little would happen to challenge this triumph. He'd been born someplace, of an unknown event, and every aspect of his arrival on this naked day could be measured against the uncomforting hypothesis that, among the local discomforts he knew, he himself was the worst.

His legs could not be moved, he could not be persuaded to move them again, and he lay with all his attention on his torso, thinking *I will be just chest and balls, I will not be legs or ankles or toes.* He panicked and felt for his legs, then moved an ankle — he yelped — in response to his fear: he did have his legs, and they would move at his command, he wasn't only a chest. *And balls?* He groaned his fear, and groaned for the pain in his legs, and then he groaned with deep contentment: he had found them under his hospital gown, both of them, and everything else, including the dreadful catheter. So all he needed to know now was when he would stop hurting over most of his body, and why and how he was here. *All right. First things first. You have legs, your balls are where you left them, and a little panic is worth a handful of testes during times of trial.*

I have not gone berserk with worry for my wife, he thought.

Do I have a wife?

How do I know my name, if I don't know whether I'm married? How did I know about balls? Are you born with a full knowledge of the scrotum? So that even during amnesia, you still —

I don't want *amnesia.*

I don't want *to be a pendulum in a ward, swinging on crutches and sucking on cold cigarettes and laughing at people forever and never* remembering.

What about my kids, if I do have kids?

The same nurse, with thin dark hair and wide white arms, was at the head of his bed, looking into his eyes this time as she wiped them. She had the voice of a twelve-year-old girl, and the teeth of someone long dead. She said, "Mr. Snuyder? Do you remember you're Mr. Snuyder?"

He tried to nod. The pain made him hiss.

"We'll give you something for pain after we X-ray your head again. But could you tell me if you know your name?"

"Thank you," he said.

"Yes. And your name?"

"Woke up knowing it was Snuyder."

"Good *boy*!"

"Woke up. Found out I had my scrotum, and I never knew if I had any children or a *wife*." He was crying. He hated it.

"You'll remember," she said. "You'll probably remember. You did take out a telephone pole and a good I say at least half of a Great American Markets rig. Worcestershire sauce and mustard and beerwurst smeared over two lanes for a quarter of a mile. If you don't mind glass, you could make a hell of a sandwich out there, they said."

"Kill anybody? Did I kill anybody?"

"Not unless *you* die on us. The truck was parked. Trucker was — how do you want me to put it? — banging the lady of the house? You must of pulled a stupendous skid. The troopers'll be by to talk about it."

"Did you look in my wallet?"

"Doctor'll be by too. I'm off duty now."

"You don't want to tell me about my family? There wasn't anybody with me, was there?"

"You're supposed to remember on your own. There wasn't anybody killed. You take care now."

"Won't dance with anyone else."

"Good boy."

"Wait," he said. "Wait a minute." He winced. He lay back. He heard himself breathe.

She said, "That's right. You lie down and be good. Good boy."

He woke again, with a thump, waiting for the nurse to speak. He saw that she was gone, the room dark, the door closed. He couldn't remember waking, ever before in his life, so abruptly, and with so much pain. And that wasn't all he couldn't remember. He thought *baby, baby, baby* to himself, as if in a rapture, and he tried to think of a lover or wife. Was he divorced? What about kids? He thought a gentler *baby* and looked within his closed eyes for children. He thought of maps — blank. He thought of cars and couldn't see the one he'd driven. He remembered that the nurse had evaded the question of who had been with him. But at least she wasn't dead.

And how had he known that his passenger was a woman? And how could he know he was right?

He was tired of questions and tired of hurting. He remembered, then, how they had rolled him through the halls for a CAT scan and how, when he'd been rolled back, they had looked at him like magic people who could make him fall asleep, and he had fallen. He wanted more magic. He wanted to sleep some more and wake again and know one thing more. A woman in the car with him. Should she have been with him in the car? Should she have come with him to this room?

And he woke again, one more question not answered, to see a light that sliced at his eyeballs and to hear a general commotion that suggested daytime and what he had doubtless once referred to as everyday life. The door opened in, and Hilary was inside with him, and through dry lips he said, "I *remember* you!"

She said, "Can you see how little I'm cheered by that?"

No: she started to; he finished her statement in his mind, fed by memory, and he smiled so triumphantly, his face hurt. In fact, Hilary said, "Can you see —"

And he said, "Hilary. Hil."

She shook her head as if winged insects were at her, and then she wept into her wide, strong hands, walking slowly toward him, a child at a hiding game. But she was not a child and there were no children — not here, anyway, because the boys were at school, of course, and he and Hilary, Richard and Hilary Snuyder, were alone, they were each forty-seven years old, and they were working at being alone together while Warren and Hank went to school in other states. The states were *other* because this one was New York. Hilary was tall, and she wore her pea jacket, so it must be autumn, and her upper lip came down on the lower one as if she wanted to make love. Richard did, then, and his hand went down to grip himself in celebration where it had earlier prodded for loss. "Hilary," he said. The catheter guarded his loins, and his hand retreated.

She wiped at her eyes and sat on the chair beside the bed.

"Come sit on the bed," he said.

She sat back. She crossed her legs and he looked with a sideways glance to see her jeans and Wallabees. His eyes stung, so he looked up.

He sniffed, expecting to smell perfume or soap. He smelled only gravy and the finger-chewing doctor. And Hilary said, "How could you decide on — going away like that?" She said, "How could you *do* that? No matter what?"

"Hil, I'm having a hell of a time remembering things. I didn't remember *you* until you came in, the boys and you and — would you tell me stuff? You know, to kind of wake me up some more? I don't remember going anyplace. They said I smacked the car up."

Hilary stood, and something on her sweet, pale face made him move. The motion made him whimper, and she smiled with genuine pleasure. Her long hand, suspended above him, was trembling. He felt her anger. His penis burned. He closed his eyes but opened them at once. He was afraid of her hand descending to seize him as if in love or recollected lust, but then to squeeze, to crush the catheter and leave him coughing up his pain and bleeding up into the blanket. He saw her playing the piano with strong bloody hands, leaving a trail of blood on the keys.

She said, "I have to go outside until I calm down. I'll go outside and then I'll be back. Because unlike you I do *not* run out on the people I love. Loved. But I'll leave you a clue. You want to remember things? You want a little trail of bread crumbs you can follow back into your life? How about this, Richard: you drove your fucking car as hard as you could into a telephone pole so you could die. Is that a little crust of some usefulness? So you could leave me forever on purpose. Have I helped?"

The awful doctor came back again, adding the insult of his breath to the injury of his armpits. He was thick, with a drooping heavy chest and shoulders that came down at a very sharp angle, so that his thick neck looked long. His fingers were large, and the knuckles looked dirtier now — this morning, tonight, whenever it was that the doctor stood at the bed, telling Richard where the orthopedic surgeon was going to insert pins of assorted sizes and alloys into the hip and femur, which the instrument panel had cracked in an interesting way. The neck was all right. The back was all right. The head seemed all right, though you never can tell with the brain. A little rancid laugh, a flicker of motion across the big jowls and their five o'clock shadow. And the ribs, of course, although CAT pictures showed no danger to the lungs. "You'll be bound."

"I'm a judge," Snuyder said.

"Good man."

"I'm a district judge with a house in the suburbs and a wife and two kids and two cars. Three cars. We have an old Volvo my son Hank fixed up. A '67 Volvo. It runs pretty well, but it's rusted out. Bound over — you say that when —"

"Yes, you're a judge. Good man. I was talking about a restraint for the ribs, is all. Two ribs. You're lucky."

"Of course, I'm lucky. And I didn't aim to hit some telephone pole."

"You remember what happened?"

"No. But I wouldn't have. People with a — people like me don't *do* that."

The doctor looked bitter and weary. "No," he said. "I can call the rescue squad, if you like, and ask them to take you back and drop you off at your car. I'd have to call the garage and tell them that it isn't telescoped. Totaled. All but small enough to use for a Matchbox toy if the grandchildren come over. Of course, you'll probably benefit by using less gas in it from now on."

Richard blushed. He couldn't shut up, though. He said, "I meant suicide."

"I know."

"I meant people like me don't *do* that."

"You want anything for pain?"

"No."

"Don't be stubborn, Your Honor. A petulant patient is still a patient in pain. Can be. Call the nurse if you hurt. I'll leave orders in case you do. I'll see you before they sedate you. It might be soon, but I think they'll wait until tomorrow, or late this afternoon. We're crowded. Sick people, you know."

"Unlike me."

The doctor let his face say that he was ignoring Richard's childishness. And Richard felt an overwhelming need to cry.

"So if you're so crowded, how come you put me in a private room. Why don't you keep a suicide watch on me? Who *says* it's suicide?"

"First of all, we didn't. Second of all: two kids in a car, one pedestrian walking her dogs, the cop who was chasing you for DWI and reckless endangerment and all the other violations you probably pronounce on people at your place of work. I'm going. We aren't having much of a doctor–patient relationship right now."

And when he left, Richard lay back, breathless with rage. He panted with hatred for his wife and his doctor, the nurse, the orderly, the hospital, the cops behind him during the chase, and the fact that he had not slowed down when they came into his mirror, no siren on but a band of white and red light that made him blink before — he suddenly could see himself — he crouched over the wheel and then leaned back, pushing his arms straight, locked at the elbows, jamming the accelerator down until the bellow of the engine and wind and, then, the siren of the following police, were almost as loud as the howl that he howled and that he kept on howling until the impact shut him, and everything else, up.

He heard his breath shudder now, in the salmon-colored room, mostly shadows and walnut veneers. Then he heard a man say, "You wanna nurse?"

"Who?"

"It's me. You can't turn, huh? Listen, Your Honor, it's such a pain in the ass as well as the armpit, the crutches, I'm gonna stay flat for a while. I'll visit you later on, you can look at me and remember. I'm the guy said hello the other time."

"You're in here with me?"

"Yeah. Ain't it an insult? You a judge and everything. Like the doctor said, it's real crowded."

"This is *too* crowded."

"Well, listen, don't go extending any special treatment to me, Your Honor. Just pretend I'm a piece of dog shit. You'll feel better if you don't strain for the little courtesies and all. Your wife's a very attractive woman, if I may say so. Hell of a temper, though."

Richard rang for the nurse.

His roommate said, "All that pain. Dear, dear. Listen, remember this when you wake up. My name's Manwarren. Emanuel Manwarren. Manny Manwarren. It's an honor to be with a Your Honor kind of deal." Then, to the entering nurse: "His Honor is in discomfort."

Richard lay with his eyes closed until the nurse returned with water and a large capsule. He looked at her. She was young and intelligent-looking, and very tired. He said, "How shall I take this medicine without drowning? I can't sit up."

She said, "He ordered it by spansule." Her voice was flat. She was expecting a fight.

"He would," Richard said. "What if I die taking medicine?" He heard himself: he sounded worried about dying.

"Don't fret," she said. "I'll telephone for an order change, and I'll bring you a shot."

"You're a charmer, Your Honor," Manwarren said.

"Are we going to engage in class warfare, or whatever this is, for all the time we're in here, Mr. Manwarren?"

"Call me Manny. Nah. I'm a prickly personality. I hate the cops, authority figures like that, judges — you know what I mean?"

"Manny, why don't you think of me as a miscreant and not a judge."

"Can I call you Dick?"

Richard closed his eyes and listened to his breathing and the rustle of Manwarren's sheets. The pain was in Richard's bones and in his breath. He said, "There *was* someone with me, wasn't there?"

"Dick, in cases like this, there usually is."

II

They lived in a renovated carriage house at the edge of a small country road outside Utica. Simple country living at a condominium price, Hilary liked to say. They couldn't quite afford the mortgage, college tuitions, cars, the McIntosh stereo rig — Snuyder felt like a pilot when he turned the power on — or the carpets from Iran or Iraq or India, he forgot which, that Hilary had lately come to buy as investments. He thought of them as insulation.

Looking at his lighted house at 1:25 in the morning, observing a close, clear disk of moon, a sky bluer than black, and veined with cloud — it was a dark marble mural more than sky — Richard said, "We get by."

Hilary was in the living room, at the piano. She was playing little clear crystal sounds with occasional speeded-up patterns of dissonance. He watched the tall, pale woman at the piano, her body rigid, neck tense, all pleasure residing below her moving wrists.

"Hello," Snuyder said softly, removing his jacket and then his tie, dumping them on the sofa. "I was working with the clerks on a case. It's a terrible case. Then we went out for some drinks."

The repetitions in the music came in miniature parts and were very simple. There was a name for that. He was unbuttoning his shirt and he had it off by the time she sensed him and stopped and turned on the piano bench to see him wiping the sweat on his chest with the wadded shirt.

"Ugh," she said, covering her eyes with her big hands.

"How."

"Richard, stop. It's ugly."

"It's a sweaty night," he said. He went for his welcoming kiss. She hugged his waist and kissed his belly.

"Yummy," he said.

"Salty," she said. "Phoo." But she held him, and he stayed there. "Vhere vas you so late?"

"I told you — clerks? case? Just now?"

Richard carried his guilt and his dirty shirt toward the shower and Hilary followed. She stood in the doorway as he slid the cloudy shower door closed and made a screen of water that sealed him away. He groaned and blubbered and shook his head and shoulders and, loosening at last, dopey with comfort, shed of the sweat and oils and inner fluids of somebody else, he heard only part of what Hilary had said.

He called, "What?"

He turned the water off, and her words came over the stall. "I said you sounded especially like a whale tonight."

"Thank you. You did not. The Satie was beautiful."

"Thank *you*. It was Villa-Lobos, a *Chôros*. I don't think it's possible to confuse the two unless you've got me at the piano, the Snuyder Variations, eh?"

"Hilary."

"Sorry. Sorry."

"A number of other performers also dislike playing to a live audience. Glenn Gould, I remind you, for the one-millionth time, stopped playing concerts altogether. He was not, I think you'll agree, a shabby tickler of the ivories."

"Can you see how *little* I'm cheered by that? I'm sorry Gould is dead. I wish he'd been comfortable at concerts. But he made *recordings*, Richard. He made wonderful recordings."

"And you will too. It'll happen." He made his voice sound matter-of-fact, sincerely casual, casually sincere. But he knew how impatient he must sound to her.

He had intended to leap from the shower, dangle his body before her, and roll her into bed — and pray for performance this third time tonight. But when he came out, tail wagging and his smile between his teeth like a fetched stick, she was gone, his stomach was fluttering with premonitions, and he was very, very tired. He decided to settle for a glass of beer and some sleep. Hilary was in the kitchen when, wearing his towel, he walked in. She was peeling plastic wrap from a sandwich, and she had already poured him a beer. "You always want beer after a day like this. At least I can make the meals."

Richard drank some beer and said, "Thank you. You're very kind, though sullen and self-pitying."

"But I make a fine Genoa salami sandwich. And I look nice in shorts."

She was crying at the sink, turning the instant boiling-water tap on and off, on and off. The mascara ran black down her face. She looked like a clown. He realized that she'd made herself up for him — when? midnight? afterward? — and had worn the face she had made for him to see. He visualized himself, proud as a strapping big boy, stepping from the shower to greet her.

He finished chewing salami and dark bread. He said, "I hate to see you so damned unhappy."

She turned the boiling water on and off, and steam fogged the kitchen window. "So you make me cry to express your dismay with my sorrow?"

"Actually, I wasn't aware that I was making you cry."

"You're such a slob, Richard."

"But well-spoken, and attractive in a towel."

"You aren't unattractive," she said. "But you're so tired, you could never make love. Could you?"

Richard sighed with fear and satisfaction as he drank his beer. "We can do some middle-class perversions if you like. Many were developed for the tired husband after work, I understand. We can —" He had by now stood and moved to her, was moving against her as they leaned at the sink. "We can do a number of exotic tricks they practice in the movies that the D.A. confiscates."

Hilary's eyes were closed. She was unfastening his towel. Her upper lip was clamped over the lower one; and he watched it when it moved. "Movie perversions?" she said. "Where would you pick up movie perversions?"

"You know those evidentiary sessions I sometimes hold? We all sit around and watch dirty flicks."

She said, "Pig."

His skin had been cool and hers hot. His body, had it been a creature with a mouth, no more, would have sung. But it was very tired, and it was crowded with his mind. He thought, now, here, in his hospital room, not about — *damn* it — whoever he had been with in a motel room in Westmoreland, New York, before he wrecked his car. He could remember that — the room, the bedspread's color, the light lavender cotton skirt on the floor, and not her face. He couldn't see her *face*.

Richard, in their house, in his memory now, had taken off his wife's clothing and had wooed her away from what was sorrowful and true. He'd loved her in their kitchen to the exclusion of everything, for a very little while. And now, in the hospital room, he couldn't see or say the name of the woman he had loved more than Hilary and whom he had washed from his body to preserve her to himself. Naked of clothes and towel and her, they had lain in a nest of Hilary's underwear and blouse and dark Bermuda shorts — skins so easily shed. And Hilary had been watching him. He'd seen her eyes rimmed with black and filling with darkness. She had figured him out, he knew. He had wondered when she would tell him. In his hospital room, he remembered hoping that she would find a way to make it hurt.

III

It took Lloyd and Pris nearly a month to arm themselves and gather their courage and rage. Then they came, through the main doors of the county office building, and past the glass information booth — "Can I help you?" the woman in beige had said to the profiles of their passing shotguns — and down one flight to the basement offices. They thought the dogs would be in the basement, Lloyd later said. "I couldn't figure on anybody keeping animals upstairs where the fancy offices was bound to be." They took eleven people hostage, including a woman who cried so long and loudly that Lloyd — "She sounded like one of the goddamned *dogs*" — hit her with the pump-gun barrel. She breathed quietly and shallowly for the rest of their visit and was hospitalized for a week. The police at first remained outside and were content to bellow over battery-powered hailers. "*I* couldn't understand 'em," Lloyd said. "It sounded like some goddamned cheerleaders on a Friday night over to the high school game. Except Pris and me wouldn't play ball."

They passed out a note that said, "26 PRIVAT STOCK CRETURS PLUS FREEDOME OF CHOICE PLUS $10,000." The money was for Pris's sex-change operation, Lloyd said in his deposition. They wanted to be legally married and live as man and wife. Pris was tired of costumes and wanted *outfits*. The police got bored and flushed them out with tear gas, then beat them badly before the arraignment. Lloyd later said, "I don't think the operation would of made that much difference, to tell you the truth. Pris, he didn't — she — whatever the hell he is. *It*. I don't think he loved me the way you want somebody to love you." Lloyd was starving himself in the county jail. Pris was defended from rape by an insurance swindler out of Fairfax, Virginia, and their prison affair was two weeks old and going strong.

And Hilary had not come back. Manwarren had paid for a television set while Snuyder had slept the sleep of the sedated, and Snuyder now lay looking at the dimpled ceiling panels, clenching his fists against the pain, and listening without wishing to. Game-show hosts with voices as sweet and insistent as the taste of grape soda cried out with delight and mortification as army sergeants and homemakers and stockbrokers selected numbers and boxes and squares marked off on walls and were awarded either bounty or a consolation prize consisting of a lifetime supply of scuff-resistant, polymer-bound linoleum clean-'n'-polisher for the busy woman who has more to do than wax, for sweet goodness' sake, her floors. Manwarren also watched soap operas that had to do with misplaced babies and frantic adulterers, always on the verge of discovery as incestuous. There were snippets of old movie, fragments of cartoon, crashingly educational disquisitions on the use of C — "C, you *see*, is also in *ka*-ristmas ta*ree!*" — and Gilligan, eternally trapped on his island with Tina Louise and constitutionally incapable of hurling himself upon her, continued to invent ways of extending his imprisonment.

Manwarren, a real critic, commented with alert smugness and an eye for the obvious. "You believe she couldn't remember who invented *noodles?*" he sang. He crowed, "Numbers are from the friggin' Arabs, dummy! No wonder he's a garbageman." Snuyder kept waiting to hear the suck-and-pour of passing traffic on the arterial highway leading into downtown Utica, but all he heard was Manwarren and the objects of his derision. "Hey," he said, "hey, Judge. You handle yourself like this 'Family Court' guy? He takes *no* crap offa nobody, you know? He's got a courtroom fulla morons, by the way. No wonder they ended up in court. They wouldn't know how to cross the *street*." A "M*A*S*H" rerun drove Manwarren into silent sniffles, but he covered well by saying, in a gravelly voice, "I don't think that's a very realistic way to talk about the Korean conflict." Of "Robin Hood," he said, for the first time approving in tone, "I never knew Glynis Johns had knockers like that, Judge."

Snuyder listened. The pain made him blink in disbelief. He looked at the ceiling panels and waited for Hilary to return. She didn't. The balding nurse, this time in a long-sleeved dress, came in with a sedative shot. He was so grateful, he felt embarrassed. His orthopedic surgeon, a tall and slender man who not only didn't smile, but who made clear both his disapproval of the patient and of having to explain to him, explained to him what he would do inside of Snuyder's hip and leg. Pins. Something about pins that would staple him together again, he remembered, after the surgeon was gone and the ceiling had dropped a few feet, and then the orderlies came to roll him away to be pinned into shape.

There was something about dogs, and their terrible odor, and somebody riding one around a muddy country lot. He said *No!* And, knowing that he dreamed while he dreamed, he awaited the dream that would tell him who had sat in the front with him while the police car chased him and he drove — by accident, he insisted to the unseen audience his dream included — into the slow breaking up of his bones. The dogs whined and whined, as if steadily, increasingly, wounded by someone patient and cruel.

The intensive care unit was dark and silent and Snuyder was in very deep pain. His hip burned, and his stomach, and the groin he ached too much to reach for. He kept seeing the skin slide open as the angry surgeon sliced. He yelped for assistance and then shuddered to show the nurse that it was he who needed her promptest sympathies. He was hooked to a drip and a monitor, she explained. Soon he would be taken back to his room. He was fine. The procedure had seemed to be effective, and now his job was to sleep. He slept, but the burning followed him, and he dreamed again of dogs whose fur was stiff with filth, whose eyes dripped mucus, and whose droppings were alive with long white worms. He heard the dogs' howling and he hated Lloyd and Pris. The television set was low, and a curtain divided him from Manwarren, but he knew, waking later, that he was back in his room, and still burning, and all right, alive, not dreaming anymore. The world was in color on the other side of the curtain where a voice electric with triumph told someone named Cecelia that the car she'd won had bucket seats. She screamed.

The woman in the car with him had screamed.

Tony Arizona, his senior clerk, was there in the morning to discuss adjustments of his trial calendar. He brought a cheap glass vase filled with blue flowers that Snuyder couldn't name, and a fifth of Powers' Irish Whiskey. He showed Snuyder how his cases had been distributed among the other sitting judges and that certain others — very few of them — had been postponed. Snuyder said, "No. You gave the boys with the dogs to Levinson."

"He wanted it. He hates queers."

"He *is* queer. I want that one, Tony. Hold it over as long as you can before you give it up. And try not to give it to Levinson. He'll be corn-holing them in chambers by the end of the first hour. Oh, boy."

"They cut you up some, I understand."

"Not to mention *I* cut me up."

"Judge. Dick. I have to give the dog people to Levinson. State wants your calendar cleared. You understand? I'm sorry."

"The suicide thing?"

"They think they might want to look into it."

"Tony. *You* think I tried to kill myself?"

"I think you bent your car around a telephone pole. For what it's worth, I don't care — I mean, I *care*, but only about you. You did it, you didn't do it, you'll work it out and the accident's over, that's that. It's not the suicide thing. It's the woman."

Snuyder heard himself sigh. He could see the letters coming out of his mouth and into a comic-strip bubble: Ahhhh. He waited for Ari-zona to tell him who she was, and whether he was in love as much as he thought he remembered he once had been.

Arizona said, "They have to do it. *I* don't know anything. And nobody else is gonna say word one. I expect a superficial investigation, announced vindication, and a prompt resumption of jurisprudence as usual."

"And then there's the matter of the law," Richard said.

Arizona, handsome and intelligent, with great brown eyes and a fondness for dark striped shirts such as the maroon one he wore, smiled a broad smile. "Absolutely," he said. "There is always the law, and the public trust, Your Honor."

Manwarren called over the curtain, "You guys believe this? They want me to believe this bimbo just won a trip around the world for two, all expenses paid, by telling greaseball over there with the micro-phone that Columbus didn't discover America?" The muted shrieks of the victor poured around Manwarren's voice.

The woman in the car had screamed. Arizona poured Powers' into Snuyder's glass with its plastic straw, then he held the straw low, near Snuyder's pillow, so the judge could suck it up. He emptied the glass. Arizona might know her, he thought. But he couldn't be asked. Snuy-der was ashamed to remember his wife and his children, his work even down to the specifics of the cases he had tried months and years ago, when he could barely remember the presence, much less identity or necessary intimate facts, of a woman he had carried with him toward jail for certain, and possibly (if Hilary was right) toward death. But she wasn't dead. The nurse had told him that no one was dead. He thought of someone with no face who sat in a wheelchair, paralyzed. He saw her — she was like a burglar in a stocking mask, terrifying because faceless, unnatural — lying in an iron lung, crushed in a fetal sleep forever, staring through a window and drooling, staggering like a monster with hands like claws at her waist, serving the judge's sentence and locked away from his mind.

Arizona slid the Powers' into the drawer of the bedside table when he left. The pain pills and the Powers' combined, and Snuyder flinched. The doctors would have to cut and cut before they found out what was wrong with such a man as he, he told himself. He closed his eyes against the undeniable blade, as if they were cutting, as if they were at the flaccid organs and slimy bone, searching for what was the matter. For him.

It was Hilary who woke him when she sat in the visitor's chair with some effort, swearing as she fell back into the deep seat. After a silence — she breathed as if she had a cold — she said, "How's your catheter, Judge?"

"Hil. Do you know who she is?"

Manwarren turned the volume down.

Snuyder whispered: "The woman in the car?" He took a breath and then shouted, "Manwarren! Turn the sound up! Mind your own business!" He felt as though he'd been running. "Bastard," he said. He shouted it: "Bastard!"

The sound came up slightly, but Snuyder knew that Manwarren was unchastened.

Hilary said, "Why, who would that be, Your Honor? How *is* your catheter, by the way?"

"I hurt all over. Okay? I'm in a lot of pain. I'm humiliated. I'm under investigation, Hilary. They're looking into my comportment on and off the bench."

"I didn't know you'd done it on the bench. And you can't really blame them. A suicide is not always the most stable interpreter of the law, never mind his other little quirks and foibles."

"It's apparently because of the woman. That was all I could get from Arizona."

Hilary said, "I wish *I* could get more from Tony. He's really a piece."

"Please don't talk like that."

"Do I really need to tell you about the hypocrisy of this discussion?"

"No."

"You know I'm disgusted with you. That's an easy one. Disgust is easy and seeing it's easy. But what *kills* me —"

"Hil, I can't remember a lot. I remember *us*, overall, you know. And a lot of times and things. But I can't remember a lot."

"And that includes the slut in the car? *That's* what kills me. It's so *sad* for you that you can't. I feel *sorry* for you. You son of a bitch."

"Hil, she's literally a slut?"

"Oh. You boy. You infant. You expect me to keep track of your infidelities and log your bedroom transactions, don't you. You'd ask me for help. You know, knowing me, I'd probably give it. You — *boy*." She wept mascara lines down her face.

Snuyder said, "I'm promiscuous? I thought I remembered that I really loved her." Their silence widened, and a woman on the television said, "I wouldn't dare tell them that!"

Hilary sighed. She said, "I think I'll go home. I understand they'll bring you back for therapy, and you'll use a walker. You'll be able to walk someday. I feel sorry it's so bad. Also, Richard, I'm moving. During the latter part of the week. I'll telephone you."

"Where?" he said. "Did we decide to do this?"

Hilary shook her head. "It started when you told me *you* were moving out."

"Yes," he said. He remembered at once, and as if he looked through transparent overlays: long arguments, slower and longer conversations, Hilary on the phone, Hilary weeping black lines while holding a teacup to her mouth, himself standing before her and wishing aloud that he were dead. He remembered the words about remorse that he had tried to say, and the fear of how they'd tell their sons. Hilary had told him about Warren, calling from college, in tears, because he had sensed that it all had gone wrong. Snuyder said, "I'm sorry. I don't remember women. A woman. *The* woman, I guess you'd call her."

"Yes," Hilary said.

"I apologize. If it's because of her, I apologize. I don't suppose it would make any difference now, seeing that I don't know her anymore. Is she the —"

But Hilary was up and moving. She was at the door. He heard the squelch of her crepe soles on the linoleum door.

He said, "I suppose not."

She said, "See you, Judge." Then, too brightly, she said, "Actually, I'll see you in court." She laughed too hard, and she left.

Manwarren called over at once. "You know what, Dick? I think you shoulda hit the pole a little harder, you don't mind my saying so. You're in a pickle, to say the least, big fella."

"You think I'm in a pickle, Manwarren?"

"Call me Manny."

"I'm going to make a call, Manny. While you sleep. I'm going to have a man who runs a chain of fish stores in Syracuse — I'm going to ask him to have an employee in the Manlius packing plant come over here while you're sleeping and kill you. He's going to open your chest with his bare hands, and he's going to tear out every vital organ in your body one at a time. And he won't wear gloves. His nails will be dirty. He picks his nose. Do you understand me, Manny?"

The sound increased in volume, and bright voices clung to the ceiling tiles. She had been in the car with him. She had screamed when they'd hit. Hilary was leaving because of her, and he didn't know who the woman was. The set cried out and the voices rose. He was alleged to have attempted suicide. He would never walk normally, and his sons would not come to him. He knew that too. Hilary would take all their money and the men on the ethics committee might remove him from the bench. He thought they wouldn't, since none of them was terribly honest either, and each was equally impeachable. They would probably reprimand him, and he would suffer a trial-by-headline. But he would return to the bench, he thought. He would live alone in an apartment such as the ones near the Sangertown Mall. Or perhaps he might move into Clinton, where the old large houses east of town were divided into Victorian cells for bachelors and men such as he. He would drive alone to work and sit in his courtroom. He would say who was right in the eyes of the law. He never would know who the woman had been, or what they had been together, or why.

It was an empty mourning, he thought — abstracted, like a statement about how dreadful the starving African babies are. He wondered if the woman he loved and didn't know might have told him she was leaving. Perhaps he had aimed at killing *her*.

He heard himself whimpering, and made himself stop. He heard Manwarren's television set, and then the dogs in the trailer who'd whimpered, he'd been told by the deputies, before they heard the foot on the door; once rescued, they'd begun to bark and wail. He thought of Lloyd and Pris, armed and marching, in their terrible fetor and loss, to recover their starved, sick dogs. They were separated now. Poor Lloyd: he had taken the hostages, and only when his prisoners lay on the floor in the deeds-recording office had he realized that he wanted to insist on one more prize, the operation that would change Pris's sex. It was then, Snuyder remembered realizing, as he'd read Lloyd's deposition, that Lloyd had understood how permanently separate he had always been from Pris and probably always would be. "He don't love me," Lloyd had said. "How could he?"

It was a case he had wanted to try. They were accused of a dozen public-health violations and twenty or more violations of the civil and criminal codes. And they were so innocent, Snuyder thought. No one should be allowed to be so innocent. Shots rang out on a TV show, and wheels screamed. Snuyder jumped, remembering the sound of locked brakes. She had been there with him, in the same small space. And he had leaned back, locked his elbows and knees, and had driven at the pole. He had. And he would not know her. And even that was not the worst part.

She *might* return. He would have to decide about trying to heal, or waiting for her next door to death. He forced himself to breathe evenly, as if he slept. The TV set made sounds. The dogs stood on the bed and chairs, they cried their pain and hunger, their fear. Manwarren cackled. The police would come soon with questions. He was held together with pins. He was going to die, but of natural causes, and many years from today. He knew it. He smelled the dark air of the trailer, and he heard the gaunt dogs whine.

One More Wave
of Fear

I DID NOT GROW UP despising nature on Argyle Road, at the far
southern edge of Prospect Park, in Brooklyn in the 1950s. But I did
come to hate the upper-case initial with which my parents said the
word. Our house was set back from a street on which few children but
a lot of lean, straight men and women lived. As I remember them,
most were white and Protestant and wealthy, and apparently convinced
that their long black cars should frequently be washed but rarely
driven. My parents also called it Natural History, or The Out of
Doors. My father taught science in a junior high school on Nostrand
Avenue, and he loved his work. It didn't seem ever to stop. Lanky,
almost thin, with great swollen knuckle joints and knees, with elbows
that were sharp and a chin nearly pointed, a nose that led him as he
was leading us, my father, with his Ed.D., was considered a master
teacher by his colleagues and his principal and many of his students
and himself. While my mother cooked, he lectured on asparagus.
When I rode with him in our DeSoto, he talked about the flowers that
grew in vacant lots and through the sidewalk cracks. And on weekends
we took wearying walks with the Audubon Society or the Brooklyn
Bird Club and, when I grew older, we hiked with the Appalachian
Mountain Club on trails in upstate New York. I remember those trips
as a blur of similarities: the same swarms of insects at the nose and
eyes; the same wet heat that was pooled about us by the same clinging
brush; the same unnatural, galloping pace that suggested flight from
the birds and plants and marshes we had come to pursue.

I sulked, at eleven and twelve and thirteen, when they forced me to stroll through Prospect Park while searching, say, for the pileated woodpecker: eighteen adults, in various stages (to me) of decomposition, and one slouching kid, who hunted through touch football games and horizontal lovers and the droppings of unleashed dogs for a bird. My mother hit me after the woodpecker trip. She swung her fists against my back, chasing me up the stairs and into my room, shouting that I'd ruined Nature for her. That night we made up. She explained, my small and never-placid mother, that her difficult childhood in the slums of east Manhattan had led her to marry my father, and to read many books, and to seek the consolations of The Out of Doors. In the darkness of my unkempt room, my mother sat on the chair at my desk, and I lay on my bed, and she told me how little fresh air she had breathed as a girl, and how she had longed even then for Brooklyn, and such a neighborhood as ours — "You know, the suburbs," she said — and how she felt at peace when with my father on what she called a Field Trip. Those words were another signal for me, like the phrase The Out of Doors, to long to get as far inside and close to walls as I could.

We forgave each other, sometimes almost daily, and my father lectured, my mother wrote her books about the children of the slums — aimed at children, and written in medicinal sentences (they were good for you, but unpleasant), and published at last by a vanity press, and finally piled in our basement, under heavy pack frames and canvas rucksacks and three sets of snowshoes that we'd never used. My father, the heir of wealthy parents, was a Socialist who used to be a Communist. The more his colleagues turned each other in to education vigilantes — those were the days of naming names to such as the House Un-American Activities Committee — the less Communist, the more Socialist, and the more secret about each, he became. I think he feared to lose his job because, like many compulsive teachers, he was a voice in search of ears on which he might fall. He forgave America, I forgave my mother, and she forgave the need to have to make me understand her. And we walked the hundreds of acres of Prospect Park, and my father pointed at leaves, and told me which were diseased and which could be brewed as a tea, and which would make me itch. I played at

"Captain Video," my favorite television show — "Hand me the atomic hammer!" he would cry to the Video Ranger, as they waged their war against the evil Doctor Pauli — in the farthest place from Nature I could find: my mind. And they *all* made me itch.

One Sunday morning, when I should have been playing stickball with other thirteen-year-old boys, or — better — looking at Don Winslow of the Navy on TV, I was entering Prospect Park with the rest of the bird club, walking from the assembly point in Grand Army Plaza, under the great arched monument. My mother wore her 9 x 30 binoculars, and my father his, on thin leather neck straps. I had been loaned a pair, which I kept in their case and carried, like a book, in my hand: I didn't want to be mistaken for someone who cared about birds. My expression, I am certain, was that of a recent lobotomy patient; it was crucial to me that no reflection of feeling or thought be visible on my flesh. Demonstrating nothing, and looking at nothing, I followed the Leader, as he was called, a man named Ted who pointed at birds and named them.

Ted, fat and round-faced and sweaty, as he looked through his binoculars suggested to me the attentiveness of U-boat captains in war. "Nothing," he said, lowering his glasses. "Garbage stuff."

"Well, a towhee," my mother said, noting its existence in a little spiral book she carried.

"No," my father said. "No. Sparrow. A tree sparrow."

"You mean eastern sparrow," Ted said.

"Well, they're one and the same," my father said, entering the bird in his own spiral book.

My mother said, patting my father's arm in a friendly way, while breezes blew her hair, "I think it's a towhee." She chanted it.

My father shook his head. He smiled at her, but I knew that smile. Its ferocity kept me in check on trips such as these. I stood and I waited. He said, "Sparrow."

My mother smiled and shrugged. I guess my father knew what the shrug said. He blushed, and his voice deepened. He said, "Your towhee is too small by an inch, lacks a round black spot on its breast, and is making the strange mistake of *calling* wrong. Listen."

Ted moved closer to my parents, while the others in the group moved on, making do without Leadership. Ted and my father cocked their heads; my mother didn't, but she stared at my father, as if he were another curious bird.

"There!" my father said. "You hear? *Teelwit!* he's calling. *Teelwit! Teelwit!* Am I right?"

My mother nodded.

He asked, "And your towhee?"

"All right," my mother said.

"Your towhee?"

"*Fine*," she said. "You're right."

"What does your towhee sing?"

My mother looked at him, and then she turned and walked to the rest of the group. Ted looked away from my father and followed her; the group moved along.

My father, his face still red, turned to me and looked, with no sign of seeing *me* in his eyes that I could find. He lifted his binoculars, then lowered them gently on their strap until they hung. They seemed to be heavy on his neck. He said, "As your mother well knows, your towhee calls *Chewink! Chewink!* You can't mistake *Chewink!* for *Teelwit!* Can you?"

In those days, there were waves of fear in Brooklyn neighborhoods — anyway, in ours. There had been a wave of fear about Germans possibly landing at night at Plum Beach, near Sheepshead Bay. There had been a wave of fear about the shabby men spotted chalking arrows in the street and on the curbs of certain blocks, one of them ours; the fear had been that Gypsies or tramps would be flooding the streets of Brooklyn, begging for food and clothing, hiring out for work they'd never perform. The men, we had finally learned, were marking routes for the delivery of new telephone directories. And of course there had been waves of fear over polio epidemics and the arrival on the block of Negro families. The wave of fear when I was six was squirrels. Brooklyn was filled with pigeons and squirrels, and the squirrels, with their thick gray pelt, their long graceful tail, their clever paws and large dark eyes, had been a part of my childhood, like curled cats and wandering dogs. But to householders they were like the rats to which they were cousins. They scrabbled in attics and ate the insulation of electrical wires, it was said. They stored nuts uninvited. They were invaders. They were part of all the movies of my childhood. James Arness and James Whitmore in *Them!* Giant ants, atomic mutation, man's meddling with nature. It invaded a small western town. Just like the squirrels in Brooklyn. Or *Invasion of the Body-Snatchers.* Or *Plan 9 from Outer Space.* Or how about all those Japanese things with one American actor and a huge *moth* running amok, everybody milling around, talking Japanese a mile a minute, which gets dubbed as "Remain calm. Tranquillity is better than dying of fear and disorder. Get your guns." It was as if the *squirrels* were pillaging and looting. In *Brooklyn.*

At breakfast, my parents discussed the attic noises they had heard at night. My mother's lips curled with loathing. My father frowned with distress, and his voice deepened. "We can deal with this," he said. "I know how to control a situation like this. I'll be home from school late, and then we'll see."

That day, he drove off to P.S. 240 with a certain harried look that I later came to associate with serious thought; he was showing my mother that he was working. And he did come home late that night, long after we had eaten dinner without him. He carried under each arm a long rectangular machine made of what I think was tin. There were tilted doors inside each contraption, and wires that banged as he walked from the back door through to the kitchen.

"Traps," he announced, slamming them onto the kitchen counter. "*Humane* traps. We catch 'em, but we don't kill 'em."

Above us, as my father in the attic labored to bait and arm the traps, the small gray squirrels ran beneath the eaves and in the walls. They had grown confident, and at night I heard their claws unhesitatingly march on our wood. At first I had been frightened that a squirrel would chew through my walls and enter my room and bite me. And then I remembered my barefoot days in the backyard during the summer — I was never allowed to go barefoot on the sidewalks because, as my mother summed matters up, "Where I haven't looked before you walk on it is dirty. That's the rule." The squirrels had never bothered me out back, and the house, I figured, was still more ours than theirs. So I grew too confident, myself, and I listened to them racing in the woodwork at night, and I smiled for my parents' despair. Cataclysm was really all a kid had going for him until he was taller than his parents.

When I woke and heard my father going to the attic to check on the traps, I fancied that I had heard them going off at night, and that I'd heard the shrill cries and frantic searching of trapped gentle Disney-creatures, prisoner in my house. Then my father would descend and say, "Nope. Nothing."

More and more, my mother greeted his report with a low and guttural wordless statement of woe — as if my father had struck her. He took to coming down in silence. I would listen to their soundless-ness as he dressed for breakfast while she, always in her robe at breakfast time, sat with him in their unstated failure. And at night, they would work again on the bait. They went through cheese, Ritz crackers, soda biscuits, Arnold bread, then cups of Planter's peanuts, then cups of nuts that my mother cracked in the afternoon while we waited for my father to come home. Finally, because peanut butter was my father's favorite food, I suggested that he use it in his traps. I was watching him eat a peanut butter and jelly sandwich, and I was think-ing that, with his thin fingers at his mouth, he seemed to nibble like a squirrel. My mother shrugged, and my father raised his brows; that night, they baited with Skippy. I recall thinking how gummy the mouths of the squirrels would be.

It worked. There had been no strangled squirrel cry, no slam of gates into place, but in the morning, as my mother waited in her gathering tension, my father went up to the attic, scrambled about a bit, and then came down slowly, clanking, and bearing trapped beasts. "*Yes!*" he called, carrying Natural History. "*Yes!*"

When I came to breakfast, I expected to find them happy. But they were — if not outright huddled — concentrated at the far end of our kitchen table, as far away from the traps on the kitchen floor as they could be. Inside each trap was a squirrel, shivering. The slanted doors had dropped to perpendicular, and the squirrels were walled inside them. Now, my father told us, sounding as if he tried to sound buoy-ant, but talking in a way that made me look at him as sharply as I looked at the squirrels, *now*, all that had to happen was that someone take the squirrels to the park — far away from the house, as far as someone might feel like walking — and then set them free.

"Someone," my mother said.

"You," he told her. "I have to teach."

"I don't *know* anything about squirrels — you're the scientist."

"Yes," he said. "And I told you everything you need to know. You carry the cages by the handles on top. The squirrel can't reach you, no matter how he tries. Then you trip the door in each cage when you're a good long distance from the house. The squirrels run away. Then *you* run away."

"That part I know about," my mother said.

So I did not wait for the school bus that morning. I dressed for autumn weather in my brown corduroy jacket and peaked brown corduroy hat. My mother, who chose to wear gloves that morning, hefted each cage by its handle — her face suggested that she carried each squirrel by its tail — and we slowly made our way up Argyle, across Church Avenue into the Parade Grounds, where kids skipping school played ball, and across which we were going to walk to reach the lowest tip of Prospect Park, near the lake.

Brooklyn in those days, and especially in parts around our neighborhood, was filled with trees and rich bushes, thick hedge, undeveloped fields that weren't even vacant lots yet — they were more like scraps of leftover forest — and everyplace in the giant trees, it seemed to me that morning in fall, squirrels swarmed, their tails floating behind them, softly flicked pennants of my mother's dismay.

We had to pause a lot, because my mother carried the traps away from her body, and her arms grew weary. I offered to carry one and was refused in the way parents decline the assistance of children — a signal that sacrifice of some considerable quantity is going on. We made our slow unhappy progress over the Parade Grounds, walking across baseball diamonds and having nothing to do with play; when I ran down the first-base line and waited for my mother to catch up, her face informed me that second base was not in my immediate future. We were on business, her frown made clear, and as far as I was concerned, from that moment on, the day was one more Field Trip.

We had a long distance to go, we were still rather far from the park itself, but the trees grew thicker, and the squirrels on them seemed to multiply. I noticed them, and I noticed that my mother noticed them. How could she not? They crawled, they scurried, they sat up and nibbled, they ran; sometimes, scrambling up a tree, one would stop, then turn, then hold there upside down, like a salamander on a stone wall in *National Geographic*. The squirrels made chattering sounds, and long loud squeaks, and some of them silently ran, in bursts, along the tree limbs. I remembered my parents talking of how squirrels hunted down birds, and I did cheer them on, though silently.

My mother said, "Enough."

"Daddy said —"

"Daddy wants to say, he can come and carry the squirrels and tell *them*. Mommy says enough. Get back where it's safe. Go back."

I retreated obediently, so that no vengeance-seeking, human-devouring squirrel, mutated by nuclear testing, or inhabited by invisible beings from another world who sought our blood or souls or air supply — or which were simply part of the enormous danger my parents always discovered — could attack. My mother, in her gloves and long, tent-shaped tan tweed coat, bent above the cages. I saw the squirrels shrink from her. I watched her shrink from them.

I heard a sharp snapping sound, and then something clicked, and a squirrel paused at the end of a trap. It moved back inside.

"Shoo," my mother said. "Go on." She waited, then kicked at the side of the trap. "Shoo!" The squirrel remained. My mother said, "Go *on!*" With the tips of her fingers, she picked up the closed end of the trap and shook it. She shook it harder, then banged on its side with a fist. "*Go!*"

The squirrel scampered down the incline of the trap and ran away, pausing to inspect; it ran again, paused, then ran farther. It went to a nearby tree and disappeared. The second squirrel went at once, and then my mother sat heavily down on an empty trap.

I watched the tree to which both squirrels had run. It was extremely broad at the base of the trunk, and its heavy thick branches were alive with squirrels. They ran, they paused, they hung upside down and right side up, they chattered and made their high-pitched sounds. As I watched them, they became the central object of vision; the tree they ran on was secondary to what inhabited it, and the tree receded, the squirrels advanced, and that was true of neighboring trees as well. The ground, too, seemed to ripple with their motion at the base of every tree.

My mother sat on her trap on the endless green-going-ocher of the Parade Grounds, looking up at the trees, the ceaseless motion of the squirrels as they worked and as the winter came in upon them. "They'll come back," she said. "You can't keep that — that" — she swung her arm in its heavy coat, she pointed with her finger in its glove, indicating trees and what swarmed in them — "there's no *way* of keeping them under control, believe you me." She diminished, staring up at them, like the pretty girl in the horror film who at last understands what has come for her.

The World Began
with Charlie Chan

WE'VE GOT SOME HOURS left to kill, and you can be the cause of death, listener. Use your clammy bedside telephone, call up Malcolm on "Late Night." Because it's night, it's late, it's getting later. Hello.

Mr. Pitkin?

You got me, listener.

How come you're so abusive to your listeners?

Me? We're talking Pitkin? Listener, I need subject matter, I *never* need whining. You can't stand the meat, stay out of the kitchen. Hey, folks, he's gone. Learn from it. We're looking for a topic, here. This is Malcolm Pitkin. Don't ask. Hello.

Malcolm?

I knew you'd ask.

Malcolm, my name is Ann. I'm a first-time caller from Fort Lee?

Wonderful, Ann. You made my night so far. Are you serious here, Ann, or do we talk ca-ca for thirty seconds?

I think you have gorgeous knees.

Whoa.

I love your knees. I saw them at the Little League the other night. I mean, I saw all of you —

Whoa. All of me? Stop snickering, Ann. I can't tolerate a woman who snickers. You're saying you saw my entire body? Stop giggling, Ann. Grow up.

Well, you do. You have nice knees. You were with this little boy who struck out, and you had your hand on his shoulder, and you were wearing Bermuda shorts and your knees looked nice. *You* looked nice.

That was Jody. He got called out on strikes by the umpire's seeing-eye dog. Jody's a nice boy. Now, *he's* got good knees, Ann. Thanks for the call. But try and control that giggle, will you? Hello. Yes?

Malcolm?

Yeah.

Oh, Malcolm.

You in ecstasy or pain, listener? Stamp your hoof if something hurts.

Malcolm. I live alone. I'm a widower.

Say widow, water, witch's wings. Say it.

Widow ought midges what? What was the other one?

That's a lush, folks. That man is pickled. Probably been, he's probably been hitting the sauce for most of the night. It ain't easy, you know, being alone. Trust me on that. Right, caller? Have I got your number?

Malcolm, I live *all* alone.

Gimme a caller, please, Frank? Francis Strunk, sitting in as producer tonight, folks. Frank! I can't see him, ladies and gentlemen, he's in another room, and I have to take it on faith he's there. I think he's working out of the washroom tonight. Frank! Will ya gimme someone to *talk* to? Hello, this is Malcolm Pitkin, and you better be sober.

I am sober, Malcolm. My name is Bob. I'm calling from Teaneck.

Nice place, Teaneck. As long as you don't need to breathe. How do you feel about breathing, Bob?

It depends on whom I share the atmosphere with. I would like to say that I am affronted by the left-wing bias of your station, your program, and most of the Jewish-controlled media, particularly but not exclusively the electronic media of this nation.

Ooh. Yummy. Are you a member of the Klan, caller? As in Ku of the Klux? Are you into, maybe, Aryan *Nation*, as they say?

My name is Bob, not Caller. I happen not to be a joiner, Mr. Pitkin. But I also happen to be sympathetic to some of the complaints of those groups, their justifiable concerns. However, I do not take the violent road.

What would be some of the roads you travel, Bob? Casual lynching in leisure suits out in the suburbs instead of shooting black guys uptown? Burn a tenement but do not dynamite a church? Yeah. But I want to hear about the Jews. You ever read *The Protocols of the Elders of Zion?* I think you might enjoy it. I mean, that's really about a *plot* against the pure of heart. Come on Bob. Hit me with it.

It is a proven fact —

He won, folks. I thought I could take it, but I can't. Dog brains are not allowed on the air. This is "Late Night" with Malcolm Pitkin, it's almost two-fifteen, and we're gonna break to sell you stuff. When I come back, we're gonna take more calls, but only from people who can show me a note from their doctor saying they have not suffered brain death. Don't go away.

And we're back. *This* is Malcolm Pitkin, ladies and gentlemen, and it's "Late Night." It's late for us all. Repent. Call and let's talk. Hello, Malcolm Pitkin, et cetera, blah blah, go ahead, caller.

Malcolm?

Somehow I knew you'd ask that.

Hi, Malcolm. My name is Asbury —

That's a name? Like Asbury Park?

Yes, except I'm calling from Cleveland.

Well, that explains it. Right. Cleveland, huh? Long distance. Glad you can hear us, I suppose.

Yessir. I have a trivia question for you, Malcolm.

You listen to the show a lot?

Only once in a while so far, to tell you the truth. Usually I work at night. I got laid off, so now I'll have more of a chance to listen.

Good, listener. A wise decision. Why make a living and keep your kids eating when you can blow your dough by calling me from Cleveland? Good. Except let me tell you how much I detest trivia. Is this — pass me the barf bag, Frank — TV trivia? Or Hollywood trivia? Or is it the lowest of the —

Sports trivia, Malcolm.

— low.

Yessir. Can you give me the number of the largest crowd the Browns ever drew at Cleveland Stadium, and the year when they drew it?

You're talking football to me, right, Passaic?

Asbury.

Yeah. Right. Listen, I want you to find a flat football, or you let the air out of a full one, okay? I want you to put your lips over the little black airhole — are you with me? Then I want you to blow. I want you to huff and I want you to puff. And when it's all hard and firm and full, then you call me back and tell me how you liked it, all right, Passaic? He's gone, folks. Because if I didn't cut him off fast, he'd have had to tell me one more time that his name's really Asbury. It's winner night out there on the airwaves, ladies and gentlemen. So I'd like to interrupt this exploration of how limited the human intelligence can become while still permitting its owner to have lips, and I'd like to send a message to my son, Jody: *Get to sleep.* Tomorrow, just before we leave for the Fort Lee Dodgers to play *hot* baseball, I want you to tell your mother to serve dinner early. Be ready for me, understand? Because I'm not coming in to get abused. You see my car, you hit the street running, got it? Tell your present mother, Malcolm's ex. And do not give her my best. All right? So who else can speak the mother tongue? I'm out here alone, folks, hovering in darkness over the eastern seaboard. I'm waiting for some *language.* I'm waiting for that rare soul who speaks in sentences I hunger to hear — direct quote from Harry Fosdick Emerson, the great New England Waldo of America's early thoughts. Each man marches to a crippled drummer. Well, limps. Of course, federal regulations require that I rephrase it: Each man marches to a handicap-intensive percusser. We'll take a call. This is Malcolm Pitkin, let's talk straight. Hello.

Mr. Pitkin. Hello. Good evening. I want to talk about garbage. Interested?

Always. It's the medium, sir. Fire away.

I can't give you the exact date, but I do know that westerners — I think it was the English, maybe the Italians. I really don't know.

All right, caller. You've established that you're an expert. I never heard of anyone before who specialized in not knowing about Italian garbage. Fascinating.

Malcolm. Really. Listen. We've been climbing Everest since in the 1920s, right? Maybe before then?

Well, *I've* only been doing it since around 1955, but I do catch your snow-drift.

And there are always these base camps, and camp one, camp two, all of that. And these guys — women too, now. They had a couple of women's expeditions. They lie around there, gathering their strength, bivouacking for the big push up to the top.

Listener, what you're describing: we call it mountain climbing. Say it after me. Mountain climbing. You got any *news?*

They throw their garbage onto the snow and ice, Malcolm. It doesn't go anyplace. It doesn't melt up there. So there's all this *garbage* on Mount Everest. Litter. Trash. We desecrate a holy place — the Sherpas call it the Mother of the World. Did you know that? It's *holy* to them. And we litter it. This is the same mentality that put us into Vietnam and kept us there. It sends us meddling into Salvador and Nicaragua and the Persian Gulf. Colonialism! Imperialism! Racism!

Listener, you're a good example of what happens to the airwaves when they're controlled by all those liberal Jews that the crazy guy a while back was complaining about. What's your name?

My name's Malcolm. It really is. I'm calling from Salisbury, Connecticut.

Your name's Malcolm? Hey, guess what *my* name is. Wow! All right. Listen, Malcolm. You have an interesting molehill to make about the mountain. It's bad to mess up anything sacred. Really. I'm with you. Littering is a dirty trick. Fine. But you can't be serious — Everest, Vietnam, the Persian *Gulf?* I'll tell you what. You prove to me that Richard Nixon put a foot on any part of Everest, or show me he had an Everest policy, I'm with you. You know what I'm talking about? Tell me Nixon was involved. That's what I'm after tonight. *That's* what I want, listeners. I want Everestgate. Tibetgate, *Dicky*gate! I want Tricky Dick tonight. Dick? Baby! Dick, you listening? I want *you!* Gimme a call here, Dick. Let's talk the truth about trash on the world's holy hills. Malcolm — gimme some Dick Nixon, and we'll continue. Otherwise, I have to tell you this, your complaint about littering is noted, and regretted, and you're gone. I'm into *policy* here, not muckraking. My advice is call the *Nation.* Maybe the *New Republic,* once, but *Nation* for sure. Maybe the *New York Post!* "POPSICLE PEAK IS RAPE ON A ROPE!" Malcolm? You there?

Malcolm gave Malcolm the H for Hung Up, folks. This is a first for tonight. Nobody else better try it, though. I'm warning you. We'll take a call. This is Malcolm Pitkin.

Malcolm? Is that you, Malcolm?

Sorry, this is Warner Oland, and we're discussing Charlie Chan tonight, here on the Network of American Failings. You know, all those Number One Sons saying to all those Caucasians posing as Oriental detectives, "*Gee,* Pop!" Remember? Then the kid would screw up by not listening to the old man, and then the old man would put him down, while continuing to serve white society. That he was always on the fringes of? You remember? He was always traveling? Always had a suitcase with him, folks? He was a visitor. An *outsider.* We're talking the American paradigm, friends. The world began with Charlie Chan. And you know who directed his first movie? Yes. The same director who brought you *Bedtime for Bonzo.* I'm not fooling. It was Richard Nixon, ladies and gentlemen. This is Malcolm Pitkin.

I won't ask if you're Malcolm.

Because you know it, right, dear? The first intelligent caller I've had tonight. Well, I really haven't *had* you. Or have I? Anyway, you're bright. You know who I am. You're ahead of the pack, dear.

Malcolm, this is Lisa.

Yeah?

Lisa.

So you know who you are too. Good. Lisa, this is Malcolm. Malcolm, this is Lisa. Hello. Hi. You come here often? Wait: *Lisa? The* Lisa? *That* one?

Hi, Mal.

Oh, my God. Lisa?

I'm not drunk, Mal. On the other hand, I have been drinking Manhattans. And it's a good idea. That's where I am when I drink them.

Don't giggle, Lisa. I hate that. You're really calling me from across the river after all these years and you're doing it in front of how many millions — well, not in front of. Let's say in earshot. You want to say it that way?

Sure, Mal. In earshot. How's that?

Geez. Lisa. You're dumb as ever. But it's *you.*

Mal, I've been divorced two times since we didn't get married.

Lisa, I'm gonna ask Mr. Strunk, the assistant producer, to keep you on the line and get your number, and I'm gonna call you back during the next break. It's coming up. Is that all right, sweetheart? Lisa, I really want to *talk* to you. I think we should, you know, do it off the air. All right?

I know you're divorced, Mal. I saw it in the papers. I thought, what the heck. Give it a shot.

Lisa, *good*. I mean, I'm really glad you did. We're gonna talk.

I thought to myself, maybe I keep on not staying married on account of I should of married Mal, you know?

Lisa, baby. Frank? You out there, Frank? Ladies and gentlemen, to add a touch of absurdity to this already ludicrous situation, Mr. Strunk and his talking feet seem to have changed venue again. Lisa? Don't hang up, Lisa! *Frank!*

I always thought about you, Mal. Even when I was happy, I kept wondering: wouldn't I be happier if I was with Mal? Of course, I wasn't happy that much.

We're gonna talk, Lisa. We have to talk. We'll talk. If I can get some *help* here. Is anybody in the building? Is anybody in a car outside the building? Lisa. Don't say your number on the air, sweetheart. The crazies'll call for a month. But don't go away. All right? I'm coming to see you. Because — you don't think it's *fun* up here at night, do you? You think somebody sits up here and talks to people at night because he *wants* to? Lisa? *Frank?*

Malcolm? Am I really talking to you?

Oh, Lisa, these *calls* are coming in. I'm gonna trust that Frank is out there in a room I can't see into, and I'm trusting he can hear me. Frank: stop listening to your sweat glands work! *Screen* for me! I'm getting dipsy-doodles here, they're talking cute knees, ancient love — Frank! Cut the crap! Lisa! You think you're fooling the *King* of the Fools? True confessions from out of the past, the thundering hooves of an old-time girlfriend still in hot pursuit . . . Are you *kidding* me? Lisa: get lost. Frank: *screen* them! Folks, okay, you heard every syllable. You know by now that I oughta be on the Broadway boards or the silver screen, but not here, right? Wasting a great talent on your lonely, midnight souls? Lisa wasn't bad, either, but we've got standards, folks. We don't believe a word. Do we? She could *not* have been *that* Lisa.

No way. And this is Malcolm Pitkin, this is "Late Night," and we'll take a break now, and then we'll talk straight. I would like to add that it was eighty-four thousand, two-hundred something, in 1964, the Browns against the Giants in Cleveland Stadium. Now, you listen to me. We are surrounded by darkness, and people tell us lies. Our children are the remnants of the bones we've gnawed. The children *are* our bones. I think we found a topic for tonight, so you stay tuned. We'll break now, Lisa.

Extra Extra Large

WHAT THE HELL, try it once or twice. Lust after everyone. Live in a sexual lather awhile. Dine on the double veal rib, the lobster fricassee, the quail. Drink Latour. And order *dessert*. Baby: order anything you want. Baby: order everything.

Bernie and I look like nearly identical twins, from time to time. He's the one with the more attractively broken-looking nose. He has a strong bald head, sloping shoulders, long arms and wide hands. His legs, if you were fitting them into designer jeans, aren't quite as long as fashion might require. He cocks his bearded chin (more chestnut, less gray, than mine) and raises his slightly more peaky brows, and he sights at you down his nose — like a boxer, calculating when to duck his chin, when to pop you with the jab.

If you took my brother for a fading, spreading middleweight, you'd think of me as a heavyweight working to drop down a class. Bernie insisted I was reducing because of happiness in love.

"Believe me," I told him, "it might be love, but it isn't any pleasure."

Bernie was under stress of his own, but it made him expand. He looked swollen with vitality, pink and broad and fit for coping. He wasn't vital, coping, or fit. As his waist widened and mine declined, as his face broadened and mine diminished, our heavy heads and thick whiskers, large nose, small eyes mounted by brows that look like accent marks in a foreign language, matched each other's as our bodies did.

I thought this as we sat in Bernie's living room, in his little house in the bright countryside that rings suburban Philadelphia. We were part of the litter of the night before, I thought, two lightly sweating, pale, hungover men who rubbed our brows, took our glasses off and wiped them on the tails of our shirts — to no avail: the spots were in, not on, our vision — and nursed at light beer, waiting to feel better. The beer tasted thin and fizzy, and I kept thinking, while I watched him considering me, We'll both be *fifty* one of these days!

Bernie nodded judiciously. His lips frowned in evaluation and then turned up in approval. He said, "Bill, you're looking good."

I said, "For a dead person."

"You keep up the regimen," he said, "and you'll be svelte. Does Joanne make sandwiches for you, with bean sprouts in them, on homemade whole-wheat bread? You're so *lucky*. Does she nag you to drink mineral water and kiss your earlobes when you push your plate away?"

"This is a professional woman, Bernie," I said. "This is a lawyer. Instead of a pacemaker, she'll get an egg timer installed. I call her up because I have a sudden need to croon vapid remarks about passion, and she tells me, 'Bill, I don't have *time*.' "

"Well," he said, "it's tough for women in the law. The guys are waiting for them to make a mistake. They call it the Affirmative Action Grace Period — usually it's about five minutes long, I hear."

"No, she's good. They wanted her. They use her for the tough cases. Felony drug stuff. She's mean. She can be."

"And this is the person you're making a physical comeback for?"

I said, "How do *you* pick the women you love?"

"Right," he said. "Pow. You're right."

"I'm sorry, kid."

"No," he said, "you're right. There's Rhonda checking me out — long distance, of course — for one more open wound to lay the salt in, and I'm telling you how to pick lovers."

"You realize something? I'm forty-four years old. You're forty."

"Possibly," he said.

"And we're sitting around here in boxer shorts, talking about the dangers of *dating*. We — Bern: we ought to maybe grow *up*."

He closed his eyes above the soft, dark skin of their sockets, and he slowly nodded his head.

"You'll get through this, Bern," I said.

"Oh, of course," he said. He opened his eyes, and I couldn't meet them. "And you," he said, "you'll get through your — your —"

"— happiness," I said.

Showered and changed, I sat in the car as Bernie made the ritual inspection. Our father had always done this when one of us drove off — the pausing to prod with a toe, but not kick, each tire; the squinting at belts and pipes and filters under the hood. Bernie even checked my oil by wiping the dipstick on his fingers, his fingers on his pants. Then he gently lowered the hood and latched it, smiling his assurances with our father's expression of grave pleasure.

"Looks like everything's under there," he said, coming to my window. He leaned in, and we kissed each other's bearded cheek. Bernie patted my face as he withdrew. I made for I-95, climbing north and east, leaving Bernie to his heat, his solitude, his turn-of-the-century woodwork, his turn-of-this-century's architecture software and computer. I thought of how you aren't supposed to die of, starve for, fatten on behalf of, or mime Linda Ronstadt songs about, love. Yet I was consuming too few calories for comfort and strength, I was groaning situps on the clammy floor of my apartment, because of what I thought of as love.

And Bernie was going the other way, and because of a dark, intense and brilliant woman named Rhonda, who, with real sadness, I think, and with a regret that hurt Bernie as much as her determination, had left. Someone hugs a middle-aged man, or suffers him to seize at her, while someone else gives him back the house keys, and hundreds of pounds of American flesh begin to shift.

I stopped on the road at one of those joints that tried to look like another of those joints. I ordered the garden salad under plastic, and a diet soda. I ate in the car so I wouldn't smell the hamburgers frying. I sighed, like a man full of salted potatoes. What I wanted to do was go back inside and call Bernie up and ask him if he remembered the time that our father's heart, swollen and beating unreliably, and independent of our father's needs, had first been diagnosed. Bernie, from his high school's public phone, had called me at college.

He'd said Dr. Lencz's name, and that occasioned a long and difficult silence into which we breathed wordless telephone noises for relief.

He'd been the doctor who attended our mother. He'd helped us be born, visited our school-day sickbeds, torn out our tonsils, lectured us on sexually communicated diseases, eased our mother — mercy-killed her, Bernie once said he suspected — and now he was fingering our father's flawed heart.

In the silence and static, I in New Hampshire and he in New York each knew what we thought: things could look up awhile, with doctors, but then they always come down. I'd traveled home by bus, I'd met him secretly at the Port Authority — he'd liked it, I remembered, that we were both playing hooky — and then, taking turns with my overnight bag, we'd stalked our father.

What can you do when you fear the man you know you can't protect, and whom you seek to shelter from his own internal organs? We needed to be underneath his skin, yet we sought to avoid his mildest displeasure. I usually called him sir. Bernie still called him Daddy. And we followed him.

Since he was at his office, we ended up standing on lower Broadway, or pacing in front of Trinity Church's wrought iron fence. At the lunch hour, we trailed him to a Savarin and watched him prod what seems now to have been poached fish. We trailed him back to his office building and watched him into his elevator car. I was broad and strong, pimple-faced, with a head of dark hair. Bernie was only slightly shorter than I, but very lean, his face full of shadows. We talked little, looked at everything, and waited until half past five, when our father emerged, one of hundreds of men there in dark blue Brooks Brothers suits and gleaming black wingtips. "Never wear brown shoes with blue," he'd warned me when I left for college, "and treat every woman with reverence." We watched his dark fedora as it rode on the large bald head that was fringed in the same pattern, I thought while I drove, as Bernie's and mine.

We pushed and pulled at each other on the rush hour subway, we instructed each other in the tradecraft of spies, his learned from TV shows, mine from the Geoffrey Household novel I'd read on the bus. At home, once we let him enter, then made our announcement of intentions, he seemed pale, weak, thin, pleased, and unsurprised. He sat in his shirt and tie while I fried the liver I'd instructed Bernie to buy. Somebody's mother, maybe even mine, had said that liver gave you strength. We sat, then, not eating, to watch our father try to chew what amounted to everything we could offer him. The sum of our courage and ability, all we could assay, was on that thistle-pattern platter from Stengl of Flemington, New Jersey — gristly, charred, oily, raw. And what he gave us in return, I wanted to say to Bernie, was his serious attention to the inedible. He let us, in our fright, push him around a little, as he pushed the liver around on his plate, bending his identical head to what we had served.

Bernie's Rhonda was tired, she had said. She was in her thirties, and too young to be so tired, she had said. She was afraid that Bernie tuckered her out by *needing* so much. "What else do you love people for?" Bernie had asked me during our weekend. We'd been walking into an art theater to watch the Truffaut film made from the Henry James story where Truffaut rants for about two hours. Good ranting, by the way: I could still remember the rhythms, and the splendid woman who loved him unrequited. "*Need*," Bernie had said as he bought our tickets. "*Love* is need."

That made sense. I thought of my daughter, Brenda, and her distant mother, removed once by divorce, then twice by remarriage. We'd been a case of need overstated, and surely our child (whose specialty these days was *under*stating need) had chosen Columbia for college because of something like a requirement for me, since I and Columbia lived in the same city. Or so I insisted. And then there was Joanne, just this side of structural steel, but happy with me, at least often, I often thought. And surely you had to *need* somehow to hang around an older man if you were young and trim and flourishing among the other assistants in the office of the Manhattan district attorney. If Joanne's schedule and attention sometimes implied other needs, I forgave them, in light of my lack of any choice. Kissing my *earlobes*, Bernie?

On the other hand, I thought, picturing him as poised in mid-chew to answer me, eating too much is need, and drinking too much, driving too quickly on Route 95, overcharging on the American Express card, or simply saying her name in despair as you reach, in the early morning, on the living room floor — your hands clasped, like a prisoner of war's, behind your head — to touch your straining elbows to your knees. Actually, Truffaut did requite her love. But it was awfully close to the end, and I thought she'd deserved far better.

Postcard, in early autumn, from Bernie to me:

> B —
> Am currently designing condos for the erotically deficient — no bedrooms, but two kitchens. All of course is well.
>
> B

All wasn't, of course. I wanted to call. I also didn't. Two nights later, while Joanne worked late, I telephoned. I held the Arshile Gorky postcard — *The Betrothed*, this serious incomprehensibility was called — when I punched out his number; I looked at the painting, and not Bernie's words, when I spoke.

"Bern, how's it going?"

"*Ça va.* Lots of *va*. Except, it seems I apparently called up Rhonda one night. On the phone."

"And she didn't tell you she was pleased."

"No."

"You didn't expect her to."

"No."

"She hung up on you?"

"Worse," he said. "She let her breath out very, very, very slowly. It was like listening to the Goodyear Blimp deflate. On and on and on and on, and then she said in that control voice of hers, the I'm-trying-to-land-all-these-jumbo-jets-at-one-*time* voice, she says, 'What, Bernie?' You know what I mean? Just 'What' and just 'Bernie.' I mean, what in hell am I supposed to *say*?"

"What *did* you say?"

"I puled."

"Well, you picked the right phone call for it."

"This is true. I was on target."

"What'd you say, Bern?"

"I believe I said, 'Oh, Rhonda.' "

"Damn."

"Yeah. I wanted, see, to make sure I didn't have any pride or anything sloshing around in the tank."

"No, I think you got it all."

"Any honor or pride or anything," he said.

"Did she answer you?"

"She waited a very long time, and then she whispered. Like a mother."

I said, "Like you were young and she was extremely old."

"You got the one," he said. "You ever do this before?"

"I wrote the lyrics and the music for it."

"Yeah," he said, "I guess we all do some supplicating now and then."

"But what'd she whisper to you?"

" 'Please,' " he whispered.

"And then she hung up."

"Really gently. No rattle or bang, just the little click. I kept listening to the phone. She sounded *good* to me, Billy."

"You know —"

"You have the solution," he said. "You're on the verge of giving me the solution, aren't you?"

"No, kid."

"No."

I said, "You want to come up to New York for a while?"

"Later. One of these days I'll come in, maybe you can get tickets for something. We can take Joanne to the Stadium, she can watch a team play ball without being distracted by winning. You believe this, Billy? A couple of middle-aged guys who *go* through this?"

"We're late bloomers," I said, "it's not our fault."

"You're still starving yourself?"

"I'm being pretty good," I said. "I don't mean anything smug."

"*Be* smug. Listen: I am almost out of the Land's End catalogue for pants. They don't believe in creatures of my proportion."

"You talk about guys like us, Bern," I said, "you're talking *about* proportion. Come on. You think Captain Marvel was sized Medium? Samson?"

"Even Delilah," he said.

"Atta boy."

I usually called Brenda's mother Susan Hayward because she made me feel and probably look like Victor Mature as Samson, pulling down the temple of the Philistines. Joanne and I were taking Susan Hayward's child and mine to an opening at a gallery on Greene Street. The artist was a man who had left off practicing law to get a degree in painting, and who taught around where he could — Sarah Lawrence, Cooper Union, NYU — and who, according to Joanne, had fallen in love with his life.

"Shouldn't you love someone else's?" I asked her. I was changing into a sport coat and long-sleeved shirt and tie because Joanne had cabbed down from Yorkville not in her jeans but in her longish black skirt, gray rayon shirt, long black silk scarf, smoky stockings and black half boots. I was angry not with the artist, and not about my clothes or hers, and not even with Joanne. I had simply been reminded once more that it took twenty minutes' cab time for me to see what she wore.

I did not again tonight raise the issue of her moving in. We were scattered all over the place, I thought: Bernie outside Philadelphia, Susan Hayward and her new husband in Maine, Brenda on the Upper West Side at school, Joanne up and east, and I, in no-man's-land, on 16th and Sixth, pulling a necktie tight and thinking that, for all our lighthearted fun, Joanne and I knew a lot about grimness.

She was ignoring me — ignoring my petulance, she'd have said. She sat on my coffee table, a big wooden crate used seventy-five years ago for shipping an Underwood typewriter, and she read the show's announcement.

I said, "I said shouldn't you love other people's lives as well as your own?"

"Well, your own isn't a bad place to start," she said. "Then you can expand the franchise. Being maladjusted's pretty overrated, don't you think, Bill?"

"Of whom do we speak, Jo?"

"Oh," she said, "*I* get it. We're having a fight." She came into the bedroom, smelling of Liz Claiborne's scent, looking (quite correctly) twelve years younger than I. "We're in a huff," she said. She pecked me on the lips, yanked on my necktie, and said, like a stiff, wary man, "Of *whom* do we speak?"

"Successful young artists make me insecure."

"Meeting your daughter makes you insecure."

"You make me insecure."

She cocked her head, considering my fear, or me, or both.

Brenda came into the gallery shortly after Joanne introduced me to the artist. He was in his early thirties, craggy, with thick, copper-colored hair, and he was possibly in love with Joanne. He looked somehow elegant in his clay-colored cotton pants (and they were well within the parameters of the Land's End catalogue) and a thick dark corduroy sport coat the color of wet stones; he hastened to find us drinks, he sought to somehow be of service, he was cordial and reticent at once.

I said to Joanne, "You call *that* well adjusted?"

She stared up from under her ample eyebrows with large, dark eyes. "I call him Nicholas," she said.

I took a sip of Perrier.

"And sometimes I call him Nick."

I watched Brenda, long-legged in a metallic-silver miniskirt over silver tights, her hair a color of yellow I couldn't name and fluffed as if someone had rubbed it the wrong way so often that static electricity held it erect. The makeup under her eyes made her face look bruised. "My former child," I said, watching her stalk to us.

Brenda said, "Hi, Joanne. Hi, Bill."

"What would it take for you to call me Daddy?" I asked. But I hugged her hard, and she did hug back. "Baby," I said.

"A low level of sophistication," she answered.

"I *have* that."

Joanne said, "Ah, but your daughter doesn't." They kissed and then left me, Brenda pulling Joanne as if Joanne were her guest. Over her shoulder, Brenda said, "See you soon, Daddy," then laughed to Joanne as if they both knew the joke.

Nicholas returned with a little sandwich on a napkin. "Smoked salmon," he said, "capers, lemon juice — good food. The bread's from Dean and Deluca." As he gently laid the napkin and sandwich on the palm of my hand, bending his head to the chore as if performing minor surgery, I was filled with resistance. I felt like an elder being shown good care by a child. But I also, still, thought of surgery: what, I wondered, were we going to cut out.

"Nice," I agreed, not eating. "And a nice show, by the way. Congratulations. The idea of spraying through the wire forms, the patterns on top of the stained canvas — really interesting."

"You really like it," he said.

"Well, yes. I really do."

He nodded and beamed. His teeth were even and white, of course. "Jo told me you were a really fair guy. A really decent guy, she said."

"Decent?"

His big handsome head bobbed quickly with relief. *Relief*, goddammit.

"About what, Nick?"

"What?"

"About what things am I said to be decent? The refusal of the Yankees to be patient with young pitching? The city's insistence on making carriage horses wear canvas diapers? Or somebody snogging my woman."

"Snogging," he said.

"I didn't want to start at too basic a level, but fine: screwing, Nick. Didn't your parents explain these things to you when you were small?"

"Jo *hasn't* talked to you, then."

"I don't know that she needs to, now."

He moved his hands as if to help me pour some language out. But I was jamming my finger sandwich into my mouth. I was chewing and pulping and sliding the slimy sandwich down. I saw Jo and Brenda across the long, pale, chilly room ringed with colors sprayed in geometric patterns. They were watching us, I realized. So Brenda, probably, also knew. I saw how much like the Susan Hayward of Portland, Maine, my daughter looked.

"Okay," I said to him as the sandwich paused beneath my breastbone. "Good pictures. Striking pictures. You probably have a mildly guilty conscience, and you probably give money to street people when they ask. All right. But I wish you'd have stuck to loving *yourself*. He humps best who humps his own. You bastard."

Bernie, on the telephone, said, "You left it at that?"

"I figured, why not take impotence as far as I could, Bern."

I was in my apartment, and it was late. I held a package of fig newtons in my left hand as if it were a loaded, cocked gun. My former lover and my former child were wherever in New York they'd got to without me. The fig newtons weren't open yet.

Bernie said, "The husband's the last to know. Or boyfriend, whatever."

"I knew."

"How long?"

"Don't ask."

"So — look: Billy. Consider that at least you don't have to wait until she moves her clothes and furniture out. You don't have to sit there and watch her do it with what's his name."

"I am blessed."

"It's a small consideration, but I *would* consider it a blessing, yes."

"I'm going to do that." I sat back and laid the cookie packet across my chest.

"And you'll stick to the diet," he said.

"I will?"

"Yeah," he said, "you should do that. I like you trim and healthy."

"And you?"

"Me, too," he said. "Now that we're both miserable, it'll be easier for me."

"I'm glad to help, kid."

"You'll be all right, Billy?"

"You need to go to sleep."

"If you're okay."

"I'm fine. I'll cry tomorrow."

"Who *said* that?"

"Susan Hayward," I said, landing on the punch line with my paws.

I was working on an article about billing practices that I owed the *New York Law Reporter*, and I was reviewing once again the Seven Hundred Signs — the indications I now knew I'd known I knew that Joanne had showed me over four months, proving we'd been an impermanence from the start. I was also framing a note, drafting something spontaneous, to send Brenda:

Here's 20 bucks, baby. Please take a cab instead of the subway
from Port Authority to your dorm late at night.

It didn't ask why she was arriving on buses at dawn, or where the
buses were coming from. It didn't go into details about the sullen
phone call from Susan Hayward, asking why she, in Maine, knew
scary facts about the safety of the child whom I, in New York, should
be protecting. I mistakenly wiped out a line about legal accounting
procedures for international matters and told the machine to save what
was left, and I went downstairs for the Saturday mail.

The warning from American Express about my overdue payments
made me, literally, blush. I hated to disappoint the man in Phoenix
who had written about my history with the firm. The postcard, addressed in Bernie's hand, made me smile: on fiscal matters, we were co-
conspirators. The reproduction on the front of the card was of a
graceful, naked Diana by Saint-Gaudens, poised on the ball of her
golden left foot, aiming a long-shafted, heavy-headed arrow at Bernie
or me. The message:

> B —
> Busted the diet last night with a grown-up woman. Long-awaited
> calories did not meet my expectations. Nor I hers.
> B

I went upstairs and fried three eggs in butter and ate three dripping
sandwiches. I spent the rest of the afternoon lugging my stomachache
from the screen showing the Texas Tech game to the screen that showed
me what I'd managed to save.

But Bernie and I, while we are mildly sorrowful people, also, often,
are capable adults. Brenda's a whacked-out late-night drifter, but also
a college kid with some sense. And her parents do love her. You always
manage to pay American Express, and they always forgive you. People
try to understand.

So imagine us, then, in Pennsylvania Station — not the arc of iron
and glass that Bernie and I knew as boys, but a large enough place for
people and trains and their echoes — as we wait for Bernie's arrival on
the Washington-to-Philly-to-New York. It's early November, I'm wear-

ing a Burberry lined raincoat that costs as much as a car, and Brenda, hair the color of neon strawberries, in her dark leather fleece-collared bombardier jacket that falls below her hips, with sleeves so long her fingertips barely protrude, looks nothing but terrific. Her mother's face every now and again shows forth, and I can only think, though I never want to say it, *Susan: not so bad.*

Bernie walks toward us, now. He's wearing the khaki fatigue jacket that our father brought home from the service. He's lost enough weight to fasten it over his sport coat, which hangs out. He's closed the jacket as our father did, snapped it and zipped it to the knot of his tie. His toes point outward as he walks, and I can see as if from the less soaring and less gorgeous ceiling how alike we seem in motion and bulk.

As if from that reduced height, I watch Brenda hug his neck and kiss his cheek, and then I watch Bernie and me embrace; our big, though smaller, bellies collide. Brenda walks between us, a little in front of us, impatient, of course. I'm back down now where I ought to be. We're going out to eat. We will watch our step. We'll look at each other, Bernie and I, and we'll see ourselves eat with a little restraint. But I'll insist on a bottle of excellent wine, and we'll take turns, I predict, encouraging Brenda with similar voices in similar tones to ask for anything she wants. Terrine of duck, the sautéed caviar, the hot scallop and avocado salad. "Anything," one of us will say.

The Wicked
Stepmother

You can imagine how much Pop wants you home. But I'm not writing to persuade you. This is, I guess, to tell you what she's like. I think she's as worried about you as you might be about her. Just think of yourself as a Pict and of her as a conquering Roman: she'd feel more secure if the outlying hordes, my barbarian brother, would only squat within the walls so she can start in *managing*. She manages awfully well.

Pop is of course goofy about her, but not in a way demeaning to him or Mom, once you swallow the enormousness of his ever marrying anyone again. At our age, and his, and hers, which is a very unleathery fifty-two, you do have to consider sex, don't you? I do. And, I must say, I am quite impressed by my ability to do so.

Part of the reason is she's sexy. A sexy middle-aged woman is not a revolutionary development, but it remains noteworthy. She is thin and strong and pretty tall — almost as tall as I am, as high as Pop's nose. She works out. They've installed one of those cross-country ski machines in what we used to call the office, but which Celia Mifflin Huytens now calls the sun room. I guess that's better, say, than The Solarium, with capital initials. I still think of it as the office, and I still see Mom at the table, with its silly curved legs, balancing the checkbook every Sunday after reading the *Times*. Except it's Celia's sun room now. Pop calls it that, and so do I. So will you when you come, because it is more Celia's house than yours or mine now, and Pop is smitten, and he's made it very clear: what Celia says it is is what it *is*.

Anyway, she's pretty convincingly herself about her workouts. She doesn't wear metallically glinting leotards or flaming pastel workout suits and $200 sneakers. She enters whatever room Pop's in, let's say the living room, wearing boat shoes and your old OSU basketball sweat pants and Pop's ratty, chewed-up cotton sweater, the navy blue job he wears for yard chores. I might have expected the sweater, because it's Pop's, and no man I have ever known could resist when the little lady volunteers to be engulfed in his big, protective clothes. But your basketball pants: the woman's a tactician as well as a strategist. She, in your clothing, brings you into the room and into Pop's mind — and of course she reminds him of your untoward absence from his homecoming with his new wife — and suggests all kinds of intimacy with her that you're engaged in without suspecting. Think of all that ladysweat, Tom.

So she strides in, all long legs and muscles up and down her back that you can just about *feel* under the clothes, and she snaps a towel at Pop, or asks me something unessential, and then off she goes around the corner. Pretty soon you hear the hiss and clack of the skis, and this kind of metal chatter that's the noise of the gear wheel on this machine — you pull back and forth on a cord while you ski to nowhere — and what's being produced, you know, is a middle-aged woman nearly five feet ten inches tall, weighing approximately nothing, with broad shoulders and an actual, verifiable waist, and a can that looks good in the short skirts she doesn't hesitate to wear. She's got one of those athletic torsos. Pop stares at it a lot — tight, a little boyish, but really not. You know? And she maintains all that in the sun room, which is hers, hers, hers.

Pop looks all right. One reason is that he is actually happy, actually glad to be alive with Mom not, and that's a tough one to say, and tougher still to resent, and toughest, maybe, to accept. Another reason he looks good is that Celia gets *him* to do the I'm-skiing-to-noplace routine. He's up to fifteen minutes a day. He *sounds* like a dying man when he's on the machine, but when he comes off it and catches his breath, his color is good, and it stays good, and he actually has this new little toe-bounce when he walks. I think he thinks he's a *jock*. And, back to something I referred to earlier, and you'll just have to get used to this: I heard him groan two nights ago.

I was reading late, trying to find something boring enough to make me sleep without pills, and I was in the middle of stark, alert outrage over an article on how the FBI got some library to disclose all the names of their patrons who were taking out books on presidential assassinations. It was very quiet in the house. I heard things as you might see them from the corner of an eye. There's a county snowplow, I didn't quite think, and there's a branch getting heavy with snow as it scrapes the bathroom window down the hall, and so on. And, suddenly, as loud as a shout in a sleeping house at one o'clock in the morning, there was Pop's voice, groaning.

It wasn't pain or nightmare or ghosts. It was full of triumph and rich delight. In the *sack*, understand? This was no abstract skiing in the name of good health. This was satisfactory sex announcing itself, and I want to admit right here that what I did, in sort of one motion, when the cry had registered, was hurl the magazine from the bed and turn off the light and roll onto my shoulder and shove my head at the pillow and lie very still — as if a grownup might somehow discover me at something very wrong.

Now, we ate breakfast together the next morning. Celia was wearing faded blue jeans and thick boot socks, no shoes, and a black mock turtleneck that announced her nipples. Pop was devouring grapefruit, which, you'll remember, Mom had to drug him to get him to pick at. Celia was drinking her strong tea and piling chunky peanut butter onto a toasted bagel. I came in for black coffee and cigarettes; she looks at them, but so far she hasn't proscribed them, though I'm sure she will. And we sit there, Pop with the papers and I with my nicotine and Celia with her self-possession, and she says, "Alexandra, you look tired, sweetie."

I tell her that I'm just waking up.

"No," she says, "you look as though you didn't sleep much at all, really. Doesn't she?" So now Pop has to look over and study these satchels under my eyes. "Alex," she says, "did we keep you up?"

You see what I mean? Nothing bitchy or cruel in the question, if you're helping a middle-aged man to rediscover sex after his wife's long dying and his own long fealty to her. It doesn't even *have* to imply what she and I know it means. And of course Pop chooses to understand only that she's concerned for his daughter. I guess he does. Maybe he's priapic over having been priapic. Men get that way. If you don't choose to admit it, you can take it from me as established fact.

I believe I reply, "Why, no, Celia. Were you up late?"

And Celia has to say, "Well, we were up. Let's say that."

Pop did have the grace to hide behind the *Times*. I sent up a smoke screen, then studied the rim of my cup. I asked no questions and she, apparently, felt no further need to assert herself as suzerain.

I seem to have portrayed Pop as the silent puppet of a cunning, dishy woman. She surely is all of each. But she is, honestly, more. So's Pop. The point of what I wanted to tell you was the groan. The — I'll admit it — enviable groan was the idea there, though what came out was *my* bitchiness as well as hers. Whatever she is, and Celia's complicated, Pop is just *glad*. And that's what I should emphasize. I have as much trouble with all of this as you do, I'm sure. So maybe that's why I told you about her planting her flag atop my tired head, that morning after. I should have emphasized how long and difficult a journey that groan suggested it had made.

Pop is, as ever, on the job. He worries about you, he worries about me, he takes calls from the office even though he's on his post-honeymoon vacation, and he has made damned certain that I understand his loyalty to everyone in his life: *everyone*.

We're in the big, handsome old house in smallish, handsome old Salisbury, Connecticut, and this big, handsome man with his tall, handsome new wife comes out of the sun room and, with a towel over his head, walks in his sneakers out and across to the backyard bird feeders, where I'm serving up the sunflower seeds.

I tell him, "Pop, you're sweating and you're going to get sick. Celia would murder you if you got yourself sick."

He gives me that dismissive shrug, the wave of the paw — you know. He says, "You can keep me warm, Alex."

This is when I surprise myself. "Pop," I say, "isn't that Celia's job?"

He steps back. I step back. He says, "Whoa."

I say it, too.

He looks at me and grins, and it's the old-time I'm-your-all-knowing-father-and-wasn't-I-right-*again* grin. I used to see it *over the phone*, calling him from college or library school or the terrible place I had for a year in La Jolla. I'd hear his voice, and I'd see that grin, and before I could calmly and dispassionately register my complaint about the flawed spin of the cosmos, I'd be up to my collarbone in tears. He flashes it here, in the snow, near the bird feeders, and there I am again: dewy, dopy, embarrassed, and possibly relieved.

"Sorry," I say, "it's not going to be that easy. The new-mother-versus-same-old-daughter number? No. It isn't that."

"I never said it was," he says. Then he does that — what's that called? The big, looping one? Bolo punch. He does that: "I didn't even think that, Alexandra. I just thought you were sad, and I wondered why."

I say, "Bullshit, Pop. You know damned good and well what it is."

This time he gets his paws on me and hugs me hard. You know. He keeps on hugging me. He says, "I've been very selfish. I know that. The thing is, Alex, I can't figure out what else I should be. What you and Tom would want me to be. What Mom would want. I don't know." He actually sounds confused. He sounds like somebody who really needs to know. "What should I be doing for you and Tom and Mom?" he says.

Here's the thing. While he's saying this, and hugging me, and maybe shaking from the cold, he lets the crying out, and I get to hear what's been in him. Tom: he is bawling. And he says, "This isn't fair. I never wanted to do this to you. I'm sorry. It is not fair." And of course that's all I need to hear, yes? So I am weeping all over him, and he's crying into my shoulder and my neck. I make a vow: if the former Celia Mifflin comes out of the house to say one perky or commiserative word, I am feeding her eyes to the bluejays. But we get to stay out there alone. After a while, he wipes my face with his towel, and then he wipes his face, and we sort of shrug and sort of laugh. We're out of it without saying what we might have said, but what should that have usefully been?

One of the tricks of my trade is what they call the reference interview. You've been through it a dozen times. You go up to the reference librarian, say someone tall and elegant like me, and try not to melt because she's such a turn-on, and you say, "I would like to read about second marriages, please." Here's where the training comes in: the librarian — let's call her she, if she's me — has to narrow down the terms of your search. In what culture? In what time-frame? By men? By women? In children's fiction? (You'd be knocked out by how many kids' books are about divorce and remarriage, death and remarriage.) In sociological research? Biological? Anthropological? And of course I'd need to know what your project is — research for practical application, thesis, term paper, curiosity, pleasure, abstract knowledge, saving your bruised young life.

I ended up working over Celia. Not that she was asking me for anything specific. She was pumping me to see if I hated her and if you, you absentee child, hated her worse. She wanted to see clearly how the land, if you'll pardon the expression, lay.

It was a very lovely late afternoon, with snow on everything and more coming down, the trains into Millerton no doubt delayed for hours, and a fire in the fireplace, drinks on the coffee table, Pop in town to buy food for a meal they'd planned together. Yup: another new Pop, constructing the menu, shopping for food. Celia and I, apparently, were to exchange confidences.

"Your father tells me that you're coming off an unfortunate passage," Celia said.

"Celia, you can call him Harold. Har. Whatever you like. I don't mind."

"It's difficult at first," she said, and she gave me a frank and honest smile that might have been a frank and honest smile. "But you're making it so easy for me. I'm grateful, Alex."

"Come on, Celia," I said. "Say what you like. Relax. We're in your house. That's fine with Tom, it's fine with me. Enjoy yourself."

She actually lowered her lashes. They are long, full, dark, and her own. "Were you in love?" she said, bringing her lashes up and then her eyes, the way you see the cannon rise in turrets on ships they show you in news footage.

I assured myself that I could meet them, and I did for as much as two or three seconds at a time. "I was," I told her. "Well, I thought I was. I think I was. When they find my ruins, the historians can figure it out. Yeah, Celia. Probably love."

"Here? In the East?"

"I left him out West. In Santa Monica, as a matter of fact."

"Is he in the movies?"

"He is actually in the movies. He writes for the movies."

"That must have been exciting, Alex."

"It was." It was. He was, the movies were, the Shangri-La Hotel across Ocean Avenue from the beach was, and so was the smell of the sea in our window. So was the smell of even the goddamned traffic. I told you this. I used to listen to the traffic when I couldn't sleep. I loved the thought of everybody driving up the coast while we were there, like an island, like a log in the water moving around us. I can't imagine why his wife would want him around after he was a log in the water with me. Yes, I can. I said, "Just as exciting as you think, Celia."

"Did you get to meet anyone big?" She asked it as though the information wasn't to entertain her so much as to give me the opportunity to offer it.

"We sat next to O. J. Simpson in the movies, one night. He's very big."

"And beautiful?"

"And beautiful," I said. I decided to use my training. Next to cops, analysts, and managers of investment portfolios, we're the best at eliciting information. "Celia," I said, "you're so easy with, well, younger people. You have a child of your own. Am I right? Pop said you have a son? Am I right?"

She said, *pong* for my *ping*, "I must say, I think of *you* as a little of my own now, Alex. And Tom, of course. I'm really eager to meet him."

"But there's a son?"

She drank at a teensy bit of bourbon she'd poured into a tall glass of diet ginger ale over ice. She said, "I have a son." She raised her chin a little, so I knew she was declaring something sizable. "I have an ex-husband who lives in Red Bank, New Jersey, with a young woman who weaves things, and I have a son who lives in an institution."

I waited for her to tell me why. I lit a cigarette, and she almost winced when I exhaled the smoke. "Should I put it out?" I said, as if I were willing to.

"Oh no, I don't mind," she lied. "Severely retarded," she said, not lying. Her eyes are dark. They got wet, then, so they were very bright.

Her hair is dark, very glossy, and her skin is beautifully pale. Her eyes made her look even more beautiful, wouldn't you know. "We took care of him," she said. "At home. We mainstreamed him in school. Have you ever seen that done? It's terrible. The parents are in the school every other *hour*, because you're entitled, the child is entitled, the law *says* he is. But the school resists, the teachers resist, the administrators resist, the other children resist — they're cruel. They're such bastards," she said. "They do the usual. They make fun, they call names, they run away screaming their little screams. Because the boy — Barry, Barry's his name. He had sudden angers, fury, you understand? He was manageable, though not very attractive, when he was a little boy. But he got big. He got big, and strong, and very frightening. One evening, when I was folding the laundry and he was supposedly helping me, he knocked me down." She touched the side of her face. "I lay on the floor, you understand, and looked up at my own child, who was my baby. And he looked down at me, and with no anger, no grudge, just curiosity, as if he couldn't understand how I'd got there. Or why I seemed so frightened of him. All I wanted to do was explain it to him. And I knew thoroughly — totally — that I couldn't. I can't."

You will be pleased to know that I didn't have a sensible word to say, couldn't find one catchphrase in the whole anthology of banalities, much less a prompt, appropriate reply. I inspected my cigarette. And then, and you're invited to blush for me, I said, "Wow."

"Wow," she said. "It is a bit of a conversation stopper. Forgive me."

"No," I said, "I was the one pumping you."

"Were you pumping me, Alex? How useful to know." She laughed her sex-goddess laugh, and all I could think to do was laugh with her. She drank a tiny bit of her horrible highball and she said, "Fair's fair?"

"I guess so."

"Tell me about your mother?"

I said, "Do you mean my mother, or your new husband's wife?" You'll recall what I said about the reference interview.

Celia said, "Did you know their marriage well enough to tell me about it?"

"I can tell you about the outside of it," I told her. "What my brother and I saw. My parents were very good friends, I'd say. I'd say they loved each other. She died hard. It took a long time. He was immersed in her dying. I don't know, Celia." When I lit my cigarette, I blew the smoke toward her. "I can tell you they kept their secrets pretty brilliantly to themselves. They were very good about not making us think they loved each other more than they loved us."

She nodded her head. She approved, I thought the nod was meant to say, and I resented it. I wanted her to feel stung, excluded, jealous, and in her place. When she moved the shallow marble ashtray closer for me, I realized that she *was*, of course, in what was officially and by virtue of possession her place.

Tom, I felt defeated. It's the only reason I can think of for how I went on to betray them to her.

I said, "Of course, that was the outer view. We've still to learn their secrets. I mean, you know — what they knew and we didn't. What they kept hidden from each other. Et cetera."

Et cetera. Truly, Latin is the last refuge of a skunk. *And*, of course, the language of imperial Rome.

Celia said, "Thank you." I knew her thanks were supposed to be for my talking to her, for describing, and with such thick-tongued unintelligence, the long romance we hope had been our parents'. But it was really thanks for letting slip the possibility entertained by any adult child — that he might have seen other women, that she might have seen other men, that they both engaged in foursomes with body builders in dirty hotels. "Thank you," she said.

And I? "Thank *you*."

She went to put more wood in the fire. She was wearing her boat shoes and no socks, and her legs looked young as she bent to the wood box. I went to help. She lifted a log too large, really, for a fire as small as the one we were burning. It needed to be split. I suggested we wait, and she, with her strong back and the attested-to thighs, must have thought I meant we ought to wait for a man to appear. She'd have no waiting. She lifted the log — there was not much effort involved for her — and swung it back before chucking it at the flames.

I said, "Let's *place* it in, Celia, you get a lot of sparks and flying coals if you —"

That was when the kitchen door slammed and Pop called out. She was distracted first by me and then by him, and the log caught on her leg and fell end-first to strike her ankle. That was all. She didn't cry out. She looked at the blood on her leg, and I replaced the log in the wood box, set a smaller one on the fire and replaced the fire screen. I heard Pop, behind me, say, "Oh, my *God*."

This was the man who bought other people's companies whether they wanted to sell them or not. This was the man who had been through a war, and the raising of us, and the death of his wife. He was on his knees, still in his coat, with her leg in his hands. "It's not a break," he said.

I said, "It's barely a bruise."

Pop looked at me the way he stared us down when we were small — head hung, eyes coming at you from just under his bushy, ragged brows, the voltage not quite enough to jump-start a truck — and he said, "Forgive her, Celia. Please."

"There's nothing to forgive," she said.

But didn't I say it anyway? "I'm sorry," I seem to have said.

She said, "Alex. Alexandra. All is forgiven. Come home." Pop nodded his head as he laughed at Celia's wit. You remember that laugh, with his teeth showing, his head nodding? It was the signal that the rest of us should laugh along. All is forgiven, come home, and a hearty chuckle with Pop and his wounded new wife. Well.

Celia said, "Let's cook. Let's eat good food and light candles and drink some of your father's wine, Alex."

So the unlamed Celia stood and we brought our drinks into the kitchen, where under her direction we chopped and julienned to compose a dinner of golden bell peppers, Gorgonzola, onions and penne. I lit the candles. Pop opened a bottle of wine about which he made those slightly smug, insightful remarks. He was *festive*. As we ate, as we drank the wine he so enjoyed naming, Vino Nobile di Montepulciano, he said, several times, "Isn't this all just terrific?" His raggedy eyebrows jumped around; his big brown eyes, which you and I have watched or ducked from over thirty years, were simply pleased.

He toasted Celia by raising his glass and saying her name. He made it sound like a quality. Then he toasted me the same way. I answered, at once, by toasting you. Pop didn't pause. "Damned right," he said.

That was when, again, I thought about Mom. I looked past Celia at Pop, and I found him staring down the table at me. He looked wistful. He looked *historical:* he was in the dangerous places, he was back in time, not safe now with Celia. I wanted to see if she knew, but I wouldn't look away from him. Tom, I am certain he was thinking of Mom.

So maybe this is what my letter's about: that in candlelight, unable to say it aloud before his sexy new wife who is far too smart for the likes of you and me, Pop was led by happiness to think of Mom. We're trained, I told you, to ferret one small datum (as the Romans would say) that is lost or hidden in the hundreds of millions of words. Maybe I just did.

Folk Tales

WHEN I KNEW HIM, when I was small, my grandpa Fine was a bony, frail man who was eager to smile when I spoke, grimmer when my parents did, secret-looking in repose. He had come from Russia, a boy, fleeing. He told my mother that everyone arrived here a fugitive. She and Uncle Bernie heard stories from Grandpa Fine, and they told them to me. Stories hiss and gurgle through the hearts of peasants, I would tell my son if I thought he could bear the news.

Most are fragments now, unfastened from the moments of my hearing them. Although I can recall sitting on Bernie's lap to watch wrestling on the black and white set in my parents' house in Brooklyn — I was never permitted to watch Gorgeous George and wonder at his golden hair unless Bernie was there to insist — I can't remember how or when he told me about Grandpa Fine and the Cossacks. But I see them in a Russian town composed by me from movies, no doubt, from novels. Cossacks ride across the square with drawn swords, and the Jews flee before them. I hear women screaming, though I don't see them, and I hear the horses' hooves. Now the Jews are fled from sight as I focus the memory of the story, or the memory that the fragments suggest I ought to retain. I see the Cossacks and then, as the invisible women cry out, a small, pale, neglected-looking boy with large teeth, short legs, small hands and nearsighted, terrified eyes, slaps at the synagogue's high wooden doors. They stay closed. I know, as he does, that the rabbi and his congregation pant shallowly inside. They will not open the doors until the riders have passed.

Grandpa Fine blamed every rabbi for his abandonment, and he never forgot. Grandma invited a rabbi into their apartment to give Uncle Bernie secret lessons for the bar mitzvah Grandpa had forbidden, and Grandpa, injured slightly at his carpentry job, came home early and discovered him. "Spitting on the rabbi!" Uncle Bernie says in my memory. His round face mocks horror; it seems, in fact, to crease with pride for the small enormity. "He drove the rabbi from the house. Imagine that."

I was an unattached, middle-aged man when Bernie brought me one more story. I was not in touch with him or his children. I was in flight from my broken second marriage. I had taken a sublet on Riverside Drive and 108th from Melissa Turnbull, a food writer, who was traveling in Europe. I'd been vouched for by her lawyer who also represented my second, former, probably final wife.

That was the year I worked for the clinic on Third and 95th, counseling the indulged and the shaky of resolve. My clothing bag hung on the back of Melissa's bedroom closet, and in it I kept my summer sport coats and slacks. I washed, dried and folded socks and underclothes, but replaced them in the two canvas satchels I kept on top of Melissa's bedroom worktable. If pressed, I would have admitted to being unable to accept the permanence of my life's large shifts. But no one pressed me, as no one ironed my chinos or the cotton shirts I often neglected to carry to a laundry service. I went rumpled and unanalyzed. I rode in taxis to work, I walked to films, I dined with colleagues when I could and alone in front of the VCR when I couldn't. I occasionally telephoned Theodore, my son, who had chosen to remain in the Southwest after college. Each time we shyly, tentatively spoke, he in fear of more bad news or a new demand on emotions he preferred to hoard, I felt grateful that in the careening course of two marriages I had been decent enough to help create only one child who carried forth a share of the genes that had survived in spite of the locked synagogue door.

On a Saturday morning in July, when damp heat lay with the density of August air, the door buzzed and Uncle Bernie, over the intercom, said, "Bosco. Hey. It's Uncle Bernie. You remember."

"Yes," I said, for the second or third time as he sprawled in the living room, furnished with white canvas covers on chairs and sofa, and monitored by Melissa from photographs, paintings and sketches that hung framed on the walls. Bernie was very small, yellow-white pale, too little and tired to have come alone from Long Island. But Bernie had always insisted on making his way. I kept looking at his lap — I had sat there, small and beloved — which was almost nonexistent. His stomach descended when he sat, and his paunch rose. His extra chin crushed the fat knot of his broad mauve tie. He was shiny with sweat, round of face. He twinkled with the gold of the rims of his glasses, the gold in the fillings of his teeth, the gold of his two rings and his wristwatch. The blue-black suit was shiny, too. When I'd shaken his hand before embracing him, the hand had been soft and broad and moist. Now his eyes were moist, and he shook his head as if to smile, as if in wonder.

"Bosco," he said. He'd named me for the chocolate syrup other children, but not I, had been allowed to stir into their milk. I had complained so bitterly that, though I hadn't received a jar of syrup, I had received a name. It only occurred to me as I spoke with Bernie, then, that being named for a childhood lament is a comment as bitter as Bosco was said to be sweet.

"So how did you find me, Uncle Bernie? What a treat!" I sounded as scared as Theodore did when I phoned. What boulder, I always felt him wondering, am I to push up which distant hill on your behalf?

"I asked," Bernie said. "Who did I ask? I did not ask the mayor of the city of New York. I did not ask the Internal Revenue, in case you was on the lam for taxes. I did not ask the Irish Republican Army because I am a Democrat. Unfortunately, I telephoned your house. Your ex-house, yes? With your angry ex-wife inside it? She helped, but she was not what you would call helpful. Was you cheating, Bosco? Or was it that thing with differences — all the phony talk meaning you're nauseous from each other?"

"She's really a nice woman," I said. "I'm sorry you never got to meet her."

"*I'm* sorry. I think I was out of town when you didn't invite me to your wedding."

"No, Uncle Bernie, there *wasn't* a wedding. One of her old college teachers was a minister. He married us in his living room."

"Ah. A minister. You don't keep kosher, then."

"Neither do you."

"Agreed," he said, flapping both hands at me as if dispelling smoke. "Never mind. There's good jokes and there's bad jokes. Guess which one I just made."

"Uncle Bernie, I never ever forgot you."

"Nice," he said, nodding. "That's nice. I'm glad. Me, too."

"Bernie, do you remember the stories you used to tell me?"

He looked puzzled. "Which?"

"Grandpa, the Cossack — you know, and the rabbi. The time they wouldn't take him in."

"That I remember," he said. "*You* remember it?"

"Parts of it. I wouldn't mind hearing it all."

"Stories? Bosco. Howie. You'll permit me to say this." He wiped daintily with the back of his forefinger at the sweat that beaded his large bald head. "You wanted stories, you could have called me up, yes? At that time, I might have had the time. No offense, kid, but — understand?"

I finally heard some of what had brought him there. "What about *time*, Bernie? What's going on?"

He smiled the smile we smile before we weep. He didn't cry, but his voice was uneven. "Tomorrow morning, seven o'clock, I go to the airport. This time, Bobbie drives me, I don't go alone. I got to fly all the way to Houston. I see the doctors in Houston. You believe it, a Jew in Texas?"

"Why?"

"Heart."

"Aw, Bernie."

"It's like plumbing, Howie. This comes out, this goes in to replace it, the thing next to it, we put new threads on, and this is the one we can't help."

"Which one is that?"

"A something or other valve."

"Something or other."

He said, "What's useful in pumping the blood. Why do I need to know its name? *They* need to know its name."

"You want me to come with you, Bernie?"

"Bosco," he said. "Sweetie." He leaned forward, offering a small red oblong with one hand while, with the other, he wiped at his eyes and then his forehead. The red was faded to nearly orange. It was about two inches long. The tiny flap was fastened with red thread wound between two small cardboard studs. The black printing said it was a safety deposit box key from a bank I remembered well.

"Corner of J and Coney Island Avenue?" I asked.

"The same. Your parents banked there all their life."

"What's there, Bernie? Why now?"

"What's there is something your mother said I should keep for you. I never looked at it because it's yours, from her. I been paying fifty bucks a year for her for a while now. Don't reach for money, please, Howie. This I did for Dora. Fifty bucks I don't have for the girl I took care of the best I could all of her life? Please. It was a pleasure. What was the question? Why now? Houston is why now. Just in case is why now."

"What's the something, Bernie? Why didn't I ever hear about it?"

"You did. Dora told me."

"I don't know. I was never told."

"You'll see it, you'll remember it. Dora said."

"Happy or unhappy?"

"Bosco! You sound a little bit like a little boy, you don't mind my pointing it out."

I weighed the key in my palm. "Maybe I am," I said.

"She told me it was precious. You could start all over with it."

"You think I need to do that, Bernie?"

"Don't be one of those men, they pout. Don't be insulted by me, Howie. I told you. I'm scared. Jews get scared, they give you advice like old ladies. All I mean, I'm touched your mother held something back for when you maybe needed it."

"When would you have given it to me?"

"When you needed it."

"How would you have known?"

His little mouth trembled, and I thought he might weep. But he was trying not to laugh.

"Bernie!" I said.

"You're right." And now he did laugh, lying back while his feet in their pointed, polished shoes tapped on Melissa's carpet.

"You forgot."

"I forgot. Bobbie found it, we was looking for some papers in case — you understand."

"Uncle Bernie," I said, "I will telephone. I'll find out how you are. If you want me there, you have the kids call me. I love you," I said to my childhood. "I love you."

"They find the right parts, and they remember how to install them correctly," he said. "You'll come out to the house when I get home from Texas."

"I will."

"You'll see my children. You'll see their children who you never saw. We'll have a complete, entire family again, almost. Yes?"

I said yes. He went down to drive himself dangerously back to Lido Beach. I stood at the elevator door, holding it open until he had wobbled inside and had turned around. I waved the short distance, and he waved back. In his face, as he smiled a frightened smile, was the face of his sister. I let go of the door, and it slid shut, but I still saw my mother's features riding forth on his.

The bank, towering and cool inside, made of marble, vast as the office of a trading company in the tropics, surrendered the flat safety deposit box. In a wooden cubicle lit by a green-shaded lamp, I opened the metal flap with damp fingers, trying to feel as fictitious people were said to feel on finally finding their legacy. I found a brown paper bag so soft with age and use that I thought, though I hadn't for so many years, of an open-air stand on Avenue J at which an old Polish woman who spoke no English sold jars of her sour pickles and sauerkraut. She saved paper bags and her customers carried their merchandise off in sacks as wrinkled and as often-used as this one. My mother used to express disdain for the woman's inability to speak in English. But she always bought her pickles. I thought I remembered a story of the woman's flight from the Nazis. Or perhaps I supplied it.

Inside the pickle lady's bag, if it was hers, was an oaktag folder. Inside the folder was a letter from Albert Einstein to me. Beneath it was the carbon copy of my letter to him. Under that was construction paper with drawings on it, men in helmets with guns, airplanes, projectiles, and in my mother's hand a notation: *Howie made hundreds like these*. Now I could save my life.

I left the box on the shelf of the cubicle, the key on top of the box. I carried off provision for my future and I drove on Coney Island Avenue toward the ocean, Coney Island itself, and Nathan's. I double-parked behind a double-parked police car, fetched two Nathan's hot dogs and a beer, and sat in the shuddering rental car while the air conditioner groaned and I examined my instructions to Albert Einstein on how to make an atomic bomb.

In 1950, at a kitchen table I remembered well, I drew in the atomic radiation that was, so to speak, in the air in those days, and I came out with this:

> Carrying in the nose a long peice of plastic about a foot long and one inch wide resting against the back of one atom two feet away, both of the atoms are on a rack. The rocket is carried in the bom bay of a B-36. When released over enemy teratory it hurtles tword ground at a fast speed. Thus if it is discovered by a lookout of the russain ground crew it can go into use before anything can be done about it. When the rocket hits ground the peice of plastic which is stickeing out propells the lower atom tword the higher atom, the big exploisen comes. P.S. This is only in case of war, beleive me I do not want war!
>
> HOWARD S. KORMAN Age 8½

P.S. Unemployed.

Surely, I thought, I must have read enough war books, for I adored them, to know how to spell "bomb bay." What seemed wholly correct, trackable back through the dark forest of my twisted little soul and lying mind, was my terrible piety about not wanting war. Like every child of World War II, weaned on toy wood tommy guns and fathers returning or failing to return from Europe or the Pacific, I had *played war*, as we called it in the neighborhood, with zeal and expertise.

I tried to remember what I had known of Einstein. I remembered only a photograph of him in a sweatshirt in *Life*, and maybe something about him and a daughter in New Jersey. Surely I would think of typing up and sending off the brilliant scheme — not only a lower atom, but a *higher* atom! Yet I hadn't typed well enough, I was sure, at eight and a half, to do the work on the crinkly flimsy from which I wiped a little Nathan's mustard. Nor would I have known to send it to Princeton, I thought. The capitalization of my name looked familiar, and of course I remembered Miss Hunsicker, my father's secretary. She'd been accustomed to typing letters about fig paste and tomatoes and corned beef, which he'd imported, but she would have done anything he asked, and she would surely have done a letter for me. She had treated me, I remembered, shamed now by my failure to ever acknowledge or requite, as if I were a princeling to the big, burly, gentle-voiced but insistent man who bought and sold foodstuffs until his heart exploded in his chest. My father had recognized genius, he must have thought, and had commanded Miss Hunsicker to let Albert Einstein know that I was thinking of him. I did remember, still, how on Saturday mornings when he took me to his offices on lower Hudson Street, I heard the *thunk* of Miss Hunsicker's Underwood as I slammed the large characters while my father sat before the telex machine and swore as his short broad fingers struck the wrong keys. When he didn't curse himself, or luck, or fate, or tinned Italian plum tomatoes in their juice, he pronounced the name of every key he sought to hit. "Eff," he said, aiming for it. "Eye. Gee. *Shit!*"

I turned the engine off and took the paper with me. Little Jewish boys from respectable neighborhoods used to take buses and trolleys to Coney Island. We feared the lethal difference of the mustachioed, pointy-shoed, peg-pantsed, blouse-shirted Italian boys who never took academic courses, we were assured, at Abraham Lincoln High School, but only vocational. They were going to work (to our horror) with their hands. They also worked with their loins: didn't we notice and lust for, dream our soiled waking dreams about, their Theresas, their Aprils, with their small waists, their skin-tight skirts, their pointed breasts that aimed directly at our inexperience? Their boyfriends, for whom they lit cigarettes, at whose every snarled remark they threw back their heads and opened their thin, bright lips and laughed to show their secret tongues, might kill us for sport, we were warned.

But now the streets of Coney Island belonged to small, slender children in enormous sneakers and bright shirts, all of whom were either bent on crucial errands, flight, or raging hunts. As crowded as the streets were with quickly moving children, they were also filled with cops — boys, for the most part, clanking in their heavy gear. I walked around the corner from Nathan's, on my way to the beach. I passed a small circular ride concession. It went around, but no one rode it. A tall, lean man with ebony skin and dark glasses drooped over the lever that controlled the ride. He stared at the ground. Sitting near him, but against a hurricane fence, in a litter of bottles and blown papers, a man in a T-shirt and filthy torn jeans, who wore no shoes, stared at me. They were stoned, and tomorrow they would have stolen something, robbed someone, or sold themselves in order to do it again. Whereas my patients, and my patients-to-be, would steal or sell in order to sit in my tasteful office, where we'd all be wearing shoes, and tell me some lies in the hope of hearing a few in reply.

No one on the beach played a radio loudly. I saw as many shells as pieces of wind-whipped trash, and, looking at the ocean, I felt the early sun on my neck and thought that it might have been so many years before, as we trudged on the sand with thousands of others to find our share of breathable air in the wet heat of a Brooklyn summer. I walked to a jetty of stone that I tried to tell myself I remembered. I failed, but sat nevertheless with my legs stretched out, the wind keeping insects off me, the heat more of a comfort than the damp stones were a nuisance, and I examined the yellowing envelope. It was about six by four inches, and it bore a purple three-cent stamp. It was addressed to me at *956 East 18. Str.* Every period was doubled, as if a colon. And the *Str.* was for *Strasse*, yes?

The return address on the envelope was *112 Murcer Str.* in *Princeton*, *N. J.* The embossed letterhead said, in steps that declined to the right: *A. Einstein*, then *112 Murcer Street*, then *Princeton*, then *New Jersey*, *U.S.A.*

Since Miss Hunsicker had typed my full name at the bottom of the letter, and since Einstein's reply (dated 4 April, 1950) was headed "Dear Howie," I wondered whether I had signed myself that way, or whether a parent had. He had written:

I received your letter of March 31st, and regret it very much
that such a young person should be already interested in such
ugly purposes as military inventions. Kindness and understanding is much more important.

Yours sincerely,
Albert Einstein

I remembered what came next. No. I remembered what I had been
told came next.

I was said to crumple the letter. I was said to have balled it tightly
and to have hurled it to the floor. I *see* myself spitting and cursing the
thief of my invention, the elder who held his approval away. I saw, as I
was certain I actually had, my mother: in a bright-orange housecoat
tied at the waist, she stood in the hallway where I'd fallen when
Einstein had discarded me, and she ironed the tossed letter, pressing
with gentle strokes his admonitions to innocence. This, I thought as I
replaced the letters and drawing in the folder, the folder in the pickle
lady's bag, was what she had planned for Bernie to pass along when
my life needed saving.

Despite the house in what they'd thought of as the suburbs, the
education I was given at a college out of town, the ranked main selections of the Book-of-the-Month Club on the shelves of what they called
their study, they had of course remained the children of peasants. Who
else would cause to be delivered the letter from the little man, who,
with his violin, his guilt, his knowledge of what was cruelest in human-
ity, took shelter in Princeton and thought about the universe and forgot
to change his clothes? Only the daughter of peasants would iron flat
the letter from such a man, related to her, I'm sure she felt, by his
having fled the ovens.

So of course I left the beach and drove to our block. The trees were
enormous and leafy, and sunlight through them lit the block with a
cool green radiance. Our house looked shabby but sound. Its roof
needed work, the paint at the window casings had to be scraped and
renewed, the brick chimney needed pointing up. But it was the same
stucco house, white now instead of the ocher it had been, with the
front porch walled in instead of screened. That was the heavy front

door with art deco metal frame around glass. This was the address to which Einstein had sent his prompt reply. Those were the steps I'd played stoopball on. And these were the houses past which I had walked, alone, on an errand I can't recall, when I heard from house after house, the neighborhood one huge radio, that Bobby Thomson had stolen the pennant from the Dodgers for the Giants. It was time to go. At parties or by myself: when I told the Bobby Thomson story, it was time to go.

In the apartment, after returning the car and riding home by cab for only the price of the *Encyclopaedia Britannica*, I changed into shorts and a T-shirt and sat at the kitchen table to reread the brief correspondence between Albert Einstein and me. I held the soft papers in the thin, gray city sunlight. I laid them before me. And all I had, at last, was one more story. What she'd saved for me, and passed to me through Bernie, was the story. I remembered, or I thought I remembered, how my mother looked on, in generous regret, in undiminished pride, while I crumpled the letter from Albert Einstein, genius, refugee from the ovens, heroic Zionist Jew. I remembered, or had been told enough to think I remembered, how my mother, pressing gently, doubtless under linen slightly dampened, resurrected the letter she would save for her son. And all I could think to do, at last, was pass the story on.

I thought of calling Theodore. But the call — I saw the low ceilings, the red tile floors, the grassless lawn, the cactuses, the basement shop where his wife said he hid when management balked at his projects — would wind through his rooms to terrorize him. He was frightened of being fired, frightened about meeting his quarterly income tax estimates, frightened of hearing from me. It's what so many of us have come to specialize in: wounded kids. His mother, not entirely without mercy, occasionally let me know that she and Theodore had spoken, and that he'd seemed well.

Well, there's well and there's *well*. "It's relative," I said, cackling. I hushed myself because I did sound mildly insane. And I would not call my son. For, if I did, I would say, "Teddy! I mean, Theodore. Listen. You want to hear the *damnedest* story?" And he wouldn't. Stories frightened him. The electronic guarantees of the binary system, as expressed in silicon chips, were where he hid from stories.

There was only one audience for this particular tale. He was in Houston being plumbed. I wished, with a physical need, like lust, to tell him that my legacy was a story, and my life would never change. I knocked like a peasant on the wood of the table for luck, and hoped for Uncle Bernie, thought of his little lap. I counted up dead parents, absent wives, unknown cousins, my distant child. Like Grandpa Fine, I had left for another country. Here I was, with my story to tell. The Einstein letter, its angry folds pressed flat, had finally caught up with me.

"Kindness," it said, "understanding": I must tell that to someone. A call would come, to the office or apartment, saying whether Bernie survived. So I would have to keep my story, while I waited, to myself. I would sleep and wake and put my unpressed clothing on and go across town and hear what my patients had to say.

Dream Abuse

LOUISE HEARD the liquid click of Gerry's eyes beneath his shut lids. He lay on their living room sofa and rubbed as he talked about the cases of a long, sour day while she sat a dozen feet from him, watching his long broad fingers. Underneath them, he said, "I get them — this is the final difference in what we do — I get them at the end. They're drooling down the barrels of their guns, or they swear they sometimes think they won't be able to put on the brakes when they're coming to a school crossing. Or a cattle crossing. They don't care which, by then. Or they tremble all the time. Or keep on rubbing their eyes, heh heh. I get them, they're just one dumb, needful statement, plus a coffin, short of a funeral. You get them, they're lying down drunk in the halls, or getting knocked up by their uncle. But they're kids. They're starting out, you figure. You work with them, you keep on thinking it's supposed to end up like *Little Women* or something."

"But you know different," she said.

"Don't I, boy," he said, sighing into his hands as, cupped along his face, they rubbed at the lids that always looked sore.

"And then you come home, and I make you forget your worries."

He stopped rubbing. He turned on one arm, blinking, and looked at her. She ducked to sip her coffee. "Yes, Louise," he said. "That's what I do. And that's what you do."

She did not say anything. But she knew that she smiled gratefully. She knew that she had just poured too much scalding coffee into her smiling mouth because her gratitude for his assurance was as powerful as her need had been to hear it. He was the counselor for the Sheriff's Department, and she was the counselor for the senior high. And every time he called it the *final* difference, Louise refused to cry.

One of Gerry's patients, a man near retirement who drove a red and white sheriff's car and who'd been said to talk to himself in public as much as he probably did inside the car out of sight, had arrested a high school junior for hanging from a pedestrian bridge near Sidney, New York while mooning. The deputy, enraged not by the boy's risk to himself, or the thought of what his body, falling from eighteen feet, might do to windshields or the amazed people behind them, had hauled the boy up and beaten him, while he was still half naked, for his nudity. "Showing your ass like that," the deputy had said, again and again, according to the boy. Louise had worked with the boy and his parents, while Gerry had worked with the deputy. During their only conference, she had heard Gerry whistling "Moon over Miami," and she'd started to giggle.

"What?" he'd said.

In the bright room, with its smell of tobacco and something like turpentine, in the steel-colored light of the Chenango Valley in winter, she had told this man who looked as much like a deputy as his clients did — tall, thick, broad of neck, slightly stooped, as though he drove all day; handsome in the way that minor actors who end up playing clever villains must once, maybe in high school, have been called handsome — "You were whistling about a moon. It made me think of that bare bottom suspended in the air over the highway."

Gerry had looked at her — had seemed to study her — as if he aimed his high forehead and big nose and little dark eyes. He moved his head as if his neck were sore, his shoulders stiff. He'd rubbed his eyes and then, the only male she'd seen do this since her second year at Oberlin, he blushed. His prominent nose and forehead made a beacon in the grim, small steel-colored room. He closed his eyes and rubbed at the lids, and she knew he was hiding.

"It's such a wonderful expression," he blurted, "*mooning.*" He laughed uncontrollably, she thought, letting his teeth show, then putting his hand to his lips as if he wished to cover them. The laughter came from his belly and his big chest so that his torso shook. He was

probably a man of coarse appetites, she'd thought. She had understood, even as she'd risen to wrap her long winter coat around her and
look at her watch and say excuses, that she was thinking less of this
competent-looking vulnerable man than someone she had left in Rochester, a lover, dark and demanding and finally cruel, whose memory
filled her with sadness about herself and what she strongly suspected,
and maybe feared, was lust.

He had telephoned her that night, and she'd felt an obligation toward
him, as forceful as if she'd betrayed him with the man in her memory.
He had been apologetic, as if he'd gone too far. A kind of pleasant
romantic duty, then, started them out, and now they had lived together, without a dog or cat or child, for almost two years, in a locked-
log house on a river flat outside of Plymouth, New York. They went to
work early, driving separately the twelve miles to the county seat to
ply their trade; they came home late, cooked together, brought in food,
and then they watched films on the VCR, or read and slept early.
Louise had told him about her former lovers — a few she'd called
boyfriends, and the other she had tried not to dwell on. He was the
one about whom Gerry had asked the most gentle, pointed questions.
She had put an end to them by telling him, "You use your mind like a
penis, sometimes, you know that?"

"Sex is in the head," he'd answered at once, his tone growing hard as
he looked over at her from the sofa on which he lay with the Science
supplement of the *Times*. "Isn't that a tenet of the feminists?"

"I'm not a feminist," she'd answered.

"Sure you are," he'd said at once, in the new, grim voice.

"I'm me. I'm only me."

"All right," he'd said, looking at the papers, "that's plenty good
enough. Be you."

They left off their lovers' archaeology until, meeting for lunch at the
Howard Johnson's near the County Office Building, when Louise told
Gerry about a girl who had sought her help in finding a doctor to abort
her pregnancy, Gerry's face had gone smooth and expressionless, then
had turned bright red.

"Only a *baby*," Louise had been saying. "And *having* a baby. And
needing to *kill* it."

"Is she finding the decision difficult?"

"Oh, Gerry, she's terrified. I have to talk to her some more. I'm worried about who the father is. I mean, I wouldn't be surprised if it were her own —"

"The decision," he'd said, his lips thin and pale against his flushed face. "Is it hard for her?"

"What?" Louise said. "What, Gerry?"

"You had your Mr. Wicked Desires. I — well, a woman, of course." He gave an imitation of a smile. "I mean, there was somebody who I — whew."

And she'd said, "Loved."

Gerry was rubbing at his eyes. She had reached to hold his wrist and pull his hand away from his face, and he had held the arm rigid. *He might be someone ferocious*, she'd thought.

The waitress had come and left their iceberg lettuce, their processed turkey strips and cold French bread, and she had never seen her do it, Louise realized.

Gerry at last had let his arm fall down into her small hand, and he had looked at her to say, "The waitress thinks we're fighting over the olives, I think. She had — not the waitress, you understand." His face had lost some of its bright color, then, and his eyes had grown less reptilian. "The woman I'm referring to. Apparently I made her pregnant. I'm assuming that. I decided I'd stick with the assumption. Well, it hadn't gone well, that's all. Our being together. Our time together wasn't going well. I think I'm not easy to live with. Do you?" He'd faked his helpless smile and laugh, and Louise had found herself rubbing at her own shut lids. "She aborted the baby, but she didn't want to tell me. First she aborted, then she told me, then she put only a few of her clothes into a suitcase — two suitcases, actually, plus a carry-on bag. It was like she was *escaping*. Well, she was. She was very pale. She was sweating. I thought she'd gone infected, from the procedure. First she aborted, then she told me, then she packed, and then she left."

Looking at him in the restaurant as he moved strips of salty meat among the lettuce chunks, she'd been able to say only, "How did you live, Gerry? How did you stay alive?"

"By not loving her anymore. I took myself away from her."

"But *how?*"

"I don't want you ever to know," he'd told her, letting his fork fall and rubbing at his eyes. She had wanted to reach across the little black shiny table to stroke him. He'd looked to her like a huge boy, like a wounded creature, Gerry, her child. That night, at home, instead of suggesting drinks or mentioning dinner, she had pulled him by the same strong arm she'd held at lunch, and they had gone to bed. But what she had thought would be a consolation turned to desperate, clever sex. It was she who had wept as they turned and plunged like drowners in the sea. Her tears, she later thought, could have seemed to be her comforting.

Gerry drove off to counsel deputies who beat their wives. He gave advice to department families about child abuse, alcohol abuse, and drug abuse. And Louise talked to girls who would not eat, and to parents who refused to give their children money for meals in school, and to boys who drove long cars and came to high school only when the courts compelled them. They watched cheerful black and white films with Jean Arthur or Myrna Loy. They read fat novels about prehistoric cave women or spies who could fight with their hands without breaking them. They paid bills with checks drawn on a joint account, and they sometimes went to Montreal or New York by plane, where they stayed in good hotels and ate too much, walked through exhibitions in museums, met with professional colleagues with whom the predication was that diseases were cured, conditions improved, and frailties strengthened.

During recent nights, in their antique brass bed that squeaked and wailed with age and corrosion, Gerry began to thrash. He'd always snored. He had, from the start, sometimes muttered in his sleep. But the deep snores that echoed in his big chest, which he never dressed in pajamas, but always in a dark blue T-shirt, now became the rumbled warnings of explosions to come. He rasped and boomed, and then went on to cry aloud, in a high, tight voice she at first didn't recognize as his when it wakened her. They were always warnings — "Do that again!" or "Go try and get in here, you son of a bitch!" And he would swing big looping roundhouse punches while he lay on his back or his side, sometimes hitting the thick brass posts of the bed and waking himself enough to say, "Oh," or "Sorry," and sleep again at once, and sometimes sleeping through it all, but always waking Louise. So that she lay in a quickly subsiding panic while he muttered and swore, worked up his dreamy rage, then threw his punch, then woke or didn't, then slept at once — leaving her to feel his face, to listen to his breathing and then, again, his snores, and to grow furious at him for doing this, whatever it was, to her.

In the morning, feeling sick because sleepless, or at best, even if she'd fallen back asleep, as weary as if she'd been up half the night, she might ask, "Do you remember what you dreamed last night?"

"Did I do it again?"

"Sure did. You were hummin' and fussin' and feudin' — you're a dangerous sleeper."

"I'm so sorry, Lou. You want to sleep in another room?"

"*No.*"

And then his quick and unembarrassed smile: "Good."

They collaborated again when a deputy was reported, anonymously, for being in the back seat of a patrol car on a country road with a high school girl of sixteen. The deputy was charged with statutory rape. The Sheriff's Department brought seven internal charges against him. Once the rape was dealt with, there would be other charges, and the man was done in New York State law enforcement, although, as his union adviser made clear, he could most likely uphold the law in any of two dozen distant states. The deputy was Joe Penders, the only African-American man in the department. He was short, thin, the brown-red color of cherrywood, with high, sharp cheekbones, a small slender nose, and hair going prematurely gray above his ears. In short, Louise told Gerry, Penders was a dish. So, she hastened to add, was Denise Bastone. "If they lynch him," she joked, not joking, "it'll be because most of the boys in school, and more than half of their fathers, were making plans to be more or less where Joe Penders apparently was, several times a week for three weeks. She has this very short, glossy black hair, and a kind of an expression — imagine a gorgeous nun without makeup, an Italian natural beauty, all right? Put too much makeup on her, so it's just short of cheap: the I'm-in-trouble signal, you know? And then have that sweet, sweet face almost ready to drop into a pout that tells you to go to hell. Okay. That's Denise, and she's wearing a skintight, crotch-high acid-washed denim skirt, rose-colored tights, and a sweater that's illegal in Utah. I asked her if she loved him."

"He said *he* thought so," Gerry said. "It's pretty clear he's desperate to marry her in the next fifteen minutes."

"Naturally," Louise said. "Of course. Which is why Denise's answer to the question consisted of lighting a cigarette, tossing the lit match behind her onto the floor, and telling me, 'He's a really sweet guy, don't get me wrong. What he mostly is, though,' she says, 'is a real wild piece of ass.' She looks me straight in the eye, and she smiles this *angel's* smile. Cue the celestial music. She says, 'You know what I mean.' She says, 'I can't figure out, like, why I can't go *get* some if I want to. You know what I mean,' she says."

"And you do," Gerry said.

"She's a *baby!* You're not supposed to make love to anybody when you're sixteen. Much less a sheriff's deputy in the back of a public law enforcement vehicle."

"Except most of the girls today who're sixteen do just that. The only aberration here is the kind of car, Lou."

"Gerry," she said. It sounded to her like whining. She watched him rub his eyes.

"But I'm right," he said. "And what about what she said? Isn't that a kind of feminist thing, too? Guys shouldn't be the only ones who can go after good stuff when they see it? Women have the right to it, too? Our bodies, ourselves, and so on?"

"And so on," Louise said, suddenly more depressed than angry, and curious now, puzzled, feeling as though she'd heard a song that she'd known but had forgotten.

They were making a salad at the kitchen window in the back of their house that night. It was near the riverbank, and they were looking outside more than at the scallions and carrots and green pepper and radishes, and more than at one another.

"I'll make a vinaigrette," Gerry said.

"Does she turn *you* on, Gerry?"

"The kid? Denise? I never met her, Lou."

"You know. The idea of all that hot teenager panting all over you."

"Well, she was panting all over Deputy Penders, not me."

"Imagining that she *might* be. *Could* be. What if she *were?*"

"Right on, Denise," he said, raising a fist betokening power to the people. "Right on. It *is* a revolution, Louise."

"You want to go out, in the garage, and get into the back seat?"

His face was so eager, so unguardedly excited in a new way when he turned to her, that she fell to studying the tender white scallops of the seed-choked green pepper she'd cut open. "Well, you're kidding, of course," he told her. "We're adults."

She said, "Of course."

As boys outside her office aimed their bodies toward accidental collisions with girls, as the noise in the corridors rose to the pitch of mass panic, Louise sat in her small room and turned her overheated metal desk lamp toward the old Modern Library edition of *The Interpretation of Dreams* that she had purchased at a garage sale in Rochester. She was comforted by the worn cloth of its red-brown binding: it was like an old dog's back, or a father's sport coat, a teacher's car — worn, even shabby, but an emblem of what was veteran, reliable, sage. Inside, on its bright white pages — she had to squint as she read — even the chapter headings reassured her: "The Dream as Wish-Fulfillment," "The Dream-Work," "The Material and Sources of Dreams." But when she read the familiar sections ("*Dr. M is pale; his chin is shaven, and he limps*"), she grew frustrated with the need to break the code — as if the dreamer and his mind were distant fellow spies, fearful of capture, unwilling to risk their location, needing nevertheless to broadcast their fears. But there was nothing on these pages about the lashing out, the violent reach, the heavy blow. There were only the undercover agents, incapable of silence, signaling in cipher.

That night, after dinner, in the broad low living room where they read, Louise pumped in coffee. She doctored it with milk and sugar, and she drank so much of it that by ten-fifteen, she felt sick. Gerry fell asleep on the sofa, and he snored at the newspaper over his face. She woke him to send him to bed, and he groggily obeyed. At ten-thirty, gagging as she poured the rest of the coffee into the sink, Louise turned the lights out and she got into bed. The sheets were cold, the comforter warm, the pillows soft, but nothing felt good; her flannel nightgown rasped at her nipples, and the back of her neck was stiff, sore. Gerry was softly burring as he lay on his back, but the snores had not fully begun. She lay with her back to him, reading by the low yellow light of her bedside lamp: *Rolling Stone* to keep her in step with her student-clients, and then *Vogue* for real pornography. She realized, after a while, that her shoulders ached from the tension with which she held them up, behind her, like a shield against his bad dreams. She realized, too, that she was looking away from him because the realest privacy lay behind his eyelids as he slept, and she was reluctant to betray him. Of course, behind closed lids in sleep, she thought, is where you get so much betrayal *done*. Where was Gerry now? With whom?

She smelled the heat of the bulb against its frail shade, and also the printer's ink on her magazine, the morning's perfume in the air around her bureau across the room, the day's labor ripening on his body and on hers, the coldness of the air from the river-bottom land around them, and the warm rich breath he breathed at her back as he shifted positions. The bed squeaked, the pages rattled and, as they did, reflections went bouncing from the photos in *Vogue* — women who had to work to look like Denise; boys who were trained to shape a mouth like the boy or man or creature in between whom she insisted on forgetting and often did — and as reflected light shimmered on the brass pole near her head, she thought, *I am a woman inside of a life. This room is dark water, and the lights are submarine, and I am floating in my whole, entire life.* She thought, *No*, but before she could marshal her argument, or mourn it, Gerry began to snore as if a motor in his chest were pumping. *He's the aerator in the tank*, she thought; she waited to hear herself giggle; she didn't.

She dropped her magazine from the side of the bed and then, as slowly as she could, she hauled herself up against the brass headboard until she sat. In the yellow-brown light of the weak bulb, she peered down at Gerry, whose snarling snores were louder now. She looked away from his pulsing closed eyes. It was rage, she realized; his shoulders jumped, his upper arms moved; his hands, she saw, were fists. She wouldn't raise her eyes above his chest. It was time to look at him, and

Louise didn't want to. When she did, the sneaky, caffeine-buzzing frightened curiosity would be treason.

She watched his fists jump, and she listened to him snore; it was, she realized, the sound that someone might make who was drowning, or being choked. And then, with a final sorrow made part of the motion itself, remembering her sad, reluctant motions with the dark, cruel man who had worked her body so brilliantly, Louise gave in, and shifted in the bed to lay her full attention on Gerry's face, as one might lay a palm along a lover's cheek, connecting, caressing, taking hold.

His eyelids fluttered. His jaw worked as he ground his teeth. In light the color of yarrow, his face seemed made of shadows. Its many emptinesses reminded her of giant boulders dragged into fields by glaciers; they were scoured, full of shallow pits, and what had sculpted them was gone. He worked his jaws, or whatever worked him made his jaws chew against each other. He had stopped snoring, now, and he was breathing enormously, taking breaths so profoundly deep that, watching the eyelids flutter, watching the bones of his face compress, she waited with her own breath held to be certain that he would finish one and start again.

That's love, isn't it? That kind of worrying?

When she heard herself think the question, she felt herself start to cry. The tears came slowly and they ran down her face. She pushed at them with the backs of her hands as she watched him in his tortured sleep. Then his eyes rolled faster under his lids, and he clacked his mouth open and shut a few times. "Blaw" was the sound his gravelly voice said. "Blaw." She recognized the noise from memories of her own scared dreams. It was what you said to ward off whatever impended in your nightmare. "Blaw." But then, and with no warning, he backhanded with his left arm and slammed his fist backward into her pillow. His voice going higher even as he shouted it, he warned, "Don't assault *me*." He threw his right, and he screamed, *"Blaw!"*

The wide, clumsy punch caught her left shoulder and pushed her back on the bed. She caught his hand. She held it. She knew its weight, and the temperature of its skin, the dark fur on its forearm. She didn't know whether to kiss it, or continue to hold it, or whisper to him that he only dreamed, then kiss him on the cheek and lie beside him until he slept without fear. *Only?*

She astonished herself by throwing his arm back against him. "Don't you abuse *me*, you son of bitch!" she shouted, and as she did she heard the echo in her words of his own dreamy voice. She punched at him clumsily, *like a girl*, she thought, swinging wildly until he woke, frightened, of course, and confused, saying, "What? What?" But he traveled all the way from the borders of dreaming, through her weeping, her shouts and her blows, to find her, to fight through her punches, to clutch her against him. She knew, as he seized her, that he did so in ignorance of what had happened inside him or inside her, or in the room between them. Gerry hugged her to himself and gave what dumb and uninvited comfort he could. She knew he did. And she, now, reached to comfort in return. She felt his drenched T-shirt and thick blunt ribs, and she held herself against them, thinking *Caught*.

The Page

THAT NIGHT I did what I had always done. It was how I'd been managing. Every morning I did what I always did, and every afternoon and night. Pooh lurched out with me while Bear slammed him into my legs and led us off the back porch. Bear was ten months old, a Labrador retriever long of muzzle and leg with vast paws. The old one, Pooh — my wife had named him — was lamed by arthritis, half blinded by cataracts, crippled by dysplasia, and still too strong to die. I placated the secrets of his physiology with Butazolidin tablets and dog biscuits. At that time, I was especially grateful when a patient or dog did not die.

It was unusually cold for early November, and the pumpkins I'd set out, because it had been the custom of the house, were settling into themselves as successive frosts softened them. No one came up our road for Halloween, but I had placed pumpkins on the front and back porches and had even fastened onto the storm doors the bunches of maize we'd always hung there. No one came to our house at Halloween because it was so remote, and because the pickings were better in town, five miles below. I had walked about, from kitchen to pantry through kitchen back to living room, waiting to give some little kids some lollipops and candy bars, but no one had come to claim them. I had thought to console myself with Tootsie Pops, but I learned from their high, artificial sweetness that I didn't believe in consolation.

Pooh staggered around the bushes in the side yard, and I heard Bear rustling in the tall, withered grass below us. He was in the field that went down a hundred yards or so to the old apple trees on which gnarled, sour apples would gleam in the morning through winter. Pooh came back and lay down beside me with a grunt. I didn't hear the puppy and I whistled him back. He didn't come. I clapped my hands and called him. I heard slow winds and the natural sway of weeds against each other, but nothing caused by the intrepid unintelligence of a young dog rushing home. I called again, and listened, and then put Pooh inside, stuck a long-handled flashlight in the pocket of my barn coat, and, leaving the porch light on, went looking.

I walked through the fields I'd last seen him in. I walked the road parallel to the fields. I went down to the old apple trees, then past them and past the old fence and over the small creek. I followed it in the dark down through the aspen forest to where it foamed in a little waterfall. My shoes and trouser legs were soaked, and my hands ached from the cold. I had fallen a couple of times and had not, I noted, sprung lithely back up. There were creatures around me, field rats and maybe an owl, but there wasn't a stalky, imperfect Labrador retriever who knew less about handling himself in these woods than the average beginning Boy Scout.

I fell again as I bushwhacked up to the house, and, speaking of tenderfoots, this time I opened up some skin and broke my flashlight. "Bear," I shouted in the darkness, a little embarrassed by the panic I heard above the grass that insisted on making noises, in the freshening wind, as if something coursed in instant response to my call.

I found another flashlight that worked, and then I drove the car back and forth on our road. I went miles in each direction, pausing to aim the flashlight through my opened windows at the grounds of every trailer, double-wide, shack and farmhouse I passed. There weren't that many, and the dog was at none of them. At home, I locked up and, sitting in wet clothes and a shirt with blood on the right cuff, I said to the old dog that the puppy would doubtless come back in the middle of the night, that he was running a deer or ferreting in somebody's compost heap. "You wake me when he comes," I told Pooh before I went up. He hadn't made it upstairs for a couple of years.

Dogs drift. They stray. They take off because of a smell, a sound, something inside their skulls that is part of what makes them other than us. I fell asleep in our bed and not that much later I woke, as I'd been waking for a while, to the sound of my voice. I took a bathrobe downstairs with me and passed the sofa onto which Pooh, in spite of his lameness, was able to haul himself every night. I went to the other sofa and lay beneath one of the heavy old quilts.

Looking out from under it, I said to Pooh, "Any word?"

His cloudy eye glittered in the darkness of the living room and then it closed.

After hospital rounds the next morning, I drove the twenty miles home because I knew that Bear would be sitting on the porch, looking, as usual, bewildered. He was not. I drove back, and I continued to wrestle with my imagination as I'd done, fairly successfully, the night before. Every time I saw the dog cringing from headlights on a two-lane highway, or, tail down and back curved in fear, crouching over his forepaws in a dark forest that felt alien, I pulled down the wide black window shade I remembered my grade school teachers hauling on small pulleys so that we could better see a film strip on how corn grows or why the washing of one's hands is a precious errand and a high responsibility. I drew the black blind between me and the terrified Labrador, who'd been struck with a stick by a man at his trap line, or who was bleeding from the flanks where he'd been shot with a hunting bow, or who ran at a sideways angle, slower and slower, because of his kicked-in ribs.

Instead of eating lunch before my clinic hours, I drove home again, pulling the blind as I needed to, and inspected the house and the grounds. I drove with the windows open and the radio off so I could hear him, and so I could whistle for him as I drove. Past Dorney Walters Road, past Sanitarium Road, I signaled to him, in case he was caught, or lost, or injured, that I was here, that this — toward the sound of my calling and calling — was how to come home.

After work that day, at a quarter of six, before I went back to feed Pooh, to maybe find a young black dog on my porch, I telephoned my daughter's office. I lay in the swivel chair and let my tired feet dangle. I thought I was in danger of talking about Bear, but I wanted to be certain I was calm for her, even casual, so I rehearsed. You know that dumb-ass puppy took off on me, I said. Probably got himself lost in the hills or near the river, I said. I thought about rivers, how fast and deep and cold they were. I'd never put ID collars on the dogs because I didn't want them getting snagged and drowned in rivers or streams. I said to her, I have to confess I'm getting worried, and if I *had* put them in collars then maybe someone, finding him, could call me. Maybe he wouldn't be lost or mistreated or frightened someplace. I pulled on the long white sash cord, and the broad black screen came down. She wasn't in, and I went out and drove back, climbing into the wild hills I lived in with, apparently, one less dog.

I remembered what I had actually said to myself in rehearsal for my daughter and then had chosen to dismiss: if they wore collars, I had said in my thoughts, then maybe someone could find *me*. I was reminded of something. I thought I knew what, but I drew the blind back down and, once I saw that nothing — *no one* were the words I heard in my head — was lying, all muzzle and ears and big, dark eyes, on the porch, I went through the business of the early evening without allowing myself a glimpse of what I didn't want to see. I took Pooh out and hung around the yard while he limped from bush to rock to fence post. "You do your rounds," I told him, "and I do mine. And you piss up posts a good deal better than I do." Then I fed him and thought about feeding me, but settled for some slices of cheddar somewhat spotted with blue-green mold. I chewed on one for a while and then, leaning over the garbage pail, which direly needed emptying, I spat the mouthful out. I was reminded, again, and again I drew the screen up. But I'd remembered by then. I thought to call my daughter and tell her how close I'd come that night to conversing with her mother again. But I put my coat on, instead, and went out with Pooh, the two of us crabbing our way up the road half a mile or so, Pooh marking and sniffing and glaring with his opalescent eyes, me calling with, I heard, such desperation that I sounded like a warning, not a request to please come back.

The next morning, I called the Sheriff's Department and spoke to one of the dispatchers I was friendly with. I worked in the jail as their doctor one night a week, inspecting prisoners, and I knew most of them well enough. I asked if the deputies on patrol could keep an eye out for Bear. I learned the names of the area dog wardens, and I telephoned descriptions to two of them, leaving a message for the third.

I called four veterinarians to ask if anyone had brought Bear in. I called the SPCA. Now everyone knew that one more dog was missing. I let Pooh out for a final pee, then locked him in and went to work. On the way, I stopped at the offices of our newspaper and paid for a large ad. I headed it REWARD. The woman behind the counter watched the pencil, then looked up at me. She looked, and then she said, "Family pet, huh? Everybody takes it hard."

"Do they?"

"Like a child's gone, sometimes," she said.

"Really," I said. "That serious."

"Look at you," she said. "Here. Let go of the pencil. I write these all the time."

"Thank you," I said. "That's tough work."

"No," she said, studying the form she printed on, "what's tough is having dogs, I'd say."

One strep throat, one battered baby whose mother was a battered wife, a half dozen leaky sinuses, one possible appendix, one definite milk allergy, a third pneumonia for the week, and the bonus — sixteen normal, healthy kids — and I was done and driving home. I stopped at the seasonal road a quarter of a mile from the house and parked with my windows open. I whistled for him. I listened to the strengthening winds in the evergreens before me on the hillside and to the dry grass rattling on the slope below. They were so much louder and more powerful, and I stopped my little noises and sat there awhile. An airplane engine tore up the sound of the wind, and I saw a light plane banking a couple of hundred feet above, then climbing to crest the hill that overlooked the house. The plane circled in slow, widening loops. I thought — the way you laugh hysterically — of finding a way to ask the pilot to look for Bear on the fields of yellowing grass and bony weed and corn stubble that lay on the other side of the ridge.

Yes, I admitted that night, while I admitted that the screen didn't work and that I dreamed the dreams and saw the sights — the whites of the eyes of a puppy in terror, the dry protruding tongue of a dog as he died of poisoned bait, the hiss on leaves of the blood that pumped from his wounds. Yes. All right, I thought, another triumph for lovers of realism everywhere. Yes. It was like mourning again. All right?

Before I left for work the next day, after I drank coffee and turned the radio on and then off, I fetched from the back pantry, from its cubby among field guides and travel books, our gazetteer of New York State with its precise topographical drawings. I looked down at the often unconcentric indications of the sloughs and rivers. There were so many roads and hillsides above them, too many forests and steep, thicketed fields.

I picked up our newspaper on my way to the hospital and I read the ad. She had rearranged my incoherent phrases well enough. It was placed at the top of a column containing three other notices of missing dogs. I visited my patients, three of whom were improving and one, Roger Pettefoy, an infant, who was dehydrated from diarrhea. We had caught his bacterial infection, but the antibiotics, I thought, had given him diarrhea. I asked Charlene Novak to throw some electrolytes into him and asked to be telephoned late that afternoon about his progress. On the way home, I shopped. Two women who had known us asked if they could help me. I smiled at one and moved on. She let me go. The other, who fell on me in an unsteady manner, all yellowing teeth and loose flesh, was not satisfied with my thanks, and she pursued me. I stopped and turned, wheeling my cart as if it were a shield. She retreated several paces with her own cart. She wore a fur coat over what looked like pajamas, and she smelled of gin. The idea of a martini became interesting. I said, "Ms. Wiermeyer? *Widdemeyer*. Forgive me. You're being kind, I know. But I really remember, if barely, how to buy short-grain rice. My hesitation, here in aisle five, is because the store seems to carry only long-grain rice. I'd intended to make myself a spinach risotto for dinner. Hence the desirability of short grains, as I'm certain you know. So I'm considering my choice, which lies between long-grain and processed. I'm only fucked up, Ms. Widdemeyer, not stupid."

That afternoon, a boy rode up on a bicycle, rare enough on our stretch of road. Pooh let him know by yelping at the bike, even after the boy climbed off it. Pooh's rich growling bark had turned to something of a yap. A lesson for us all, I thought, as I went out the front. The boy was fourteen, probably, pimpled over a pallor he owed to canned gravies on dehydrated mashed potatoes and plenty of sweet sodas. I smelled his cigarettes and unwashed skin.

He said, not looking at my face, "You the man advertising the reward?"

"For a dog," I said stupidly.

"Dog," he said, patting Pooh's head. "Black puppy, it says, except he's pretty damned big for a puppy."

"Kind of dopey-looking ears and a little white spot on his chest?"

"Yupper," he said, breaking the word into two syllables and landing heavily on the second. "Kind of cute."

"Did you call him by his name?"

"Bear," he said. "Pretty near tore the damned chain off of him."

"Chain," I said, taking my wallet out and counting to a hundred.

He described the trailer off the road and its short gravel driveway, the long chain fastened to its riserless wooden steps and the black dog held by a collar that looked to be made of chain as well.

"A choker, maybe," I said. "It tightens up the more the dog pulls on it."

He nodded. "Could have been," he said. But I knew that he'd agree, now, to anything because he saw more money in the wallet.

"When you go home," I said, "be sure and keep one of those twenties to yourself, if you know what I mean."

"Yupper," he said, mounting the bike and looking like all these big country boys caught between handlebars and steering wheels — too long and lean for the squat kids' bicycle, and a little bit angry, as if he knew how he looked.

I checked Pooh's water dish, then locked him in and drove to the trailer. I had paused at the door of my house, wanting to heft something. This was an emergency, and it might require equipment. I thought about flashlight, ax, splitting maul, garden spade, a serrated bread slicer, or one of the French cooking knives. Finally, I took my medical bag. I wanted to know what I was doing, no matter what I had to do, and my professional tools seemed best.

I turned up a road I rarely traveled because it was not only seasonal — unplowed during the winter — but because it was unpaved and seemed to be made of potholes linked by rocks. I went slowly, rehearsing my conversation with whoever had Bear. I would have to pay another reward. I would have to have a discussion, I supposed. I would have to perhaps undergo a berating for carelessness and maybe listen to complaints about scattered garbage or the scratched-up walls of a shed or the stain on a rug. The trailer was at the edge of a state hardwood plantation. Once a year, those who'd been chosen in a lottery were permitted to log firewood. For a few weeks, the forest screamed and trees fell and pickups tottered back and forth under heavy loads. Then these woods felt dark again when I drove past the road that went through them, and there was a good silence from them — unless you had driven there to call the name of a missing dog.

I'd noticed the trailer before, its trim fence taut on pressure-treated four-by-fours, but I hadn't thought about the posts in the gravel drive, nor the very large links of chain that hung between them, nor the sign that said, in high, childish letters, *KEEP OUT*. I saw a thinner, brighter chain that was looped around the steps in front of the darkened trailer in the darkening woods. I didn't see Bear.

I was breathing too quickly for the effort involved in parking a car and walking from it to step over a thick chain and go up the little hillside to climb four steps and knock on the aluminum door of a white metal and plastic trailer with blue trim that was maybe twenty feet long. I raised my hand to rap at the storm door when someone opened the interior door a crack and said, "Get off of my property."

"Give me back my dog, and I will." My voice was so high, I hardly recognized it.

"There isn't any dog here. Get out."

"I know my damned *dog's* here. I want him back."

"He's mine."

"Bear!" I called.

"You stay right there, Buddy," the man's voice said. It had a flat dullness to it that seemed strange, since it also sounded angry. "His name's Buddy," the man said, "and my brother bought him for me over in New York. Now, you get the hell off of my property."

"I guess you want to talk to the cops," I said.

He said, "I knew it was you. I knew it was you. I knew it was you. Goddamned Howard, huh? All the way over from Ohio, huh? Big undercover motherfucker Howard, huh? I *knew* it was you!"

The door opened a little wider, and I called, "Bear!"

The barrel of a rifle came out. I remember staring at the sight because it seemed to stand so high. I heard a metal sound, and I jumped off the porch and ran down the gravel drive, falling near the bottom and letting myself roll under the chain. I ran around to the far side of my car and crouched there. I thought I saw the trailer door close. I sat on the ground and shook. Everything shook. When I finally inched myself into the car and turned it around, driving almost too low in the seat to see, and when I was back in my own driveway, I thought that I could use some of my professional gear once I pulled the gravel out of the cuts and washed my hands.

I thought: The barrel of a *gun*.

I thought: I did hear him lunge inside the trailer when I called his name.

I told Arch Constantine, the deputy who arrived forty minutes later, and he wrote an incident report for me to sign.

He asked, moving his three-cell flashlight on the table, and studying his juvenile handwriting, "Did you feel menaced, Doc?"

"Menaced. Arch, you're damned right I felt menaced. I was *scared*."

"Scared's fine, but menaced is what the law's about. Menacing. Was he menacing you?"

"There's a law against it?"

"There sure is. I believe we've had him on it before, this Lester Scott guy. The sheriff knows about him. A number of us do. He's a head case. And you felt menaced, then."

I nodded. I hesitated, but he smiled. He had a sweet smile for a man who was almost seven feet tall and perhaps as heavy as two of me. It was a crooked face, as if he'd been broken and put together again with some difficulty. "Menaced," I said. "I ran."

"I understand," he said, tapping the report.

"I ran away, Arch. Like a kid."

He said, "I'd just as soon you did, Doc. I'd like to keep you alive. You take care of two of my nephews and you're the only fun we get down at the cells unless one of the prisoners gets a package of food. You let us deal with the perpetrators and you forget about them until we lock them up. That strike you as fair?" He smiled the smile I often enough used with the parents of my patients. I thought of the tiny clenched face of Roger Pettefoy in the ward and of his mother, who'd trembled when she spoke with me.

"Deal," I said.

When he was gone, I fed Pooh and then walked around the house, waiting for word. I watered the plants, many of which looked sicker than the children I'd treated that week. I let Pooh out and called the hospital. I shouted at the Head of Shift because I hadn't been called about Roger Pettefoy. She told me, stiffly, that no instructions to call had been left. I told her how wrong she was, that when Charlene Novak heard orders she wrote them into the chart. She told me how improved the baby was, and I gave her orders and insisted that she read them back. Then, of course, I apologized. I said, "My dog —" I was able to stop myself, so that when she asked me what I'd said I could reply, "It's been a long day. Forgive me. Please call me if the child's signs change." I said, "Deal?"

She didn't know what I meant, apparently, and she disconnected.

Pooh barked at Arch when he returned. He ducked as he came in and he refused to sit. There was no dog in the car and none beside him but Pooh. The deputy said, "I've dealt with him before. I was right. He's crazy."

"I believe it."

"No," he said. "He's *crazy*. He thinks your name's Howard."

"I know that."

"He thinks you work with the DEA."

"Drugs?" I said.

"He thinks you followed him from someplace in Ohio, and before that from someplace down South, and he thinks you're a spy for the DEA. You're some kind of undercover agent. I thought he was going to shoot me, sure as shit. He hates law officers. He hates uniforms. Mostly, right now, he hates *you*. That's why he's got your dog."

"He admitted it was mine?"

"Sure did. Dog came wagging to the trailer, and he just chained him there. Wants you to know it."

"Why?" I tried not to let it sound like *Why me?*

"He's not sure, he says. He says he *thinks*, maybe, he'd enjoy shooting you through the chest. He was particular about that, about the through the chest part. He says he's got a load of guns and ammunition, and he would take great pleasure in killing you and any of your cop friends."

"Jesus," I said, "you were —"

That was when he did sit down and lean over his legs and look at the clouded blue linoleum of the kitchen floor. He nodded. Then he whispered, "I did think he was ready to put me down."

"Jesus," I said, "you can't get killed because of a dog, Arch."

He looked up, suddenly. He smiled his sweet smile. "Thank you," he said. "I'd at least like a chance to talk it over with my sergeant and more than likely the sheriff. We can't have him doing whatever he's doing with guns, that's for sure. And if he's got your dog, we have to get it back. There's the drug thing, besides. The marijuana. You've heard about it. Let me talk to people about warrants or whatever, and what to do next. You do me a favor?"

"You bet."

"Don't go back there. He *will* kill you."

"That's a deal," I said.

Later, when I sat in the kitchen and wondered for some reason whether I smelled to my colleagues and nurses and patients like a sour old wooden house inhabited mostly by dogs, I thought of how noble I had been. Well, of *course*, we can't have deputies murdered for the sake of a dog.

Well, of course, I thought.

I heard from the hospital, with a dutiful report on Roger Pettefoy bouncing back. In the morning, I woke on my sofa across from Pooh, who glared from his, and I heard the sound of an airplane flying low. It was just light, it was Sunday morning, and I would have to be in the hospital to check on the kids, but not until nine or ten. I had five hours on my own, and I knew how I would spend them. Pooh lay still, pretending not to be there, until I was in the kitchen, making coffee. I heard his groan as he half slid and half fell onto the floor.

By six I was in the car, parked at the intersection of Lester Scott's road and mine. I walked through brush, keeping parallel to the road. I had my flashlight, but only used it with my hand cupped loosely over the lens. I wore a dark, heavy Irish sweater we had bought maybe fifteen years before in Clifden, and it almost fit. Putting it on, fighting my way up into its bulky sleeves, I had realized how little I'd been eating. I wore an old tan tweed cap, dark work gloves for no reason I could give, and I carried the heavy pocket knife I kept sharpened in case I had to do an emergency tracheotomy. I had carried it for years and never used it. I'd no idea why I brought it with me now. Maybe, if he shot me in the head, I would need to cut an airway in so I could breathe while dying.

Of course, I was panting. I sweated heavily, and I imagined myself as pale, as radiating my feeble heat and light through the woods like a beacon. The light plane gargled and buzzed not far above, a couple of hundred feet, maybe less. I progressed by staggering, by falling, by taking short, uneven steps, by gasping and muttering, by pulling myself ahead, this hand on that branch, this foot pushing off that unsteady rock I hadn't, anyway, seen in time to not fall on, but for all of my inability and fear, I felt something I can only describe as health.

We'd heard the stories for years, and Arch Constantine had more or less repeated them, but with more detail. Although I live on shale, clay, and bony ridges, I also live on water. The high valley that runs along the spines of hills a thousand, two thousand, feet high has water that drains off it. These mountain streams continue as creeks and brooks and branches — so they're named on the map — to the Chenango River and the Unadilla. These empty into the Susquehanna, and that runs as far as Chesapeake Bay, and there you are, from here — from this little nowhere anyone heard of — gone to everyplace else.

Farmers with moving water of any reasonable depth are attached to the rest of the world, in other words. You can bring a shallow-draft boat up into river-bottom country. What you load it with is the marijuana you've been growing half a mile back off the road, out of sight of troopers and deputies, accessible only to the harvesters, who work there while they're screened off by the harvesting of soy or corn, or the spreading of manure. So the marijuana is grown behind the grass, then it's ferried to deeper waters, and it's taken farther by lazy-day fishermen in Boston whalers through a system of rivers as complicated as a network of human nerves, or by high school dropouts in fast, converted cars who use the Onondaga reservation as a distribution hub for shipments north to Canada, south down the thruway to New York.

The plane came back over. Why Mr. Lester Scott decided I was working for some antidrug agency couldn't have had much to do with what he saw. I was a scrawny, middle-aged man who hung around with dogs. I never carried a shotgun or a rifle, never paid attention (I was told) to anyone nearby. I couldn't have the look of a narc. I felt myself smile. I was flattered.

I was also winded. I was also near the trailer. A yellow light lay around the doorway and the top outside step. I heard the jingle of the chain as Bear moved away from the trailer. I heard the click as Scott locked himself back in. Commando-Doc peering through the brush on the subject's perimeter, I needed only cork blacking to look like an unmuscular joke about films. His small lot was perfectly rectangular, I thought; all the corners were right angles. A small shed — garbage and tools, no doubt — was plumb in its relation to the trailer. His woodpile was neat, and what he'd split of the mound of round sections was piled in face cords between studs he'd spiked into the ground. Moving around the lot, I saw at the back of the trailer a single cinder block step beneath the rear door. From it, I could see a trail. It probably went to his marijuana crop. I could follow the path, set his crop on fire, then steal back Bear while Scott was distracted. Since I didn't smoke, however, and since my emergency rescue kit consisted of Agway reinforced gloves and the tracheotomy knife, I needed another plan.

I stepped out onto the back of his lot. I would like to say I glided, but in my rubber-bottomed winter boots I thumped. I walked alongside the trailer and, at the corner that would take me around to the side of his wooden front steps, I paused. I hissed. I gave the low, coded whistle that would bring my dog and, if they held him back, the steps and trailer too. He paused, I whistled again, and then he bent again to lick his loins. So much for Lassie, so much for Lad and Rin-Tin-Tin.

As I bit on my lips and tongue and cheeks, and worried what I could reach of my head for a practical thought, I found myself stepping around the corner and walking to my dog. I whispered, "Bear, goddammit." Probably, the goddammit did the trick. He looked and stiffened, he leaned forward — they are all myopic until they're blind — and then he galloped, ass high, tail corkscrewing, big jaws open in what everyone who owns a dog will call a smile.

The chain scraped as it tightened at the step, and Bear winced, a step or two short of me. Scott had put him in a choker meant for a smaller dog. I could see the furrow in his fur as it bit. I pushed into him, and back, so that the pressure eased. He burrowed into me, put his paws on my shoulders as he tried to swallow my face, and knocked me over. So there I was, one hand hooked inside a binding choker chain, flat on my back with my black dog standing on my chest, inhaling my nose and mouth.

I heard the trailer door open and a flat, thin voice: "Get away from Buddy. Get off of my land."

I lay back. Bear had gone stiff. I closed my eyes and I said, "Fuck you."

"I did grant you the sporting chance," he said.

I heard a soft sound, the closing of a little metal latch. I heard the grate of some other metal mechanism, and I opened my mouth and eyes at once. I was on my feet, and I don't remember standing. I kneeled at Bear and worked to loosen the choker. He had retreated as far as he could from the porch, so he'd tightened it, and the only way I could set him free was to push him toward his captor. There was some kind of important Zen semiautomatic large-magazine coveting-of-property message in that action, I think I thought. Scott put six, seven, eight rounds into the earth around me. Bear growled low, but also drooped with fear. He shivered, and so did I, but without the growl. I finally somehow pulled the collar off, tearing away some of Bear's ear. He screamed, and they later found a chunk ripped open where the ear meets the head.

The plane flew low above us, and I heard other engines and so did Scott. A yellow power company truck was almost out of view where it idled, to the left of his house. I couldn't see its cherry-picker crane, but as the yellow light inside his doorway vanished, I knew they were cutting his power off. A big ambulance slid up, and so did two navy blue state police cars, and then the red and white sheriff's cars, one after another, maybe half a dozen, and then several unmarked cars pulled in. By then, I was holding Bear against my chest with his paws folded in against my arms.

I said, "I'll tell them you could have killed me and you didn't. I'll tell them how you fired into the ground."

He looked up at the plane as it returned. He raised the rifle and he fired. He said, as he shot, "A man gets a vote in this country. A man still gets a vote. Man good as niggers and DEA sneakthief undercover lawyers, keeping him from what's his due and guaranteed Constitution rights. Spics in Talladega get the vote, and so do I." He squeezed off round after round. I heard the cops calling, as if to warn, by sheer power of their cries, the unprotected pilot in his plane. I turned my back to Scott because I was afraid he was going to shoot us, and I didn't want the dog to be my shield. I couldn't move my feet. I knew I had wet my trousers, and then I felt the warm trickle as Bear took my cue. He didn't feel heavy, though he must have weighed close to eighty pounds. It wasn't his weight. It was my legs. They wouldn't move. So I crouched with my back to Lester Scott as the plane came back — this time I heard the troopers and deputies cursing the pilot — and flew in, slow and low and large above us.

Scott fired a round a second, it sounded like, and though I thought I was deafened by the noise of his rifle, I heard one of the lawmen call *Down!* at the same time that I heard Lester Scott say in his flat, uninflected voice, "I know you. I know you. I know who you are." He fired twice again, and then the rescuers fired. They must have posted snipers with military rifles because two shots, which boomed and echoed in the forest, struck him at once. Imagine swatting a side of beef with a breadboard. I heard the bullets go in. I was on my knees by then, unable to breathe. The right side of my back was numb, and I figured out, at about the time that I registered the second volley of shots — lower in register, tinnier — from everyone else firing, that one of the troopers or deputies had shot me. I figured it was a mistake, though you never know how angry someone in that situation might become at a civilian fouling their rural drug bust.

It was a high adrenaline morning, all right, with men screaming commands through bullhorns, the airplane roaring back and forth, lower and lower, it sounded to me, and everything in my body pumping head to toe and side to side. I lay on top of Bear, unable to move. The numbness on my back had been replaced by a very deep and profoundly disabling pain. I didn't think I could breathe anymore. I hadn't the breath to tell them. I knew that Bear, beneath me, hadn't moved. So I didn't, anyway, want them to pick me up. I lay as still as I could, shaking and feeling wet all over and breathing very shallowly. I heard them gabbling and laughing and commanding one another to perform all sorts of actions.

Someone said, "Most of the motherfucker's plastered onto the trailer, and the rest of the trailer is halfway shot to shit. I believe we have lowered the resale value for his motherfucking estate." They laughed high up in their throats, and the smell of cigarette smoke poured over us.

I was going to croak a brave and wounded doctor's joke about smoking and its toll on one's health. I remember that. I remember opening my mouth, timing myself against the pulses inside my ribs and under my lungs, but I couldn't shape the big, hissing syllable I'd need to start with. The spotter plane went over, and then someone turned me. I gagged and started to cry, I'm afraid.

It sounded like Arch Constantine, a deep voice in genuine sorrow. He said "Aw," the way we said it as kids when something that seemed as important as our lives — a skate key, a baseball glove — was lost or stolen. He said "Doc." Then he said "Aw" again. I drifted out and then came back to hear him tell me, "Here's the gurney, Doc."

I timed it. "Dog," I said.

Arch didn't answer me. He said, "There you go, Doc" in a voice gone high and false. I knew not to ask them again.

Great Brook, Morris Brook, Handsome Brook. I thought of water over rocks someplace. West Branch and Canasawacta Creek, the Gene-gantlet. I saw them, though I had only heard their names from fisher-men or patients, had only driven over them in ignorance or heard them cited by cops. I saw them as fine blue lines on a map. I saw small-eyed, pale and hungry men in skiffs, wearing gumboots, their bodies tight-ened, as if toward pain, against the inevitable treachery. But the rivers ran to the edge of a page, as if I held a map in a book before me on the kitchen table in our house, sitting over coffee while the old dog snored and Bear, not killed by the shots going through me, ate a shoe. The creeks and rivers dripped their wavering paths to the blank bottom margin of the gazetteer.

Only the pilot could see it all. Drifting low, hanging, he could crook his wrist and cover thousands of yards as we bent our necks back and watched him veer. He could twitch his hand and turn the page we lived on.

Berceuse

Berceuse: *n.f.* Woman who rocks an infant;
rocking chair; cradle that rocks; lullaby.

IT WAS THE SUMMER of 1973 when we lived in the country and I
read stories about white girls kidnapped by Indians, stories about
children who sometimes came home. I read Richter's *Light in the Forest*,
I read North's *Captured by the Mohawks*. I read so many. The mother
and father and brother and sister were stabbed or shot or burned or
clubbed, were flayed and hacked and butchered, and one small girl was
left alive by mistake or out of evil intention. She was held in her terror
on a horse and ridden back to an Indian encampment. She was raised
by the Indians as their own. Some of the books insisted on rape.
Nevertheless, silent men with hairless chests took care of the girls as
they grew, and often, somehow, there were infants born to them, and
that was one of the times in the course of the summer, coming to such
a moment, when I would start to cry.

It was the summer after my miscarriage, and we had come from
New York City to the country for our vacation. For three weeks my
husband Sonny Schiff would not have to copy-edit texts on subjects he
despised like economics and sociology. He could lie in the sun and read
a Horatio Hornblower novel, immune to the black flies that sought my
nostrils and mouth and eyes and drove me indoors, where I read about
being taken away and raised in an alien culture but being somehow
retrieved and then, as they say, being of two minds. Sonny then had
big knuckly cheekbones under fair skin. He had green eyes and ginger-
colored hair, wide shoulders, long, strong arms. A fireman, I called
him, a New York Irish fireman. But Sonny was a Jew whose grand-
parents came from Germany. I am the only daughter of a Lebanese

Catholic from Utica who married my mother in Ulverston, Lancashire, on the western edge of the Lake District. I have my mother's eyes and skin, and I look best in the summer if I stay indoors. That summer, though I stayed indoors, I did not look my best. And I have the reproductive organs, apparently, of a different species. My womb is crooked and pinched. I did little good for the seed of the Schiffs. It took me a year and a half to get pregnant. It took me one morning of bloody thighs and knees and shins to not be pregnant anymore.

So we were recovering our equilibrium. We were composing ourselves. I was reading about white girls captured by Indians, and Sonny was staying outside, away from the little woman who was a little quick on the trigger. We housesat for a friend of Sonny's cousin Miriam, the well-known literary Schiff. In Dutchess County, we lived under copper pans and Le Creuset pots on a ceiling rack in the kitchen. We made tunafish sandwiches on a butcher's block that seemed wider than the dining table in our apartment. An eighteenth-century Dutch cupboard in the living room grinned shelvesful of spongeware at us. And in the front hall, a two-drawer cherry stand — which would have cost us three months' rent — held a scratch pad and a telephone. In the garage was a gray, high-nosed Volvo we'd been invited to use for errands. Sonny said he thought it suitable for a state burial.

We spent a week reading books and slouching around in little stores. We watched the television set, I fell asleep during movies and, according to Sonny, I snored. He scratched in the large garden behind the house, assuring me that vegetables would be on the table by the middle of our second week.

"It's the Hudson Valley weather," he said. "This humidity makes stuff grow faster. You ever notice that about the South? Tobacco?"

"I wasn't ever in the South," I said. "Neither were you. And what about tobacco?"

"That's right," he said. "Exactly. What?"

I smiled through the screened French door outside of which he made his tedious jokes and capered with a hoe for my distracton. The least I could do for him was smile.

He said, while I was doing the least I could, "Don't do that, Kim, all right?"

"What?"

"That thing with your face."

"I was responding, Sonny."

He turned back to the row of seeds that would rot in the ground, I knew, or become tight and hard as stones. He wiped his arm across his forehead like a farmer in the sun, and he clawed with his hoe at the ground.

I said, "I was responding, you son of a bitch."

Cousin Miriam came at the end of the second week to collect her pound of flesh. I couldn't tell her that. Sonny said that Miriam had called while I was in Poughkeepsie, reading in the Vassar library about an alumna who'd been written up by her daughter in the *Pine Plains Register*. This woman, after graduation in the 1930s, had gone to China to assist a Methodist medical missionary, and she'd been kidnapped by Mongol traders. I remember that I was eager to tell Sonny I was branching out. I remember that I thought I was cute. I saw myself walking from the garage across quartz pebbles to the white Colonial house with a kind of ass-twitching swagger, my head waggling a bit. I remember smiling what seemed, then, a droll and satisfied smile.

I brushed at my hair in case black flies had ridden in on me, and in the cool darkness of the hall, I shouted, "You'll never guess what I read about, Sonny. Hey."

He leaned around the corner from the living room and said, "Boo."

"Yeah?"

"I was scaring you."

"You can't scare me."

"Cousin Miriam just called," he said.

"Yes, you can."

"She's coming for a visit."

I couldn't stop. "Are you saying that she called to *ask* if we would *like* for her to *think about* coming up for a visit?"

"This is Wednesday? She's here, where you stand, in two days."

"Bitch," I said. "Bitch and bitch and *bitch*. She finds us the house, she sets up the vacation, then she comes — she did the whole thing for this. Didn't she. *Didn't* she? So she could come up and collect her pound of flesh?"

"Don't say that when she's around, right?"

"She's a collector, Sonny."

"Shylock, the Jew-dog loan shark, you remember, was the pound-of-flesh collector. Would you consider not saying anything about Jewish compound-interest fiends while she's here?"

"How about you ask her if *she'd* consider not saying everything about murdered Jews while she's here?"

Sonny smiled. When we first were married, I loved it when he smiled because his eyes wrinkled up and his forehead lost its tense, stretched look. Even in the summer of 1973, I was pleased for him when that happened. But this time it was one of his phony smiles, a pacifying smile. He used it on me when I was being hysterical or difficult or stubbornly unpersuaded.

I said, "You're doing that Sonny Schiff's Greatest Smiles Collection smile."

"No," he said.

"Yeah."

He said, "I'm sorry, Kimmy."

"Okay. Okay. I'm not making it easy. I know. Okay. But I would like to know something."

"The answer is: she does not have the hots for me."

"Bullshit, Sonny."

"And it's incest for first cousins to have the hots for each other."

"Each other?"

"I'm telling you I don't have a crush on goddamned Miriam!"

"Don't shout, Sonny. Don't be abusive. I'm not the one who told his wife she couldn't say Jew or the thing about *The Merchant of Venice* because the world's most hate-filled woman is coming to stay for the rest of the century."

"Weekend," he said.

"Long one or short one?"

"Friday, Saturday, Sunday."

"Will we sacrifice a gentile child for her, or shall I simply bake a ham? And did you *admit* a minute ago that Miriam walks around throbbing for your Jewish bone?"

"That's so vulgar, Kim."

"They raised us that way in the bazaar. And she did set us up so she could come out here and get at you and hang around the way she always tries to do in the city."

"Kim. Be reasonable. Be logical."

"Talk like that a little more, Sonny. I'll punch you out. I mean it."

"Don't punch. Don't yell. Don't fight." He walked into the living room and pitched onto one of its three sofas we could never, ever afford. He dropped hard, and the sofa didn't move. Ours, in the West 22nd Street apartment, would have slid screeching from wall to wall. I sat across from him on the coffee table with brass fixtures. I remember hoping that its legs wouldn't buckle and crack. "Yes," he said, lying on his back, his face beneath his broad, long hands. "Yes."

"Yes, she set us up?"

"Of course. Didn't you figure it when she told us we could have this place? The woman is lonely, Kim. She has no social life. She goes to lectures. She goes to poetry readings. Men never like her for very long."

"Isn't that strange," I said. "When all she really wants out of life is a roll in the hay with an Israeli tank battalion. I mean, a few hours of gunnery practice is all the wee thing really needs. And the occasional shiksa to cuff."

"Nice," he said.

"Oh, Sonny, I'm not being nice. I'm picking a fight."

His voice came through his fingers. "Kim, can you feel good about somebody? Can you feel good about anything? Anything. Fall in love with the black flies. Like the way you look in shorts again. When we're in bed, when we roll over to go to sleep, touch my back."

"If you murder Miriam for me, I will eat the black flies in a pudding," I said. I felt inconsolably embarrassed for us.

Sonny said, "That's all right. We'll handle it."

"What's all right?"

"Everything," he said. He kept his hands on his face. He sounded so young and uncertain. "Miriam and all," he said.

"Sure," I said. "She might wreck her car on the Taconic and crash and roll over a few times and catch on fire and burn and die."

"I knew you'd understand," he said.

⋅   ⋅   ⋅

Enter Miriam Rozcwicz, the daughter of Sonny Schiff's mother's older sister who, in Hartford Connecticut, married an immigrant whose building-supplies income sent his daughter Miriam to Brandeis and, for her master's degree, to NYU. Miriam was short, slight, pale, unmuscled, sometimes pretty, always smart, aggressive even in her sleep, and quite certain that death had been invented as a way of getting at the Jews. She touched her younger cousin Sonny whenever she could, and she always smiled at me as if I had just mastered the ability to burp with my mouth closed.

"So," I said, as Sonny took her bag to an upstairs guest room, "did you have a nice drive?" She examined the question, fruit of an evening's preparation, the way dogs inspect bones for scraps of meat.

She looked at me in a way I suppose Bluebeard might think of as loving, and in her soft, high, small-child's voice, she said, "It's so pretty. Did you know, when Khrushchev — the Russian premier?"

"I heard of him one time," I said.

"When he came to the UN, Eisenhower —"

"And I heard of him."

Miriam giggled. It was like watching a crocodile giggle. "He had Khrushchev taken for a drive on the Taconic Parkway because it's so pretty. Yes. I had a lovely drive, thank you."

"You're welcome," I said.

"So!" Sonny shouted, returning to the front hall where Miriam and I still stood. "Here we are!" he shouted.

"I love your blazer," I told Miriam. I always thought of her in peasant blouses with puffy short sleeves, the seams decorated with bright stitching. She tried, in fact, to look fashionable, though the effect at last was that of someone who ordered clothing over the phone in response to the sales clerks' descriptions.

"Drinks!" Sonny shouted desperately.

Miriam said, "Seltzer. With some lemon?"

"Perrier," I insisted. "We bought Perrier."

"That's seltzer," she said agreeably.

"It's French seltzer," I said. "Sonny, I will have a very, very, *very* large gin and tonic." I smiled my most responsive smile. He looked away from it.

"Maybe I'll have one too," he said.

"And Kim and I can meet you outside," Miriam said. "Let's see all this *nature* you're living with."

"Lots of flies out there," I sang.

"They never bother me," Miriam said.

I said, "Great."

So we went out the French doors and walked in a fog of black flies. They hovered around me and welts blew up on my arms and neck as they ate. I told Miriam that Sonny had tried building a brush fire so the smoke would drive the bugs away. It hadn't worked. I pointed with my toe at the remains. "Smudge fire, I think they call it," I said, risking flies on my tongue, hoping she would say that, for heaven's sakes, we ought to go *in*.

Looking down at the charred sticks and blackened grass, watching me blink and swipe and shake my hair, Miriam said, "Bonfire. I was reading about fires, bonfires. In the Middle Ages, they used bonfires for, you know, the bodies. The people who died of plague. *Bonefires* they were called. So, I was thinking. The good Germans of the thirties and forties, they had them both. They had *bon*fires when they burned the Jewish books, the books by Jewish writers and of course the Torah. They burned the scrolls whenever they could. You knew that?

"And, of course, then they had their *bone*fires at the camps. Those you know about, too. So there was ash, and then there was ash. Here's Sonny," she said, in her little girl's voice, as though she had caused him to appear expressly for my pleasure.

We walked in the yard outside the garden, though Sonny wanted us to return to his almost-instant produce. Miriam talked about Manhattan and its politics, turning from Sonny once in a while to politely check that I had heard of this politician or that crossroads issue. Having learned the city, having inspected the trees and lawns, we returned to the garden.

"I put corn in here," Sonny said, pointing to some disturbed soil. "Over here's the lettuce." The thirty-foot garden was vacant, stony, untilled, surrounded by tall weeds and patrolled by chiggers, mites, gnats, stinging horseflies, breath-sucking black flies and, probably, grudge-bearing copperheads three feet long. Sonny's rows of crop looked like small, superficial wounds.

Miriam was silent at last. Then she said, "But everything here is dead, Sonny."

"It was nice of you to notice," he said.

"Well," she said, "I do have to tell the truth."

"Oh, I think truth can be overrated," Sonny said in fulsome tones. "Why not lie, and spread a little joy?"

"You want me to *lie?*" Miriam said. She folded her arms across her shapeless chest.

"He'd welcome a useful lie," I said. Sonny looked unfriendly, and I shrugged. "Just showing off for company," I said.

Miriam said, "You two," and patronizingly smiled.

I felt constrained to make the sound that old men make on subway platforms just before they spit on the tracks. "I swallowed a bug," I explained. I slapped at the air and led them back to the house.

At dinner — which I cooked wonderfully, knowing that Miriam was incapable of heating soup — she told Sonny about his aunt and his mother. She took the tone of someone who had come upriver on a primitive vessel, bearing news to an outpost a thousand miles and a dozen months from home. She assured me that Sonny's mother sent her love. I thought this, in fact, to be true — we enjoyed one another — though Miriam coated her words with secret nuance and each syllable she spoke fell to the tablecloth and glistened.

Sonny listened politely. This was his cousin, and he would offer his attention; he would work his mind on what she said. His forehead looked as though the skin might burst if a butterfly brushed it. Miriam spoke of an exhibition of children's books held in Munich shortly after the end of the Second World War. It was like sitting with my father in our seats on the third-base line when Robin Roberts pitched. Roberts would lean into his windup, and I would think: here it comes.

Miriam was going to review a study of fairy tales, she said. Here it comes, I thought. She was going to surprise a few people, going to say a few things. "Believe me," she said. "For example, the Munich thing." She waved her fork at my marinated lamb without tasting it, enchanted as she was by my husband and herself.

"The book fair?" Sonny dutifully asked. He twirled his knife like a baton. Often, at long dinners, he twirled his flatware and silently craved cigarettes.

"Exhibition, they called it. I don't know German, the German word for it. I wouldn't know German. But yes: the fair, let's say. The authorities were quite horrified when several handsome editions of 'Hansel and Gretel' were offered."

Here it came. I said, "What's wrong with 'Hansel and Gretel'?"

"After the War?" she asked triumphantly.

Sonny said, "No. I don't get it either."

Miriam sighed through her nose. I had visions of jet black nostril hair, dense as scouring pads. "Do you remember the story?"

Sonny said, "Wicked stepmother, a father, they take the kids into the forest. They lose them. The kid leaves bread crumbs to follow back home, but birds eat the bread, the kids —"

"Something with a witch," I said, looking at Miriam.

"Right," Sonny said, twirling his knife, "the witch in the ginger-bread house. She wants to eat the kids. No — the boy. Right? Maybe both of them. I forget. His sister helps him with something. I don't remember what. And they get home, with money, I think."

"Gold," Miriam said. "Of course. It's German. It's bourgeois, so of *course* it celebrates money. *Looted* money. But you're forgetting *how* the witch wants to cook the boy."

"In a big kettle," I said, envisioning a vast black kettle in a children's cartoon I had seen on TV one Saturday morning. I now saw Miriam in it, up to her neck in greasy liquid, a fricassee of harridan. "A giant caldron of a kettle," I said.

Miriam looked pleased. "Oh, no, dears. In an oven. Ovens? Right after the War?"

"The Jews," I said, as if I'd just discovered them. "In Auschwitz. The ovens."

"The ovens," Miriam said. She added, "Good, Kim." Then, not waiting for me to wag my tail and pant, she said, "The German ovens. The reminder made the German bibliophiles a little uncomfortable. Ovens." Miriam smiled as if she had tasted something wonderful. I knew it wasn't on her plate.

Miriam slept at the distant end of the L-shaped upstairs hall, far from our bedroom, but we whispered nevertheless. In the darkness of the strange room, under strangers' sheets and cotton blankets, we lay on our backs and we whispered. Our voices sounded harsh and frightened.

"Her hair looks better short," I said. "She doesn't look bad."

"She walks, she says."

"Walks?"

"She takes a long walk every morning. She walks from West Fourth to Gimbel's and back. For her health."

"Does she have something bad?"

"No," he said. "I'm sorry to disappoint you. She decided, she says, that an intellectual has to have an understanding of the body."

"Yeah. Your body."

"No, Kim, not my body. This is Miriam in full song. It's *the* body. Something about action, Albert Camus, Algeria, colonialism that becomes a something-else in America, and the Frenchman who — I forget. Wait. Crèvecoeur! I knew I knew it."

"And that's why she cut her hair short?"

"And takes long walks."

We were quiet. I heard the crickets or frogs, or whatever it is that you hear all night in the country. It only stops when there's a loud noise. Then they all start again at the same instant, rubbing their wings or singing, whatever they do. I was learning that summer that you can stop hearing them and then start hearing them again, just the way they stop making their noise and start again. It's like turning down the sound on the radio, I was learning.

Sonny said, "So how do you feel?"

"Fine."

"No," he said. In the dark, whispering, he sounded angry, desperate. "I mean, in your heart. Inside. In your heart. How do you feel?" I didn't answer. He said, "Kim?"

"You make me feel like I'm ruining the summer if I don't feel like the opening number in *Oklahoma!*"

"I don't want you to feel like *Oklahoma!* Just tell me how you do feel."

"I feel fine, Sonny. How do you feel? I mean, it's not like I'm your patient or something. How are *you?*"

"I'm fine if you are," he said.

"Well, we're both fine, then." His face was closer to my neck. I said, "You think she does have a boyfriend? Miriam? I can't see her smooching in the Lion's Head with some poet in a leather jacket. Can you?" His nose touched my neck. In the dark, I closed my eyes. After a long time, he let his breath out and out.

I said, "What?"

"When will you be happy again, Kimmy?"

"Let's just talk about Miriam, Sonny. Let's not talk about things like being happy." We were silent again. His breath washed my neck. I said, "I read a book the other day called *House of Sixty Fathers*. It's set in the Sino-Japanese War. This little Chinese kid has to find his way back home to his mother."

He put his lips on my neck. He said into my skin, "Was he kidnapped by Chinese Indians or Japanese Indians?"

I sat up. Then I leaned back down on one elbow. I touched his cheek. It was rough with whiskers. I sat back up.

"What?" he said.

"Your five o'clock shadow is a little heavier than Miriam's, I think. How come I don't belt her for treating me like the resident brain-damaged child? Is it my good Catholic upbringing in suburban Phila-delphia, or is it that if I deck her really hard and break something — you know, really *crunch* something — I'll end up feeling like I've struck a terrible blow against all of the Jews, all of the persecuted Jews? Which returns us to a good Catholic upbringing in suburban Philadelphia. Guilt and partial penance our specialty."

"She doesn't think of you like that."

"No?"

"Not brain damaged."

"Thank you, Sonny."

"She's Miriam, Kim. That's all. Miriam. She takes these things seriously."

"Everyone in any area code you can pick takes these things seriously. She take them *personally*."

"Maybe it's good that she does. You know, that somebody does. Even if it makes them a pain in the ass."

"And a bigot," I said.

"Well."

"And a bigot."

"And a bigot," Sonny said, sighing.

"Sonny, you sound like I'm giving you one more little problem to contend with."

"No, you're not," he said. "I'm sorry if I sound impatient."

I lay back down. I was at the edge of the bed, facing outward. I said, "I think maybe I'll try and get a teaching job again. And I'm thinking maybe I should look into taking some courses at night."

"That takes care of the daytime and the nights. Can you come up with something to get you out of the house on weekends?"

"You're really pissed off at me, huh, Sonny?"

I thought he said, "You." Then he made a strange noise, muffled by his pillow.

"What?"

I heard him move on the sheets. I felt him shake. I felt the bed shake on its springs, and I knew he was crying into his pillow. The two of us, then: we cried alone together.

Sonny was pushing a big, noisy power mower around the back lawns while Miriam lay on a white chaise longue, her legs and arms spread to, presumably, the sun. She wore a patterned blue bandeau that clashed with her long, pink bermuda shorts. She wore sunglasses, and I couldn't see if she stared at Sonny, who had removed his shirt and whose underpants showed above the waist of his loose, stained chinos. He wore a rolled red kerchief as a sweatband. He had worn sweatbands like it in Vietnam, unloading cargo planes at Da Nang. Though her eyes were hidden, I was certain that the witty reviewer, the panelist on forums about politics and language, was staring at her cousin's belly and chest, dreaming about what remained beneath his clothes. I was at the kitchen window, tuning the sound of the mower out and then in, watching Miriam watch the boy I was married to.

The mower stopped. I waited to see whether I had stopped hearing it. But Sonny had shut the motor off to come in for a drink. Miriam followed. He ran with sweat, and I saw her nostrils widen as if to inhale his smell while I put ice cubes in tumblers. Miriam needed to share even his thirst. I thought of her licking the sweat on his chest. She wouldn't, finally, have the appetite. She wouldn't have the tongue. I smiled into the refrigerator as I took out lemonade.

She removed her glasses, and I was pleased to see that her blue-white skin had burned around their shape. She would return to New York looking like a singed albino raccoon.

"Ah," Sonny said as I poured more lemonade for them. "You want some, Kim?"

I shook my head.

"It's good."

I nodded.

"It's good for you — Vitamin C."

"It's mostly sugar," I said.

"Vitamin C and sugar — guards you from scurvy, keeps you from bitterness. Here." He held out his glass. I reached out, not watching Sonny but Miriam, as I took the glass and turned it around so that the pulp gathered in the shape of his lip below the rim was turned toward me. I fitted my mouth to the shape of Sonny's, and I sipped. I licked my lips and held the glass out to Sonny. Miriam stared into my face.

Then she shook the Saturday *Times*, which Sonny had fetched for her when he ran his early-morning errands. She folded it and slapped it hard at the table. "You've seen this?"

I shook my head. Sonny picked up a dishtowel and wiped at his neck and chest and arms. He lay the towel around his neck and said, "I'm off."

"Stay and chat, Sonny," I said. But he smiled for his escaping, and then he escaped.

Miriam sat before the book I'd been reading, and she once more shook the *New York Times*. "Troop movements," she said. "Iraqis, the Syrians. Egyptians, of *course*."

"I haven't been paying attention, really," I said.

"Too bad. Because it's coming. Ask your husband."

"What, Miriam?"

"Israel. Another war. What else am I talking about? Another attempt to eradicate a small state because it happens to be the home of the Jews."

I tried to pull my book back across the table, but I could see her eyes as she read the title upside down. "*The Searchers*," I explained. "It's about a family that gets wiped out in a frontier Indian raid, in the West. The sisters get taken off, but their brother survives. He and this uncle —"

"Cowboys and Indians," she said. "Israel is going to be ganged up on. Again. Israel is going to have to fight for its life."

"I'm sorry."

"The rest of the world will go to church and say, like that, 'I am sorry.' And once a year, in the name of a Jewish man whose Jewishness is conveniently overlooked, they will smear a little ash on their foreheads, and they will say, 'I am sorry.' The ash, of course, will come from the fires. The bonefires. Those you remember."

While she spoke, her little eyes in their white-flesh frames in her crimson skin were going over the pages of *The Searchers*, which she held close to her face. Deep lines like large parentheses ran from the outside of each nostril down to her chin. The lines framed her mouth. The lips were tight with disdain. She tossed the book onto the table, and lost my place.

"I am saying to you," Miriam said, "that the entire world wants every Jew on the surface of the earth to die."

"Oh, Miriam."

"Each."

"You dislike me," I said. "Okay. I think you try to put up with me for Sonny. Though you also try to put me *down* for Sonny, if you know what I mean. No, listen. I don't understand you very well. I don't have any right, I suppose, to comment on what you're saying. Except you always tell me so much. You lecture me a lot —"

"It could help you," she said, "if you knew what Sonny knows, knew what matters inside of your husband's soul."

"That would be nice, I guess, if you meant it. But what matters to you doesn't necessarily matter to us. Miriam: all that seems to matter to *you* is death."

"And you find that disturbing? *You?* What *about* death, Kim? Kim. Kim. Kim. Kim. What *about* death? What about the meaning of the six million dead? The smell of the camps. The chimneys. Can you imgine the smell coming up the chimneys and out into the Polish air at

Oswiecim from the ovens? The tiny bloodied ashes that flew in the air? What would the townspeople have pretended to think the SS were baking in their ovens? Yasir Arafat has the *recipe* for what they were baking. Fairy tales, they were baking. Hansel and Gretel, they were baking. Over and over again. First Hansel, then Gretel, then little Hansel and Gretel babies, then wicked stepmothers, then softheaded fathers, then Hansel and Gretel again. Also at Maidanek. Also Treblinka. Hansel and Gretel and Hansel and Gretel. *That* is what you don't care about. *That* is why Israel. And *that* is why the Arabs want Israel burned down to the sand. The entire desert will be their oven. Millions of Hansels and millions of Gretels again. And that, wife of my Jewish cousin, is what you do not understand. Put the mark on your forehead this Easter and mourn your dead God."

She shook. Tears ran down the creases on her face. Sweat pasted the fringes of her pert new haircut to her burned forehead. The sound of the mower had stopped again. "You are so smug and narrow," she said. "You mourn your one child. Not even an entire child. You mourn the death in your Christian womb. Let me tell you why your baby died, wife of my Jewish cousin."

"Don't tell me, Miriam," I said.

"Oh, yes," she said. "Your baby died because you murdered us. Every one of you murdered our dead. Ask your priests. Ask your dead God. The fruit of your womb is death."

Sonny moved from the doorway, then, where he had stood to listen. I had watched his face as her words broke over it. I saw in it only the sadness for me that I always saw. When he spoke at last, he spoke softly. "Miriam, you must never talk that way to Kim. Especially now. How could you hurt her like this? How could you hurt my wife?"

"I'm not your wife," I told him. "I am *death*'s wife. Ask Madame Defarge."

He said, "Miriam: go home, please. Don't change your clothing. Don't do anything but go, I think. This has been a terrible thing, Miriam. Leave her alone. Leave us alone. You have to go home now."

She said, "When will *you* go home, Sonny?"

He shouted, "*Now*, Miriam!" His voice rose very high, and his face was as red as hers. His eyes were wet. He stepped between Miriam and me, and she flinched, stepped back, and then went out of the kitchen. He said to me, "I am sorry. I am so sorry."

I sat down on the far side of the table from where Sonny stood. I didn't want anyone embracing me and telling me how sorry anyone was.

He gestured gently toward me, after a while, from the far side of the table. "Kidnapped by Jews," he said.

"She'll tell your mother and your aunt how you were kidnapped by the goyim."

He smiled a sad, exhausted smile. I thought that if I ever had a baby who grew up to be spirited but ill, he might one day be my brave friendly child who looked like that.

Sonny said, "Please don't try and smile. Just feel the way you feel. It's all right. I know she hurt you terribly. I wish you wouldn't look like that, Kim."

We heard the screen door gently close. We listened as her car door opened and shut. We heard the car start up and roll on the pebbles in the driveway with a slow, bouncing crunch.

"Now it's only me and you," I said.

Sonny said, "Please help me find you a way to be happy." He said more, maybe about Miriam, and maybe about me, and maybe about sorrow, and maybe about us. I wasn't hearing anymore.

"I am happy," I told him, trying to sound the way you sound when you answer people. I told him, "I'm on my way to it. I'm going to be." That was what I promised Sonny Schiff on a summer afternoon when we lived in the country for a time and were married.

It was a tricky shot because we had an old farmhouse burning to the ground and blowing in on itself. We were using two cameras, and we were shooting an actor who wasn't quite physical enough for the part but who was pretty and whose presence in the movie got the deal made. We were scared that he would drop the make-believe child before he staggered to the door of the house. We were scared that he would muff the shoot as the house blew and we would have to send me careening around the countryside, trying to buy the right-sited farmhouse in this scrubby New York State landscape where you either farmed or did chores for someone professional or you made what you thought of as retirement money by selling your house to a production company filming someting gothic and urban about what its producer thought of as rural life.

Our female villain had lived upstate for part of her childhood, and she pretended not to miss Santa Monica. She was, in fact, a genuine trouper, pretending not to need to be one as she played a country girl whose movie part was that of a country girl. Our male lead was tall and quite frail and could not bring himself to lie to anyone about his discomfort. The days were sunny and hot with high skies, the nights were cool, and flying creatures the local boys called sweat bees landed in our hair and stung our necks. A few harmless garden snakes were by now in our conversations approaching the size of anacondas. The producer, Sid Gallery, for whom I had worked on two other films, enjoyed the misery of the players. Like all film executives, he was contemptuous of actors. He hung with the crew, playing cards, drinking beer judiciously, reading the New York papers that his wife mailed up along with coffee beans that he ground fresh every morning and from which he brewed a dark and sinister beverage.

I drove to the nearest town to use the photocopier in the post office, I got everyone's mail, and I stood behind Sid when we rehearsed and then filmed scenes. I held the latest script revision in case he wanted to consider it. I held a book with numbers for the cellular telephone he used so frequently, and I was the designated responder to his rhetorical questions.

"How can he think of shooting in light like *this?*" he might say.

"Murky," I'd agree, in case he was really conducting a conversation. Usually, he'd have thrown his question over his shoulder at me — it kept him from pestering the director, whom he always nauseatingly assuaged — and he more than likely would not have expected a reply. I always prepared one in case he did.

Here we were, then, at a tense moment for the film. Time and therefore money was at stake, and we were close to being over budget, a situation Sid was on location to prevent. It was half past seven; people with allergies were muffling sneezes as the air cooled off and pollen flew in the wind. Gold light was on everything. Each stalk of grass threw a shadow. They called it Magic Time. The low white farmhouse, leaning in at the sills and doorframes in a nicely knock-kneed way, erupted in smoke as the clapper came down and Rocky Zimmerman's assistant called for action. The boom swung smoothly in. The crane rose then dipped in front of the house. From the side, a tracking camera trundled past the windows — we'd built in two extra windows for the shot — and our hero, holding his dead girlfriend's baby by him, given up in adoption when he had left her, was now reclaiming the child, a year older, from abusive religious zealots. Or something.

And here he came. There came the fire behind him. The roar would be supplied in the studio, though we indeed burned creosoted wood behind the house and would be blowing in the walls as our hero narrowly escaped. He didn't drop the blankets that passed for the kid. We would shoot him in closeup holding a genuine year-old baby, framed by a studio door. All we needed him to do, now, was make for the front-yard tree with the new old swing we'd hung on it, to slump there and watch the flames and bursting wood and collapsing roof and, while the glare reflected from his polished cheekbones, sing a fragment of husky lullaby to the baby he would cherish, now, forever. WIDE TWO-SHOT. TIGHTEN. HOLD. FREEZE. FADE TO BLACK.

Tomorrow we would shoot the hunt that took place early in the film near a shale cliff I'd found off something called the Skaneateles Turnpike, a narrow road between parallel two-lanes that took you to points between Binghamton to the south and Utica to the north. We were going to use the crumbling rock face for a fight in which our hero would pry the cliff loose and let it cut his pursuers to pieces with the sharp edges of falling rock.

I was in Sid's trailer, then, drinking a beer from his little refrigerator and laying out script for the next morning. He liked to look at a day's work at a time instead of organizing it from the shooting script on his own. Producers get babied by women like me who are paid to be adults for them. The *New York Times* of the day before was open to the sports, and I took a break in his camp chair and turned past the sports to anything else. Anything else, that day, was the obituary section. I always read the obits. When you're in your forties and you live alone, you read about the dead.

There it was. Richard "Sonny" Schiff, well-known publishing figure, long-time activist in freedom-to-write activities for PEN America, was dead at forty-four of an aneurysm.

Sid stooped to fit through the trailer door. He was very nearsighted, and he aimed his vision along his beaky nose, turning his awkward, thin body toward me.

"What's an aneurysm, Sid?"

"You — there's a — something's wrong with an artery. Vein? Weak wall of an artery. Or maybe a vein."

"You had a paperback dictionary. It isn't on your table."

"It isn't?"

"Where's your *dictionary*, Sid?"

"You bet your condo on a Scrabble game?"

"Sid."

"In front of you," he said. "Under the scripts I was looking at. Not looking at."

I didn't listen after that. I looked up "aneurysm" and then "dilatation" to be sure I understood. I said, "You're right. But what's it mean?"

By then, he stood behind me. He put his big hands on my shoulders. "It means," he said gently, "that the blood vessel bursts."

"How do you die of it?"

"If it's in the brain, you have a stroke. Other places, you bleed inside, into the body. Usually, they don't know you have it until it's too late. It can also happen in the heart, I think. Anyplace, really. Tell me what, Kim."

"My husband died," I said. "The man I used to be married to a long time ago died. Of an aneurysm. He was a very healthy man when we were married."

The woman who was with the film designer gave me a lift to the Utica airport where I got a flight that put down in Syracuse and took off almost at once for New York. I still wore sweaty jeans and scuffed work shoes and an old chambray shirt. I had a carry-on bag, but I didn't know what was in it. Sid had given me cash for cabs. He always carried a lot of cash in an oversized gold money clip shaped like the Brooklyn Bridge and sold by Tiffany. His wife claimed that he refused to tell her who had given it to him. I remember saying to her, at a post-shoot party, where everyone was a little smug with relief and because the editing hadn't begun, "We all have our secrets."

I remember how stiff and blank her face was as she answered, "Yes, but having a secret should really mean that no one knows we have it. Don't you think?"

I took a cab from LaGuardia to my place on 92nd and Central Park West. Hector, the doorman, asked me a question. Raymond, the elevator man, asked me a question. I recall giving answers but not what any of us said. It was a large apartment from which I could see some of the Central Park reservoir, but I didn't choose to look that night. I threw the air conditioners on and I opened and closed the refrigerator a few times. From the Utica airport I had called New York Information for the numbers of funeral homes. I'd written down a dozen and on the fifth call, they'd told me that, yes, Sonny was in their care. In their care. Well, he had been in my care, and I had been in his care, and then we had been careful and then we had been careless, and then we'd been in the care of others and now he might as well be theirs. I noted the time of the service and the address. When I hung up the phone, a fat girl at the rental car desk a few feet away said, "Are you all right, ma'am?"

That was what I heard as I walked in my apartment and looked at mail but without opening letters. When she asked me, I cried for the first time since reading of his death. I stood in the airport and I nodded my head and I cried. I felt like one of those plastic dipping birds on the back ledge of someone's sedan: they dip their beak as the car rocks. I dipped and nodded and wept.

I took the subway and sweated through my black knit cotton dress. It was a long ride to Park Slope in Brooklyn. Walking in the narrow streets, I realized I wasn't far from the bridge that would look like Sid Gallery's money clip. I wondered if he had loved a woman in Brooklyn. It hadn't been his wife, I knew, because she had made it clear that she would only live in Pacific Palisades, Manhattan, or Aix-en-Provence. I wondered if I cared to make anything of Sid's commemoration of a love affair with something that held money. But what else would a producer use as a sign of great emotion?

Harnik's Funeral Home looked like a vast factory made of cinder blocks, and it enclosed the usual hush. I was admitted to a room larger than I'd expected it to be. I wore a large-brimmed black felt hat in which I knew I looked good. I pulled it down hard and walked in. At the front of the room, a low door was sliding to. A woman fell forward, then caught herself. Everyone else sat stiffly, looking toward the small door. Then I saw the little trundle wheels and realized that Sonny Schiff had just gone into the gas-fired flames. The woman who had moved so suddenly just as suddenly stood. She turned, and I saw that she had dived to embrace her children. A café-au-lait girl of eight or nine and a twelve- or thirteen-year-old boy with ebony skin held her waist. The boy was in a dark gray suit, the girl in a navy blue dress that matched her mother's blue-black long-sleeved shirtwaist made of a shimmery rayon that bulked out at the shoulders. There seemed to be a point announced by their refusal to wear black.

The woman was tall and very slender, almost bony. Her skin was a dark tan, her cheekbones prominent, her forehead wide and high, her hair cut short, her arms and legs very long. She had elegant hands with which she held her children's shoulders. She was Sonny's wife, I thought. She was the woman he had gone to after the women who came after me. Sonny had married me and then, eventually, he had married her. I knew her name: Eloise. I didn't know her children's names. I knew that she was a curator at the Museum of Natural History. I had probably passed her, on the Upper West Side, a dozen times in the street. We were Sonny's wives.

A man in a black suit stood impatiently at the side of the room. He was waiting to pray. Eloise Schiff wouldn't, she'd decided, let him start. I smiled for her will, and she saw me. Maybe she recognized me. I hoped she did. She smiled back. Sonny, I thought, she *is* beautiful, and so are your babies. On the wall was the usual wooden cross. No figure was spiked to it. Eloise, in front of it, ignored the cross and the minister. Then she took a breath and seated herself, pulling her children down too. I wondered if she knew my name and what — whatever — in Sonny's life I had meant.

So Sonny was cremated. Sonny was off the earth. Maybe she would scatter what was left. Maybe he'd remain someplace. Hello: I wonder if I could borrow a teaspoon of ashes? I thought of Sonny's cousin, Miriam, who had hated me for an Arab whore and who had lusted for him just this side of drooling. She would be mourning him, I thought, by rejoicing for the pain: that these gentiles-upon-gentiles had burned the Jew she loved — just as they (she would say) and I and the others so yearned to burn every Jew off the earth. She would cradle the satisfaction of that pain, she would rock it slowly within her as she mourned.

The minister spoke. I turned the sound away. I looked at heads and faces, but though I recognized a few, I knew none of them well. I did not collect friends. I had lovers and then I didn't have them. I had a husband, then didn't. The Schiffs weren't there — none of them. But *he* left *us* for the cross, they would say. I looked at the babies Sonny had made with his wife. I thought of him with her in their bed, of her long brownness and his paleness against her. I thought of his face in the contortions of effort and pleasure. And I thought of Eloise giving birth, and of Sonny holding his children. Eloise stirred in her seat, and then she turned. She looked down the room to me. Her children turned with her. The man in the black suit spoke louder, sharply. People behind her turned to see what had drawn her attention. I nodded slowly. She nodded in return and looked. Then she faced the front of the room, and then her daughter turned. Her son kept studying me. I tried to smile. I tried to learn his features. He turned away.

I walked out the broad wooden door and downstairs and out to the street. Park Slope was full of heat and stale air and smoke. I wondered if Sonny was part of the smoke. I raised my head. I breathed deep.

They sent the designer's girlfriend, Charlie she called herself, to pick me up. She was a chunky, sweet-faced blonde who could stay there after the shoot if she wanted, I thought, and ride around in the pickup trucks of local men, smoking cigarettes and sitting close to their side of the bench seat, one hand lying behind their shoulders.

"So how was the funeral?" she asked, sucking soda through a straw from a big paper cup.

"I tried not to pay too much attention."

"Yeah? So what'd you do?"

"A lot of deep breathing," I said. I heard myself titter, so I shut up and leaned against the door and looked out at the harsh, hilly countryside. After a while, as we approached the compound, I said, "Charlie, let's drop you off and I'll take the car. An errand."

"We're going dancing tonight. There's some kind of a local native *square* dance or something. You want to come?"

"Can't dance," I said.

"Don't ask me," she sang.

She left me with the car. I drove back out and into the hills. I knew I should be watching for deer and taking care not to skid on the scree at the edge of the narrow, rutted road, but I simply drove into my lights. After a while, I caught myself thinking that I wasn't thinking. My self-consciousness annoyed me. I slowed down and looked at dense brush that gave way to long fields that ran to the low hills where I'd found the cliff made of shale. Then I was at the broad fields where we'd bought and repaired and burned down the farmhouse.

I stopped and turned off the lights. As I got out, insects were at my nose and mouth. I slapped automatically, not in anger. I still had the funeral hat on, and I pulled it low on my forehead. I looked at the standing front wall, the chimney, the remains of the other walls, the moonlight shining through the empty window to the right of the ruined front door. I remembered the minister: I should have listened for something that might help. Sonny had worked his way from me, a Catholic, through some (no doubt) Jewish literary ladies in New York, to marry a black Christian woman. Maybe he'd been fleeing his mother and his aunt, his cousin Miriam, his father, and all those European Jews who themselves had fled. Maybe he just didn't care. Maybe Sonny had been a man who simply didn't care about anybody's notion of God and the color of anyone's skin. That would make him better than anyone I knew, I thought.

"I am so sorry," I wanted to say. "I am so sorry I didn't love you the way that I should." I didn't say it, though. You do not stand at a burned farmhouse-turned-movie-set and say that. You're conscious enough of self-consciousness to give yourself pause about ever trusting yourself again. And Sonny wasn't, after all, the only person I didn't love. Sonny was the most important, but there were others I had been successful in managing not to love.

I did not look over my shoulder to see if anyone was watching, but I wanted to. In lieu of apologizing, then, and instead of discussing with myself how well I had done at doing ill, I went through the wet grass and the scuffed hardpan near the stoop to the front door. I leaned in without touching the doorframe and saw by moonlight through the floorboards and stringers to the darkness of the packed-earth cellar. I retreated, then walked around the fallen sides to the back of the house, where we'd burned enough creosoted wood to generate a nasty, stinging smoke that the fans had blown through the house at our hero and his rescued child.

I remembered Miriam shrieking about the Jews burned by the Nazis. Hansel and Gretel and Hansel and Gretel, she had cried, cooked and spewed out into the air of Poland. I walked back to the car and found Charlie's soda cup. I tossed away the dregs and went back out behind the gutted house. Spring peepers in some nearby marsh made their noise. I remembered learning, in the country house where Sonny and I had lived one summer, how to tune out their sound. The pungency of creosote, like deep kerosene, was powerful there. I couldn't smell the grass or wind, only what had burned.

I squatted at the fire site and seized handfuls of burned-through wood and ashes. I stuffed them into the cup very quickly, and then I crushed the lid on and rose so fast that I grew dizzy. I wobbled a little as I walked to the car.

When Sid came into his trailer, I was already in bed. He said, "Hi, babe. You make it all right?"

"I made it," I said.

"Yeah, but you're all right?"

"I'm all right," I said.

He laughed a breathy, almost apprehensive laugh. "You are one tough babe," he said.

I heard his clothing and the *chunk* of his money clip as it hit the table. He came to bed, breathing a little raggedly. He had just turned fifty-eight, and he wasn't in wonderful shape. I was trying to convince him to eat less meat and to run a few mornings a week. He stuck with beer and card games with the crew. He sighed and reached his hand up my leg. He cupped my bottom and gently squeezed. Sid was always very gentle with me.

"Yes?" he said. "Yes, you're all right now that you've gone and come back? You'll tell me about it?"

"Yes," I said.

He sniffed. "What's that smell?"

"I was out at the house."

"The house we burned? Bitch of a good fire, wasn't it?"

"It was good. You're always so high on your catastrophes." He had produced a film in which a library was flooded, and he spoke with pride of his management of what he called the elements.

"But what were you doing out there?"

"Thinking."

"Thinking and getting smelly," he said with a parent's uninterested affection.

He rolled to me and nuzzled my breasts. He lapped at me as his hands worked, and he didn't see the soda cup I'd left on his worktable. It glowed in the moonlight that pressed through the trailer's little windows. I knew that in the morning, very early, while Sid brewed his dark, strong coffee, I would take the cup outside to one of the covered barrels that stood near the bus, the location trailers, the rented cars. I would carry it out and throw it away. I cried harsh and loud and I stopped myself. He probably thought it was the sex.

I'd heard nothing of what the driver said, although he talked all the way to the corner of Central Park West and 90th. I wished that I could skip across the street on my toes with long strides and look like one of those New York women who had studied dance very seriously once upon a time. But I walked slowly through slush, my eyes slitted against a damp, persistent snow. I felt unwilling to walk, much less pretend to be light on my feet. All I was, on this December night of red lights blinking in reflection on the wet street, was very, very tried.

Sid Gallery, once a steady-working film producer, was now managing to earn a living from development deals that sometimes resulted in two-hour TV films and an occasional cable movie, which, he liked to tell me, showed some class. We had spent today shooting a film for HBO in a rented townhouse on East 67th Street. I saw him much less than when I'd worked on his staff. We no longer made love, although his wife continued to detest me. But when he had a complicated job, Sid still tried to hire me first, and when I could, I worked for him. He was, I once told him, the only man I had stopped sleeping with who still liked me. His reply was to reach with his long left arm from the camp chair in which he sat and slide his hand up under my dress along the back of my leg and into my crotch, saying, "I wish this still was mine."

I was careful not flinch. "Who said it ever was?" I answered.

He yanked his hand down, but then gently touched me from outside my dress, and then removed his hand entirely. "Point well taken," he said.

So there I was, not skipping lightly, but at least not falling down, and on my way to the 92nd Street apartment and something hastily cooked and a long night's sleep. It was the night of my forty-sixth birthday, and I was eager to be unconscious of that fact for as much of the evening as possible.

Our doorman, Hector, nodded at me and pointed at the corner of the alcove in which the big glass doors were set. In the shadows of the alcove I saw a slender person with very large eyes.

"Hello, Hector. Someone for me?"

"Black boy," he said.

"Black *man*," that party said.

I stared at him. He looked like a child dressed for church, in his thin, polished black loafers, his pressed trousers with cuffs, his thin-looking coat that almost touched the cuffs. His shirt was white, his tie a bold floral pattern. His big eyes kept blinking at the snow. He wore a narrow-brimmed hat, but he didn't look like someone who usually wore one.

"Yes, sir," I said. "Do we know each other?"

He took the hat off. His hair was cropped very short. The gesture with which he held the hat before him, the clearly innate courtliness, his tall, lean body with its long arms and legs — all were familiar.

"Yes, ma'am," he said.

"But not really, right? Just kind of?"

He shrugged and smiled, and the shrug went back very many years. "You're his son," I said. "You're Sonny's son."

And that is how I came to cook a dinner for two on the night of my forty-sixth birthday. Gibson Schiff, just eighteen, wearing his dress-up suit (its jacket hung in the hall closet with his overcoat at my request), sat at the small table in the front of my narrow, tiled kitchen and drank a can of soda while I cooked for him.

I heard a woman chattering. I heard the nervous monosyllables of a deep-voiced child, in a noisy and maybe threatening woman's apartment, who apparently felt that he had no choice but to stay. "This is just a little slivered smoked salmon," I said, "and some oil-cured olives, some sun-dried tomatoes, chopped scallions, all in olive oil and a lot of fresh rosemary. Sound appealing?"

"Yes, ma'am," he said, bending to dip his long upper lip into the glass of soda.

"Can't you call me Kim?"

"No, ma'am."

I started to laugh, because I'd heard in his answer a fine commentary on himself. I stopped. I saw that although he knew himself, he didn't know me well enough to celebrate his ruefulness. I asked, "How did you find me? In this whole city, how did you find the right trail and follow it to me?"

"I looked you up in the telephone book. I knew your name from the end of a movie on television. My mother was watching and she saw your name and she said, 'That is your father's first wife.' So I looked it up."

"I'm so happy you did. Do I call you Gibson?"

"Pop called me Gabby. My momma doesn't."

"What does — it's Eloise?" He nodded. I was pitting the olives, drinking wine from a bottle of Chardonnay that Sid had given me. "What does Eloise call you?"

"She isn't calling me anything right now," he said. "She doesn't want to *know* me. I don't live there."

"In Brooklyn?"

He nodded again, smiled nervously, then went very somber.

"Your mother's so elegant and lovely looking," I said. "You two don't get along?"

"Not at the moment."

"So where do you live, Gabby. May I — Gabby's all right?"

"If you don't mind it, I don't care."

"Gabby," I said. "Where do you live, then?"

"My girlfriend's parents said I could sleep on a sofa in their basement. Not for long. For tonight, maybe tomorrow."

"Does your mother know that's where you are?"

"I didn't want her to worry."

"You knew she'd worry."

"My mother loves me," he said.

"So then what's —"

"My mother also hates me. On account of you."

I was careful not to look up. I used scissors on the sun drieds and then wiped the blades and started cutting the rosemary. "Do you know why?"

"Sure," he said, "I started it."

"You want to tell me, or anything?" I tested the penne and gave it a minute more to cook. The salmon and olives and sun drieds and scallions were ready, so I turned them off, then drained the pasta, poured a half ladleful of pasta water back into the bowl of penne, stirred in the sauce, added lots of ground pecorino and pepper, then brought it to the table and dished it into big bowls. I brought another can of soda for Gabby, the wine for me, and told him, "Nobody can eat this stuff without slurping. Okay? Gabby?"

"Slurping," he said. "Yes, ma'am."

"Mm. That's not bad, you know? For a scratch little supper? Edible?"

He picked at what he could, mostly the pasta, leaving everything else he could at the edge of his plate underneath his knife. I had never, I realized, seen a child do that before. I had heard about it. I felt my eyes fill up. He was watching me.

"Spicy," I said, sniffing. "Too spicy for you?"

"No, ma'am, it's very good."

"Yeah. Listen. Eat whatever you can. I've got cookies in the freezer that have macadamia nuts and enormous chocolate chips. I'll get you filled up one way or another."

He smiled his shy, polite smile. It was what he gave when he knew nothing else to give. It wasn't insuffcient, I thought.

"But will you tell me what kind of trouble I got you into? With your mother? I'll get you out, if I can."

He was shaking his head. He'd raised his large, light palm, an automatic gesture of beneficence. I saw Sonny's hand and fingers. I saw Sonny, almost twenty-five years before, sitting across a table from me, raising his hand in assurance. I shook my head slowly.

"It wasn't anything you did on purpose," he said. "It was a letter."

"From who?"

"You, ma'am."

"Kim. Please."

"Yes," he said.

"Whose letter?"

"Yours."

"A letter I wrote?"

He nodded, probably to negotiate his way around using my first name. "After my father died," he said, "I felt like I didn't know much about him."

"No," I said. "I found that out while my father was still alive. And then it gets worse when they're dead. Except it maybe happens with everybody, not just fathers, you know?"

"He didn't save much in the way of what you would call personal papers. He had stuff me and my sister gave him, stuff our momma gave him. Not a lot from his friends or work or anything."

"No. Sonny traveled pretty light. But he saved my letters?"

He shook his head. He held up one long finger. I couldn't stop myself. I reached across the pasta bowl and between the ivory-colored candles to take hold of it. He moved, but didn't remove it. When I let go, he dropped his hand to his lap. "One letter is all," he said. "I asked my mother who it was from and she told me who you were."

"Was that before or after she told you my name?"

"Long time after," he said. "Why?"

"Had she seen the letter before?"

"No. She said it was private, and we weren't meant to know my father's secrets."

"But they felt like secrets anyway, and a secret is a wound, isn't it?"

"I don't quite know what you mean, ma'am. But maybe. I certainly wanted to know who he was. Who he used to be."

"Your mother could live without knowing. She's strong."

"She's angry. She's mad at him for dying."

"She's right to be."

"Yes, ma'am. Maybe so. All *I* wanted was to know about him."

I went to the back of the kitchen and from the freezer I took the bag of cookies not quite rich enough to kill you where you sat. I brought out dessert plates. He politely declined more penne. I cleared the table and put coffee water on. I ground the beans as Sid did on location, and I set up a filter. "Have some of those cookies, Gabby. Then I can eat some and tell myself I'm being polite and keeping you company.

We both chewed away, and in the light of the candles I watched his jaws work. They could have been tiny and at my breast and working as he ate from me, I thought. Well, with some modifications. And then he wouldn't have been him, and that would be so unfair. I said, "Shit."

He looked up. His eyebrows rose as Sonny's used to.

"So your father was difficult to know."

"He was real nice. Gentle and nice. He loved us. He handled the, you know, color thing, too."

"How?"

"I don't know. He always touched me. He always like told everybody by the way he touched me. Held me by the hand. Put his hand on my shoulder. On the top of my head. That way we were part of each other. The rest of that shit — I beg your pardon —"

"Aren't we a couple of tough-talking guys," I said.

"The other part of black and white, he was just as scared. He worried about it like me and my mother and everybody else. Like, who do you hate and who do you love and who do you hang with and how do you handle it when people start using their mouths. All of that. But it started with him holding on to me when we like went out *into* it."

"It sounds like him. So what didn't you know?"

"All the rest. Who he *was* when he wasn't being who he felt like he had to be for me."

I made sure he saw me nod. "Don't we all want that, though. I don't know anyone who —" He held the envelope out. It might have been under his leg on the chair or in his lap. I hadn't seen it, though, until he offered it between the candles and I reached out in response. My spiky handwriting embarrassed me — the way your voice does when you hear it on a tape. I remembered the light-gray stationery. I had used it when I was a hard-ass, combat-weary graduate student in the spring of the year after my miscarriage. I'd gone back to teaching, and then back to being a student, though never back to where Sonny and I had been when I'd conceived for my first and only time.

I looked at the back of my hand: veiny, bony, arched by tendons, a distant relative of the strong young hand that had written whatever was in the envelope I held.

"You told your mother you wanted to return this to me?"

"I told her that and I told her I would ask you about him."

"Maybe you shouldn't have told her."

"And still come and see you?"

"Oh," I said, "I didn't mean you should betray her."

"I wouldn't do that," he said.

"Gabby, you're too young to know what in hell I mean and you know it. I'm old enough to be your mother. But that isn't the topic under discussion, is it? What I'm saying is just never mind whatever it is I seem to be saying. This is all a little bit of a shock. Would you like to read something, or watch TV? Or — look, I'll read it and we'll see. All right?"

I pulled the candles a little closer and squinted.

Sonny —

One of us is always asleep when the other one's awake. I just made the sweet, clean subway ride from 116th and Broadway — the usual delight — people raping corpses, etc. I'm OK. Are you? Tonight we discussed deep-focus shots in Orson Welles. Since a lot of us hadn't seen many, he felt compelled to describe every scene. He even passed around some promotional stills. It was kind of silly and funky. All that dusty old yellow light. All those schoolroom desk chairs. The smell of chalk and hairy overcoats and bodies that sweated all day and everybody's day's worth of breath. I love it. He talked about a scene in the movie I saw and you slept through at the New Yorker. The Magnificent Ambersons. When this couple realizes they won't ever be together ever. Or we know it, anyway. It's the saddest scene. He does it all with the camera. Kids dancing together behind them, and this older couple just losing *it all. He said, How does this scene work? I answered, It made me feel crummy. He said, Can you work with any more precision than that, Miss Schiff? I got so angry at the* Miss! *I felt like he was kidnapping me away from you. He saw my face, I guess, so he changed it to* Mrs. *And I felt like he was making me go away from that wonderful stinky old room. I started crying. So what I want to ask you is this. Do you think I was crying because you and I have it so good or because I know something about how we're losing what it used to be or I'm just crazy? Can you figure out what we need to be talking about? Am I right that we* need *to be talking? I am wondering this, Sonny — am I coldhearted and a bitch and halfway to death? I keep thinking about your brilliant monster cousin Miriam, the Jewish Nazi. The fruit of my womb is death, she told me. Maybe she tagged me right. Sonny, can you talk to me about this? By this I mean either us, me, deep-focus lenses, or the absolute monsters who serve coffee in the Chock Full o' Nuts on Broadway, across from campus. Sonny. I haven't said any of it. Sonny. It feels like we're in the frame but not behind the camera, Sonny.*

K

I breathed out for a very long time. When I had the nerve to look up he was, sure enough, staring at me. It was a sweet, childish, hungry stare, far from offensive. I felt like a source of food for him. I took the last of the cookies from the bag and put them on his plate.

"Gabby, did you get a chance to read this?"

"Oh, no," he said. "It was addressed to you."

"No, hon. I addressed it to *him*."

"Right," he said. "Right. I meant that. I meant, it was private. Nobody wrote it to *me* is what I meant."

"You did read it."

"Yes, ma'am."

"I was so young and sad when I wrote that. I was even kind of seeing another man. I used to have coffee with him at the place across the street from where we had our class. We used to talk. He liked me. The thing is, this doesn't tell you about Sonny. I barely knew who *I* was, much less him. Is there anything here you can use?"

He folded his hands — almost Sonny's hands — on the edge of the table. "It was the best clue I could get hold of," he said. "Also, it belongs to you and you should have it."

"You're a lovely young man, Gabby. Sonny must have been very proud of you. I'd be. I *am*. Aren't I a kind of relative? Ex in-law once or twice removed? I wish I were your aunt." I said it too passionately and too suddenly and it wasn't what I meant. I think he felt that. "Anyway," I said, as much to keep him from flight as to inform him, "anyway, here's what I know: Sonny Schiff was one of the most intelligent men I ever knew. He was very patient with me. He was scrupulous. He never cheated me or anyone of anything. He seemed to publish good books. He was known to be tough, honest, and a little annoying about *being* tough and honest. He was one of those men who would walk two miles to return seven cents to somebody, and nobody cares, but he tells you partly so you can honor his good deed — he didn't mind that — and mostly so you'd understand he had done a good thing and you could learn from it and be like that."

Gabby was grinning. I could almost hear Sonny's deep and solemn voice delivering Gabby his lessons about principled behavior.

"He was born Jewish. He was a bad Jew. He didn't worship the god of the Jews or their history. He hated all religions equally, I think. He hated all tribal loyalties and all religious credos. He married a Catholic — that's me — a half-Lebanese, half-English Catholic, and then he married your mother, who's —"

"Black," he said, bewildered.

"Protestant of some sort," I said, laughing.

"Unitarian."

"See? He couldn't stand to do what he was told. What he was expected to. But I do think he married me because he loved me. Not only because I was some kind of escape from his family. Have you met them?"

"They never came around."

"They wouldn't. Believe me, you missed out on zero. Their favorite record is *Europe's Best Bigotries*."

"He loved my mother," Gabby said.

"I know that absolutely. Just as I know how much he loved your sister and you."

"But what I mean," he said, "I was looking for the *other* stuff."

"Something you never suspected, right?"

"Yes, ma'am."

"He didn't clip his toenails enough."

"My momma always got on him for it. She called him a barbarian."

"So did I! Same *word!*"

"Yeah," Gabby said. "But under all that."

"What am I going to find for you, I wonder?"

"I guess nothing," he said.

"I'll tell you what. I'll start looking for things. After we split up, I hid my pictures, the photographs of us and the family and all of that. I hid them from myself, understand? I'll dig them up. I'll find some pictures of your father when he was a young man. I'll show them to you. I'll tell you about who he was when we look at them, and maybe you'll get a feel for him. Instead of just words. All right?"

"I'd be grateful," he said.

"If you could only stop talking like I'm your — I don't know — your teacher or something. Grandmother. Don't you have an aunt you like? Somebody who's family but safe?"

He grinned his very good grin. "Yes, ma'am. Kim."

"Yes," I said. "But there's a condition: only if you go home. I know I'm meddling. But if I were your mother, I would want you home with me every night I could get. Are you planning on college? Going away someplace?"

"Ithaca. I hope to go to Cornell University — if I survived the College Boards."

"Oh, Gabby, that's hundreds of miles away," I said. "So then you have to hang around with her now. You go home to Eloise. You make her forgive you. Can you talk her around?"

"Nobody does that on her," he said, smiling. "But we maybe can do a truce."

"You ask her permission. I know you don't think you need it, but you ask her anyway. And she'll say yes. I hope she will and I think she will. You take my telephone number — well, you found me in the phone book, of course. Then, you call me and we'll set up a time. I'll cook you something you like next time. We'll look at your father when he was a boy."

So that was how I came to place a subtly striped suit coat on the narrow but rising shoulders of a tall, slender child inside of whose gleaming dark skin my pale former husband's body worked. On top of the jacket, I draped his dress-up overcoat. I gave him a twenty-dollar bill for a cab. He refused. I insisted. I told him that whoever was on the door would call him a cab. And he was to go home, to the woman Sonny had married after me.

"Do it, Gabby," I told him at the door. "It's our deal."

"Yes, ma'am. Kim."

"No," I said, "call me ma'am if you need to. I'm getting used to it. I love your manners. Don't get hung up on my name. And you come back here. Kiss me goodnight."

His eyes widened — again, Sonny's arching brows — and then I saw them close as I leaned in to kiss him where I'd often kissed his father, just above the corner of his mouth. I pressed in, he held still for it, then his hands cupped my elbows and for an instant he leaned in to accept my lips. I kissed them both, one goodnight and the other goodbye.

"Gabby," I said, like a love-struck girl. "Sweetheart, tell your mother — I don't know. Tell her I saluted her. Go home."

That was how, on my forty-sixth birthday, I sat at the crumb-littered table and touched the envelope of my letter against the lit wick of a candle in my kitchen. That was how I came to hold it, burning, and to drop it onto my dessert plate. That was how I came then to burn the letter itself — that long complaint in what must have been for Sonny a terrible repetition, like illness not fatal but never cured — my deep, unspecified lament.

I dropped it burning onto the plate. I put my hand on the hot ashes that instantly went cold. Little bits of ash were printed on my fingertips. One by one I tried to suck them clean.